NOT MY DAUGHTER

"A topical tale that resonates with timeless emotion."
—*People,* 3½ stars

"Delinsky proves once again why she's a perennial bestseller with this thought-provoking tale . . . Timely, fresh, and true-to-life." —*Publishers Weekly*

"Emotionally intelligent . . . Mother-daughter bonding, knitting, and a ripped-from-the-headlines plot from Delinsky offer her fans what they want—high drama and realism."
—*Kirkus Reviews*

WHILE MY SISTER SLEEPS

"Graced by characters readers will come to care about, this is that rare book that deserves to have the phrase 'impossible to put down' attached to it. Delinsky does a wonderful and realistic job portraying family dynamics; the relationship between Molly and Robin, in particular, is spot-on. This touching and heartbreaking novel is highly recommended."
—*Library Journal*

THE SECRET BETWEEN US

"Barbara Delinsky can be counted on to deliver straightforwardly written, insightful stories about family relationships. Her new novel, *The Secret Between Us*, is one of her best."
—*Boston Globe*

"Relationships are brought to the limit in Delinsky's splendid latest exploration of family dynamics."

—Publishers Weekly (starred review)

"[A] page-turner . . . In addition to being immensely readable, Delinsky's latest is thought-provoking; readers will inevitably pause to consider what they would do . . . Highly recommended."

—Library Journal

"A polished drama . . . Delinsky does a fine job creating sympathetic characters with personal problems . . . Well-crafted and satisfying."

—Kirkus Reviews

FAMILY TREE

"In frank, unencumbered prose, Delinsky's sixth novel raises intriguing questions . . . making for engrossing reading."

—People

"An illuminating view of one family's search for the truth when their world turns upside down. The characters are vividly drawn with masterful detail in this one-of-a-kind book. As the author delves deep into a controversial and timely social issue, she exposes the societal hypocrisy and the ramifications of events that hit too close to home."

—RT Book Reviews (Top Pick)

AN ACCIDENTAL WOMAN

"Warm and charming . . . The multiple layers of interlocking characters and plotlines add up to one transfixing and thoroughly satisfying story."

—RT Book Reviews

Also by
Barbara Delinsky

warm hearts

barbara delinsky

St. Martin's Paperbacks

This is a work of fiction. All of the characters, organizations, and events portrayed in this novel are either products of the author's imagination or are used fictitiously.

Previously published separately as *Heat Wave* and *A Special Something*.

WARM HEARTS

For information address St. Martin's Press, 175 Fifth Avenue, New York, NY 10010.

ISBN: 978-1-250-01895-3

Printed in the United States of America

St. Martin's Paperbacks edition / October 2012

St. Martin's Paperbacks are published by St. Martin's Press, 175 Fifth Avenue, New York, NY 10010.

10 9 8 7 6 5 4 3 2 1

Dear Reader,

I'm a woman with a past—namely, a group of novels that have been lost for nearly twenty years. I wrote them under pseudonyms at the start of my career, at which time they were published as romances. In the years since, my writing has changed, and these novels went into storage, but here they are now, and I'm thrilled. I loved reading romance; I loved *writing* romance. Rereading these books now, I see the germs of my current work in character development and plot. Being romances, they're also very steamy.

Initially, I had planned to edit each to align them with my current writing style, but a funny thing happened on the way to *that* goal. Totally engrossed, I read through each one, red pencil in hand, without making a mark! As a result, what you have here in this dual volume are the originals in their sweet, fun, sexy entirety.

The first of the two, *Heat Wave,* is set in Washington, D.C., but rest assured that it has nothing to do with politics, which is one of two topics (religion being the other) that I do not touch in my writing. That said, I have loved the nation's capital since my first visit there when I was eleven. Tourists then, my family visited every major monument, plus the Smithsonian, Mount Vernon, Arlington National Cemetery, and the White House.

Young as I was, I saw a charm in the city. The irony here? I wrote *Heat Wave* in 1987, a full four years before my oldest son moved to Washington. Little did I know back then how important the city would be in my life today!

There are vintage elements in *Heat Wave*, most noticeably the absence of cell phones and sonograms during pregnancy. Beyond that, though, the fantasy of falling for an irresistible stranger across a sultry courtyard is as electric today as it was in 1987.

Another timeless fantasy is at the heart of the second book of this pairing. Have you ever fallen for a guy in a magazine ad? The Marlboro Man is one example, but in 1984, when I wrote *A Special Something*, another ad was making the rounds. This one was for cologne and featured a searingly handsome guy in a bed, not wearing chaps or much of anything else. I stared at that ad for days before realizing what a perfect story it would make.

A Special Something is set on the island of St. Barts, where the Caribbean heat is in sharp contrast to the February chill in New York, from which hero and heroine have escaped. I've never been to St. Barts, but with its reputation for topless beaches, it struck me as the perfect locale for a tryst. So I researched the island, reading everything I could find in the library—which was where we did research back then. Now, a click of the mouse would do it. But I did love library time.

Why have I bundled together these two particular books? Both involve the fantasy of instant attraction between strangers. Both involve hot weather. Each features a strong heroine who is wary of commitment, a hero who seems too good to be true, and a raft of family complications. That said, there are more differences than I can count in plot setting and detail. So alike, and yet so different. In this sense, *Heat Wave* and *A Special Something* are a perfect pair.

Enjoy!

Barbara

heat wave

1

Caroline Cooper untied the wilting bow at the neck of her blouse, released its top button and peeled the damp fabric from her sweaty neck.

Beep. "You're working too late, Caroline. It's eight o'clock your time now, and Lord knows when you'll be hearing this message. . . . I'm worried about your father. The X rays of the leg look good, but he's in terrible pain. I'm beginning to wonder if he'll ever walk right, let alone play golf, and so help me, if he doesn't we'll sue. Maybe we'll sue anyway. The doctor who set his leg wrong last fall shouldn't be practicing medicine." Sigh. "Call me when you get a chance, sweetheart. We need to talk." *Click.*

Freeing the last of the buttons, Caroline carefully separated the blouse from her shoulders and arms.

Beep. "Ahh, Caroline, still out on the town. How I envy you your energy. Can you loan me a little?" Groan. "The baby's getting bigger. I'm getting bigger. Where I get the strength to keep going I'll never know. I think it's defiance. The men in the firm are worried that I'll give birth in the office. What sissies they are. Of course, they've never been pregnant. For that matter, neither have you, but I need a pep talk. Call whenever." *Click.*

Caroline breathed a sigh of relief when she stepped out of her skirt and an even greater one when she rolled the nylons from her legs.

Beep. "Would you like to know what your good friend did today? She demanded—not asked but demanded—to keep the lake house. It's not enough that she has the Colonial, the Camaro and Amy. She's a greedy bitch. I don't know what you ever saw in her as a friend." Grunt. "I don't know what I ever saw in her as a wife." Pause. "Catch you another time, Sis." *Click.*

Clad in panties and bra, Caroline padded wearily to the bathroom. The light there was oppressive after the dimness of the larger room and, if anything, exaggerated the heat. Wetting a cool cloth, she pressed it to her face.

Flowers. That was what she wanted to come home to after a long day's work. A bouquet of fresh, sweet-smelling flowers. Not an answering machine spouting complaints.

With a sigh, she dragged the cloth down over her neck and held it to her pulse. A bouquet of flowers . . . or a bunch of brightly colored balloons . . . or a gorgeous guy with a sympathetic smile and a frozen daiquiri in his outstretched hand. She moved the cloth around to her nape and realized that just then she'd take the daiquiri over the guy.

With a wistful sigh this time, she unsnapped her bra and let it fall to the commode before rewetting the cloth and dragging it slowly over those parts of her that hadn't breathed all day—the insides of her elbows, the curve of her waistline, beneath and between her breasts. The relief was wonderful, if short-lived. She debated taking a cool shower, decided it was too great an effort. She felt drained. What she wanted— given no bouquet of flowers, no bunch of balloons, no gorgeous guy, no frozen daiquiri—was to wipe her mind clear of all thought and relax.

Dropping the cloth in the sink, she flipped off the light and returned to the large single room she called home. It was a loft apartment, the third and top floor of a Georgetown town house. She'd been working in Washington for three years before she'd found it. Miracle of miracles, she'd been able to afford the rent, so the last thing she'd begrudged was the lack of air conditioning.

Until tonight. The dog days of summer had arrived suddenly and with a vengeance, but it wasn't even summer. It was the sixth of June. She shuddered to think what July and August would be like.

Her movements were sluggish, legs seeming to lack the strength to cut through the opaque heat. The Casablanca fan on the ceiling stirred the air some, but because the only air in the room was sweltering, the improvement was negligible. Her feet made a sticky sound on the large adobe tiles as she crossed to the closet. Even the thin batiste shift she slipped on felt heavy.

Opening the broad French windows as far as they'd go, she put one knee on the window seat, gathered the mass of her thick hair in her hands and held it off her neck. The courtyard seemed devoid of air this night. Still, it was peaceful—another plus for the loft. Cars were parked around the cobblestone drive; at its center was a small cluster of trees and shrubs, a patch of grass and a modest wrought-iron bench. Sharing the courtyard on its far side were town houses just like hers. All in all, the effect was charming.

Or claustrophobic. She'd begun thinking of open spaces, of fields filled with wheat that swayed in the wind or meadows dotted with willows and irrigated with bubbling brooks, when the sound of the telephone rent the still night air. She closed her eyes for a minute, took a long, deep breath and pushed away from the seat. Her hand hovered over the phone in a moment's indecision before it finally lowered.

"Hello?"

"Hello, yourself," came a pleasant male voice. "Just get in?"

She didn't know whether to be relieved or annoyed. Though she'd been dating Elliot for several months, she wasn't in the mood for him just then. She was hot and tired. After a long day of talk, she craved silence. Still, she supposed Elliot was better than her family.

"A few minutes ago. What's up?"

"It's been a hell of a day, but I'm in heaven now. No more than two hours ago, we signed the contract on the shopping mall, but you wouldn't have believed the last-minute glitches. It was touch and go for so long I thought the whole thing was going down the tubes. But we did it, we actually did it. Do you realize what a coup this is?"

Caroline gave a weak smile as she daubed her beading forehead with the back of her hand. Predictably, Elliot babbled on.

"My firm is about to build the classiest mall Arlington's ever seen. For a young firm, that's not bad. The developer may be a tough nut to crack, but the architectural plans are great, and our reputation's bound to soar. So—" he paused and spoke with an audible smile "—how about you and I go out for some champagne and caviar?"

The frozen daiquiri still sounded better. She closed her eyes and let her head fall back, bracing the lax muscles of her neck with her hand. "I'm really exhausted, Elliot."

"But there's cause for celebration. It's not every day I land a deal like this."

"Shouldn't you be celebrating with your partners?"

"Spent the last hour doing that. The next couple of hours are for us."

She stifled a moan and worked at summoning compassion. "I'd really love to, but it's been a hell of a day for me, too, and I don't have a contract to show for it."

"Come out with me and I'll share the excitement."

"Nah. I'd only drag you down."

"Sweetheart," he drawled, "that would be impossible. Nothing's about to drag me down tonight. I'm on a first-class high. Join me and you'll see."

She rubbed an incipient tension from the bridge of her nose. "Thanks, but I'd better take a rain check."

"Rain checks aren't offered on bright nights like this. Who knows how long the high will last? Once the reality of the job sets in, I'll be a nervous wreck. Now's the time to celebrate."

She sighed. "Elliot, I don't think I could hold my head up for long in a restaurant."

"Then take a cab over here and we'll do it big with take-out or something."

"I'm not dressed."

"So much the better," he said in a tone that immediately

told her she'd said the wrong thing. He'd been making suggestive noises for the past few weeks, and she'd held him off with one gentle quip after another. It wasn't that she didn't like him; she did. He was a good conversationalist and he was polite. He enjoyed concerts, lectures, fine restaurants. She could forgive him his self-centeredness, because she understood that it came from insecurity. But she felt little for him beyond friendship. He didn't turn her on.

"We'll have dinner another night," she said.

"I'd offer to bring food over there, but your place is probably hot as hell. What if I come rescue you, myself? You must be dying."

"I'm fine, just very tired."

He was quiet for a moment. By the time he spoke again, he'd apparently acclimated himself to Caroline's refusal, because there was a jauntiness in his voice. "You're missing out on a good thing."

"I know. Forgive me?"

"Don't I always?" he countered with such flippancy that she wanted to scream. But she didn't have the strength. Or the heart.

"Yes, Elliot."

"We're on for Saturday, aren't we?"

"Uh-huh."

"Okay, sweetheart. I'll talk with you later, then."

"Right."

"Think of me tonight?"

She left that one alone. "I'm really glad you got the project, Elliot."

"So am I. Bye-bye."

Replacing the receiver in its cradle, she stood for a minute with her head bowed, rubbing the throbbing spot between her eyes. It occurred to her that with increasing frequency Elliot made her throb that way. Too bad the spot was wrong.

Rolling her eyes at the twist of her thoughts, she made for the refrigerator and a pitcher of iced tea. She'd no sooner grasped the handle, though, when there was a knock at her door. Reluctantly closing the refrigerator, she shuffled across the room and put her eye to the peephole. The cone-shaped face with an absurdly large nose in the lead was that of her downstairs neighbor.

She opened the door with a smile. "Hi, Connie." Her eyes widened. "You look super." Freed from the distortion of the peephole lens, Connie Halpern's face was exceptionally pretty, but Caroline had already known that. What impressed her now was the chic and daringly cut lounging outfit Connie wore. But then, Caroline shouldn't have been surprised. Connie was forty-two and divorced. A small designer boutique in Georgetown Park kept her busy by day. A congressman from Idaho kept her busy by night. "Big date?"

"Mmm. And I promised him *café kirsch*," Connie answered with a grimace, "but I'm out of eggs. You don't . . . by chance . . ." Her eyes finished the sentence by wandering toward the wall that was Caroline's kitchen.

"Sure do," Caroline said. "How many?" she called over her shoulder as she returned to the refrigerator.

Connie was right behind her. "Two, if you have them. Whew, is it hot up here! What's wrong with the air conditioning?"

"There isn't any."

"Why not?" Connie asked with endearing indignance.

"Ask Nestor Realty."

"The creeps. My place is delightfully cool." She took the eggs from Caroline. "I'd invite you down, but . . ."

"You have a special guest and I look like something the cat dragged home."

"Actually," Connie said, tipping her head and giving Caroline a good once-over, "you look kind of sexy. Where's Elliot?"

"Home."

"Oh."

Caroline smiled again and gave her friend a nudge. "Go on. He's waiting."

But Connie just stood. "I feel guilty as hell leaving you up here alone and sweltering."

"Alone I don't mind, and as for sweltering, it's really not that bad. I was just about to help myself to a tall glass of iced tea when you knocked."

That was enough to let Connie off the hook. "Go to it, then, girl," she said, heading for the door. "And thanks for the eggs. You're a lifesaver." With a wave, she was gone.

Closing the door behind her, Caroline promptly poured the drink she'd promised herself. No sooner had she replaced the pitcher in the refrigerator, though, when the phone rang. She stared at it, wishing she had the nerve to either ignore it or unplug it. But the caller could be her mother again, this time in a real panic. Or her sister, Karen, saying that she'd gone into premature labor. Or there might be an emergency involving one of her clients.

"Hello?"

"Caroline?"

Her pulse faltered at the familiarity of the voice. It had been six months since she'd last heard it, but when one had been intimately involved with a man for over a year, there were certain things one didn't forget. Like his voice. And the promises he'd made . . . and those he'd broken.

"Ben."

"How are you?"

"Just fine," she said. Actually, she was trying to figure that one out. The initial sound of his voice had touched off a reaction, but it seemed to have been more one of surprise than anything else.

"I'm back in town."

"Oh?"

"Uh-huh. I finished up in Madrid."

Benjamin Howe was a floating member of the diplomatic corps. Only after the fact had Caroline realized that he manipulated his assignments to coincide with his love life. Or vice versa.

"How was it?" she asked, plucking uncomfortably at those parts of her shift that were clinging to her skin.

"Interesting. But it's good to be home. Tell me about you. What have you been up to?"

She shrugged. "Same old thing, Ben."

"Still counseling?"

"It's my field."

He paused as though trying to think of something else to say. Or waiting for her to pick up the ball. Eventually he asked, "Have you had any interesting cases lately?"

"They're all interesting."

"I mean, anything out of the ordinary?"

"Unfortunately, broken homes aren't out of the ordinary nowadays. Neither are disturbed children, unfortunately."

"Fortunately for you, or you'd be out of business."

She tried to take his words for the humor she knew he'd intended, but still they sounded crass. She was beginning to feel uncomfortable in ways that had nothing to do with her stifling apartment. Ben, who'd once fascinated her with his good looks and exciting position, no longer did. She wasn't sure why he'd called.

"I'd be very happy to be out of business," she said, "if it meant there was less unhappiness in the world, just as I'm sure an oncologist would be thrilled by a cure for cancer."

"Ah, so lofty."

"No. But I do mean what I say."

There was a long pause, then a quiet "Touché."

Caroline's lips formed the reluctant beginnings of a smile. Ben had always been astute to the nuances of words. It was necessary in his work. Apparently he hadn't lost his touch while he'd been in Spain.

"You're still angry at me," he decided. If his perceptiveness was off just a hair, it was because he couldn't see her indulgent expression.

"No." She'd grown a lot since she and Ben had broken up. "I'm not angry."

"But you haven't forgotten."

"No woman forgets promises of undying love. That doesn't mean she has to wither and die when the promises are broken."

"So you've moved on? That has to say something about the love you felt for me."

"I never said that I loved you. Not once."

In the lengthy silence that followed, Caroline tugged open a kitchen drawer, took out an elastic band and, balancing the phone between jaw and shoulder, scooped her hair into a high, makeshift ponytail. The ends were wet. Her neck was even wetter. She wanted that iced tea. She wanted the window seat. She wanted peace and quiet.

"No, you never did say that, did you?" Ben asked, then went on before she could agree. "But, look, I didn't call to re-hash the past. I just thought it'd be fun to get together. How about a drink? For old times' sake, if nothing else."

"Tonight?"

"Sure."

"Uh, thanks, Ben, but I'm beat. Maybe another time."

"How about tomorrow?"

She shook her head. "Late meetings."

"Then Friday. I could meet you after work."

"I'm sorry, but I have other plans." Opening the freezer, she dropped several ice cubes in her drink, holding one out to rub on her neck.

"You really are seeing someone else?"

"You could say that," she said with a touch of humor. The ice felt good, though it was melting on contact.

"Anyone I know?"

"I hope not. That'd be pretty uncomfortable, comparing notes and all."

"Is he good?"

"At what?"

"You know."

She hesitated for only the short amount of time it took to straighten her spine. "And you don't. Why don't we leave it at that?"

"You're trying to make me jealous. It won't work, Caroline. I know what we had, and it'd be pretty hard to beat."

Caroline heard his defensiveness and surprised herself by feeling remorse. Then again, she should have expected it. She was a softy at heart. Ben had always prided himself on his sexual prowess. Teasing him about finding a replacement was hitting below the belt in more ways than one.

"I'm not denying what we had," she conceded. "It was good while it lasted. But it's over."

"So what's the harm in going out for a drink?"

"Maybe another time. Listen, I'm really glad you're back. I hope things go well."

"What's his name?"

"Who?"

"Whoever you're seeing."

She debated telling him to mind his own business, but she knew Ben too well for that. He was persistent. When he set his mind to something, he usually got it. He'd wanted her and he'd gotten her. He'd wanted out and he'd gotten out. If he wanted back in now, for whatever his reasons, she was going to have to close the door in his face.

The problem was that she wasn't naturally cruel or vengeful. She didn't want to hurt him; she simply wanted to be free of him. And the best way to do that, she realized, was to paint herself as being unavailable.

She could lie and say that she was wildly in love with another man, even engaged to be married, but she'd never been good at lying. On the other hand, she wasn't opposed to presenting the facts and letting him jump to conclusions.

"His name is Elliot Markham. He's a builder. We've been seeing each other for nearly four months."

"Is it serious?"

Certainly not, she reflected. But if Elliot was to serve as a buffer, she couldn't be that blunt. So she said, "Give me a few more months, then ask me again. I'm being cautious this time around."

"I see. Well—" he sighed "—maybe I'll call you another time and we'll have that drink."

Persistence. There it was again. Or maybe it was pride. Ben didn't like being refused. Of course, chances were that before "another time" rolled around, he'd find another woman. Knowing Ben, she mused wryly, he'd invite her for the drink anyway and then have his new lady friend pick him up afterward.

"We'll see. Take care, Ben."

"You, too, Caroline."

This time when she hung up the phone, she did switch on the answering machine. There was something deceitful about doing that, but she was just hot and tired enough to stoop to deceit. She'd about had it with phone calls.

Ben. Of all people, she'd never expected to hear from him. Six months before, he'd made his plans without telling her, then hadn't looked back when he'd left. She'd been stunned and deeply hurt. Anger had eventually set in, but relief had followed. Ben wasn't right for her. She'd been too involved in the relationship to see it at the time, but it never would have worked. His phone call proved how thoroughly she was over him. And Elliot . . . well, she was grateful to have had him in the wings.

The ice cube she'd held was nothing more than lingering streaks of wetness on her neck, forehead and cheeks. Taking the glass of tea from the counter, she settled on the window seat with her shoulder and head braced against the wooden jamb. She tried to concentrate on the small stirrings of air, but there were few. The night was a thick blanket of heat. Little moved or breathed.

Unable to draw her mind into a total blank, she found herself thinking of life's little complications. There was her work, for one thing. On the plus side was her love of it. She was in partnership with three other therapists; their offices were in newly renovated and comfortable quarters within walking distance of her apartment. When she'd first joined the practice, she'd assumed that her work would consist of references from her partners, who'd already established themselves in the area. And indeed, that was how she'd started. But one client had led to another, and to a consulting position at a local prep school, and to leadership of a group session, and to more clients. Her practice was full, evenly split between children and adults. She found it incredibly rewarding.

There were days like today, though, when things just

hadn't worked. Her eight-o'clock appointment, a troubled high-school junior, had stood her up. Her eleven-o'clock appointment, a woman struggling to make her marriage work, had spent the hour evading issues of dependency by asking how Caroline could possibly understand what she was going through if she'd never been married herself. Her three-o'clock appointment, a ten-year-old girl, refused to talk. And her four-o'clock appointment, a divorced pair whose two children she was also counseling, skirted every pertinent issue by accusing her of a conflict of interest in working with the whole family. It didn't matter that they'd been the ones to initially request it; when the therapist herself became a negative factor in the proceedings, the prognosis was poor. Though Caroline had promptly referred the parents to one of her partners, she'd been saddened by the loss of therapy time and effort.

After swirling the ice cubes around in her glass, she took several sips of tea. The drink soothed her throat but did little to cool her thoughts. Frustration at work was part of the job. Even on the best of days, the intense concentration she gave her patients was draining. Still, when four setbacks occurred in an eight-hour span, she was discouraged.

A trickle of sweat crept into the hollow between her breasts. She dabbed at it lightly with her shift, then, prying the undersides of her thighs from the seat, drew up her knees into a more comfortable pose.

It was the responsibility that was so awesome, she decided. Clients came to her with issues of mental health. When she let them down, she felt let down herself. Which was pretty much why, she mused as she cast a glance at the telephone, she felt guilty about the answering machine. She had a responsibility toward her family, too.

Wishing she could be a little more selfish, she set down her tea, went to turn off the machine, then returned to her perch. How could she say no when they wanted to talk? She might not be the alarmist her mother was, but if her mother felt in a panic, then the panic was real. Likewise, she could remind her sister that no one had forced her to juggle a marriage, a law career, and a pregnancy, but still she was proud of Karen and had encouraged her from the start. And as for her brother, Carl, her sadness over his pending divorce was made all the worse by her fondness for his wife, Diane, and the knowledge that she'd been the one to originally bring the two together.

Little complications? She supposed. But they weighed her down. From the time she'd reached her teens, she'd been the Dear Abby of the family. Just as she couldn't heal her father's leg, erase her mother's worries, ease the burden of pregnancy for Karen, or miraculously mend Carl's marital wounds, she couldn't turn a deaf ear to their pleas.

She gave a great sigh, then a tiny moan. Her shift was quickly growing damp from perspiration. Leaning forward, she peeled the light fabric from her back, gave a lethargic twist, then returned to her position against the window frame. She straightened each leg in turn to wipe moisture from the creases behind her knees. Then, planting her feet flat and apart, she gathered the short hem of her shift and tucked it with some decorum between her legs.

One part of her wished she'd taken Elliot up on his offer of air-conditioned solace, but the greater, saner part knew she'd made the right decision. She and Elliot were on their last leg as a couple. He wanted sex; she didn't. If that little complication hadn't cropped up, they might have continued a while longer in a pleasant relationship. But it was only a matter of time before he pushed the issue too far. She would be as tactful as possible, but there was no way she'd go to bed with him out of pity.

Breaking off was going to be awkward. Elliot happened to be the brother of one of her partners. Another little complication. And now Ben had popped back into the Washington scene, apparently willing to pick up where he'd left off. So she needed Elliot a while longer. But she hated to use him that way. She hated it.

With another soft moan, she shifted languidly on the window seat. Sweat trickled down her neck. She pushed it back up with a finger that tangled in loose tendrils of hair fallen from her ponytail. When the wisps fell right back down and clung damply to her nape, she left them alone. Closing her eyes, she tipped her head toward the night and raised the glass of tea to her neck in the hope that the condensation would cool her heated skin.

Then she opened her eyes and saw him—a stranger, far across the courtyard. He was sprawled on the tiny fire escape just beyond his own third-floor window. The night was dark, but the pale golden glow from his apartment outlined his shape, and she couldn't look away.

His hair was thick, spiked damply on his brow. His legs were long, lean and firm, bent at the knees and spread much like hers. He had large shoulders, one slightly lower than the other as he propped his weight on a hand. The other hand dangled over his knee, fingers circling what she assumed to be a beer can. Other than a pair of brief shorts, his body was bare.

Caroline had no idea who he was or where he'd come from. Though she knew her immediate neighbors, his row of town houses faced a different street. She wouldn't have passed him coming or going, and since she didn't own a car, she wouldn't have bumped into him in the courtyard.

She'd never seen anyone on the fire escape before, not that she'd done a lot of looking. Only the heat had brought her to her window tonight; she wondered if it had been the same for him.

With fifty feet of night separating them, she couldn't see his face. But she wanted to. She wanted to see his eyes, or at least his expression, which would be telling. She imagined that he was every bit as hot as she was, and every bit as tired. Was he as frustrated with the little complications in life? Was he feeling the brunt of a million demands? Was he, too, wishing he could escape from it all for a time?

There were no answers to her questions, of course. He was an unknown, a man she had little likelihood of actually meeting. The pace of life in the capital kept people on the move and wasn't at all conducive to leisurely run-ins.

But he was at the right place at the right time. She needed

an escape, an outlet for secret thoughts. Features softening in a shy and feminine way, she tipped her head a bit more and gave vent to her fantasies.

He'd be tall. At five-seven, she needed a man who topped six feet. She liked feeling petite and protected, though she hadn't had much experience in being either. She'd always been the protector, it seemed. Granted, it was a psychological distinction, but it wouldn't hurt to set the stage right.

He'd be dark. She fancied that their coloring would be similar. She rather liked the idea that people might take them for brother and sister, while they shared secret smiles at the truth. Her own hair was dark brown, often mistaken for black. His would be the same. And it would be on the long side. There was something rakish about a man with long hair. She could see that it was thick, because it capped his head well, but the shadows on his neck hid its length. Which was okay, because she was only dreaming.

He'd be handsome. His features would be well-defined and boldly cut, giving him a distinctly aristocratic look. Mmm. An aristocratic look. She liked that. She'd never mingled with the aristocracy. Her parents were solidly upper middle-class, but aristocratic? Not quite. Not that she had aspirations of running with the hounds or boogying with the jet set. She'd be bored to death—not to mention the fact that she thought the hunt was cruel and discos gave her a headache. Still, it'd be nice to know that he could have had that and had opted out.

But she was getting away from looks, and she hadn't finished with handsome. His nose would be straight, his cheeks lean, his jaw firm and his lips expressive. She could read a lot in people's lips—relaxed or tight set, chewed or sucked or pursed, curved up or down or drawn into straight lines. Not that she'd have to rely on his mouth to convey his feelings, because he'd have the deepest, most inviting and eloquent brown eyes.

The last thought surprised her. She had brown eyes. She'd never thought them particularly gorgeous. But his would be, she knew, because of all that went along with them.

Oh, and he'd have a heavy five-o'clock shadow. That was

because he'd just come in from work or from running. She
pictured him a runner. Of course, if he were coming to pick
her up, he'd shower and shave first. He'd want to look his
best for her. She'd have to tell him that he looked fantastic
all grubby and sweaty.

She brought the glass of tea to her cheek and rubbed wet
against wet. Tall, dark and handsome. That was what he'd be.
People would look at them when they passed, thinking what
a stunning couple they made.

She smiled in self-mockery. She wasn't stunning. Attractive, yes. But with him, she'd be stunning. Or she'd feel it,
and that would be all that mattered.

Having dispensed with physical attributes, she moved on
to other vital statistics. He'd be in his late thirties, just about
right for her thirty-one years. She wanted someone older than
she was, someone more experienced. If he was in his late
thirties, even early forties, he'd be well established in his chosen field. He'd be successful, of course, but more important
than that, he'd be confident. She needed a confident man, because she was, overall, a confident woman. She was also in-
trospective and insightful, qualities that intimidated a man
who was less sure of himself.

She intimidated Elliot, who compensated by artificially
inflating his strengths and successes. To some extent she'd
intimidated Ben. At least, she'd assumed that was what she'd
done, because she couldn't find any other reason why he'd always felt the need to come on so forcefully. She was by nature
a watcher and a listener; when she spoke, she had something
pertinent to say. Some men found that to be a threat.

He wouldn't. He'd be a strong man but one who welcomed
her opinions. He'd appreciate the fact that she thought about
things, that she was fascinated by her own motives and those
of others. He'd be able to listen without getting defensive. At
the same time, he'd be able to offer his own opinions without
insisting that they were law.

Open-minded. She figured that summed it up. He'd be
open-minded, thoughtful and intelligent. His career? She
straightened one leg on the seat and flexed her toes while

she thought about that for a minute. He'd have to be in a caring profession. A doctor? Perhaps. Maybe a psychiatrist. That way they'd be able to bounce cases off each other. Then again, many of the psychiatrists she knew were weird. Chalk psychiatrist and put in teacher. Mmm, that idea appealed to her. He'd be involved with kids. Maybe college kids. She had her share of clients from local colleges and found her work with them to be particularly rewarding. They wanted help. They could respond.

She brushed her arm over her forehead, pushing back damp strands of hair. The stranger didn't move, other than to occasionally take a drink from the can he held. It was a light beer, she decided. He wasn't really a drinker, but he needed something to quench his thirst and beer was the best. Light beer, because he didn't want to develop a beer belly, though he was more health-conscious than vain.

Health-conscious was a good thing to be at his age. It was a good thing to be at any age, but if he was approaching his forties, it was all the more important.

She paused for an instant as a new thought struck. If he was nearly forty, tall, dark, handsome, self-confident, successful and caring, there had to be a good reason why he wasn't married. Because he wasn't. She didn't fool with married men. Besides, if his apartment mirrored hers, it wasn't suitable for two.

Perhaps he was divorced. He may have married young and none too wisely—she'd forgive him that early innocence—then redeemed himself by ending the union before two lives, or more, were ruined.

Maybe he'd never married at all. He'd been too involved in his career. Or—she rather liked this idea—he'd been waiting for the right woman to come along.

Well, Tall-Dark-and-Handsome, here I am. But she didn't have to tell him that. He'd know. One glance and he'd know. She wasn't looking her best just then, but that wouldn't matter to him. He'd want her for better or for worse. And worse wasn't all that bad. Hadn't Connie said she looked sexy?

Well, Caroline decided with a fanciful sigh, so did he.

There he was on his fire escape, tired and sweaty and, really, when she came right down to it, not much more than a full-bodied shadow. Still, she imagined that he was sexy as hell. True, her opinion was tinged by everything else she'd conjured up, but since she was into the fantasy, she'd do it right.

He'd be the epitome of raw masculinity. One look at him close up and she'd feel those awakening tingles deep inside. She tried to remember when she'd felt them last. It might have been with Ben, at the beginning, when she'd been snowed by his style. Or it might have been with Jonathan Carey, her first and only other lover, but she suspected that what she'd felt then had had more to do with the excitement of being a freshman in college and finally "doing it." Then again, the last time she'd felt those tingles, really felt them, might have been when she was seventeen and necking in Greg O'Malley's Mustang. When Greg had grazed her breasts, her insides had come to life. It had all been so new then—new and mysterious and forbidden.

It would be new with Tall-Dark-and-Handsome, too. New as in mind-boggling, heart stopping and soul reaching. He would be a stupendous lover. Caroline could see it in the way he held himself. His body was well tuned and coordinated. Ropy shoulders, tight hips, long, lean legs . . . sexy . . . oh, Lord . . .

She clamped her thighs together and took a shaky breath, a little shocked by her physical reaction to thoughts alone. And just then, in that moment of reality's intrusion, she noticed something. The profile of the dark stranger across the courtyard had changed. He'd turned his head. He was looking at her.

Her heartbeat tripped. A flush spread over her cheeks, deepening that already created by the heat. For a split second she feared that he knew all she'd been thinking. She wondered how long he'd been looking at her and wondered why she hadn't noticed sooner. Perhaps because it was normal for a man to look at a woman when they were making love?

But the fantasy was over and still he looked. She averted

her gaze for a minute, then looked right back. Her embarrassment eased. Her chin came up a notch. She knew that he couldn't possibly know her thoughts. And if he did, what of it? She was an adult. She was free to dream as she saw fit.

That brought her to the fantasy's bottom line. She would be swept off her feet by Tall-Dark-and-Handsome, swept up, up and away from the hassles of her life, but there would be no strings attached. She could come and go as she pleased. She would feel neither responsibility nor guilt. No restrictions. No little complications.

It sounded divine.

But there was another sound just then. She swung her head around. Her telephone. She glanced back at the stranger. He didn't move. The phone rang again. She wasn't sure whether he could hear the ring, but on the chance that he could, she had to answer it. Pushing herself up, she crossed the floor in resignation.

"Hello?"

"Gladys?" asked an elderly male voice.

"Excuse me?"

"Is this Gladys?"

She couldn't believe it. "You must have the wrong number."

"Oh," said the man, "I'm sorry."

No problem, she thought with a sigh as she hung up the phone. Her hand remained on the receiver for a minute, thumb rubbing across its smooth grip. Then, straightening her shoulders, she crossed to the side of the room where she would be out of sight. She ran her tongue over her bottom lip. She curved one hand around her neck. Then, trying to be—feel—nonchalant, she worked her way back to the window. When she reached it, she stopped. She took one baby step, then another. With her hand still on her neck in a thoughtful pose, she turned her head and peeked out.

He was gone.

2

Caroline returned to work the next morning feeling refreshed. A thunderstorm at midnight had brought relief from the heat. Thanks to the ceiling fan, her apartment had cooled nicely and she'd been able to get a solid seven hours of sleep. She didn't mind that the temperature was again on the rise. Her office was cool. She'd face the loft later.

Every one of her morning appointments showed up, and on time. There were several tough sessions, but nothing as frustrating as what she'd faced the day before. Given that bit of encouragement, she decided against running out for lunch. Instead, she sat at her desk, opened a carton of yogurt and put through a call to her mother, who had been at the back of her mind since she'd woken up. Experience told her that the guilt she felt about not calling sooner was worse than the call itself would be.

Naturally, there were explanations to be made; Madeline Cooper was slightly miffed. "I was hoping you'd call back last night, Caroline. I didn't get a wink of sleep."

"I'm sorry, Mother."

"You must have been out very late."

"I didn't get in until ten—"

"But that was only nine here. You could have called."

"—and I was exhausted," Caroline went on. "I wouldn't have been much good to you."

"You could have called and told me that. I spent the night worrying about you, on top of everything else."

Caroline might have reminded her mother that she was thirty-one, that she'd been away from home since the age of eighteen, that if something were desperately wrong the police would call—but it wasn't worth the effort. She had made each of the arguments before. She knew that she could make them until she was blue in the face and still her mother wouldn't hear.

So she changed the subject. "How's Dad?"

"Oh, he says he's all right, but I see him wince every time he moves." Her voice dropped to a mumble. "I'm sure there's something the doctors aren't telling us."

"I'm sorry, Mom. I didn't catch that."

"Hold on a second, dear. I'm going to pick up the phone in the den so I can sit comfortably."

Caroline could picture the scene; it was a recurring one. Her father was no doubt nearby, and her mother wanted privacy, which did not bode well for Madeline Cooper's frame of mind. That was nothing new.

"How are you doing, Caro?" came a deep, affectionate voice.

"I'm fine, Dad. How about *you*? Leg aching?"

"Nothing I can't handle, despite what your mother says—"

"You can hang up now, Allan," Madeline shouted the instant she picked up the extension.

"Bye-bye, Daddy. We'll talk more another time."

"Sure thing, sweetheart." The line clicked.

"That's better," Madeline said. "I don't want to worry your father, but I do think the doctors are hiding something."

"Why would they want to do that?"

"I don't know, but I feel it."

"You're imagining it, Mom. Believe me."

"Bone cancer. That would account for the pain, wouldn't it?"

"Dad does not have bone cancer."

"How do you know?"

"Because he broke his leg when he tripped in the garage. It was set wrong the first time, and now they've rebroken and reset it. There's the clear-cut cause of his pain."

"But you don't know it isn't cancer."

"Dad has seen more doctors in the past few months than he has in his entire life. They've taken blood and done a dozen other tests. If he had cancer, they'd know it. Doctors today are very cautious. They have their eyes wide open. My guess is they've ruled out everything from asthma to corns."

Madeline seemed momentarily pacified. "Still . . ."

"There's no 'still' about it. You're working with the best orthopedic team in the state. They're as sure of their work as any doctors can be. You said that the X rays were okay. Didn't they tell Dad to expect some pain?"

"Some pain I don't mind. Plenty of it, well, that's another story."

"Dad sounded fine to me." In fact, he'd sounded fine each time she'd spoken to him since the surgery, which was one of the reasons she felt so complacent.

"He tries to hide it, but I can see it in his face. It's difficult for him even to shift position."

"It'd be difficult for anyone with a full-leg cast. That thing's heavy."

"I suppose."

"Look at it this way, Mom. You know exactly what the problem is. We're talking bones here, not heart or lung or some other vital organ."

"But if he never walks right—"

"You don't know that that'll be so. The doctors have said that he'll spend six weeks in a cast, then another month or so in therapy. Wouldn't it be better to wait and see how things go before' assuming the worst?"

"He's an active man, Caroline. You know that. If the leg doesn't heal right, his whole life-style will change."

"That's not *so*," Caroline insisted. She was trying to be patient, but after years of hearing the direst of dire predictions from her mother, her own patience was in short supply. She was by nature an optimist, very likely in reaction to Madeline's pessimism.

Tempering her voice, she projected the confidence she felt and that she knew her mother relied on. "The fact that Dad has always been active is to his benefit. He'll make the leg work by hook or by crook."

"And speaking of crooks," Madeline rushed on as though grateful for the lead, "I meant what I said last night. I'm seriously thinking of suing that first doctor."

"Wait, Mom. Just wait. See how you feel in two or three months. You may have a case for a lawsuit, but Karen would be the first one to tell you that a suit will take time and effort and money."

"We have a lawyer in the family."

Caroline had to laugh at that. "Good Lord, that's just what Karen needs. She's a corporate lawyer, not a litigator. And she's in Pennsylvania, not Wisconsin. *And* she's going to be slightly busy for the next eighteen years or so, or have you forgotten that you're about to be a grandmother?"

"I'm already a grandmother, but with the mess your brother's made of his marriage, it'll be a miracle if I get to see Amy once a year."

Which was another absurd comment, Caroline mused, but she didn't want to go into the issue of Carl's divorce, so she said, "Trust me, Mom. Dad will recover beautifully, and the two of you will be able to fly in often to see Karen and the baby, and Amy, for that matter." She paused. "Have you given any thought to what I suggested last week?"

"That I get a job? How can I get a job when your father needs me?"

"Dad has his own work, which he'll be getting back to as soon as he can manage with crutches." Caroline would have added that he'd do that much sooner if Madeline didn't hover so much, but she had to be tactful. "You need a diversion. We're all grown and away. Dad will be as active as ever. You should have gone to work years ago."

"We don't need the money."

"I know, but you'd feel better if you had something to take your mind off your worries."

"I can't think about that now," Madeline said, her words clipped. "Maybe later."

"I'll hold you to that," Caroline warned, then went on in a softer tone. "Would you feel better if I give the doctors a call?"

They were the magic words, just as Caroline had known they'd be. She could practically see her mother's face break into a relieved smile and could easily hear that relief in her voice. "Would you, sweetheart? I know how busy you are, but that would put my mind at ease. They don't listen to me," she complained, and, facetiously, Caroline wondered why not. "But they'd tell you the truth. They'd know that you couldn't be fooled. I have the number right here. Have you got a pencil?"

Caroline quickly scribbled the phone number her mother rattled off. "I'll put in a call now, but it may be a while before I reach one of them. Don't panic if I don't call right back, okay? It'll simply be because I haven't talked with them, not because they've said something I don't want you to know."

"You won't try to spare me?"

"Of course not, Mom."

"You'll call me either way?"

"Yes. And, Mom?"

"Yes, dear?"

"Try to relax. Dad is going to be just fine." Caroline looked up to catch the eye of one of her colleagues. "I've got to run now. I'll talk with you later."

She hung up the phone and tossed a glance skyward. "Role reversal. I sometimes forget who's the mother."

Pushing off from the doorjamb, Peter Hollis crossed the carpet to stand before her desk with his hands in his pockets and his legs planted wide. "Problems?"

"Nothing out of the ordinary."

"Good, 'cause I need your help."

"Uh-oh. Your group again?"

"Yeah. I have this seminar to give tonight, and if I don't spend some time preparing, I'm going to make an ass of myself."

Caroline could believe that. Peter was wonderful with individual clients, even group-therapy sessions, but he tended to clutch when it came to formal deliveries. It didn't surprise her that he'd waited until the last minute to prepare. It was a phenomenon called push-it-out-of-your-mind-until-you're-up-against-the-wall.

"I'll take the group," she said. She'd done it before. She never minded filling in for one of her partners, if only for the solace it gave her that they'd do the favor in return. Not that she'd ever had to ask. But someday she might. "It's at two?"

"You're free. I checked."

She made a note for herself, then eyed Peter without raising her head. "You're really nervous?"

"You could say that."

Propping her elbows on the desk, she smiled. "You'll do fine, Pete. Just sit down and plot out what you want to say. Make notes for yourself. You'll do fine."

"I'm supposed to speak for forty-five minutes, then open the floor for questions. Knowing my luck, there won't be any."

"Make a list of your own questions. If they're tongue-tied, you can get them going."

"I think I should take a course in public speaking."

He was probably right, but it was a little late for that now. "Just blot out the crowd and pretend that you're speaking with a small, cozy group."

"Easier said than done."

"It's mind over matter."

He shot her a crooked smile. "Where have I heard that before?"

They both thought of the cubby of a kitchen down the hall. Weeks ago, someone had taped that very message on the small refrigerator. Caroline guessed that it had been Maren, who was forever fighting the battle of the bulge. Then again, it could have been Norman, who was trying to cut down on canned sodas. Or Peter himself, who had an ice-cream habit he was trying to break. For that matter, she mused, the others could suspect her. Beside her supply of yogurt was a bag of bite-sized Almond Joys; choosing between the two was often a trial.

"Y'know," Caroline said, "it was probably Jason who put up that sign." Jason was a part-timer, their work-study secretary, and he teased them all mercilessly about their weaknesses. More than once she'd caught him with an Almond Joy, so she'd been able to tease him back. "Think he snitches your ice cream?"

"Let's just say that I found a paper cup with mocha remains in his wastebasket last week."

"You're into scavenging?"

That coaxed a chuckle from him. "Looking for the notes that I've never written for this speech." He drew himself up to his full five foot eight and headed for the door. "I'd better get to it. Thanks for this afternoon, Caroline. I appreciate it."

"No problem," she said sincerely. She'd simply write up her reports later.

With a glance at the small digital clock on her desk, she lifted the phone and punched out the number her mother had given her. As she'd suspected, neither of the doctors was available. She left a message and hung up the phone, then had just enough time to finish her yogurt and freshen up in the ladies' room before her one-o'clock appointment arrived.

That meeting went well, as did the group session at two. She'd conducted it before and knew the eight teenagers, all of whom were plagued by social insecurity. They accepted her as part of the therapy team, and after the first predictably slow fifteen minutes, things picked up.

She was pleased about that, particularly when her three-o'clock appointment turned out to be the pits. She'd been counseling Paul and Sheila Valente for five months. In their mid-thirties and married eight years, they'd developed communication problems that were putting a definite crimp in their relationship. They both worked full-time at high-pressure jobs, yet they managed to spare an hour a week to see her. She'd always seen that as a positive sign.

Suddenly Paul decided that they were wasting their time. "I don't see any progress," he announced the instant they were seated. Caroline was amazed he'd been able to wait even that long; she'd seen the thunder in his eyes when she first greeted him back in the waiting room and knew that the clouds had been gathering for some time. "Sheila goes to work. She comes home and thinks about work. Once in a while she remembers I'm there, but for the most part I could be a picture on the wall. If she's not willing to make an effort, no amount of counseling will help."

"I make an effort," Sheila argued, as eager to fight as he, "but each time I suggest we do something, either you have your own work to do or you want to work out or watch the baseball game."

"Those are things that I enjoy," he said, thumping his chest self-righteously. "There are plenty of other times when I'm doing absolutely nothing. That's when you choose to open your briefcase."

Sheila glared at the wall. "I see no reason why it always has to be me accommodating you, rather than the other way around." She turned her glare on Caroline. "I have to time my getting up in the morning so that the steam from my shower will have gone by the time he reaches the bathroom."

"That's not true. You need the extra time to fiddle with your makeup and try on three outfits before you finally decide what to wear."

"I have to look good at work. Clothes and makeup are important."

Sheila headed her own beauty-consulting service. Caroline had to admit that she always looked stunning. Not that Paul was a slouch. He was blond and good-looking, not overly tall but well built. He managed a large hotel not far from the Capitol, an enviable position for one so young.

"See?" Paul asked. "It's always work. When we finally manage to be free on the same evening, she doesn't want to go anywhere. She says that she dresses up every day and needs a break." He turned to his wife. "Well, I need a break, too. I need a wife who tries to please *me* for a change."

"You want to be doted on. Paul, that's passé. I'm not your mother. And do you dote on me?"

He snorted. "If I started, there'd be no end to it. Give you an inch and you'd take a mile. Look what happened with paying the bills. We agreed that we'd each take care of our own. Then one month you were too busy, so I gave you a hand. The month after that it was—" he affected a whiny soprano "—'You're so much better at it than I am, Paul,' so I did it again. Since then you've just assumed I'd do it."

"I work, damn it. I face bills day in, day out."

"Well, damn it," he yelled, throwing his hands in the air, "so do I!" He turned to Caroline. "She's obsessed with her role as the working woman. I didn't ask her to work. We don't need the income."

"We do if we want that house in Silver Spring."

"*You're* the one who wants it. I'd be just as happy to stay in the condo we have here and look for a house when we really need one. Like when we have kids. But that's a whole other can of worms. When we were first married, we said we'd wait two or three years before having children. Then you felt that the opportunity to consult at Bloomingdale's was too good to pass up, so we agreed to put off the kids a little longer. Then you started your own business—things were hot, you said, and you didn't want to lose your contacts—so it was shoved off again. Why in the hell do we need a big house if we don't have a family to fill it?"

"A family's a moot point when we can't stand being near each other in bed."

"Speak for yourself. I reach for you and either your nails are still wet or you've just creamed your face or you have cramps—"

On and on they went, while Caroline listened silently. At last, she held up her hands to signal a ceasefire. "You're both angry, and that's okay. It's good that you can let go here. I only wish you could do it at home."

"He'd turn up the television."

"She'd lock herself in the bathroom."

Caroline raised a single hand this time. "I want you to sit back for a minute and think. You're both bottlers. We've talked about it before. You hold things in until you're ready to explode. It was my impression, though, that things had been getting a little better. I thought you were beginning to talk. Either I was mistaken or something happened this week to set you back."

"Nothing happened," Paul said. "*Nothing* happened. That's just the point. I want *something* to happen. I want a show of her feelings, one way or the other, but she says nothing."

Caroline looked at Sheila, inviting a response. What she got was a belligerent "Why do I have to take the first step?"

"Why not?" Paul countered. "I take the lead in just about everything else. I was the one who suggested we come here. I was the one to compromise when you said you wanted a woman therapist." He turned to Caroline. "But it's not working. She doesn't want therapy. I don't think she ever had any intention of changing. These sessions are pointless."

"That's the most intelligent deduction you've made in years," Sheila decided. With that, she rose from her seat and left the office.

Paul stared after her in disbelief, then shifted his disbelief to Caroline. "Why didn't you say something? You could have stopped her."

Caroline was disturbed herself, but she was trained not to show it. "Not if she wanted to leave. She knows how I feel about our sessions. She knows that I think they're helpful, even when they become free-for-alls."

"So what happens now?"

"We let her cool off."

"We?"

"You. You give her a little time. Tomorrow or the next day, you can broach the subject of coming back."

"Tomorrow or the next day—that's optimistic. When Sheila's angry, she can go for a week without acknowledging my presence."

"And you?" Caroline asked gently but pointedly.

He considered that for a minute, then shrugged.

"What set things off this time, Paul?"

He rubbed a hand across the back of his neck. "Who knows? We had the big guns visiting the hotel this week, so I spent three nights there working late. Each time, she was in bed when I got home, and she's never been a morning person." The hand kept rubbing. He looked legitimately tired.

"So you didn't have a chance to talk. How about this week? Will your schedule be as bad?"

"No."

"Why don't you make a date with her?"

"If she doesn't want to talk, she'll turn me down."

"You could try."

"I doubt it would work."

"What do you have to lose?"

He looked Caroline in the eye and said, "Pride."

She had to credit him with honesty. Pride didn't make her job any easier, but the client's recognition of it was a first step. "Well, then," she said, "what do you want to do?"

"About these sessions?"

She nodded.

He dropped his hand to the armrest. "If Sheila and I don't work something out, we might as well call it quits."

"Is that what you want?"

"Deep down, no. But I can't stand the way we are together. We share an apartment. That's about it. Once in a while we share meals. But fun? Laughter? I want a wife who's a friend. Right about now, I don't like Sheila very much."

"Right about now, you're angry and hurt."

"You're right. So what do I do?"

"Calm down. Wait for Sheila to do the same. Then talk. Quietly and sensibly. Tell her what you just told me. See what she says."

Caroline could see the argument forming on Paul's lips. He paused, clamped his lips together and finally nodded. When he stood to leave, she accompanied him to the door.

"If either of you wants to talk during the week, you have my number. Try to get her back here, Paul. Even if you decide to terminate, a final session would be wise. We've left too many things up in the air. If I can sum up a little, share my thoughts with you both, you'll be in a better position to decide what to do from there."

He nodded, thanked her, then left. Returning to her desk, Caroline sat quietly for a bit. As always happened at times like these, she reviewed the session, wondering what she might have done differently. Unfortunately, as always happened at times like these, her next client arrived before she'd reached any conclusions.

By the time that client, plus two others, had come and gone, it was six o'clock. Pushing aside mental exhaustion, she joined her partners for their regular Thursday-night meeting. At its conclusion, she returned to her office to find her sister-in-law, Diane, slouched in a chair.

"I need to talk."

"Oh, Di," Caroline whispered.

"He's impossible. I know he's your brother, but I'm your friend. I have no idea how to handle him."

"And I do?"

"If anybody does, it's you. You know where he's coming from, and besides, this is your specialty."

Caroline thought of the session with the Valentes and felt a heavy weight inside. She thought of the follow-up phone call she still had to put through to her father's doctors, and the one to her mother. She thought of the folders piled on the corner of her desk, waiting for the addition of notes from the day.

"Let's go for drinks," Diane suggested. "You look as discouraged as I feel."

At least she'd noticed, Caroline mused. There were times when she wondered whether anyone thought of her feelings. But Diane was a friend, a good friend. They went back a long way and she felt deeply for Diane's present turmoil.

"Okay," she said as she began to load the folders into a briefcase to take home. "A drink. Just one. I can't begin to tell you all I still have to do tonight."

* * *

It was after nine when she finally reached the loft. She didn't begrudge the time she'd spent with Diane, because it had been productive. Over glasses of wine, they'd discussed Diane's resentment of Carl, who was having a tough time at work and had chosen to blame it on his marriage. Over chef's salads, they'd discussed the effect of the separation on Amy, who was four years old and devoted to both her parents. Over raspberry sherbet, they'd discussed the tug-of-war that the divorce settlement was becoming. And over lingering cups of coffee, they'd discussed the fact that, when all was said and done, Diane still loved her husband.

Caroline had every intention of telling that to Carl, but not tonight. Not tonight. There was too much else to do. She was bone tired and mentally saturated.

And hot. The loft was as bad as it had been the night before. As she'd done then, she flipped on the fan, opened the French windows, then stood in the semidarkness and played back the answering machine.

Her mother had called, bless her impatient soul. And Ben, no doubt checking to make sure she hadn't lied about late meetings. And one of her clients, who was sick and wanted to cancel her next day's leadoff appointment. Caroline didn't stop to wonder whether the sickness was real; she was too grateful to have the extra time to make up for the work that she suspected she might not get done tonight.

There was no return call from either of the doctors. She phoned their number and left her name as a reminder, then phoned her mother to relate the non-news. Dripping with sweat by this point, she peeled off her clothes, took a quick shower to wake herself up, pulled on a sleeveless nightshirt and, bending forward, secured her hair in a barrette at her crown. Then, pushing aside the small plant that was normally her centerpiece, she sat down at the round kitchen table with a low lamp, a tall glass of iced water and her briefcase.

Concentration didn't come easily. That morning seemed so far away that she had to struggle to recall the contents of those early sessions. Her mind wandered to the Valentes, to

her parents, to Carl and Diane, while her eye wandered to
the window.

His apartment was dark. She wondered whether he was
out on a date or simply working late. Propping her chin on
her palm, she closed her eyes and pictured herself out with
him. They wouldn't go to the symphony, or the theater, or a
movie. They'd go to an intimate restaurant where the ambience would more than make up for the lack of conversation.
Even without that ambience, they wouldn't have to talk. He'd
understand her exhaustion. He'd know that it was the quiet
companionship that mattered.

Opening her eyes with some effort, she trained them on
the folder marked Meecham, Nicole. She squared a pad of
paper before her, lifted her pen and began to write. *Client
initiated discussion of her superior at work. She resents what
she sees as condescension on his part, and this fuels the anger she feels toward her parents. Independence is becoming a
central issue in therapy, as is self-worth.*

She dropped the pen and took a cool drink. Independence.
In some ways she'd always been independent, in others never.
What was independence, anyway? Was it a state of mind or a
physical state? And self-worth? Oh, she had a sense of that, all
right. The people in her world wouldn't let her forget that she
was their mainstay. She wished they would, once in a while.
There were times when she wanted to lean on someone else.

What she needed, she decided, dropping her head back
with a tired sigh, was a vacation. Not the kind she usually
took—visiting her parents and her sister—but a real, honest-
to-goodness vacation. A remote spot. No telephone. No responsibility. Total anonymity.

Well, almost total. Her gaze crept out the window and
across the courtyard. She'd take a vacation with him. He'd
pick the spot, a sparsely populated island in the Caribbean. . . .
No, no, a remote cabin in northernmost Maine, where the
nights were blessedly cool. He'd drive her there in his Jaguar.
It'd be a long drive, but she'd sleep most of the way. She
wouldn't have to keep an eagle's eye on the road as she did

with Elliot, who, she was convinced, had done his driver training at Macy's. Tall-Dark-and-Handsome would be a careful driver. She'd be able to relax and rest.

Without conscious thought, she rose from the table and went to the window. Tucking one leg beneath her, she perched on the end of the seat with her arms wrapped around her waist and her shoulder braced against the frame.

He'd wake her when they reached their remote cabin, but he'd do it gently, and the first thing he'd do after he unlocked the door would be to pull back the sheets of the bed. They'd be crisp cotton sheets, smelling of the fresh outdoors in a way no dryer could simulate. She'd stretch out and soon be asleep, but when she awoke in the morning, he'd be with her.

And then . . . And then they'd make long, sweet, passionate love.

She drew in a wispy breath at the thought, then held that breath in her lungs when the light in his apartment came on. His window was already wide open. Either he'd been home earlier or he was more trusting than she. Whatever the case, she could easily follow his movements, which she did with more fascination than guilt.

He wore a body-molding tank top, a pair of running shorts and sneakers, and his skin glistened with sweat. He was tall indeed, she discovered with pleasure. His head well exceeded the top of the refrigerator, from which he was taking a drink. His back muscles flexed with the action; they weren't at all bunchy but were nicely formed and well toned. As he straightened, held the can to his mouth and tipped his head back for a drink, she saw that his shoulders were broad without being inflated and his torso tapered to wonderfully narrow hips.

The tingles were off and running. She was a little appalled, because she'd never been one to sit ogling men. But those tingles felt so good and healthy that she gave them free rein. More than that, she encouraged them as she mentally transferred the body in her sights to that cabin in Maine . . . to that bed . . . to that exquisitely gentle but fiercely satisfying lovemaking.

When Tall-Dark-and-Handsome turned toward the window, she held her breath. She knew she should move away, but she couldn't. The best she could do was avert her eyes for a minute, but, with a will of its own, that gaze quickly returned to watch while he flipped a newspaper open on the table and stood reading.

The *Wall Street Journal*. She couldn't possibly see, of course, but she knew it was that. No stuffy journals dealing with medicine or education or psychology for him. He'd be one to broaden himself.

But she didn't really want to think of his mind at the moment, when his body was hers for the looking. Gorgeous. That was all there was to it. He was gorgeous. His hair wasn't as long as she'd hoped, but it was well mussed and clearly sweaty. His chin—only one, not even a hint of a double—was tucked neatly to his chest, which was hugged so snugly by his tank top that she wondered at its purpose. It had to be to absorb sweat, she decided, because if he'd worn it for propriety's sake, he'd failed. There was nothing remotely proper about the way he looked in the thing, or the way it met his low-riding shorts . . . or the way those shorts cupped his sex.

When a shiver coursed from her shoulders to her knees, she wondered if she'd gone too far. Shivers—in the heat? But, oh, Lord, he was combing a handful of fingers through his hair now, and the way he raised his arm, the shadow beneath, the delineation of his collarbone, the prominent veins on the inside of his forearm—more shivers, delicious ones, frustrating ones.

Tearing herself from the window, she made a beeline for the table, sat back down and clutched her pen. Only after the fact did it occur to her that she should have been more subtle. If the abrupt movement had attracted his attention, he'd be watching her now. She cast a glance at the lamp. To turn it off would defeat her purpose; she really had to work. It didn't light much of the room, which had suited her fine in terms of the heat, but it did light *her*, and if he was looking across the courtyard as she'd been doing seconds before, he'd have a clear view.

Donning an expression of intense concentration, she began to write. *Client is deeply into fantasizing. It's a rather new experience for her. Either she's been too busy to do it before or she didn't have the need. I suspect that it's a combination of both. Then again, she may have repressed the need. Or she may feel herself above it. Counselors do that sometimes.*

Slowly setting down the pen, she carefully tore the sheet of paper from its pad, folded it in half, then in quarters, and tucked it into the space between the small clay pot that held her creeping Charlie and the slightly larger and more brightly colored pot in which the clay one sat.

With that touch of self-analysis out of the way, she settled down to work in earnest. Discipline had always been her strong suit, and she called on it now to guide her through the reports that she wanted to have done by morning. From time to time she paused for a drink, or to brush dots of moisture from her nose, or to massage the muscles of her lower back.

By eleven, she was ready for a break. Unfolding herself from the chair, she arched her back and stretched, then raised both hands to the top of her head. When the phone rang, she slowly looked its way.

Not exactly the break she had in mind, but beggars couldn't be choosers.

"Hello?"

"I didn't wake you, did I?"

"Of course not. What's wrong, Elliot?" The flatness of his voice, an about-face from the night before, was a dead giveaway.

"Celebration's over. Did I say that this developer would be tough to work with? Make that impossible. We spent the whole day arguing with him about the architect's specs. They're absurd. Half of the stuff he's got listed can't be bought."

"Why did the architect list them?"

"Because he's an arrogant S.O.B. who did his training in Milan. Well, hell, we can't go to Milan for materials. Not if we want to make any profit on this thing."

"The developer must know that."

"Sure he knows it. But he doesn't give a damn about our profit. He's out for himself."

"Oh, Elliot, there must be some way to make him understand," she said. Grabbing a nearby dish towel, she began to dust the peninsula on which the phone sat. When Elliot said nothing, she remarked, "At least you have partners to argue on your side. It's not your responsibility alone."

"That's the problem," Elliot said in a quiet voice.

"What is?"

"I was the one who came up with the bid on these particular specs."

"You bid on the wrong materials?" She couldn't believe he'd do something so stupid. Then again, he'd been desperate to land the job.

"I bid on materials that I felt were of equivalent quality. The developer knew what I'd priced, but now he's decided that he wants the originals."

"Can you charge him for the difference?"

"Not with the contract already signed."

"So what will you do?"

"Either absorb the difference or fight."

Caroline's hand stilled on the cloth. She didn't feel like dusting. It was too hot. She sighed. "I guess you have a decision to make, then."

"I'm damned either way. On top of that, we found out today that we'll have to do a whole lot of blasting if we want to put in an underground parking lot."

"You didn't know that before?" she asked. By the time he'd launched into a long story about topographical charts, she was seeking diversions. While she'd never found Elliot's trials and tribulations fascinating, they'd been interesting enough. It was his petulant tone that put her off now. That and the heat.

She ought to get a small air conditioner, she decided. But where to put it? She couldn't set it in one of the French windows; that would ruin their look, not to mention the luxury of being able to open both wide. The only other window was in the bathroom, so a window unit was out. She could have one installed in the wall, but that would take major construction, which she doubted her landlords would condone.

Hell, she didn't want an air conditioner. She wanted a magic carpet.

"It'll probably be awful," Elliot was saying. "So give me something to look forward to. I can pick you up at work and we'll do something wild."

"When?"

"Tomorrow night."

"But we have plans for Saturday."

"We can do something tomorrow, too."

Shifting the phone to the other ear, she rubbed her stiff shoulder and leaned back against the counter. "I can't, Elliot. I'm so far behind with paperwork that I'll be late at the office."

"Name a time and I'll come."

"If I don't get my work done, I'll have to spend part of Saturday at it, and I've already got a list a mile long of things to do for Saturday."

"I need you, Caroline."

It was a cheap shot. He was playing on her softness, and actually, she couldn't blame him. It usually worked. But not tonight. She was tired of being a doormat. "Elliot, I can't. Really. Saturday night has your name on it in big red letters."

"If I didn't know better, I'd think you were two-timing me."

"With work?" she asked. Her eye crossed the courtyard.

"With a man. Are you seeing someone else?"

Tall-Dark-and-Handsome moved through her line of vision. She couldn't see what he was doing, because he was fast moving out of sight, but a hunter-green towel was draped around his neck. He must have been wiping off sweat.

She gave a helpless little moan. At its sound, she bit her lip, then realized that it wasn't so bad; the moan could be taken two ways. "I don't have time to see two men," she answered, realizing only after the fact that her words could be taken two ways, too.

Elliot took both moan and words to his benefit. "Good. I'm feeling possessive."

She was careful to stifle the moan this time. "When should I expect you Saturday?"

"I'll give you a call during the day."

"Better tell me now," she warned in as teasing a tone as she could muster. "I'll be running all day, and I don't want you to have to talk to the machine."

"Okay. How does six-thirty sound?"

"Fine, Elliot. See you then."

She hung up the phone and slowly turned to face the window. As slowly, she began to walk, stopping only when her thighs touched the window seat. Lowering herself to her customary position against the jamb, she wrapped her arms around her legs and looked over the cars and trees to the opposite loft.

From what she could see, it was set up almost identically to hers. The living area was in the foreground. Beyond it and taking up most of the wall to the left of the front door was the kitchen. To the right of the door was the sleeping area.

The similarities to her own place ended there. His furniture was of a soft brown leather and distinctly masculine, while hers was upholstered in a bright floral print that favored pale greens and pinks. His kitchen table was square and lacquered in a dark shade of tan with chairs of leather and chrome, while her table was round and its chairs of matching light birch. And while her bed was a double and wore a quilt to match her sofa, his was king-sized and covered with . . . covered with . . . a jumble of sheets.

She smiled. He was a slob. His bed wasn't the only thing in a state of disarray. Mail littered the peninsula by the door. Magazines and newspapers were strewn on the coffee table in the living area. A suit jacket, replete with tie, had been draped over the leather side chair. And she swore she could see the very tip of a pile of dishes in the sink.

If he thought she was going to clean up after him, he had another think coming. Still, there was something appealing about his mess. It suggested that he was laid-back, and she liked that. Ben had been a compulsive cleaner, and the compulsiveness had carried over into other aspects of his life. He'd been ultraorganized, both at work and at home, and punctual to the extreme of sitting in his car until the stroke of eight, if that was the time they were to meet another couple for dinner.

Tall-Dark-and-Handsome wasn't hung up that way. He didn't stand on ceremony. He was spontaneous and took enjoyment from the sheer act of living. She decided that his apartment looked more lived-in than messy and she liked that, too.

Just then, the object of her speculation came into view. She clutched her knees tighter against the impulse to hide from sight, for she couldn't do that. It was too late. He'd come to lean against the window and was looking straight at her.

Her toes curled. She began to tingle. A knot of excitement formed in her chest and worked its way to her throat, making each breath an effort.

Gone were the tank top and running shorts. The towel that had earlier been draped around his neck now swathed his hips. He'd come from the shower. She didn't ask herself how she knew that the moisture on his skin wasn't sweat. She couldn't possibly tell the difference from where she sat. But she knew.

His body shone. For a fleeting second she imagined that it was wreathed by a halo, but she caught herself on that particular bit of fantasy. He wasn't a saint. Lord, she didn't *want* a saint. She wanted a man, just a man, sweet idiosyncrasies and all.

He didn't nod his head or lift a hand. There was no movement except the slow, barely perceptible rise and fall of his chest.

Sweat trickled down her cheek to her jaw. Her skin grew warmer, this time from within. She had the split-second vision of her body sparking, then disintegrating into a little puff of smoke. Before the vision had passed, she knew she had to move.

Turning her head first, she very carefully pushed herself

from the seat. As calmly, she crossed to the kitchen table, neatly returned her papers to the briefcase, then switched off the light. Knowing that he could no longer see, she gave vent to the tiny tremors in her limbs and less steadily pulled back the quilt on her bed and stretched out atop the smooth sheets.

She didn't look back at the window. Her head was turned away, eyes closed. But the last images to register behind those lids before she fell asleep were of a cool cascade of water, a bar of Irish Spring and a hunter-green towel lying discarded on the floor.

3

Brendan Carr was bewitched. That was the only conclusion he could reach when at the oddest moments of the day his thoughts turned to Sweet-and-Sexy. He'd come to think of her as that. The name fit. There was a sweetness to her—in the lyrical way she moved her hands, the girlish way she gathered her hair into a ponytail, the graceful way she roamed her apartment. He might have called her innocent, for he imagined he saw that, too, but sexiness overrode it.

Was she ever sexy! The thin bits of cloth she wore in the heat hid everything essential while hiding nothing at all. She was slender without being skinny. He knew that her breasts were small but well rounded, that her waist was narrow, that her hips flared just enough to flaunt her femininity. She didn't flaunt it knowingly; he was convinced of that. She couldn't see the way the dim backlight of her loft passed through material to outline her curves. He sensed that she'd be embarrassed if she knew, or maybe that was what he wanted to believe. He wanted to believe many things. Hell, what man wouldn't, when a woman turned him on the way she did?

He wanted to believe, first off, that she was single. She lived alone, but that didn't mean that she wasn't separated from a husband or engaged to another man or biding her time until the object of her true love returned from a faraway place. He'd seen a man in her apartment several times, and though she'd kissed him goodbye when he'd left, she'd deliberately freed herself from his embrace before it had escalated. They'd certainly never made it to the bed.

With the march of those words through his mind, he grimaced. He wasn't really a Peeping Tom. But the French windows were huge in relation to the loft, and he was only human. At night, with the lights on, little was hidden. She hadn't covered the windows with drapes, apparently seeing the travesty of that, a woman of his own mind.

Actually, he'd been acutely aware of that loft since he'd moved into his own two years before. Its previous tenants had been a pair of coeds who had partied nonstop. Even in the dead of winter—though Washington's winters were far from frigid—they'd had no compunction about throwing the windows open wide to share their raucous gatherings with the world. The noise had been horrendous. He hadn't been the only tenant annoyed, but he'd been one of the few who'd dared speak up. Toward the end of their stay, the two girls had taken to tossing derogatory cracks across the courtyard at him. He'd been relieved when they'd moved out.

That had been six months ago. Naturally, he'd been curious about the new tenant. He'd assumed that the realty firm—the same one that owned the entire block of town houses—had been more careful this time, particularly since they'd been left with a monumental cleaning and painting job. The winter months had been quiet and he'd been busy, but when the first of the good weather had rolled around, he'd cast an occasional curious glance across the way.

He'd never forget the night he'd first seen her. He'd been scanning the front page of the *Journal* when the sudden illumination of her apartment had caught his eye. Unable to resist, he'd leaned back against the counter and watched over the top of the paper.

She'd just come in from work. At least, he'd assumed that was it, since she was dressed more smartly and seemed older—strike that, more mature—than a student. She'd shrugged out of her blazer and laid it on the bed, then transferred a frozen dinner from the freezer to the microwave.

He remembered feeling badly that she was eating alone, then wondering why he should. She was attractive. If she'd wanted a dinner partner, she could have found one.

So he'd thrust aside any feelings of guilt and gone back to his paper that night, but he hadn't been able to keep his eye from wandering on other nights.

You could learn a lot about a woman by spying, he mused. You could learn, for example, that she was dedicated to her work, if the long hours she kept and the homework she did were any indication. And that she was a creature of habit— entering her apartment each night, flipping on the light, placing the mail on the counter, opening the French windows, weather permitting, and turning on the answering machine, in that order. And that she was neat—unless she had a daily maid who cleaned up after her. He couldn't possibly know about that, since he was at work himself and, anyway, couldn't see into her loft in broad daylight. But when she came home at night, the place was always tidy. Of course, in contrast to his own place, anything would seem tidy.

Over the weeks, he'd come to think about her more and more. Somehow, returning to his apartment hadn't seemed quite as lonely when he could look forward to a glimpse of her. For the longest time she'd been unaware of him, and he'd had mixed feelings about that. On the one hand, he'd wanted to be able to wave or smile or call across the courtyard to her. On the other hand, he'd been satisfied to set reality aside and simply dream.

He'd done a lot of that. He dreamed that she was his ideal, and though he'd never spent a great deal of time formulating ideals, she embodied them all. She had a career but wasn't an ardent feminist, never letting her job take precedence over the personal life she wanted. And she did want a personal life, he dreamed. She simply hadn't found the proper channel.

He dreamed that she was warm and giving, a dream abetted by the amount of time she spent on the phone. He knew that they weren't frivolous, chatty little calls, because she'd often rub her neck or hang her head. The calls frustrated her, but still she took them. She was a selfless sort.

And a loaner. More than once she'd answered her door to find one of the neighbors in search of something—butter, sugar, eggs. Usually it was Connie. He knew Connie. He bumped into her on and off by their cars in the courtyard and found her to be a little too aggressive for his tastes. And too old. He was thirty-eight. Though Connie was a looker, she was over forty if she was a day. Perhaps it was a hang-up of his, but he wanted a younger woman—not a teenybopper, simply one who hadn't been around quite so much.

Sweet-and-Sexy looked to be in her late twenties, which was just about right, as far as he was concerned. The nine-or ten-year advantage meant that he was well established at work and could provide for her as he saw fit.

If she was in her late twenties, she'd have completed her education and had time to put down roots in a career. Money wasn't the issue; it was more one of self-respect. Her self-respect. The stronger an image she had of herself as a person, the more comfortable she'd be with herself as a woman.

And she was comfortable. He could see it in the unself-conscious way she dressed and moved. Actually, sexy was the wrong word, because it implied that she was aware of the effect. Sensual was more apt, but Sweet-and-Sensual didn't roll as well off his tongue, and sexy was what she made him feel.

Particularly over these past few days of intense heat. When he was home he wore shorts and little else. It wasn't that his own bareness turned him on, but feeling half-naked as he watched her floating in whisper-thin shifts was phenomenally erotic. As was sweat.

He'd always known he had an earthy side, but it had never before emerged as strongly. He loved the way she looked when she was hot, when her skin was flushed and silky tendrils of hair clung to her neck. He didn't want a woman who perspired daintily. He wanted a woman who produced real, honest-to-goodness sweat, like he did. And he wanted a woman who reacted to it like she did—gracefully wiping her brow with the back of her hand, arching her spine in a catlike stretch, tipping her head to place a tall, cooling glass against her neck, slanting against the window in an unconsciously sultry pose.

Then, two nights ago, she'd looked up and seen him. Fantasy and reality had suddenly blurred, which was ridiculous, since he didn't really know anything more about her than he'd known before. But there had been something about the way she'd looked at him—as though she was a little shocked, a little fascinated, more than a little unsure of what to do about either—that focused things a bit more.

Was it time to act? He'd asked himself that question dozens of times in the past two days. He wanted to make that first verbal contact, but somehow that would bring reality even closer, and he wasn't sure if he was ready. His hesitance seemed silly, when he thought about it, because he'd never been diffident or shy. He attributed it to the fantasy, which was so lovely that he didn't want it to end.

Of course, if reality were to prove even better, he'd curse himself for the waste of time. She was so pretty, so sensual, so gentle looking. He could imagine himself relaxing with her, and he badly needed to relax. He could imagine the soft conversations they'd have and those times when they wouldn't even have to talk, feeling perfectly comfortable sharing the silence.

He could also imagine her in bed. Not just *in* bed. He'd caught glimpses of her there moments before she'd turned off her light. It was enchanting the way she'd stretched out, curved around, found a pleasant spot beneath the sheet. But that wasn't what he'd had in mind. He could imagine her in bed *with him*, offering the deepest softness and the sweetest fire.

"Hey, Brendan. We've got a problem."

His head came up and he straightened in his chair, but only the long finger he used to brush sweat from above his lip suggested that his mind had been on anything but work.

His underling seemed not to have noticed, but then, Kevin Brauer had never been particularly observant. He wouldn't notice a man sweating in an air-conditioned room any more than he'd notice the black ink on a counterfeiter's thumb. He was a technician, good for researching, chasing down leads and setting up schedules—the last of which, Brendan assumed correctly, was what had brought him around with such an aggrieved expression on his face.

"Smith doesn't want to testify."

Brendan flexed his sore racquetball shoulder. "That's nothing new. He's said so before."

"But he's refusing to show for the hearing. He says that he has to fly to Dallas on business and won't be back until next Wednesday. If the hearing's set for Tuesday—"

"He'll have to change his plans. We've already postponed things twice to accommodate him. Accommodating time's over."

"What should I tell him?"

The set of Brendan's jaw hinted at impatience directed more toward Kevin than Harold Smith. "Just what I said. Accommodating time's over."

"And if he balks?"

"Subpoena him."

"Subpoena," Kevin echoed with a vigorous nod as he withdrew his head from the door. "Right."

Brendan let out a mocking snort and wondered about the Kevins of the world. They were, by and large, bright and had graduated law school with honors. But the regurgitation of book facts was one thing; creative thinking was another. Lawyers like Kevin were misplaced in the criminal division, where instincts were crucial. They'd do far better in antitrust or civil or tax.

But the Kevins of the world specifically wanted criminal. They envisioned high intrigue and action. Little did they know that the highest intrigue at this level of law enforcement was strictly intellectual and that the heart of the action was a war of wills.

Kevin Brauer did not have the personality to win a war of wills. Brendan did. A patient man, he spent a lot of time thinking, just thinking, mulling over the scores of documents he read each month, trying to identify patterns and anticipate moves. It was puzzle solving at its best, a battle of wits. Given his natural curiosity, the ability to project himself into other worlds and minds, an intricate knowledge of the law, an uncanny sense of timing and staunch determination, he had the edge.

The Smith case was a perfect example. Harold Smith owned a chemical plant similar in size and structure to two others that had been threatened with sabotage in the past year. Brendan's instinct, aided by voluminous research and an unconfirmed source, told him that Smith's plant was next in line. Though they all knew that the threat of chemical contamination of food sources or water supplies was a lethal weapon in the hands of terrorists, Harold Smith was resisting. He downplayed the vulnerability of his plant and the possibility that one of his employees was on the take. He didn't want adverse publicity to result from an investigation that he believed would go nowhere.

Brendan's job now was to quietly but firmly convince him that the publicity would be that much more adverse if he failed to cooperate.

His intercom beeped, jarring him from his thoughts. He jabbed at the button on the speaker phone. "Yes, Marge?"

"Miss Wills on line four. Are you in?"

He wished he weren't, but he'd already put off the persistent Miss Wills twice today. "I'm in," he said with a sigh, then switched off the speaker, pressed line four and lifted the receiver. "Hi, Jocelyn."

"Does Marge hate me?" came the soft female voice.

Brendan had to smile. "Of course not."

"I think I annoy her when I call."

"Only because when I'm not here she has to make excuses, and too often I'm not here."

"I keep missing you," Jocelyn said with such genuine sadness that Brendan felt more than a twinge of guilt. Jocelyn Wills was a very lovely woman whom he'd dated on and off in the past few months. He liked her, but that was all, and when he'd sensed that her feelings had grown deeper than his, he'd tried to cool it.

Jocelyn wasn't taking the hint. With the license granted

the modern woman, she called him often. She even showed up at his apartment, "just to say hello." He wouldn't have minded the impromptu visits if it wasn't for the fact that, when she put him on the spot that way, he felt like a heel if he didn't ask her out. Inevitably he did. Inevitably he felt worse afterward. He knew that he should be more honest about his feelings, but he couldn't hurt her. She was sweet and innocuous. She'd been living in the capital less than a year. Her circle of friends was small. She was lonely.

But when she said things like "I keep missing you," the best he could do was play dumb to the double entendre.

"Things have been hectic here. We're trying to tie up all sorts of loose ends before people start taking off for summer vacations."

"Have you made your own plans yet?"

He squeezed his eyes shut and made a good-going-Brendan-you-jerk face. "Not yet, Jocelyn. I'm still waiting to see what the others plan to do."

"Why? You have seniority over most of them. Tell them when you're going away and let them plan around you."

"It doesn't work that way. With seniority comes greater responsibility. Besides, I can be more flexible than those who are trying to coordinate plans with their spouses and kids."

When Jocelyn didn't answer immediately, he knew precisely what she was thinking. She'd invited him to spend the last week of July with her at her family's place on Martha's Vineyard, and he'd been putting her off as tactfully as he could. No doubt she was hurt to have to play twentieth fiddle to his colleagues.

"I have to let my family know whether we want the house. My sister wants it the same week."

"Let her have it," Brendan said as gently as he could. "I honestly don't think I'll be able to get away for more than long weekends here and there."

"But you need the time off. When was your last vacation?"

"March."

"That doesn't count. You went to a conference."

He didn't bother to say that he'd taken several days for

himself when the conference was through. He hadn't felt he'd been dating Jocelyn long enough to merit a joint vacation, or so he'd told himself at the time, but even back then he must have known that his feelings for her were finite. He wasn't a prude. If he'd wanted her, he'd have had her join him in a minute. But as pleasant as she was, she didn't excite him.

On the other hand, he could seriously consider kidnapping Sweet-and-Sexy and whisking her off for a month. Martha's Vineyard, Bar Harbor, Hilton Head . . . hell, he could take a suite at the nearest Marriott and be happy.

"Well," he said with a sigh that had nothing to do with vacation schedules, "conference or no, I was out of the office, so it was a break."

"I was looking forward to the Vineyard."

"Why don't you go anyway? The place is swarming with people in the summer."

"I was looking forward to going with you."

"I can't make it, Jocelyn."

"I'll hold the house for the week," she said with sudden resolve. "My sister will just have to make other plans."

"That's not fair."

"I'm tired of being fair. If I have the house, maybe you'll join me, even for a day or two."

"Jocelyn—"

"Don't say a word. Just know that the invitation is still open, okay?"

"It's not okay," he said in frustration. "Listen to me. If I take time off this summer, I'll be going off where no one can reach me. I'll want to be alone, isolated from everything to do with my life here."

"Isolated from me?" she asked in a small voice.

"Isolated from everyone."

"Oh." She thought about that for a while; then, for whatever her reasons, she decided against arguing. "Okay. But you'll still be welcome at the Vineyard during that last week in July." She took a quick breath. "But the real reason I'm calling is that there's going to be a lecture on Soviet-American relations next Thursday night at school. The Soviet ambassador will probably be there. I was planning on going and thought you might like to join me."

"Thursday night?" he echoed, buying time to decide what to do.

"At eight. Will you be busy that night?"

There was busy and there was busy. A quick glance at his desk calendar told him that he didn't have anything formal on the agenda. But if he didn't have work to do at home, he might want to play raquetball or read a good book . . . or sit in his darkened apartment and stare across the courtyard.

"Uh . . ."

"If you have plans, I'll understand."

If only she *wouldn't* understand. When she spoke so gently and sincerely, he felt badly all over again. "No, I don't have plans."

"Would you like to go?"

Soviet-American relations? Hell, the topic was good. He always enjoyed hearing a new slant. "Sure, Jocelyn. Should I meet you there?" She worked at American, which was how she came to be on the inside track for the university's lectures.

"Unless you want to catch a bite to eat beforehand," she suggested hopefully.

It occurred to him that that sounded too much like a date, while the beauty of meeting her at a lecture was its impersonality. He doubted she'd be any more attuned to the subtlety now than she'd been in the past, but he had to give it a try.

"Better let me get as much done here as I can. That way I won't feel as guilty about taking time for the lecture."

"Guilt will be your downfall, Brendan," she teased.

You should only know, he thought, but rather than follow up on her jibe, he simply asked her in what room the lecture was being held, promised to meet her there at eight and signed off.

That night, Brendan sat in his living room taking a good, long look at himself and his life. Sweet-and-Sexy's apartment was dark, but his self-examination had less to do with that fact and the possibility that he was bored than it had to do with the fantasy itself.

It frightened him a little, the depth of that fantasy. He'd always been more a doer than a dreamer. He'd always been active and busy, and he was now, but still he was dwelling on a fantasy that could prove as insubstantial as a wet tissue. He wondered why he was doing it. Was the void in his life that great?

He supposed, when he thought about it, that he was lonely. He was surrounded by people all day and by rights should be thrilled to spend his nights alone, and for the longest time that had been okay. Now, though, it seemed wrong. He wasn't sure when the change had taken place. Life had a way of speeding by, a blurred panorama of events that came into focus only when one slowed down to make a turn. He hadn't planned on turning. His subconscious must have stuck a hand on the wheel.

He wondered if it had something to do with his age. Women weren't the only ones aware of biological clocks. Any man who was active in sports knew that at thirty he was a tad slower than he'd been at twenty, at thirty-eight a tad slower than he'd been five years before. Brendan had never been bothered by that; what little he'd lost in speed he'd gained in finesse.

Nor was he vain; he didn't fear going gray or needing glasses or getting wrinkles. It was more a matter of health and strength. He wanted to be able to enjoy a wife and kids when he was in his prime, which brought him back to the biological clock. He was reaching his prime damn fast.

Sprawling lower on the sofa, he steepled his fingers against his mouth. Where *was* she? Her apartment was still dark as pitch, and it was nine o'clock. The thought of her on a date made him jealous. The thought of her away for the weekend left him in despair. Feeling distinctly antsy, he bolted from the chair and stalked into the bathroom. A tepid shower brought relief from the night's heat, but it did little to settle his mind. Moments later, barely dry, he tugged on a pair of

nylon running shorts, grabbed a Miller Lite from the fridge
and climbed onto the fire escape. Popping the tab with his
thumb, he chugged a third of the can before setting it down
on his knee.

He'd be a good catch, he argued in his own defense. He
was easy to look at, easy to be with. Having lived alone for so
long, he was self-sufficient. Okay, so his apartment wouldn't
pass a white-glove test, but he knew the rudiments of cooking, regularly emptied the trash and, when inspiration struck,
could make his bed. He came from good stock, had a solid
education, a stable job in a stable profession. Granted, as a
public servant he didn't earn the big bucks that he might in
the private sector, but he had lived modestly over the years
and had saved. If she gave the word, he'd buy a house. He
kind of liked that idea. Something out of the city. Something
with lots of privacy. Something with acres of land for the
kids.

She'd want kids; he knew she would. She'd even want to
put her job on hold while the kids were young. He'd never
ask her to do it. It would be her own decision, but it would
please him. He was a modern male and all, and he'd insist
on doing his share when he was home. Still, that old-
fashioned part of him believed kids did best in those early
years when they were with their moms, particularly with
moms like her.

He took another drink, then stared grimly into the dark.
So he was into the fantasy again, and the scariest part was
that it seemed so real and so right picturing Sweet-and-Sexy
in his future.

My man, you're in for a fall, he told himself. *She'll turn
out to be an accountant with a squeaky voice and an aver-
sion to sex.*

But all such thoughts flew from his head then, because
the light in her apartment came on. Teeth against his upper
lip, he watched closely while she set the mail on the counter,
laid down the blazer she'd been carrying along with her
briefcase, opened the French windows wide, then turned on
the answering machine. As she listened, she was working at

freeing the buttons of her blouse. His teeth sank deeper when the blouse flared open, and though she kept her back to him, his imagination went wild.

That was all she allowed. Skirting the bed, she passed from his line of vision.

He was aching for more, his entire body tight. Exhaling the breath he'd held, he slowly drew in another, let it out, drew in another, let it out. By the time he'd gained a modicum of self-control, she was returning to the answering machine, wearing a very large, very long, pale-yellow T-shirt. No sooner had she switched off the machine than she walked to the window.

He held his ground. His pulse quickened, but he didn't look away.

Her shoulders were straight. Her arms hung gently by her sides. Though her face was in shadow, he knew the instant their eyes met. He felt it viscerally, that silent hello, and, counting on the force of brain waves, sent back his own.

How was your day? he asked.

Better now, she answered, *And yours?*

Likewise. Is your apartment very hot?

She trailed the flat of her hand down her neck. *Yes. But I don't mind. Air conditioners are noisy.*

There wouldn't be anyplace to put one here. It'd be a shame to block the windows.

I agree.

You have a ceiling fan, don't you? I can't quite see.

Her fingers crept up her scalp, drawing the weight of her hair from her neck. *I do.*

I'm glad. It helps, doesn't it?

Yes.

Why don't you get something to drink? I feel guilty sitting here with my beer.

In a minute. Her hand fell from her hair and came to rest lightly on her stomach. *I don't want to move just yet.*

But she did move, casting an abrupt glance over her shoulder. Only when he'd pulled himself from the fantasy did he hear a faint jangle. She looked back at him.

It's the phone. Will you excuse me for a minute?
Sure.
You won't leave?
Nope.
He imagined he saw the faintest smile curve her lips before she turned and trotted to the phone.

"Finally!"

Caroline's heart skipped a beat. "Karen? Is it the baby?"

"No. It's you! You're finally home! I tried you twice last night and then once earlier tonight."

That explained the clicks on her answering machine. "Why didn't you leave a message?"

"Because it didn't work last time. You didn't return my call."

Caroline felt duly chastised. "I was planning to call this weekend, when I had time to sit and really talk."

"Can you talk now?"

Could she talk with her sister? Of course she could. *I mean, enough is enough. When it gets to the point that you're imagining conversations with a man you've never met . . .*

Arcing an apologetic glance toward the window, she drew out one of the kitchen chairs and sank down. "Sure, Karen. I'd love to talk. Tell me how you're feeling."

"Fat and heavy and hot."

"That great?"

"Yeah."

"How's baby?"

Karen's voice picked up. "Kicking up a storm. Really hardy, says the doctor."

"That must make you feel good," Caroline returned with a smile. "I wish I could see."

"None of us can see."

"I mean touch."

"Everybody touches. It's weird, Caro. Everybody touches. I mean, it's my body, but everybody touches. *You* can touch. That's okay. Obviously *Dan* can, and my friends, even the people I work with every day. But clients?"

Caroline heard the tension in her sister's high-pitched babble. "They're envious," she said, but the soothing words were far more than mere platitude. She knew what she was saying. She felt that envy herself. "You have something they want."

"I try to remember that when my back aches and my ankles swell to twice their normal size."

"Twice?" Caroline chided.

"Well, maybe not twice, but close."

"That's normal, Karen. So are the backaches. Maybe you ought to take it a little easier."

"With work?"

"Mmm."

"I wish I could. But I'm just an associate."

"You're a *pregnant* associate."

"And the big boys are watching me closely. I'll be up for a partnership in a year. If I can't show them that I'm serious about my career, I can kiss that partnership goodbye."

"What does Dan say?" Dan was Karen's husband, and a nicer man Caroline couldn't have chosen for her sister. "He wouldn't care if the partnership was deferred, would he?"

"He wouldn't, but I would. I've worked so hard for this, Caro. To come so far and either have it postponed or lose it completely would break my heart."

"But you do want the baby."

"Yes, I want the baby. I want the baby and Dan *and* the partnership. I can do it, Caro. I know I can."

"So do I, but that doesn't mean it will be easy."

"Nothing's easy for a woman—especially in law. You wouldn't believe the discrimination that still exists."

"You've managed to handle it up to now," Caroline said by way of encouragement.

"But it's a constant fight. I think that's what discourages me most. In the best of circumstances I have to be twice as good as any man on my level, and now, with this pregnancy, I have to be *three* times as good. You'd think I had a terminal illness, the way the partners try to hide me from clients. I can understand in a way; a client doesn't want to come to rely on a lawyer who will be disappearing for a couple of months. But that's all it's going to be. Ninety days. The firm knows that. Ninety days!"

"Shh, Karen. It's okay."

"I'd really like to believe that. I have my moments of insecurity, too. Times when I think of what might happen if the baby is a screamer, or there's some physical problem—"

"The baby won't be a screamer," Caroline interrupted, "and there won't be a physical problem. Don't be like Mom, Karen. It's self-defeating."

"That's what I tell myself," Karen said with a sigh. Her voice wobbled as she gave in to that insecurity she'd mentioned. "You don't think I'm tackling too much, do you?"

"If anyone can do it, you can."

"But can anyone do it? Can anyone be a wife, a mother and a lawyer and do all three jobs well?"

"I don't see why not, as long as you recognize the limitations and deal with them as they pop up. You've done well so far, haven't you?"

"The baby's not born."

"But Dan will be there to help you. He's been supportive from the word go. He wants the baby as much as you do and he knows how much your career means to you. That could make all the difference, Karen—having a husband who's behind you."

"Mmm, I am lucky, I suppose."

"I *know*. So. Do you feel any better?"

"Yeah. It's good to be able to let off steam, but I feel guilty bitching all the time to Dan."

"Your bitching isn't so bad."

"That's 'cause you're used to it. And because I'm the only little sister you have."

Caroline glanced at the microwave clock. "Don't you think it's time you got some sleep, little sister?"

Karen sighed, but it was a sheepish sound this time. "Yeah, I think I should get a little sleep. Thanks, Caro. You always do make me feel better."

Caroline thought about that for several minutes after she'd hung up the phone. She was glad her sister believed in her, because she was wallowing in her own quagmire of guilt—guilt that she wasn't in Wisconsin helping her mother, guilt that she couldn't spare Carl and Diane their pain, guilt that she could freely build her own career while her sister struggled so hard. She wished she didn't take their troubles so personally, but she always had and feared she always would.

She wondered what her colleagues would say to that. No doubt they'd say she had very strong maternal instincts. They might also suggest that she fostered her family's dependence by being on twenty-four-hour call. If so, she'd been doing it for so long she wasn't sure how to break the cycle.

Rising from the chair, she went to the window. Tall-Dark-and-Handsome was still on his fire escape. She felt a little better.

Do I do that—encourage their dependence?

I don't know. Do you?

I suppose. Maybe it is a need I have.

Maybe the need is for a family of your own.

But in order to have a family of my own, I have to have a husband. If I don't find the right man, I'll be complicating things that much more. I've seen what can happen if a marriage isn't right. The guilt feelings are worse. I'm so tired of the guilt.

Come on, where's that optimism?

Her lips curved at one corner. *Gone with the wind?*

Sorry. No wind tonight.

She drew her hand across her cheek, catching rivulets of sweat before they dripped to her jaw. *Tell me about it.*

No wind. No air. Just us. So what are we going to do about it?

I don't know. I don't know.

We have to do something. We can't go on meeting this way.

But what if we don't get along when we come face-to-face? Things will grow awkward. I won't be able to talk with you the way I have.

Ahh, but what if we do get along? Think about it.

Caroline thought about it all that night and well into the

next day. She thought about it while she wound her way up one supermarket aisle and down the next. She thought about it when she was having her hair trimmed, when she was buying stockings, when she splurged on a new sundress that was a little too casual for work. She thought about it while she was at the laundromat and later while she cleaned the loft.

And she thought about it when she was out with Elliot, which compounded her guilt all the more.

4

If Elliot was perturbed when she staved off his advances after dinner Saturday night, he didn't press the issue. She almost wished he had. She was feeling worse and worse about leading him on, but she didn't have it in her to bring things to a head. She knew that she should free him—force him—to see other women, but she dreaded having to do it. Elliot was a kind soul with a fragile ego, particularly when he was on edge at work.

Ben's showing up unannounced on Sunday evening didn't help. She'd been trying to work—between glances at Tall-Dark-and-Handsome's apartment—and the interruption was unwelcome. Tall-Dark-and-Handsome had had his own guest, a petite and attractive woman whom he'd soon ushered back to the door, and Caroline had wanted to study him in the aftermath of the visit. But Ben had come.

"Nice place, Caro," he said, glancing around from the door.

"Thanks. I like it."

"All you need is an air conditioner and it'd be perfect."

"It's fine without," she said, clasping her hands at her waist. She was feeling awkward about not inviting him in, but she didn't want him in. Besides, there was her image to consider. Tall-Dark-and-Handsome might be watching. She didn't want him to think that she had a whole string of men.

With characteristic pertinacity, Ben barged forward. Short of physically restraining him, there was little she could do.

"How about a cool drink?" he asked. The look he sent toward the kitchen said that he wasn't planning on taking her out.

She gestured toward the table, where her files lay open. "I'm really busy, Ben. You should have called ahead and saved yourself the trip."

He shrugged and started wandering around. "I was in the neighborhood. I wanted to see your new place."

Standing beside the open door, she followed his progress. He nodded at the prints she'd hung on the wall, tested the toe of his tasseled loafer against the small area rug before the sofa, ran his well-manicured fingers along the back of the armchair. "Same furniture. It fits in well."

"I thought so."

His gaze idled on the bed. "We had some good times there."

She remained quiet.

"Didn't we?" he asked, facing her.

"Uh-huh."

"At least we agree on that."

"Ben, I really have to work."

His blue eyes grew more so. "You're looking good, Caro. There's something alluring about a T-shirt and shorts. Maybe no air conditioning is a plus."

She could have been the first to say that he looked good in his sport shirt and slacks. He was as cool as ever, despite the three-floor walk up and the warmth of her apartment. Benjamin Howe didn't sweat. Ever. Nor did he affect her the way he once had. The last thing he needed was encouragement, so she said nothing, simply continued to eye him.

"Are you afraid of me?" he asked.

"Of course not."

"You're looking wary."

"I'm just waiting for you to take the hint and leave. I don't know how much more blunt I can be," she said, but innate affability took the edge off her words. "I do have work to do."

"Really?"

"Really."

"And you really want me to leave?"

"Yes."

He sliced another glance to the bed, then skimmed her body from head to toe. His message couldn't have been more clear if he'd written it in blood. "Not even a quickie . . . for old times' sake?"

That was too much. "Don't be crude!"

"Crude, or honest?"

"You'd think that was all we'd had!" Then her lips thinned and she nodded slowly. "But it was, wasn't it? Only there was a lot of other garbage parading as something else that went along with it. Well, I hate to be the one to tell you this, but some women get tired of garbage. I've cleaned house since you left."

"So you don't want the garbage. How about the sex free and clear?"

"No way."

He arched a single brow. "Not even with Mencken, or Malken, or whatever the hell his name is?"

"Not even with him."

"Well," Ben said, grinning, "at least now I know. Okay." He sauntered toward the door. "I'll leave you to your work. If you get lonely, you'll know where I am."

She was bristling with fury, but she refused to let it show. "Goodbye, Ben," she said calmly.

He nodded as he stepped into the hall. With measured movements, she closed the door, then leaned back against it for a minute, took several deep breaths and looked across the courtyard. The sight of Tall-Dark-and-Handsome leaning against his window was an instant balm.

Ben's nothing but a pest, she assured him.

I hope so.

And your visitor?

No one important.

A sigh of relief slipped through her lips. *I really do have to get this work done. Did you finish the Sunday paper? If not, you could bring it over here and read while I work.*

Thanks, but I've got work to do myself.

Want to bring it over?

I'd like that, but I don't think we should.

Why not?

Because you'd be a distraction. I'd keep looking at that bed of yours and thinking that we ought to be there.

But we don't know each other.

Do you honestly believe that?

Caroline hung her head for a minute and ran a finger over the moisture of her nose. *No. I don't believe it.* She looked up. *But I meant what I said to Ben. I don't want the garbage. I can't handle it right now. Maybe what I do want is pure sex.*

It'd be more than that with us. And there'd be no garbage.

Are you sure?

Yes.

She smiled sadly. *That's a lovely thought, but it's only a dream, and I do have work to do.*

Okay. Another time, then.

With a chuckle, she pushed away from the door. *Another time.* That was the nicest thing about a fantasy, she decided, as she sat down and focused on the notes she'd written earlier. A fantasy didn't suffer with postponement. It was always there, a carrot that dangled sweetly and in secret, to be called forth again and again and again.

Caroline called forth that fantasy many times in the next few days. But even aside from the fantasy, she learned a great deal about Tall-Dark-and-Handsome.

He very definitely lived alone. Aside from his visitor on Sunday—and she dropped in again on Tuesday evening but left as quickly—he seemed a private sort. Except where Caroline was concerned. It occurred to her that he made no attempt to shield his apartment from her view, which made her feel a little less guilty that she did the same.

He ran. Some nights he came home wearing a business suit, changed into a tank top and shorts and went out, only to return after an hour looking tired and sweaty but healthy. Other nights, when he came home, his shirt was wide open and he was already sweaty. She wondered if he'd come from a health club.

He worked. She could see him poring through papers during the evenings—papers of the file type, rather than the newspaper type—and though she continued to speculate on his occupation, the specifics came to matter less than the fact of his diligence.

He didn't drink beyond that one beer an evening; at least, not that she could see. He didn't own a television, or if he did, he rarely watched it. She couldn't tell if he had a stereo; she never once heard the noise. And occasionally she could see him reading a hardcover book.

Sometimes he talked on the telephone, and then she was a little uneasy, for she sensed he was talking with a woman. His expression was gentle, understanding, often beseeching. She doubted it was the same woman she'd seen, since these calls lasted longer than the visits ever had. She told herself that if there was another woman in his life, surely that woman would appear. When she didn't, Caroline could only imagine that she existed, and that was nearly as bad as what she imagined on the nights he didn't return home until late.

It wasn't that she was jealous. She had no claim on the man. It was more that she feared she'd lose him, which was absurd, since she didn't have him to start with. It was all a fantasy, she reminded herself, but that didn't help when she sat at her window staring into his dark apartment. She missed him during those times, just as she welcomed him when he returned. Not a night went by that he didn't come to the window at whatever time he got home.

It became a ritual—a welcome home, a shared drink, a sweet good-night. She had come to depend on it, as they reached what she thought of as their first-week anniversary. When Friday night rolled around, she was particularly needful of that silent shared drink.

She'd had a rough week. The heat had held up—an unusually static high-pressure system, said the weatherman—and she hadn't slept well on many of those nights when the air in her apartment had been hot. It was hot tonight, too.

She'd changed into shorts as soon as she'd come home and was reclining against the window, a glass of iced tea in her hand, while Tall-Dark-and-Handsome took his beer from the fridge.

He wore a charcoal tank top over lighter gray running shorts, which, despite their color, made his hips look sleek and narrow. He paused only to take a quick swig of beer and kick off his sneakers before sliding onto the fire escape.

Hi, she thought breathlessly.

Hi, yourself.

How was your day?

He drew away from the wrought-iron railing and flexed his upper back before relaxing again. *Hot. And yours?*

Ditto.

At least it's the weekend. What say we take off and go someplace cool?

Like . . . ?

Alaska.

She gave a sultry half smile. *Mmm. That sounds nice.*

Ever been in an igloo?

No, but it sounds real good right about now. Sweat dotted her neck and pooled between her breasts. She took a drink, then held the cool glass to her cheek.

Would you really go there with me? she imagined he'd ask.

Sure.

Don't have any other plans for the weekend?

No. I told Elliot I needed a break.

He put the can to his mouth and tipped his head. In silhouette, his Adam's apple bobbed gently as the cool liquid flowed past. Turning his head slowly, his eyes found hers. *How did he take it?*

Not well. I feel guilty.

You shouldn't, you know. You have every right to refuse an invitation.

Still . . .

He's a big boy, Caroline.

That's the first time you've used my name. I wish I knew what to call you.

Tall-Dark-and-Handsome is fine.

But it's not real.

None of this is real.

That's not true. She sucked in a shaky breath and admitted what she'd been trying to ignore. *What you make me feel is real.*

Tell me what you feel.

She pressed her lips together, then slowly moistened them with the tip of her tongue. *Excitement. I look at you and my heart pounds.*

In this heat?

Crazy, I know.

What else?

Heat inside. I can't really see your face, but your eyes make me sizzle. Or maybe it's the set of your shoulders or the shape of your chest. She watched him wipe a damp palm on his thigh. *Or your legs. You have beautiful legs. Do you know that?*

They're not beautiful.

Maybe not to you, but to me they are. Lean and tight.

They're hairy, too.

I'm beginning to sound like an ape.

No. Just a hairy man.

Do hairy men turn you on?

I never thought they did, but the hair on your skin is masculine. So different from a woman's.

I should hope so.

Her insides were beginning to knot. Closing her eyes for an instant, she arched her back, then brought the glass to her forehead. *I don't know why I'm doing this to myself.*

Maybe you're sex starved.

No. Sex is nice, but I've never really hungered for it, if you know what I mean.

And you do now?

With you. But maybe you don't feel the same way.

Are you kidding?

You do want me?

Why do you think I've got my knees bent up this way?

Oh. The color in her cheeks deepened. *That's nice.*

It's not nice. It's damn frustrating. What are we going to do about this?

I don't know.

He shifted, straightening one of those knees, seeming to find comfort elusive. Not once did his gaze leave hers; it penetrated the night and the distance between them, searing straight into her heart. *Maybe if we just give in to it and make love, we'll get it out of our systems.*

Maybe.

Should we try it?

Her breath was coming faster. *I don't know.*

You could invite me over there.

She bit her lip. *We're strangers.*

I could invite myself over there.

I don't even know your name.

Or you could come over here.

I couldn't.

We have to break the ice somehow.

I know. I know. She whipped her head toward the door in response to a loud knock. *I don't believe it. Someone's here.*

Maybe it's Connie.

She returned her gaze to his. *No. She's gone for the weekend.*

One of your other neighbors?

Maybe.

Or Ben. Maybe he's still at it.

I hope not. The knock came again, even louder this time. Again she glanced toward the door.

You'd better get it.

I know.

Go on. I'll be here.

With a sigh of frustration, Caroline set her drink on the window seat and went to the door.

Brendan couldn't take his eyes from her. She looked so sweet, so agile as she trotted across the floor. And sexy. Her shorts were short, but her thighs and bottom did them proud.

And that T-shirt . . . If she was wearing a bra, he'd eat his hat. Not that he owned a hat, but the bet stood; he was that sure of winning. Her hair was caught up in a clasp that left loose strands caressing her damp neck. He could think of all kinds of things he'd do with those loose strands and her neck and his tongue.

Damn. It wasn't a neighbor. It was the guy she dated, but she didn't look pleased to see him. She had a tight grip on the doorknob, and her back had stiffened. Brendan's eyes narrowed. He could see that the man was talking, gesturing toward the inside of her apartment. She shook her head, but he ignored her and took several steps into the loft.

Brendan felt his body grow tense in ways vastly different from the sexual tension of moments before. He watched closely. Her guest continued to talk. She shook her head again, more slowly this time, but whatever she was saying seemed to annoy the fellow, who proceeded to rake a hand through his hair, then fling his arms wide in frustration.

Brendan could almost sympathize with the man. He didn't look like a mean sort; he was clean, nicely dressed, and there was a defensiveness about him. If he was half as hung up on her as Brendan was himself and she was denying him what he most wanted, Brendan could indeed understand the frustration.

His feelings of sympathy vanished, though, when the man clasped her arm. She quickly pulled from his grip and took a step toward the door, but her visitor kept pace, kept talking, kept gesturing. She pointed to the door. The man shook his head. When he snaked an arm around her waist and brought her body flush with his, she arched away and tried to push.

The harsh sound of the beer can crushing in his hand brought Brendan to life. He'd seen enough. Sweet-and-Sexy didn't want that man there. If the guy wasn't willing to accept that on his own, Brendan intended to help him.

Blindly pitching the can toward the sink on his way out the door, Brendan flew down the three flights in record time. He didn't have to pause when he reached the street; he'd traveled the route in his mind so many times that he knew the fastest way around the block. He also knew that since her apartment faced his, her town house had to be the fourth from the corner. He ran there full speed and yanked the door open. When it collided with his toe, he swore, but that was the extent of his self-indulgence. Ignoring the pain, he took the steps two at a time.

He might have taken it as a good omen—to his fantasy or his calculations or whatever—that the door to the third-floor apartment stood open, but he wasn't taking time to think of omens, good or otherwise. He slowed his pace and jogged to the door, coming to a full stop with his hand high on the jamb before calmly ambling inside.

Caroline's head shot to the door the instant he appeared. She'd already freed herself from Elliot's hold, but the threat of his presence remained. Now, abruptly, it was gone and forgotten.

Tall-Dark-and-Handsome? It had to be! The way he looked at her spoke of all she'd imagined and then some.

"Hi, hon," he said softly. Strolling to her side, he wrapped an arm around her shoulder and pressed a warm kiss to her forehead. "Sorry I'm late. I took a detour. Nearly got lost." He gave her a smile and a squeeze, then released her shoulder and extended his hand to her guest. "Brendan Carr. And you are . . . ?"

Elliot stood very still. Only his eyes moved, jumping from Brendan to Caroline and back. He looked totally confused, all but paralyzed, and seemed to be rescued in the end by nothing more than the reflex of manners.

"Elliot Markham," he said, letting his hand be shaken.

"Nice to meet you," Brendan said, then headed for the refrigerator. "Man, is it a warm night." He pulled open the door, extracted the pitcher of iced tea that he knew was always there, took a glass from the adjacent cabinet and poured himself a drink. "Anyone else want some while I'm at it?" he asked, shooting a glance over his shoulder.

Caroline could only manage to shake her head. Her eyes were wide, glued to Brendan—*Brendan*—and she doubted she could swallow air, let alone tea.

Elliot wasn't quite as awestruck. Recovering from the shock of Brendan's appearance—more than that, from the shock of Brendan's obvious familiarity with Caroline's apartment—he narrowed his eyes on Caroline and murmured under his breath, "What's going on here?"

Under normal circumstances, Caroline would have shrugged. But these weren't normal circumstances. Brendan, her hero, had come to her rescue. She couldn't take her eyes from him as he calmly downed his drink and set the empty glass on the counter.

"I asked you a question, Caroline," Elliot said in that same low murmur.

Her eyes flew to his and she blinked, as though surprised to find him still there. "Excuse me?"

"What's he doing here?"

In that instant, Caroline realized that she had to pick up the ball. Brendan's entrance had been stupendous. She couldn't flub her part and let him down. "He's just come in from a run."

"In his bare feet?"

"It's the newest trend," Brendan injected nonchalantly. "I think it started with Zola Budd in the Olympics." He dropped his gaze to the toe that hurt like hell and was beginning to swell. "I have to admit that it has its drawbacks."

Caroline, too, saw the toe. "How did you do that?" she asked, raising hurting eyes to his.

It was all he could do to think of a response when she was looking at him that way. Her eyes were brown, like his. He'd never thought his own particularly scintillating, but hers were. And so soft. And filled with worry.

"I'm afraid—" he made a face and scratched the back of his head "—that I wasn't watching where I was going. There was this Lamborghini that passed me and I made the mistake of turning my head to look at it. I ran into a trash can." He shrugged. "I suppose I could blame it on the dark—"

"Let me get some ice."

"No, no, hon, it's okay." He came to stand by her shoulder, close enough for her arm to graze his chest. "Will Elliot be joining us for dinner?" he asked softly.

Elliot was staring hard at Caroline. "I thought you said there was no one else."

"There hasn't been—"

"—until now," Brendan finished.

"We've just recently met," she explained, but she didn't feel guilt. She knew that would come later. For now, she couldn't think of anything but the large, firm body beside her. Its warmth, a world apart from the June heat, drew her closer. Its scent, ripe with maleness and sweat, filled her senses. Its sheer size made her feel safe and alive and very, very feminine. "Brendan lives across the courtyard," she added a trifle breathlessly.

Mistaking breathlessness for weakness, Elliot lashed out. "You told me that you needed a break this weekend. That you wanted to be alone. That you had work to do and sleep to catch up on. Is this what I get for squiring you around town for three months straight?"

"No one asked you to do that," she said quietly.

"But I did it, and you didn't say boo. Now, all of a sudden you don't need me anymore, so you throw me every excuse in the book."

"I meant what I said."

"Is that why he's here?" Elliot shot back with a dagger's glance at Brendan. "How do you think this makes me feel?"

Caroline knew how Brendan's presence made *her* feel— warm inside, a little giddy and very excited. Because of those feelings she was having trouble sympathizing with Elliot. "I'm sorry if you're upset."

"Upset?" He started to raise a hand to his face but dropped it before it reached its goal. "That's a mild word for what I feel."

Brendan leaned closer to Caroline. His arm crossed her back, hand coming to rest on her arm in light possession. He liked the way her slender body felt by his, liked the smoothness of her skin, the gloss of her hair, the faint floral scent that was so in keeping with his dreams. Most of all, he liked the fact that she was no longer a dream but real.

"Maybe you'd better leave," was his quiet suggestion to Elliot.

But Elliot didn't hear. He was too busy working himself into a self-righteous rage. "I don't deserve this, Caroline. For three months I've been indulgent. I've let you call the shots. If you wanted to see a particular show, I took you. If you wanted to eat at a particular restaurant, I took you. When you were busy with work, I said, 'Okay. I respect you for that.' Where's the respect I deserve in return?"

"Elliot, please don't," Caroline said.

"Why not? Do you find the truth unsettling?"

What he had said wasn't exactly the truth. She knew that he was trying to save face in front of Brendan, but, in his indignance, he was digging the hole deeper. "Nothing will be accomplished by—"

"Shouldn't I fight for what I want?"

"Is that what you were doing just before I got here?" Brendan asked, his low voice cutting through the air like the purr of a whip.

Elliot grew rigid. His eyes widened. He opened his mouth and shut it in the same breath.

Caroline turned her head to meet Brendan's gaze, then promptly forgot both his words and Elliot's presence.

Brendan was beautiful. She couldn't think of another word, and she knew that an impartial observer might think her daft, but she didn't care. His jaw was firm, square and covered by the dark shadow she'd come to expect. But she hadn't expected the tiny white scar on his chin, or the quick softening of his lips when she'd turned, or the faint crookedness of his nose. And though she'd hoped that his eyes would be brown, she hadn't expected that they would be like thick, rich velvet, stroking her deep inside. She hadn't dared hope that they would hold such longing.

He gave a tiny, secret smile. *Hi, Caroline.*

She returned both the smile and the greeting. *Hi, Brendan. Did we finally do it?*

I think so.

His hand left her arm. The backs of his fingers lightly brushed her cheek. Her lips parted. She tipped her head until those lips touched his thumb.

"Shit, I don't need this!" Elliot growled.

Jolted by the intrusion, Brendan and Caroline whipped their heads around in time to see him stomp to the door, grab the knob and slam it shut on his way out.

Then, more slowly, they looked back at each other.

"Hi," he said aloud. His voice was nearly as velvety as his eyes, but a smokiness underlay that velvet to produce something extraordinarily manly.

"Hi," she whispered. Standing there, looking up into his eyes, she nearly melted. Her limbs liquefied; her blood flowed faster. Any tension that Elliot's angry departure had caused seemed to gather, break apart, float away.

Brendan's gaze shimmered over each of her features. "I was beginning to think it would never happen."

"Me, too."

"I didn't plan it this way."

"I know."

"But I couldn't just sit there and let him paw you."

She knew that she'd been far from helpless, but that didn't matter. "I'm glad you came," she said, then, unable to resist, raised a hand to his jaw. His beard was rough and spoke of strength. She shaped his lean cheek with her palm and whispered her thumb over his chin.

He closed his eyes for a minute. When he opened them, they were darker. "Your touch is gentle. Nice."

"I kept imagining what you'd look like." Her fingers crept to his lips. Her eyes crept higher, meeting his in a wordless expression of admiration.

The compliment touched him to the core. She made him feel ten feet tall and quivery. He opened his mouth to say something but couldn't think of the words to express what he felt. So, instead of speaking, he touched his tongue to her finger and very lightly put his hands on her waist. Almost instantly, they began a feathery rotation.

Caroline felt the movement clear to her toes. His fingers were long and strong but gently enticing. Dazed with sensation, she closed her eyes and looped her hands over his shoulders. If it was an invitation, it was a subconscious one, but far more than her subconscious felt the glide of his hands on her bare skin as the hem of her T-shirt rose from her shorts. She sighed at the divine pleasure, then sighed again when his lips touched her forehead.

How fantasy paled, she thought. Had she never gone so far as to imagine the way her inner wrists would feel on his shoulders, or the way his chest would press closer with each breath, or the way his thighs would brace hers? She wondered what it was about this man that was so special; then she gave up wondering and simply savored his touch.

Soft. Moist. Sweet. Brendan couldn't believe how perfect she was. He'd held many a woman in his arms in his day, but none had felt so right. Caroline. Her name was as lyrical as she. Caroline. He might have said it aloud, but he didn't know for sure, because the effect she had on him was mind numbing, the pleasure deafening.

He caught a trickle of sweat as it left her hairline and it was on his lips as they moved over her eyes to her cheek. He didn't stop to ask himself if he was rushing things when he sought out her mouth. Hers was waiting and parted.

He kissed her with whisper-soft touches at first, enjoying those exploratory forays. Caroline enjoyed them, too, for her hands had slipped to his back, and the tight cording she found there stood in leashed counterpoint to that gentleness. His tank top was damp, the skin nearby slick with a sweat that lubricated her fingers in their slow journey of discovery. His breath mingling with hers bore the cool, fresh scent of tea. She felt the beat of his heart against her breast, heard its echo in her bloodstream, and she opened herself to him as she had to no man before.

Details blurred then amid an overall air of bliss. Mouths, tongues, hands, bodies—slow, languorous movements gradually speeding with sensual demands. There was heat within heat. The sultriness of the air lent a sultriness to their passion. One kiss led to the next, wider and deeper; one touch led to intimate others. If either of them had been asked if this was a dream, each would have been hard put to answer. The fine line between fantasy and reality ceased to exist.

"I need you," he gasped in a moment's lucidity. Her bare breasts filled his hands; her own hands had slipped beneath the waistband of his shorts and were palming his naked flanks. They were mouth to mouth, chest to chest, belly to belly. His arousal was full, pressed so hard against her that he had to force himself to think. But think he did, even though his voice emerged husky, ragged and rushed. "You know my name, I'm thirty-eight, a lawyer, stable, not married, and I won't give you anything you wouldn't want to write home about except maybe a baby—are you protected, Caroline?"

"Yes," she breathed, "yes."

Within seconds, they'd sunk to the rug. Caroline's T-shirt fell aside, followed quickly by his tank top and then their shorts. They reached for one another, for the only vibrant touch that mattered in that instant out of time.

Caroline had never felt so filled as when Brendan buried himself in her depths. He had never felt so fully received as when she closed herself around him. Though they shared the trust reserved for longtime lovers, each minute, each movement was new and priceless. And whether it was real or imagined, neither could say, but an aura of invincibility gave force to the fire.

The still of the night was broken by soft gasps and breathless sighs, by whispered words of praise and encouragement and, incredibly, by the laughter of two people delighted with themselves and the moment. It was the echo of that laughter that remained long after the gasps had risen to cries and their bodies had erupted in climax.

5

They lay on the rug, bodies limp but entwined. Caroline was sprawled half over Brendan, anchored by the dead weight of his arm and one very long, very masculine leg. With her hair tangled, her cheeks flushed and her lips moist and full, she was the image of a woman well loved. He, with half-lidded eyes and a curling grin, was the cat who'd gotten the cream and then some.

"I feel happy," he announced just for the hell of it.

She was every bit as ebullient. "So do I. I should be feeling guilty or embarrassed, even horrified." She raised her head and sought his gaze. "I don't make a habit of going to bed with strange men."

"I am not strange," he assured her as he pressed her head back down. "And we didn't go to bed."

"All the more horrifying. On the *rug*."

He gave a smug chuckle. "Actually, it was nice. Spontaneous. A little unusual, in keeping with our relationship."

"What relationship? We barely know each other."

"We do."

"It's only been eight days."

"Are you kidding? I've been involved with you for weeks." Her head bobbed up. "Weeks?"

Patiently, he returned her head to his chest a second time. "Weeks."

"But why didn't I know?"

"Maybe because you were too busy. Or because you weren't looking for anything. Or because you're a lady. I'm not."

She grinned against his warm skin. "True. But still, if someone was watching me for that long, I should have felt it."

"Actually, I had reason to start looking," he confessed, and went on to explain about the two girls who had lived in the loft before her. "You are a pleasant turn."

She considered that. "I don't think I've ever been a turn before."

"Forget turn. Think pleasant. Then again, that's a gross understatement."

She grinned again. "If you say so."

"You don't think so?" He was the one to lift his head this time. "Hell, you're spectacular! You handled Elliot perfectly and didn't miss a beat when I arrived."

"I missed a couple right at the start. I never expected to see you sauntering in that way."

"But you knew who I was."

She nodded, then dropped her chin to his chest. "How's the toe?"

"Don't feel a thing."

"That could be good or bad."

"I'll worry about it later."

Her lips twitched mischievously. "How did you really bang it?"

"On the front door downstairs, when I was in such a hurry to rescue you from Elliot." He narrowed one eye. "How did you know I didn't run into a trash can?"

"You wouldn't run into a trash can," she said. "Besides, I knew you hadn't been running. You were in your apartment right up to the point when Elliot arrived, and within five minutes of that you were here." She paused. "You do run, though, don't you?"

"Not as much as I should. Mostly I play racquetball."

"Ahh."

"Ahh what?"

"I was right. Those nights when I'd see you come home

looking all grubby with your shirt hanging wide open, I guessed that you were coming from a club."

"If I had any brains, I'd shower there. But I always figure it'll be a waste of time, since I'll be sweaty again by the time I get home." Abruptly he looked stricken, almost comically so. Closing a hand over each of her arms, he tried to raise her. "Lord, I didn't think! I haven't showered tonight. How can you stand me?"

She denied his attempt to hold her away by exerting that little bit more force and said in a soothing voice, "I haven't complained, have I?"

"Maybe you're too polite."

"And maybe I have a head cold." But they both knew it wasn't so, which made her point. "Relax. I like the way you smell."

Given her obvious sincerity, he did relax. Rather, he tried, but the directness of her gaze did something to him. It seemed to enter through his eyes and move downward, squeezing his heart, buzzing his stomach, settling with a hot thud in his loins.

"Ever think of getting an air conditioner?" he asked. It was the first thing he could think of to say, and even then his voice sounded odd.

"Yes, and decided no."

"Me, too."

"How long have you had your loft?" she asked, feeling slightly muddled herself. The husky sound of his voice, the solidity of his long body, the same scent he'd worried about— all conspired to stoke the desire she'd thought sated. And when she looked at him—looked him directly in the eye— she was lost.

"Two years." His hand began to move on her back, palm light, long fingers gliding over silk-smooth skin. "I had another place before that, but it wasn't half as nice."

"Me, too. I can walk to work now."

"What do you do?"

She inhaled a deep breath and rubbed her nose against his chest, then found that so delightful that she repeated the move with her cheek. His skin was warm, lean over muscle, softened by hair. And he smelled . . . so . . . good.

"Caroline?"

She raised her head. "Hmm?"

It was a minute before he remembered what he'd been asking. He had to clear his throat before any sound emerged. "Work. What do you do?"

"I'm a family therapist."

He smiled somewhat distractedly and murmured, "A helping profession. I figured something like that."

"You did?"

He nodded, but very slowly. He was enchanted by the way her brows went up, widening her eyes. And those eyes . . . good Lord, he could drown. "It's the way you walk," he said in a sandy voice.

"It can't be."

He nodded again and as slowly.

"That's crazy," she whispered. She was propped up on a hand that covered that faint rise of his chest, and she'd discovered that the slightest movement not only ruffled his chest hair but brought his nipple to a peak against her palm.

Brendan shifted her gently until she was more fully atop him. His hands formed Vs beneath her arms, supporting her upper torso. His eyes slid from her mouth to her neck, then slowly, helplessly, drifted lower. "Not crazy. You walk lightly and quietly—" he took an unsteady breath "—but there's a gentleness in your stride and a gracefulness in your legs. And—" his eyes grew smoky "—patience. You exude patience, all round and creamy, tipped with rose—"

"My legs?"

"Your breasts." With ease and fluidity, he raised her until one of those breasts met his mouth, which latched on and began a sucking motion that brought a sweet cry to her lips.

"Caroline." His voice was hoarse around her budding flesh. "Caroline what?"

She sucked in her breath and managed a strangled "Cooper," as he tongued her nipple.

It was a minute before he spoke again, and then it was in

the thickest of whispers. "I want you again, Caroline Cooper. Slower this time. I want to savor every . . . single . . . sweet . . . spot." He punctuated each word with gentle nips that left her a writhing mass of awakened sensuality.

They did go more slowly this time, and Brendan wasn't the only one to savor the details. While he worshiped her breasts, she ran her fingers through the vibrant tangle of his hair. While she delineated the virile contours of his chest with her mouth, he familiarized himself with the ivory sheen of her shoulders and back. While he explored her legs and thighs with hands that trembled, her own, trembling, too, discovered the flatness of his belly and the smooth, soft skin by his groin.

The time for fantasy had passed. Everything they touched and tasted and felt was real. They flowed around and about each other, seeming suspended in time and space, yet acutely aware of each slow caress. The sweat that covered their bodies was an erotic conduit; the heat in the room was forgotten, overshadowed by the heat of desire.

But there was a price to be paid for slowness. Their limbs began to quake with the burden of harnessed desire. Sweet torture, pleasure and pain, contorted their features. Anguished cries tore from their throats.

When he could stand no more, Brendan turned them so that they were on their sides facing each other. He slid a leg between hers, then a hand to fill the gap he'd opened.

At the first such caress, Caroline tightened her arm around his neck. She needed to hold on; the world seemed to be falling away with sudden speed. She didn't know if it was the newness of Brendan that was so exciting, or if her reaction to him was pure chemistry, or if there were deeper factors at work. She did know that his most gentle touch was frighteningly intense—and that she needed more. With a low whimper, she arched closer.

"Is it good?" he whispered as he watched a myriad of expressions cross her face. By concentrating on those expressions and on the sheer act of speech, he was hoping to stave off his own hunger a bit.

She nodded. Another whimper slipped out.

"You're very soft there." His fingers slid lower. "And moist here."

She whispered his name, nothing more, but the wonder that filled her eyes was all the encouragement he needed.

He continued his low crooning. "Do you know what it does to a man to touch a woman here? Such a private place. And here." His finger entered her with ease and was quickly joined by a second. "No, no, don't shut your eyes."

"I can't help it. . . ." Barely a whisper.

"Look at me, Caroline."

Only with great effort did she manage to obey. She felt dizzy, on a drugless high that threatened to blow her mind. Her fingers bit into his shoulders, and her whisper was broken. "When you do that to me . . ."

He repeated the slow inner stroking. "This?"

She groaned. "It's not enough."

"What do you want?"

She lowered one hand and touched him.

The effect was like fire. He jerked, took several quick, shaky breaths and knew that he couldn't last much longer. Her fingers surrounded him, knowing just what to do. He was almost as moist as she and from the same cause. Still he spoke, albeit in a voice rough with strain. "Do you want me inside?"

She gave a vigorous nod. Her lips formed his name, then went on to whisper, "Now!"

"My tongue?"

"Oh!" she cried. The image he evoked was too strong. With a loud indrawn breath, she stiffened, then began to pant with the force of the inner explosion he'd caused.

But the image had worked on him, too, or maybe it was the feel of her hidden flesh pulsing, or the closeness of her body. Within seconds, he'd withdrawn his hand, rolled her over and surged inside. The last of her spasms was more than enough to send him into euphoria. But that was only the beginning, for no sooner had that climax passed than they worked together toward another, then another.

It was a long time before either of them was able to breathe with any degree of steadiness, and a lot longer before either spoke. Between utter exhaustion, intense satisfaction and the enervating heat of the night, they couldn't move. The silence seemed enough.

"Powerful," Brendan whispered at last. His breath couldn't begin to ruffle her hair, which was dripping with sweat but no more so than his own, which clung to his forehead.

Caroline made a sound that was part hum, part moan, entirely in agreement with his assessment.

"In all my dreaming I never imagined it quite like this," he added.

"I never let myself go half as far."

"You dreamed, too?"

She gave another agreeing hum.

"Tell me what you dreamed."

"I dreamed that you were tall and dark and handsome," she said, nestling more comfortably against him. "And you are."

"I could argue, but if you think so, that's enough. What else?"

"I thought your nose would be straight."

"Sorry."

"And that you'd be aristocratic."

"Oops."

"No problem. In my dream, you'd renounced all that decadence, so the end result is the same."

"That makes me feel better. What else?"

"That you were in your late thirties. I was on the button there."

"I dreamed that you were twenty-eight."

She tipped her head against his arm and awarded him a grin. "I like that."

"Was I right?"

"Nope."

"Twenty-seven?"

"What a diplomat you are."

"Okay. How old?"

"Thirty-one."

"You're kidding."

"Nope."

"The body I just ravished has been around that long?"

"Now, wait a minute. I'm not exactly Methuselah. And who are you to talk? You have seven years on me."

"Which is just about right, don't you think?"

She caught in a breath, then let it out in a soft "Yes."

He seemed very pleased with that. "Okay. Go on. What else did you dream?"

"That you were a doctor or a teacher." When he raised a hand, thumb down, she hastened to add, "But a lawyer's okay. My sister's a lawyer. I can take it."

"Thank heavens for that."

"What kind of law?"

"Criminal work."

"À la Perry Mason?"

"Not quite. I work for the Justice Department."

"Do you now?" she asked with enthusiasm. Mentally she shifted the white hat from the head of a doctor or teacher to that of a loyal government employee.

"'Fraid so."

"Why afraid? I think it's great."

"There are many who'd disagree," he said, thinking of one in particular, then quickly pushing her from his mind. "There is a stereotype of government bureaucrats sitting at their desks shuffling papers."

"Is that what you do?"

"I often sit at my desk, but the only shuffling of papers I do is to organize one file and move on to the next."

"What's in the files?"

"Investigation reports, witness statements, a million documents. I work full-time on domestic terrorism."

"Bombings?"

"Those and kidnappings and scores of other crimes or would-be crimes."

She couldn't quite hide a shiver. "Sounds frightening."

"In the sense of the crimes being real, it is. Would that I were out of a job."

In spite of the subject matter, she had to smile. She'd said something very similar to Ben when he'd been so blithely commenting on her work, and it warmed her no end to know that Brendan shared her feelings. That warming livened her curiosity.

"I don't usually think of terrorism in relation to this country."

"Most people don't. Maybe that's because the most brutal acts of terrorism are still committed abroad. I'd like to think that the way this country's run has something to do with that. We're more vulnerable abroad, because we don't have the same controls there that we do here."

"Controls and democracy—a strange pairing."

"Not really. The Declaration of Independence pledges to protect the rights of our citizens to life, liberty and the pursuit of happiness. Certain controls are necessary to protect those rights. The occasional traveler may complain about the security measures in airports, particularly when he's stopped and searched for whatever set off an alarm, but, by far, the majority of us understand that our own safety is at stake. We appreciate the measures taken to secure it."

Caroline had been watching him as he talked and was fascinated. He was articulate, never slipping into the legalese some lawyers hid behind. He was also sincere. Honesty radiated from his eyes, and the relaxation of his mouth reflected his ease with his thoughts.

"Don't look at me that way," he whispered. "It turns me on."

She blinked once, unaware of what she'd been doing. "I'm sorry. I didn't mean to do that. It's just that you have such strong conviction. It's written all over your face."

What was written all over her face was admiration, but it wasn't the kind that an empty-headed woman showed for a man snowing her with rhetoric. It was grounded in respect, and that was what was having such an effect on Brendan. It surprised him, actually. He'd never attributed sexual urges to respect. Of course, he realized they were indirectly related; if he respected the woman he was with, the sex was better. But the fact that the look on Caroline's face excited him had deeper implications, ones he wasn't quite ready—or able—to consider just then.

"I think I need a cool shower," he said.

"Is there danger involved?"

"In a cool shower?"

"In what you do. If you're dealing with terrorists, you have to be putting your own life on the line."

The concern he heard in her voice was adding to his woes. Concern . . . a sexual turn-on? He'd never have believed it before, but the proof was growing quickly. He tried to drag up an image of the most dangerous, the most despicable, the most offensive of terrorists. "I don't deal with them directly, not often."

"Do you try cases?" she asked, raising herself to see him better. The movement shifted her legs between his, brought her tummy warmly against his hip and her breasts against his ribs.

"On occasion." He cleared his throat. "Caroline, I do need a shower. How about we take one?" He felt he could handle showering with her better than he could handle lying naked with her. It would be all too easy to make love to her again, when what he really wanted was to talk, which they wouldn't do if they stayed as they were.

Caroline, who'd been totally immersed in thoughts of his work, wasn't quite sure what to make of his sudden wish for a shower. Though the room was still hot, the sweat had dried somewhat on their bodies. She wondered if he was looking for an excuse to get away. Some men wanted to be left alone after sex. He'd seemed perfectly comfortable to lie with her up until now, but maybe restlessness had caught up to him.

Her expression dropped, torn between apology and disappointment. "Am I asking too many questions? You're probably bombarded with the same ones over and over again. I'm sorry. It must get a little tedious . . . but I'd really like to hear more. I haven't known many lawyers. My sister is in corporate work, which is completely different—"

He stilled her babbling with a single, firm finger against her lips. "No, you're not asking too many questions. I'm glad you're interested, and I'll tell you everything you want to know later, but I'm gettin' pretty hard with you snuggling against me like this. I don't want you to think I have a one-track mind, because I really don't. It's just that my hard part doesn't want to listen to my softer parts. In short," he said, catching a breath, "if we don't get off this rug right now, you'll have raw buns tomorrow."

Caroline's cheeks grew red and she said, "Oh," so sheepishly that he gave her a fierce hug.

"Come on," he growled. "Let's shower. I want to know if your water pressure is as lousy as mine."

It was, but that took little pleasure from the time they spent under the spray. They were completely at ease with each other, talking gently as they soaped, shampooed and rinsed themselves.

Brendan was pleased that Caroline showed neither coyness nor modesty. As he'd dreamed, she was comfortable with herself as a woman, and the idea that she was comfortable enough with him to relax in such an intimate, if nonsexual, activity was gratifying.

Caroline was pleased that Brendan, who was very clearly aroused when they first stepped into the shower, made no attempt to slake his need. It wasn't that she didn't want him again, but somehow, being in such close confines yet foregoing sex made a statement that their attraction went beyond the physical. And that was something she needed to know— particularly after Ben's crude words the weekend before.

"Next order of business," Brendan declared, patting his stomach. "Food."

They were out of the shower, dried as much as the humidity would allow, and dressed again.

"I could make something," she offered hesitantly, "but the choice would have to be between a frozen dinner, a peanut-butter sandwich or scrambled eggs. I haven't much else that's fresh. Tomorrow's market day."

He waved aside her apologetic look. "I feel like Chinese. How about I bring in some take-out?"

"Would you rather go to a restaurant?" she asked, but her reluctance to do that was reflected in Brendan's eyes. Neither of them wanted to eat out. They weren't ready to share themselves with the world, air-conditioned or otherwise.

"We'll eat here." He headed for the door. "I'll just run back to my place for some money."

She reached for her purse. "I have money—"

"No way. Besides, you've got fresh clothes on. I want some and—" he paused to send a rueful glance at his toe, which was less swollen than purple "—a pair of sneakers." At the threshold, he turned and looked back at her. *I could be gallant and go by myself, but I don't want to leave you alone. You might start thinking and have doubts about what we've done, and I don't want that. I need more time with you. We have to talk about where we go from here.* "Come with me?" he asked quietly.

Caroline broke into an open smile. She hadn't really wanted to let Brendan out of her sight so soon, and while she'd never have told him that, she was relieved by the invitation. Holding up a single finger, she ran toward the closet for a pair of sandals.

Moments later, they retraced the route Brendan had taken with such haste earlier that evening. By the time they'd reached his apartment, he'd grown sheepish.

"You'll have to excuse the mess." He made an endearing and hurried—hence, futile—attempt to neaten the mail and newspapers that littered the peninsula jutting out by the door. "I wasn't expecting guests."

"It's okay. I already know you're a slob." Physically removing his hands from the mess, she shooed him away. "Go change. I'm starved." She finished neatening the counter, then stood against it and watched while he tugged on a pair of khaki shorts, shimmied into a clean white polo shirt and laced on a new-looking pair of sneakers. Sitting on the bed, he stuck out his foot and said with pride, "I knew I was saving these for a purpose." Then he stood and advanced on her with one hand low on his hip. "And how do you know I'm a slob?"

"I've seen the way you live, Brendan Carr." She tried to be stern faced, but her eyes danced. "You leave clothes on the chair and magazines all over the coffee table, and you rarely make your bed." She cast a glance at the sink. "I was right. Those *are* dirty dishes piled up."

"You must use binoculars."

She shook her head.

"It's really that bad?"

She nodded.

"I'll have to have the cleaning service more often."

She laughed.

"You're enjoying this, aren't you?" he asked, feigning hurt, but when she nodded again, he grinned. "Let's get that food." Throwing an arm around her shoulder, he guided her toward the door.

"Tell me more about your work," Brendan said, dropping a denuded sparerib into the dish Caroline had set out for that purpose. "How long have you been a therapist?"

"Officially, for seven years. I got my degree at Duke and spent four years working in the Raleigh-Durham area before I came to Washington."

"Why Washington?"

Wiping her greasy hands on a paper napkin, she reached for an egg roll. "I've always been intrigued by the capital. When I got wind of an established group looking for an additional member, I jumped at the chance. It's worked out well. My partners have their little quirks, but they're capable therapists and they gave me more than a fair start. Things have built to the point that my schedule is pretty full."

"Hence the long hours doing reports at home each night?"

"Do *you* have binoculars?"

"Nope. Just a knack for putting two and two together.

Hardly a weeknight goes by that you don't spend time at this table."

"There never seem to be enough hours at the office."

"But you do work late there some nights." He was watching her plate as she tried to break into the egg roll with her chopsticks. "Why don't you just pick it up and take a bite?"

"Because this is where the challenge lies."

"To hell with challenges." He reached for his own egg roll, brought it straight to his mouth and devoured one-third of it in a single, neat bite. After he'd swallowed, he gave her a winsome smile. "That wasn't so bad, was it?"

"You have a bigger mouth than I do."

"True," he said, and continued to smile for a minute. She could match him quip for quip. He liked that in a woman.

"What?" she asked, simultaneously amused and bemused by his lingering smile.

He shook his head and forced himself to tone down the smile. "Nothing. We're getting off the subject of your work. When I think of family therapy, I picture an entire family sitting around a table yelling at each other with the therapist serving as referee."

She chuckled. "Close. There's no table to sit around, but I do referee at times. Actually, my practice is broader than what you've described. I work with families who can't get along, couples who can't get along, kids who have self-image problems or problems coping with a divorce or a death, fathers who feel left out, single mothers . . ." She paused for a breath. "The list goes on and on."

"Pretty heavy."

"Sometimes."

"Does it get you down?"

"Sometimes. Well, not so much the subject matter, because I'm one of those who believe that every cloud has a silver lining. What really gets to me is when I can't reach a client or when outside factors come into play that ruin the momentum of what I feel has been productive therapy."

"Such as . . . ?"

"When a parent gets tired of paying the bill. He sees a

superficial improvement in his child's behavior and decides that, presto, the problem's gone. I'm not one to carry on therapy ad nauseam, but superficial changes are superficial. It's like taking penicillin for a strep infection; the symptoms disappear after the first few days, but if the patient doesn't continue to take the full ten days' worth or whatever, the deep-down germs live on."

"When the problems recur, do you see the child again?"

"Once in a while. Usually I'm the scapegoat. The parent tells himself that I did a poor job and goes to another therapist. I've had clients who've already seen other therapists come to me with the same premise."

"Do you take them on?"

"How can I not?"

"You're a softy."

"My own words exactly," she said with a grunt as she stabbed at the egg roll in frustration. Her delicate picking had done nothing but shred the wrapper. "My heart bleeds easily." She raised the mangled piece of food with her fingers. "Too easily." She bit into it as Brendan had done to his. She wasn't quite as neat; half of the stuffing fell to her plate. "Right about now," she said, then waited until she'd swallowed what was in her mouth before continuing, "I'm feeling badly for Elliot."

Brendan had felt it coming. Strangely, though, he didn't feel threatened. He did feel curious. "What does he mean to you?"

"He's a friend. Nothing more. Tonight was a blessing in some ways. I've been tactfully trying to give him the hint for a while, but he hasn't caught on. At least now he knows. He's probably sitting in his apartment, feeling humiliated and very down on himself. Despite his bravado, he's a little weak in the ego department."

"I pretty much guessed," Brendan said through a dry half smile, "that his accusations were lopsided."

She gave a one-shouldered shrug. "Elliot did his best. He made up his mind about what he thought I wanted to do—"

"And you were too polite to argue."

"Not too polite. . . ."

"Too good-hearted, then."

"It's just so . . . *painful* to disappoint someone that way. His intentions were always good."

"Will you call him?"

Fiddling with the chopsticks and the scraps of egg roll on her plate, she mulled over that possibility. "I think I have to. I'd like to tell him my feelings. It's overdue—I should have said something sooner—but if I can make him feel a little better about things, it'd help."

"You don't think he'll be even more humiliated if you call?"

That hadn't occurred to her, or maybe it had and she'd ignored it. She had to admit to the possibility that, by calling Elliot, she'd be easing her own feelings of guilt far more than his sense of rejection. "Do you think so?" she asked cautiously. "You're a man. What would you want, if you were in Elliot's shoes?"

"That's hard to say."

"Would you feel that I was rubbing salt in the wound?"

He forked in a mouthful of Moo Shu Beef and chewed pensively. "Probably. At least, at the time I would. Later I might realize that what you said made sense. 'Course, that would depend on what you did say."

"That there isn't any future in our relationship, that it could linger for months but that that wouldn't be fair to either of us."

Brendan nodded. "I could probably buy that if I were Elliot, but there's more that he'll want to hear." The inflection of his voice suggested that she'd know what that was, which she did.

"He'll want an explanation for you and me," she supplied with a smattering of guilt.

"Right."

She took a deep breath. "Then I'll just have to repeat what we told him tonight."

"A lot's happened since then."

She dropped her gaze. "I know."

"Are you sorry?"

Her eyes flew back to his. "No!" After a moment's pause, she asked softly, "Are you?"

He shook his head firmly and with finality.

That satisfied Caroline. Out of sheer curiosity, she asked, "Who is the pretty blond-haired woman I've seen at your place?"

Brendan answered in a similarly straightforward tone. It was as though they'd already agreed that the blonde was no threat, simply an incidental to be explained. "Jocelyn. We've dated some. It sounds as though my situation with her is very much the same as yours has been with Elliot."

"She wants more, but you don't?"

"That's it."

"She doesn't take hints."

"Nope."

"And you can't just tell her to get lost."

"Right. She's new around here. A mutual friend back in Detroit told me she was coming and asked if I'd show her around. She's a very nice, very gentle lady. I've been trying to think of men to introduce her to, but the ones I know are either too young, too old, too married or too tough."

"How about you give her Elliot's name?" Caroline suggested tongue-in-cheek.

He answered in the same mischievous vein. "How about you give him her name?"

"On second thought—"

"—we ought to wait a bit. It'd be pretty awkward breaking up and arranging a fix-up in the same breath."

Caroline grinned broadly, then took a loud breath and sat back. "Well, now that we have that problem solved . . ."

"What about the other fellow who was here?" Brendan asked. "The one who stopped by last Sunday."

Her grin faded into something less gentle and she set down the chopsticks. "That's Ben. We were together for a year, but it's over and done. He's been in Spain for six months. I guess he was hoping I'd fill the gap until he could find someone else."

"But you won't."

"Absolutely not."

"Good." He, too, sat back. They continued to regard each other in silence for a minute. Then he said, "Which brings us down to the nitty-gritty. Are we . . . a couple?"

She didn't have to give it much thought. Though their lovemaking played a role in her decision, it was far from the deciding factor. She felt comfortable with Brendan, but more than that, he excited her. There was so much in his eyes as they held hers now, so much in his expression, so much in his mind. She'd be a fool not to explore all those things. And Caroline Cooper was no fool.

6

"I'd like that . . ." Caroline began.

Brendan worried when her voice trailed off. "But . . . ?"

"I'd like it more than anything. But there's something you ought to know. There have been times lately . . ." She frowned, struggling to verbalize her thoughts. "There have been times lately when I've felt . . . used."

He nearly sighed in relief. For a split second, thoughts of a dire illness or a dark cloud from the past or even an impending move that would take her from Washington had flitted through his mind. "Used" he could deal with, once he knew what she meant.

"By men?" he asked.

"No, no. By . . . oh, Lord, by *everyone*." Her eyes widened emphatically. "Maybe 'used' is the wrong word. It sounds malicious, when there's never been malice intended." She continued to struggle, finally eyeing him helplessly. "But I can't find a better word."

"Just take it slow and tell me what you feel. There's, no rush. We have all night."

His soothing tone was a help, and his eyes held all the patience in the world. Encouraged, she began to explain. "When you asked me how long I'd been a therapist, I answered in terms of 'officially.' Do you remember?" He nodded. "Well, unofficially I've been one for nearly twenty years."

"An eleven-year-old therapist?"

She acknowledged the absurdity of the claim with a feeble smile. "Actually, I was probably twelve or thirteen, but it all begins to blur from there. I had a good-sized group of friends, and we were all pretty close. Somehow I emerged as the confidante. They poured their hearts out to me, and I listened and soothed as best I could. My brother and sister—he's a year older, she's two years younger—did the same, and I don't remember when that began. I was the one in the middle, the one with a level head on her shoulders, the Rock of Gibraltar, the Wailing Wall, the Solomon. My brother is a bright guy but he's always been impulsive. He leaps before he looks, then falls apart when something goes wrong. My sister is every bit as bright, but she's always had a talent for biting off more than she could chew. Given that she's a perfectionist and that she can't always meet her own high standards, she ends up tense. It's always been my job to help her work through that tension."

"I would have thought that to be your parents' job," Brendan observed gently.

Caroline shot a helpless glance at the ceiling. "My parents are a whole other story. My dad is the sweetest guy in the world. He runs a successful business and he's a crackerjack at what he does, but when it comes to dealing with other people's emotions, he's helpless. Unfortunately, my mother is a whirling dervish of emotions. She worries about anything and everything. If there aren't any problems, she creates them."

"So your brother and sister turned to you."

"And my mother. She turned to me, too! She'd be right there when I got home from school to tell me of her latest trauma. And I listened and commiserated and said whatever I could to make her feel better." She held up a hand. "Please don't misunderstand me. It wasn't that I had any answers, that I was a genius or anything—simply that I had a positive attitude and some common sense."

"And patience," he said with a smug grin.

She blushed, recalling the observation he'd made while they were making love. "And patience," she admitted softly. She reached for the pitcher of iced tea, refilled both their glasses, then took a long, cool drink from her own.

Brendan was thinking about what she'd said. "You were obviously a born counselor. Your family must have seen that early on."

"I'm not sure that they were aware of what was happening back then. Now they say things like 'I knew I could count on you, Caro,' or 'What would I do without you, Caro?' or 'You're a good soul, Caro.' "

"Now? You mean it's still going on?"

She nodded and scrunched her face up in despair. "My mother still calls me several times a week from Milwaukee, my sister from Philadelphia, my brother from Baltimore. I do love them and I'd be lonely if I didn't talk with them, but to come home from work and have to deal with every one of their problems and non-problems and worries and fears . . . it's too much. Maybe if I were in a different profession, if I weren't dealing with other people and their problems day in, day out, I'd have emotional energy to spare. But I've begun to feel so *tired* of it all, so—"

"Used."

Her gaze grew beseeching. "Then you understand?" He barely had time to nod when she sat forward and rushed on. "And it isn't only my family. It's my friends. Old ones drop by when they're in Washington, and I love seeing them and exchanging news, but somehow or other we always revert to the same pattern. They pour out their hearts, I listen and counsel. I mean, it's always been this way, so I don't know why it's bothering me now—except that maybe it's finally hit me that there ought to be two sides to a relationship.

"Okay—" she held up a hand "—you're probably thinking that I'm a stable person who solves her own problems rather than seeking out the advice of others, and to a certain extent you're right, but not completely. I have needs, too."

"Do your friends know that?"

"On one level they do, but I don't harp on it. And I know

that's my problem, too. If I were to say something or be more demanding, things might be different. But I get so wrapped up in their lives that I don't think of my own until afterward. Take Jessica Wright. We met at an aerobics class two years ago and became friends. I really like her. She works at a local TV station, so she's interesting and she's fun. But her social life is like a soap opera. She called me last month—I still can't believe this—she called me in a panic because she'd mistakenly made dates with two guys on the same day. Now, theoretically she'd have been okay. She was seeing Donald in the afternoon and Malcolm in the evening. Except she'd promised Malcolm dinner at seven, which was just about the time Donald said he'd have her back."

Brendan could anticipate the problem. "But she couldn't say anything to either, because neither was supposed to know about the other?"

She nodded. "Would you believe that both men work at the station?"

He winced, but his thoughts were already moving ahead. "What did she have you do?" he asked cautiously.

"I went over to her place at five, set the table and put dinner on to cook—none of which she could do earlier, or Donald would have suspected something when he picked her up."

"Couldn't she have said a girlfriend was coming over?"

"With fine china, starched linens and candlelight?"

Brendan conceded the point with an appreciative "Not bad. So, what happened then?"

"By the time seven rolled around, I had everything ready. Jessie had Donald drop her at another friend's apartment. She raced through the back alleys and climbed up the fire escape to her bedroom, while I did my best to occupy Malcolm." She combed her fingers through her bangs, which were damp again from the heat. "Forget the fact that I was late for a date myself. Jessie was so apologetic and so grateful that it didn't seem to matter at the time. I told myself that it was one instance, that's all. But if it isn't Jessie, it's someone else." She paused for the quickest of breaths before barreling on. "Take my partners at work. They're all wonderful, and I never mind covering for them when something comes up, but there has to be a limit somewhere, somehow, on their other demands. Maren insists that I take her shopping—"

"You have great taste in clothes."

Caroline didn't have to ask how he knew what she wore, so she asked more softly, "Do you think so?"

He nodded.

The pleasure his compliment brought broke the momentum of her diatribe. She smiled and sat quietly for a minute.

"Go on," he prompted.

Her shoulder settled with the release of tension. "I can't believe I'm doing this. I sound just like my mother."

"You're human. You need to sound off once in a while. When was the last time you did it?"

She shrugged.

"Then it's long overdue. Please. Go on."

She gave a quick shake of her head. "You don't need this."

"Go on."

"I must be boring you silly."

"You're making me feel useful. Besides, there's a message that's coming for me at the end—that 'but' about our future together. Since I'm not sure I want to hear it, the longer you take getting there, the better." He cleared his throat. "Now, then, you were talking about your partner, Maren, with whom you go shopping. I take it she has lousy taste in clothes?"

Caroline sent him a you-should-only-know look. "On top of that, she has bright-red, almost orange hair and she's on the chubby side, so the challenge of finding things that become her is that much greater."

"How about your other partners?"

She raised a finger. "There's Peter, who is a single father and needs a recreation director when his thirteen-year-old daughter is with him, which is every other weekend." A second finger joined the first. "There's Norman, who's at war with his mother-in-law and needs a full-time strategist—and who, by the way, happens to be Elliot's brother, a lovely situation." A third finger went up. "And there's Jason, our part-time secretary, who has discovered that he gets better grades on his college papers after I've done some editing."

"And you can't say no?"

"How *can* I? They're my friends. They need help, so they come to me. They know I won't refuse. But it's been so tiring lately. Always another demand. Maybe it's the heat—" The phone rang. Her gaze flew to the offensive instrument, and her voice dropped to a conspiratorial whisper. "I knew it was too good to be true. Not a call all evening. This one is bound to be a doozy."

Brendan had to work hard to keep from laughing at her beleaguered expression. The phone rang again. "Should I get it?"

She seriously considered that, then shook her head. "If it's Elliot, he'd be crushed." She glanced at the digital clock on the face of the microwave oven. "It's pretty late. With the time difference, though, it could easily be my mother in some kind of dither. Even without the time difference, it could be Karen going into labor, or Carl about to strangle Diane—" A third ring came and Caroline pressed a fist to her forehead. "I can't stand this." Jumping up from the table, she snatched at the receiver. "Hello?"

"Gladys?" asked a slow, elderly male voice.

"Gladys," Caroline echoed in a chagrined whisper, then said full voice, "No, this isn't Gladys."

"Well, may I speak with her?" the man asked haltingly.

She closed her eyes and shook her head, unable to restrain a smile at the humor in the situation. "I'm sorry, but there's no Gladys here."

"Could you . . . tell me when she'll be back?"

She pressed two fingers to her forehead, rotated them in a slow circle. "You misunderstand. No one by the name of Gladys lives at this number."

"What number is this?"

"What number are you calling?"

There was the rustle of paper over the line. Lifting her hair off her neck with one hand, Caroline waited patiently. She looked first at Brendan then at the ceiling.

"Here it is," the man said slowly, and read off the number he wanted.

"You've dialed wrong, sir. Why don't you hang up and try again?"

"Oh, *I'm* sorry," he said in genuine dismay. "My fingers aren't as steady as they used to be. I'm so sorry."

"It's perfectly all right," she said, and hung up the phone. "That's the second time he's called," she told Brendan. "Poor old fellow—he sounds to be close to eighty. Why do you think he's calling Gladys so late at night?"

"Beats me," Brendan said with a grin.

The grin was a little too smug. "Do you *know* that man?"

"Of course not."

"But you know something."

He shrugged. "Just that certain urges are timeless."

Caroline looked doubtful as she returned to the table. "You don't really think that that old man . . ."

Brendan shrugged again. "You could always ask him next time he calls."

"Mmm. Now why didn't I think of that?"

"Because," he drawled, "you're a la-dy."

The smile she tried to hide came out crooked. She didn't know how any man could be as adorable as Brendan. He was sprawled in his chair with his legs crossed at the ankles. He'd long since kicked off his sneakers. His arms were folded over his chest, and his shirt had come free of his shorts. The way he was looking at her made her heart melt, and when he used that playful drawl . . . On impulse, she coiled an arm around his neck, leaned down and planted a wet, loudly sputtering kiss on his beard-shadowed cheek.

"What was *that*?" he asked, pulling her onto his lap.

"A zerbert."

"What's a zerbert?"

"Haven't you ever watched *The Cosby Show*? No, you haven't, because you don't have a television, but I do. When I heard all the hullabaloo about this terrific show, I had to watch it one time. Actually, it was funny enough to tune in more than once, but either I'm not home at the right time, or I'm on the phone, or I don't think to turn on the TV until it's too late."

"So what's a zerbert?"

"It's the thing that Rudy gives Cliff, the thing I just gave you." Levering herself from his lap, she reached for the container of Moo Shu Beef.

"What are you doing?"

"Reheating it."

"You don't like sitting on my lap?"

She was facing the kitchen, with her back to him. At his question, she dropped her chin to her chest. Didn't she like sitting on his lap? A foolish question. Her arms were alive where they'd made contact with his shoulders, and the backs of her thighs weren't the only things still tingling. "I think," she said, letting her head fall back with an intake of breath, "that I could happily sit on your lap for the rest of tonight and most of tomorrow."

"I wouldn't mind that," Brendan murmured in her ear. With barely a sound, he'd come up behind her. The length of his body conformed to hers. His arms framed her sides.

Sighing, she closed her eyes and relaxed her head against his shoulder. "Make that a week," she breathed.

He touched his lips to her temple. "Uh, could be a problem there. I'm supposed to fly to Detroit on Monday."

"For how long?"

"Four days."

"Do you do things like that often?"

"Several times a month."

She turned her head so that her face was against his neck. "Then I won't have your light to look forward to at night?"

"I could buy a timer."

"Not the same."

"You could come with me." He made a low crisscross of his arms on her middle, bringing her that much more snugly against his thighs. "We could do all kinds of naughty things before and after my meetings."

"But I have to work." Of her own accord, she turned and wrapped her arms around his neck. "You're an awesome temptation, though," she said, and met his lowering mouth. His kiss was deep and thorough. By the time he let her up for air, she was clinging to his shoulders for support. "And an awesome kisser," she added breathlessly.

"Look who's talking. Here I am, doing my best to show you that I have drives beyond the sexual, and you move this way or twist that way or come up with an expression that reduces me to a mass of live-wire hormones, when we still have to talk."

The moment's silence was profound. Caroline could clearly feel both his arousal and the tiny tremors caused by the flow of desire through his limbs. She was similarly aroused, though less visibly so, and one part of her wanted nothing more than to reach down and touch him. The other part recognized the truth in his words, and her facial expression acknowledged it.

He took her face in his hands and bent his head until their eyes met. "Tell me you'll sleep with me tonight. I can take all the talking in the world as long as I know that."

"I'll sleep with you tonight."

He sighed in relief, then abruptly shifted gears. Grabbing the carton of fried rice from the table, he set it in the microwave beside the Moo Shu Beef. "How long?"

"Uh . . . uh . . . two minutes?"

He programed in the time, turned on the microwave, then put some very necessary distance between himself and Caroline by walking around the far side of the table and resuming his seat. "Where were we?"

"Kissing."

He punished her with a scowl. "Before that."

"Zerberts?" The teasing was a help. Her heartbeat, racing moments earlier when she'd been in his arms, was gradually returning to normal.

He made a rewinding gesture with his hand.

Caroline complied. "Way back then I was complaining

about the people at work. But I need a break from ranting and raving. Tell me about you."

Brendan didn't respond at first. He was trying to gather his wits. From time to time—like now—he caught an overall glimpse of what was happening to him and he was shaken. He couldn't quite believe that Caroline was Caroline and that she was real and that he was suspiciously close to being head over heels in love. The last thought was the most incredible, but he didn't know how else to explain the way his heart seemed to open up and reach for her each time she looked his way.

"Brendan . . . ?"

He blinked once and regained his presence of mind. "You haven't finished telling me about you."

"I'll finish later."

"But I need to hear the moral of your story."

"It'll come."

"You'd leave me in suspense?"

She nodded. "Have you ever been married?"

He wanted to argue more, because, despite the lighthearted tone he worked so admirably to produce, he really *was* anxious to hear what she had to say. But he understood her curiosity. She had a right to it. Hadn't she just agreed to spend the night with him? Besides, it wouldn't hurt to lay his cards on the table at the start.

"No. I've never married. I came pretty close once, but the relationship died a very vocal and angry death."

Caroline tossed a glance toward the window and spoke softly. "When I was . . . fantasizing, I made a list of the reasons why you might still be single."

"How did you know I was—I mean, before tonight?"

"I don't get involved with married men," she said, as though the simple statement answered his question.

"You were planning on involvement?"

"Not planning. Fantasizing. I thought that maybe you'd had an early, unhappy marriage and were divorced. Or that you'd been too involved with your career to marry. Or that you'd never found the right woman." She paused, and her voice gentled all the more. "What happened?"

Before he had a chance to explain, the microwave dinged. She held up a finger, pivoted to remove the containers and set them on the table. Only after she'd doled out first rice, then beef did she give a go-ahead wave with her chopsticks.

Brendan gaped at the mound of food on his plate. "You didn't divvy this up too evenly."

"I just want a little."

"Do you want me to talk or eat?"

"Both."

"That'll be cute."

"You'll find a way."

Indeed, he found that by alternating between talking and eating and looking at Caroline, there was less pain in the telling of his story. "Gwen and I met as first-year law students in Boston. She was different from me—very aggressive, very sophisticated—and I found that exciting. As a couple, we worked well. We saw different sides of issues and argued them through until we'd both benefited from the debate. I had imagination, she had technique. We learned from each other." He took time to eat some, then resumed. "I really thought that was it. We were in love. We'd graduate, get jobs, live happily ever after."

In her customary role now, Caroline listened intently. Brendan had no idea that her heart was beating faster as she waited for the punch line.

"The trouble probably started in the summer before our third year, when we took jobs that theoretically were apprenticeships for what we'd be doing once we passed the bar. Gwen was interning with a corporate-law firm, I was in the district attorney's office. We'd have good-natured arguments—at least, I thought they were good-natured, though some of them were pretty heated—about private practice versus public service. Gwen felt that the true prestige and the only stability were in private practice. I felt that the real respect and the major challenge were in public service. We each had our own, very different convictions, and they became a constant issue between us. Our arguments went on through that entire third year, and toward the end, heated was a mild word to describe them." His features wore the memory without grace.

"So you went your own ways after graduation?"

"Oh, yes. I could have accepted Gwen's work—even though she talked like a fat cat—if she could have accepted mine. But she wanted money, and I knew damn well that as a public servant I'd never earn it in the big way she wanted."

"You were angry."

"Yeah, I was angry. And hurt. I felt as though she'd rejected me for the pettiest of reasons. Then I realized that the reasons weren't petty at all, and the rejection wasn't one-sided. Gwen and I had totally different value systems. The money issue was just the final straw. In hindsight, I'm amazed that we lasted together as long as we did. I could only guess that it was because we were students and living in that kind of limbo."

He paused to eat, but his heart wasn't in it. After pushing a piece of beef around his plate, he set down his fork and raised his eyes to hers. "I live well, Caroline—not extravagantly but well. Over the years I've saved and invested, but I've never been impressed with conspicuous consumption. The loft may be modest by some people's standards, but it suits my needs. I choose to live there. Someday I may choose to live elsewhere. If so, great. Likewise, when I take a vacation, I do it the way I want. That may mean staying in a posh Caribbean resort or in a crude ski lodge, but I have the option of choosing and I exercise it."

Caroline could find no fault with his philosophy, which was similar to her own. Nor could she fault the candor in his eyes, the urgency, the vulnerability. Knowing that he wasn't finished speaking, she remained quiet.

"I guess what I'm trying to say," he went on, propping his forearms on the table, "is that I don't have all the money in the world, nor do I want it or need it. I love my job. Working for the government gives me rewards far beyond green stuff. Sooner or later, this attorney general will resign or be replaced in the natural transition of power, in which case I'll be looking for a new job. Given my record, it won't be a problem. Don't ask me where I'll look, because I don't know. But I do know that I want to remain in public service."

Caroline felt admiration and a great deal of pride. "You sound defensive about it. There's no need."

His eyes were scanners, picking up every nuance of her reaction. "I just wanted you to know."

"Okay. Now I know."

Very slowly, his mouth softened from a firm line to a tentative half smile. "Aren't you glad you asked about marriage?"

She nodded. "It taught me more about you." Her eyes twinkled. "And just for the record, the last vacation I took was a long weekend this past February. I stayed at a farm in Vermont, where I shared a bathroom with eight other guests. We ate family style, sitting around a long table with the couple who owned the farm and their three kids, and we helped pay our keep by doing chores. Mine was to collect fresh eggs from the henhouse."

"Did you enjoy that?"

"I enjoyed walks in the nearby woods better than collecting eggs, but I'd go back to the farm in a minute. It was relaxing. Restful. A nice change of pace."

With a suddenness that startled her, Brendan bolted from his chair, rounded the table, scooped her up and carried her to the window seat.

"What are you doing?" she cried.

"Abducting you. You're perfect. You have the right answer for everything." He lowered himself to one knee on the seat and settled her sideways between his thighs. His arms closed around her, gently locking her in.

"You're abducting me to my own window seat? What kind of an abduction is *that*?"

"You had something else in mind?"

She said nothing, simply slipped her arms around his waist. He spoke against the top of her head. "Let's go to Maine."

"Hmm?"

"I said let's go to Maine. We can fly up to Bangor first

thing in the morning, rent a car and drive north. There are secluded little cabins for rent along the banks of the Penobscot. It'd be quiet and cool."

"That's incredible," she murmured.

"Not necessarily incredible but certainly—"

"No, no." She raised her head until their eyes met. "I don't mean Maine, but the fact that you suggested it. When I was fantasizing, I pictured us doing something like that. I pictured your sweeping me off somewhere where I'd . . . be . . . free of responsibility and guilt." She sucked in a sudden breath. "Brendan?"

He loved the way she said his name. "Mmm?"

"That's the moral of my story. When you ask me if we're together, and I say 'yes, but,' that's what I mean." She responded to the confusion in his eyes by hurrying on. Her own gaze had taken on the same candor, the same urgency and vulnerability she'd seen in his moments before. "If there's one thing I want—no, *need*—in a relationship it's freedom. I'm tired of feeling responsible for people. I'm tired of feeling guilty when I want to do my own thing. I'm so *tired* of the strings and the obligations and the little catches. There are so many hassles in my life. I don't want us to be a hassle." She paused, and the pleading quality in her voice grew even more so. "Can we do it?"

He was quiet for a minute, pensive as he studied her face. At last he said, "I don't know. I'm not sure any relationship can be as free as that. By definition, a relationship implies some kind of tie."

"Mutual attraction is a tie, and that's okay."

"What kind of attraction are we talking—physical or emotional?"

Caroline was in the process of deciding that when his features distracted her. They were honest, open features, inviting honesty and openness in turn. "That's exactly what I want," she whispered. "Honesty and openness. I want to say only what I want and what I feel. I want you to say only what you want and what you feel. No lies. No little fibs or empty platitudes. No game playing. No bartering with vows and promises."

"I can buy that—"

"But there's more. I want to be able to lean on you. I want to be able to complain, to let off steam, to ask for sympathy and advice and coddling. I'm tired of being the mother in relationships. I'm tired of being the caretaker. I want to be the one taken care of—" Her voice broke off sharply.

"What's wrong?"

"I don't believe I'm saying all this," she muttered, averting her eyes. She tried to put some space between them, but Brendan's arms tightened around her.

He could see her embarrassment and touched those telltale spots—her cheeks, her lips, her forehead—with his fingertips. "You're saying what you want. You're being honest and open."

"I'm being selfish."

"Maybe you need to be selfish."

"But I can't expect you to put up with that."

"Why don't you let me decide what I'll put up with and what I won't? Right now, I'm trying to understand exactly what it is you're saying."

Her earnest eyes went to his. "I'm saying that I can't promise you anything."

"You want a straightforward, uncomplicated, pleasure-as-long-as-it-lasts relationship."

Very slowly, she nodded. "I think that's all I'm capable of right now."

"Because you're being pulled in so many different directions?"

"And because I feel used up . . . burned out . . . drained."

Brendan didn't have to consider his options. Nor did he have to argue with Caroline about her capabilities. She might tell him that she felt used up, burned out and drained, yet she'd given him more in the past few hours than any woman had given him in years.

"I accept your terms," he declared.

"You do?"

He nodded. "I don't need a mother. Or a therapist. I can't promise to be a yes-man, because that's not me. I can't lie about my feelings and I don't think you'd want that, anyway.

But I won't take advantage of you. I won't expect or demand. I'll be yours to use as you want."

Caroline wasn't quite sure what to make of his easy compliance. She'd expected some sort of argument. Or was it that she'd hoped for one?

"You . . . really don't mind?" she asked hesitantly.

"Nope."

Her skepticism lingered for just a minute longer. In the end, it was destroyed by the very selfishness she'd worried about. She had what she wanted. Brendan Carr—secret friend and neighbor, white knight, lover extraordinaire—had agreed to honor the terms of her fantasy. He was what she needed right now. If he had no complaints, who was she to argue?

"Okay," she said, smiling. "We're a couple."

"How about Maine?"

"I still can't believe you've suggested that. When I was fantasizing, I thought of someplace up north where the nights would be cool. Only I imagined we'd drive the whole way."

He gave a quick shake of the head. "Not enough time. It's a ten-plus-hour drive. We'd have to turn around as soon as we got there and drive right back in order to get to work on Monday. If we fly, we'll have nearly twenty-four hours up there. Do you have anything here tomorrow or Sunday that can't be missed?"

"No."

"Me, neither. So what do you think?"

"I think that I've never thought of doing anything half as impulsive as this before."

"Wrong."

"Wrong?"

He took her face gently in his hands, fingertips tangling with the damp tendrils by her cheeks. "Making love with me earlier tonight was more impulsive, don't you think?"

She blushed and nodded.

"Which goes to show that our impulses are good where each other is concerned, so let's go to Maine."

"Okay."

7

It was a lovely idea, "was" being the operative word. But to have caught a flight to Bangor and allowed for driving time from there would have meant leaving at seven, and at seven that morning Brendan and Caroline were dead to the world. After a night of much loving and little sleep, it was no wonder.

Brendan was the first to awaken. Sprawled facedown on the bed, he turned his head on the pillow, dragged in a sleep-roughened breath, then stretched. His body felt utterly spent, but it was a relaxed kind of exhaustion, a lovely lethargy that spread from his neck to the tips of his toes.

Satisfied. He felt incredibly satisfied. It was a new sensation and it puzzled him, until he managed to pry open one eye and see where he was. Unable to resist when his gaze lowered over a disheveled head of hair, an ivory-smooth back and a softly rounded bottom, he broke into a very slow, very smug, very male grin.

A minute later, the grin vanished and his head popped up. "Oh, no," he whispered, focusing on the nightstand clock. *"Eleven?"*

A soft moan came from Caroline, whose head was tucked by his ribs. She curled a leg sideways and straightened one arm on the rumpled sheet, then, with another moan, reversed each of those movements and slowly turned toward him. He knew the instant that awareness hit her, because she went abruptly still. She extended the fingers of one hand and tentatively touched their tips to his waist. Then, as tentatively and almost disbelievingly, she raised her head and met his gaze.

"We overslept," he said. His voice, still sandy with sleep, held the same element of unsureness that he saw in her gaze. He didn't know whether she was pleased, displeased or indifferent, and the matter of the trip to Maine was the least of it. Hard as it was to believe, when he felt as though he'd known her forever, this was the first time they'd faced each other in broad daylight.

Caroline's only problem was an initial disorientation. She wasn't accustomed to waking up with a man, and his sheer physical presence with its distinct warmth and scent confused her—until she realized that this was Brendan. Her confusion vanished quickly. Brendan. It seemed perfectly natural that he should be in her bed. With the softest of smiles, she lay her forehead on his middle.

"Caroline?"

She yawned.

"Are you okay?"

She hummed a yes.

"I think it's too late to try for Maine."

"S'okay," she murmured. "This is nicer."

He gently twisted her hair off her neck. "Anyway, it's raining."

She hummed another yes.

He wondered if she knew what was going on, because it sounded to him like she was falling back to sleep. At least she seemed content, he mused with another smile as he looked down her prone form.

She was a sprawler like he was. There'd been some tight moments on her double bed during the night, times when, in their sexual abandon, they'd nearly toppled to the floor. Even now he was perilously close to the edge, while she angled out from his side. But he didn't mind.

Lord, was she sweet. Sweet and natural and uninhibited. She was perfectly at ease with him. They were made to be together.

Unfortunately he couldn't tell her that, though every instinct inside him wanted to. She'd think that he was trying to put ties on her, and he'd promised her that he wouldn't. He'd also promised that they'd go to Maine, but he'd broken that one.

"I should have set an alarm," he said in a soft apology to himself as much as to her, then mumbled something resembling "Guess I had other things on my mind."

For someone who was allegedly falling back to sleep, Caroline's good-humored if groggy-sounding "I'll say" was prompt. She knew precisely what Brendan had had on his mind, and she'd been guilty of the same. She couldn't begin to review each single instance when they'd turned to each other during the night. At times he'd been the initiator, at times she had been. Who had moved first hadn't mattered, though, because they'd shared a fierce and endless hunger. Even now, when she opened her eyes to the lean, manly lines of his torso and legs, she felt a stirring inside. Slightly dismayed by that, she stirred the rest of her body, maneuvering up to meet his head on the pillow. She couldn't restrain a moan in the process.

Rolling to his side so that he faced her, he put a hand on her hip. "What's wrong?"

Her cheeks grew pink. "Nothing. Just a little sore."

His hand slid down her thigh, then up its inside. "Here?"

She nodded.

"You haven't been with a man since Ben?"

"No. And I never did this with him."

Brendan's lips twitched. "Marathoning?"

She laughed. It was a soft sound, feather light and gay. "Mmm. I guess that says it." She was quiet for a minute. "Where do you get your strength? You're probably not the least bit sore."

His dark eyes twinkled as they held hers. "I wouldn't say that. I thought I was in good shape, playing raquetball and all, but this morning my upper arms and shoulders are protesting something or other I did to them."

She pictured precisely that something or other he'd done,

and her skin warmed. "I'm glad to know it's not only me," she said more softly. Looking into those velvety brown eyes, she was mesmerized. But it wasn't only his eyes. It was his tousled hair and his stubbly jaw and the breadth of his chest and the fullness of his sex—all of which were powerful items in her periphery.

He caught her lips in a soft, sweet kiss. The backs of his fingers feathered the warm curls at the apex of her thighs. Gently, so gently he touched her, but it was enough to generate all sorts of fiery little responses. When she moaned again, it had nothing to do with the soreness.

Riding on the pleasure brought by his stroking fingers, she whispered his name, then said in the same awe-filled breath, "This could go on forever."

"Let it," he whispered back. His fingers sank deeper and he delighted in the audible catch in her breath.

"I've never been like this," came her soft words of denial, but her eyes were closed, her lips remained parted, and she'd bent one knee to give him better access.

He was up on an elbow, alternately watching her face and the action of his hand. His voice was thick. "It's good for you."

"So much?" she whispered.

"Uh-huh."

She gave a tiny gasp and undulated against his hand. "We have to stop . . ."

"Not yet."

"I don't know . . . how much more I can take."

"Just this."

Her fingers dug into his shoulders. "Brendan!" Her breathy cry held both surprise and wonder, which was incredible to Brendan, since he'd brought her to many other climaxes in the course of the night. But her body rocked under the force of this one, and by the time the spasms had begun to wane, she had her face buried in the crook of his shoulder.

In time she let out a long, ragged breath.

"Good?" he whispered huskily.

"Mmm."

They lay for several minutes listening to the gentle sough of the warm rain falling in the courtyard and, beyond that, the distant sounds of traffic.

"Whatever must you think of me?" she murmured, raising sheepish eyes to his.

"I think," he said, "that you're a very passionate woman."

Her hand was resting on his stomach. She slid it lower, whispering, "And you? You share the passion. Will you let me pleasure you, too?"

His fingers closed around hers, guiding them back the way they'd come. "Not now." He kissed her forehead.

"But you're hard—"

"And enjoying the knowledge that I've satisfied you. It's enough this time."

Caroline found it hard to believe that a man could be so selfless. Yet, studying his face, she saw nothing but sincerity etched in his features. "Are you sure?" she asked in a whisper.

He smiled and nodded.

What a handsome smile, she thought. A confident smile. A gentle and generous one. It caused a distinct tightening in the region of her heart.

To counter that tightening, she sent him an accusing look. "You've bewitched me, I think. Either that or there's something in the air. Do you suppose exhaust fumes from the courtyard could be an aphrodisiac?"

Barely restraining a grin, he shook his head.

Her grunt held begrudging agreement. She didn't smell exhaust fumes; she never had. At the moment, though, the air surrounding them was musty, a mixture of humidity, sleep and sex that she found to be delightfully earthy.

Closing her eyes, she fit herself more snugly into the arm Brendan offered and smiled in contentment when he began to stroke her hair. It amazed her that she welcomed the physical contact, particularly given the weather. But then, physical contact with Brendan was like nothing she'd ever known before. It was new and refreshing, offering a counterpoint to the heat. His firm body supported hers even as it yielded to her curves. Regardless of how casual or incidental, his touch was exciting in the tremors it caused, and in the case of deliberate provocation it was stimulating, sensual and satisfying. It was also a total distraction from the rest of the world.

Body and mind, both buzzed with lingering pleasure. Caroline was thinking that she could spend the entire day with him this way when he gently eased her aside and rose from the bed.

Bending down to kiss the tip of her nose, he whispered, "Be right back," before disappearing into the bathroom. When he reemerged moments later, he crossed to the refrigerator, poured a large glass of orange juice and delivered it to her in the bed.

"I'm impressed," she said, propping a pillow between her back and the headboard. She accepted the orange juice, took a healthy drink, then handed it back. "Breakfast in bed. Not bad."

He took a swallow of juice. "If I were truly chivalrous, I'd be making an exotic omelet."

"It's okay. I'm not a breakfast person." She smirked. "But you don't know that, do you?"

Pursing his lips, he shook his head slowly. "Can't see in during the day. I only know you as a creature of the night."

She chuckled at that. "You make me sound wicked."

"Not wicked. Maybe wild or sensual, even wanton, but never wicked." He slid down against the headboard until they were flush side to side and slanted her a glance. "So. Since we've blown a trip to Maine, what's your pleasure? Washington is a romantic city. We could play tourist and walk around in the rain."

"In the rain?" she echoed meaningfully.

"Mmm. Forget walking around. We could take a drive to the country."

She considered that, but again there was the rain and somehow the thought of being restrained for hours in a car with Brendan's hands stuck on the wheel bothered her. She crinkled her nose in rejection of the idea.

"I could leave you in peace," he suggested cautiously. "You could do whatever you'd do on a normal Saturday—"

She interrupted him with a vigorous shake of her head. Relieved, he spread his arms in a gesture of self-sacrifice. "I'm at your disposal. You name it."

What she really wanted to do was to stay right there all day. She felt pleasantly tired and thoroughly sated. Her body's soreness would respond to a warm bath, and she rather liked the idea of taking one with Brendan, then just lying around talking, making love, thumbing her nose at the busy pace of the rest of her life.

But, Lord, what would he think if she suggested a full day of lazing around? He might revise his assessment of her to wicked after all. What she needed, she decided, was for *him* to suggest that they idle away the day together.

The phone rang just then. She shot a glance in its direction, then returned her gaze to Brendan. When the second ring came, she plopped a wet kiss on the tiny white scar on the tip of his chin, climbed over his body and padded across the floor to the peninsula. She had the instrument halfway to her ear before she thought twice, but by then it was too late.

"Hello?"

"What's going on, Caroline? I got a call from Elliot a few minutes ago. He's furious."

"Norman," she breathed, looking distinctly regretful as she turned around to face Brendan. If only she'd stopped to think before she'd picked up the phone. If only she'd let the damned thing ring. If only she'd put on her machine. "How're ya doin', Norman?" she asked conversationally.

"Not real well, considering that my brother just ruined the peace of my Saturday brunch."

She felt a surge of guilt. "I'm sorry," she said on impulse, then added, "He shouldn't have done that."

"What I want to know is why he did. What happened between you two?"

Caroline's eyes were on Brendan, who was lounging against the headboard with one knee bent and an arm folded behind his head. She had his full attention, which, thank heavens, wasn't a problem. He knew about Elliot. He knew about Elliot's relationship to Norman. And the sight of him—his mere presence—calmed her.

"What did he say?" she asked quietly.

"He said you'd been two-timing him."

"He's upset."

"He said you'd been using him."

She felt another twinge of guilt. True, she'd used Elliot as a buffer between Ben and her, but Elliot knew nothing of that. As for the accusations he'd made the evening before—accusations she was sure he'd repeated to his brother—she was innocent.

"He's misinterpreted things, Norman."

"So, what's the story?"

She shook her head in dismay. "I can't believe he called you."

"He's my brother. My *younger* brother."

"But he's still thirty-six," she argued, tamping down a spurt of annoyance. "Did he really expect that you'd come running to his rescue and make everything all right?"

"I'm not sure what he expected. Maybe he just had to let off steam. But if I can help him, I'd like to."

Caroline gave a tiny sigh. Norman was a good guy. For that matter, so was Elliot. Between them, though, they were going about things the wrong way. "I'd like to help him, too," she said, "which is why I was going to call him later."

"He seems to feel that it's over between you."

"It is."

"Because of another man?"

She felt another little burst of annoyance and had to remind herself that this was Norman, her partner. If she lashed out and antagonized him, things would be uncomfortable at work. Besides, she really did like him. While he had no business prying into her personal life, his heart was in the right place.

"No," she answered calmly. "It's over because of Elliot and me. We're not right for a long-term relationship."

"I thought you were perfect for each other."

"Oh, Norman," she said with a sad smile and a sigh. "You *wanted* us to be perfect for each other."

"Sure I did. He's my brother and you're my partner and I like you both. What could have been nicer?"

" 'Nice' doesn't necessarily make for a good marriage."

"You know what I mean."

"Yes."

"Were you really planning on calling him?"

"Yes."

"Please do, Caroline. I think you owe it to him."

"I know that, Norman."

"I've never heard him so angry."

"His pride is hurt."

Norman hesitated for an instant, clearly trying to be diplomatic about something he'd already mentioned once but unable to restrain his curiosity. "He did say something about another man."

She gnawed on her lower lip. What she had with Brendan was private. Still, she wondered if a touch of the truth wouldn't go a long way toward pacifying Norman.

Her lip slid free of her teeth. "Elliot asked me out for this weekend and I refused. In spite of that, he showed up last night. While he was here, a friend of mine—a neighbor—arrived."

"A man?"

"Yes."

"Are you dating him?"

"I hadn't been before last night, but now, yes, I think so."

"So Elliot saw you with the guy, after you'd turned down a date with him."

"Elliot was in my apartment uninvited when he saw my neighbor arrive," she argued. "To tell you the truth, I was grateful my neighbor appeared. Elliot was being a little pushy."

"Pushy? What do you mean?"

"I think you know," she murmured, quickly regretting she'd mentioned it. "Listen, Norman, all I can say is that I will call Elliot. If you want to know anything more, you really ought to ask him."

"He's apt to tell me to take a flying leap."

She snickered softly. "Why didn't *I* think of that?"

"Because you're too diplomatic. You really would be good for Elliot, you know. You'd tone him down—"

"Norman . . ."

"Okay. Go back to whatever it was you were doing. I'll talk with you later. Bye-bye."

Very quietly, she replaced the phone in its cradle. Averting her eyes from Brendan, she set to work putting a pot of coffee on to drip. "He told me to go back to whatever it was I was doing," she said self-consciously, "He should only know."

Brendan had easily gotten the gist of the phone conversation. He was wondering whether this unwelcome intrusion from the outside world would sour her on their relationship. "How do you feel?"

"About what we've been doing?" She indulged in a private smile. "Perfectly justified and content."

"How do you feel about Norman's call?"

The smile faded. "Badly. It was enough that Elliot was upset. Now he's upset Norman, so things are worse." Setting down the coffee canister, she turned pleading eyes to Brendan. "Why did he do that? Why did he have to call his brother right off the bat to complain?"

"Maybe he just needed to talk to someone."

She considered that for a moment, then gave a negligent shrug.

Brendan tried again. "Maybe he thought that Norman could straighten you out."

She gave a soft snort, but she supposed that possibility was real.

He regarded her more soberly. "Maybe he wanted to beat you to the punch. Maybe he was afraid you'd get to Norman first with a report of attempted assault."

She had to admit that that did make sense. She hadn't thought of what Elliot had done as an attempted assault, since she'd handled it and emerged without a bruise. But a court of law certainly might see things differently. Perhaps Elliot realized that. "It wasn't really . . . so bad," she said in Elliot's defense. And I pretty much did tell Norman about it."

"Only at his goading. At least, I assume he was goading."

"Yes."

She'd turned back to the coffee when Brendan rose from the bed and came to her side. "Don't let it get you down. You handled Norman well, and you'll do the same with Elliot."

"Why do I feel like such a crumb?"

"Because you've conditioned yourself to feel that way." He tipped his head and gave her a humorous once-over. "You don't *look* like a crumb. Do you realize that you're parading around here stark naked, without a stitch of clothing, much less modesty?"

She returned the once-over indulgently. "Look who's talking."

"Isn't it great?" he asked with such a boyish grin that she had to shake her head in chiding.

"You are impossible. Here I am, trying to grapple with a serious dilemma, and your mind is in the gutter."

He hooked an arm around her waist and anchored her to his side. "The gutter? No way! I'm simply saying that we're perfectly at ease with each other, and isn't that nice? Besides," he rushed on, "I think you have to put your 'serious dilemma' in perspective. Norman knows about what's happened. You were dreading his finding out, but that's over and done now. He's been mollified, hasn't he? And you've already made the decision to call Elliot. So, what's to grapple with—other than deciding what you want to do today?"

Before Caroline could answer, the phone rang again. This time she did think twice. After another ring and continued indecision on her part, Brendan lifted the receiver and put it to her ear.

She offered a hesitant "Hello?"

"It's me. Did you speak to Diane?" The accusation in Carl's voice left no doubt that his question wasn't idle.

She mouthed, "my brother," to Brendan before speaking

into the phone. "We had dinner together last week, but I already told you about that. She's called several times since then. Why? What's happened?"

"She informed me that I was being impulsive and that, according to you, if she gave me a little time I'd come to my senses."

Caroline closed her eyes and slowly shook her head. She wasn't denying what Carl said, simply trying to understand how her good friend Diane could have been so tactless as to repeat her advice verbatim and then quote the source.

With a squeeze to her shoulder, Brendan left her side. She opened her eyes to watch him as he finished making the coffee. The sight of him gave her resolve.

"It's true, Carl. You are being impulsive."

"Since when are you the authority?"

She was careful to keep her voice gentle, though she had no intention of backing down. "Since we were kids and you dumped every little problem in my lap. Since I was an undergraduate psychology major. Since I earned a Ph.D. in counseling."

At the last bit of news, Brendan's brows went up. Caroline waved away the significance of the degree with her hand.

Carl was equally unimpressed. "Don't throw fancy qualifications at me. I'm not your client."

"Right. You're my brother, which means that I know you better than I know most of my clients. You've always been impulsive. Things get a little rocky between you and Diane and you throw up your hands and decide that that's it, it's over. You move out of the house and start divorce proceedings without ever sitting down and trying to talk things through with her."

"She's making crazy demands."

"Do you have any idea why? Because she's trying to shock you into slowing down and thinking, really thinking, about all this. She doesn't want a divorce, Carl. She loves you."

"Oh, yeah."

"She does."

"Then she has a strange way of showing it."

The coffee started to drip. Brendan paused in his hunt for the mugs to give her an encouraging wink.

Caroline didn't take her eyes from him. "You've backed her into a corner. Maybe if you offer her a hand, she'll be able to express herself better."

"Offer her a hand," Carl retorted, "and she'd take both, and where would that leave me?"

"Happily married?"

"Fat chance."

Dropping her gaze to the floor, she sighed. "Look, Carl, you have to do something. I've suggested marital counseling, but you've vetoed that idea more than once. You and Diane have to talk. If you don't you'll find yourself all alone down the road."

"You're on her side."

"I'm not on anyone's side."

"Bullshit."

"No, Carl." Her patience was beginning to wear thin. "I'm rooting for you and Diane as a couple. You have so much going for yourselves. Take my word for it, your problems are minor compared to some that couples work through."

With a vocal growl of frustration, Carl hung up the phone.

Caroline stared at the silent receiver for several long moments before slowly replacing it. She stood with her fingers curled around the edge of the counter and her head bowed. "I feel useless. Nothing I say seems to help, which would be fine if they didn't keep dragging me into it."

Brendan reached over and tucked a wayward lock of hair behind her ear. "You've tried. What more can they ask?"

"Nothing, I suppose. But, damn, it's a little like the teacher whose own kid is flunking out of school. My field is counseling, but when it comes to the marriage of my brother and my best friend, I might as well be a . . . a caterer."

He laughed. "Where'd that come from?"

A crooked smile stole to her lips. "It's my secret ambition. I've never been able to cook for beans."

"I take it that's a warning."

"Uh-huh." Her eyes had grown teasing as they clung to his. She didn't want to brood. She couldn't possibly brood—not with Brendan here. He lifted her spirits, removing the weight that would otherwise have dragged them down. Yes, she felt badly about the call from Carl, but she felt something else. She felt like a person. Brendan's presence was a reminder that she had a right to her own life. "You're good to put up with all this," she said in thanks.

"All what?" Brendan asked. He had been momentarily distracted by that look in her eye and had been thinking that she could make him feel like a million without uttering a word.

"My phone calls. Another man would have had his pants on long before Norman had finished."

He shifted those marvelous shoulders of his. "I like being naked."

She shot a glance toward the window and tempered a grin. "Lucky for us it's daylight. Who knows what that pervert across the courtyard would make of our dancing around in the nude."

"Since I'm 'that pervert' and I'm here, not there, I give us permission." He drew her into a snug embrace, took a long, deep breath and gave a loud sigh of satisfaction. "This is what I like."

She nodded her agreement against his chest, then opened her mouth to tell him what she'd really like to do all day when the phone rang again. Instead of speaking, she gave a growl much like the frustrated one Carl had made before he'd hung up.

"Does this happen every Saturday?" Brendan asked.

"Yeah. Let's go to your place."

"My place is a mess."

The phone rang again!

"But at least it's peaceful," she argued in a higher voice than usual. "That has to be either my mother or my sister."

"You're not the only one who has 'em," he drawled.

She held him back and looked up. "Uh-oh. You get calls, too?"

The phone rang the third time. Scowling, she reached over, snatched it up and would have bellowed into it had Brendan not put a timely thumb against her lips. Very slowly he drew the thumb away. Very sweetly she said, "Hello?"

"Hi, Caro. I'm not in labor, but let me tell you, I have a pain in the butt! Mom is driving me nuts! She called me two minutes ago babbling on and on about a malpractice suit, and it's not the first time she's mentioned it. But it's so *pointless* for her to go on about it when she doesn't even know how much of a case she has. She has to wait to see how dad's leg heals. Do you think she's asked him how he would feel about a lawsuit? He probably wants no part of it. She has no *idea* what a suit like that will entail. She'll have to hire a lawyer—I told her *I* couldn't do it—and go through the hassle of collecting evidence, not to mention putting Dad through more and more exams. It'll take tons of time, a load of money and the case could piddle around in the courts for years. By the time she's done, they'll put *her* on the stand and prove she's loony!"

Since Caroline hadn't been able to get a word in, she'd shifted the phone away from her mouth and was filling Brendan in on the side.

Somehow, between her own words, Karen managed to overhear the low murmurs. "Who's there?"

"A friend," Caroline answered, giving her sister the perfect opening to apologize for interrupting and say she'd call back later.

Karen did neither. After a short and distracted "Oh," she barreled on. "You have to help me, Caro. Get her off my back. I can't take her paranoid nonsense on top of everything else that's happening."

"There's not much I can do."

"Call her. Let her babble away to *you*."

"Thanks a lot," Caroline mumbled. If Karen heard, she ignored the sarcasm.

"You have so much more patience, Caro!"

"And you're the lawyer. You have the credence. I've told Mom that she'd be foolish to think of suing right now, but she won't listen to me. I've tried, really I have." Gratefully, she accepted the cup of coffee Brendan pressed into her hand, then shook her head when he made a stirring motion with his finger, silently asking if she wanted cream or sugar.

"Try again!" Karen ordered on a slightly hysterical note.

"Karen, calm down. If she's already called you today, you're off the hook for a while."

"For a day."

"No doubt she'll be calling me, and when she does, I'll do my best to divert her."

"Just tell her to leave me alone."

"I can't do that."

"Sure you can, if you do it nicely."

"I have a better idea, Karen. Why don't you let Dan answer the phone and say that you're working or shopping or sleeping?"

For the first time Karen paused. "I hate to put the burden on Dan."

What about the burden you're putting on me? Caroline asked silently. Aloud she said, "Dan can handle it."

"I'll tell him you said so. Oops, there he is. I've got to run, Caro. He'll be loaded down with grocery bags. I'll call you later. Bye." She was already yelling, "Coming, sweetheart," before she'd hung up the phone.

Caroline hung up on her own end and, turning to Brendan, rolled her eyes in frustration. "She's incredible! She knew someone was here, yet she babbled on and on about Mom's babbling." The phone rang. Her voice dropped to a low, stiff monotone. "That's Mom. Don't touch it."

"She'll keep trying. Why not get it out of the way?"

Squeezing her eyes shut, Caroline pressed her fingertips to her forehead. It was an instinctive gesture, made in anticipation of the headache she was sure to get if she spoke with her mother."

Since she wasn't looking, Brendan picked up the phone. His deep voice rang out with just the right amount of deference. "Cooper residence."

Caroline spread her fingers and dragged them downward,

peering through the cracks at Brendan. His grin was a dead giveaway of her mother's startled sputter at the other end of the line. With little effort, Caroline could imagine her mother's words.

Who is this?

"This is Brendan Carr."

Who is that?

"I'm a friend of Caroline's."

What are you doing there?

"Visiting."

At this hour?

He squinted back at the clock. "It's nearly noon." Winking at Caroline, he asked innocently, "Who is this?" Caroline could just imagine the tone in which her mother informed him of her identity. "Ahh. Mrs. Cooper. How are you?"

It was the wrong thing to ask. Caroline knew it the instant the words left Brendan's mouth. She stood back and watched while he listened to a prolonged monologue, no doubt about Madeline Cooper's raw nerves, her husband's broken leg and the weather, in that order.

Brendan shifted from one foot to the other. He hooked his hand on his hip, alternately nodding in silent sympathy for Madeline and ogling various parts of Caroline's body. It was all Caroline could do not to laugh aloud at the abrupt switches.

At some point, though, the direction of Madeline's talk changed, because he said a bit defensively, "I was next to the phone. It made sense for me to answer."

Picturing her mother getting huffy, Caroline reached for the phone. She got Brendan's hand instead, long fingers threading through hers, curving around them, holding firm.

"Her hands are tied up at the moment," he dared say when Madeline asked to speak with Caroline. "Perhaps she could get back to you."

Caroline tried to free her hand without success, so she reached for the phone with the other one. Brendan simply turned to render the instrument beyond reach. In doing so, he brought their bodies into contact. Caroline stopped struggling.

"She won't be here then," Brendan was saying. "We're just getting ready to leave." Caroline arched a single curious brow, but he was a step ahead of her. "We thought we'd take a drive down to—" He was interrupted. "I know that she doesn't have a car. I have one." He stopped again. "It's a Toyota. Very safe. And I'm a good driver. I have never had an accident in—" He broke off for a minute while Madeline talked. "Please, Mrs. Cooper, there's no need to be superstitious. I'm not 'due' for an accident. I have a perfect record because I'm careful."

Caroline was enjoying herself. She'd offered to take the phone; Brendan had refused. Now he was seeing firsthand what it was about Madeline Cooper that could drive a sane soul mad.

"The drivers are no worse here than anywhere else," he pointed out patiently, then said a minute later, "I'm sure you're right, in terms of expense if nothing else. If Caroline doesn't need a car, it's pointless for her to have one." He listened to something Madeline said, then blinked. "I suppose you could say that we're dating."

Had he been wearing a shirt, he would have been growing hot under the collar. Caroline could see that his pleasant expression was more forced with each of Madeline's questions. She would have felt sorry for him had he not asked for the torture himself.

"Fairly recently," he said. Then, "Yes." After a longer pause, he looked at Caroline. "My intentions?"

Caroline's smug grin disappeared. "Oh, no," she whispered plaintively, "she can't ask that!"

"We've only just begun to date," Brendan reminded Madeline. "It's a little early to discuss . . . of course I'm an honorable man. I wouldn't do a thing . . . you shouldn't be worrying about that."

When Madeline jabbered on, he took the phone from his ear and belatedly offered it to Caroline, who opened her eyes wide in an are-you-kidding look and shook her head. Reluctantly he returned the phone to his ear.

"Uh-huh . . . of course I understand . . . would it be possible for her to call you Monday?" He shut his eyes briefly at whatever it was Madeline said. "No, Mrs. Cooper, that's not so . . . no, I am not trying to keep you from talking to her . . . excuse me? Holding her prisoner?" Wearing a look of utter incredulity, he murmured to Caroline, "Tied up and gagged?" Clearing his throat, he returned to Madeline. "Please, Mrs. Cooper, if you'll hold on a minute, I'll see if Caroline can come to the phone."

Exasperated, he thrust the receiver at Caroline.

I warned you, her eyes said.

His answered, *Next time I'll listen.*

Caroline spent the next several minutes assuring her mother that she was well, happy and free. No sooner had that been accomplished than Madeline wanted to know— from Caroline's lips, despite the fact that Brendan had already given her much of the same information—who Brendan was, where he lived, how she'd met him, how long she'd been seeing him and what he did for a living. Caroline's answers varied from straightforward to evasive. She kept them brief. She did *not* ask how her mother was, instead repeating what Brendan had said about getting ready to leave. After promising to call at the start of the week, she hung up the phone.

Brendan instantly snatched it up, punched out information, then, with his eyes glued to Caroline's, asked for the number of the Canterbury Hotel. Moments later, he had reserved a suite for the night.

Caroline hadn't said a word. She was watching the expressions that crossed his face, expressions ranging from frustration to determination to desire. Now there was caution.

"Is that okay with you?" he asked. His hand remained on the telephone receiver. He would cancel the reservations in an instant if she had qualms.

Caroline had no qualms whatsoever. The Canterbury was reputed to be one of the most charming hotels in Washington. Though she'd never seen it herself, she'd been told about the classical music in the lobby and the period furnishings in the rooms. It would be cool and comfortable and quiet. She could laze around with Brendan to her heart's content.

A smile tugged at the corners of her mouth. "No one will know we're there."

He slid an arm around her waist. "That's the idea."

"I like it. What should I bring?"

"Not much. We could dress up for dinner if you want."

"I'm sure they have room service."

"Uh-huh."

"Have you ever done this before?"

"Nope." His eyes had grown darker, more luminous. "It's been a fantasy, though, and since we're into living out fantasies . . ."

Very gently, almost hypnotically, he reached for her. Her arms quite naturally looped around his neck. Her flesh met his with the same ease but with excitement, as well. It was incredible, she realized, the ease and the excitement— incredible and unique. But then, wasn't that what a fantasy was all about?

8

The twenty-four hours that Caroline and Brendan spent at the Canterbury were heavenly. They didn't leave their room during that time, and not once were they bored. They made love, slept and talked about most anything that came to mind. When they felt the need for food, they called room service.

Caroline surprised herself. She'd been exhausted all week; her dream cure should have been a restful and companionable silence. But with Brendan she wanted to talk. He fascinated her—his background, his lifestyle, his work. She devoted herself to feeding that fascination. And when he asked her questions in return, she found that she could tell him anything.

She did call in early Sunday morning for an automatic playback of the messages on her answering machine. She told Brendan she wanted to know that her sister was all right, but they both knew it was something more. No one knew where they were. Caroline didn't miss the nagging phone calls, but she couldn't shake the fear that if something did happen to one of the family, no one would be able to contact her and therefore she'd be unable to help.

It was a catch-22. She wouldn't have had to worry if she'd left Karen or Carl the number where she could be reached in an emergency. But if she'd done that, she'd have opened herself to unnecessary calls—precisely what she was trying to escape.

With Caroline, responsibility was a habit of long standing. Brendan understood that. He couldn't equate it with a habit like smoking, because it was neither life-threatening nor undesirable. A sense of responsibility was a good thing to have—unless it became a detriment to one's own peace of mind, in which case it had to be put in perspective. That was what Caroline was going to have to learn how to do.

In the meantime, Brendan could be patient. He knew that she couldn't just snap her fingers and, presto, set aside all family concerns. He wouldn't have wanted her to. It would have been out of character, and he was finding that he adored her character. She was proving to be the kindest, most interesting and uninhibited woman he'd ever met.

He wondered whether she was this way with everyone—talking freely, asking questions, sometimes doing the opposite and listening so quietly that he was convinced he was boring her to tears, only to have her come back with an insightful, thoughtfully presented response that forwarded the discussion, often lifting it to a higher plane. He felt intellectually challenged. By virtue of the questions she asked or the comments she made, he was thinking about things in ways that he hadn't done before. He felt productive.

Selfishly, he wanted to think that she was this way only with him. He wanted to think that, even beyond their agreement, he offered her something that she'd previously been without. The key, if it was true, was in making her see it.

While not thinking quite as far down the road, Caroline couldn't remember a time when she'd felt so free of the burdens of the world, and she said as much to Brendan as they gathered together their single, embarrassingly light bag of possessions and prepared to check out of the hotel early Sunday afternoon. "I'd like to stay here forever."

"No, you wouldn't," he countered only half in jest. "You'd get itchy to be up and out and around in the world."

Wrapping her arms around his waist, she turned her face up to his. "Are you?"

"No."

"Then why should I be?"

"Because you said you wanted freedom. You want to come and go as you please. No strings. No restrictions. No hassles."

"In a manner of speaking, I've had all of that here. It's been idyllic. Maybe that's why I want to stay." The thought of returning to the real world was making her feel a little blue.

Brendan didn't want to push his luck by exploring her feelings more deeply than, in fact, she was ready to do herself. So he said, "I guess we both needed a vacation."

"It's more than that. We didn't get away, but we . . . got away." She crinkled up her nose. "Do you know what I mean?"

"You bet."

"I wish we'd had more time."

"We can always come again."

"I'd like that," she said with a soft smile and a resurgence of enthusiasm.

Brendan felt his breath catch in his throat. The soul touch of her eyes did that to him. Add to it the softness of her smile and he was a goner.

Several minutes passed before he was able to respond, and then his voice had a gruff edge to it. "You're too agreeable, Caroline. I can see how you get yourself involved in doing things you don't really want to do."

"But I *would* like to come here again, or go to another place like this. Maybe we could try an inn in the country next time. I have a terrific book that lists them."

"You're a fan of country inns?"

"I like reading about them."

"Have you visited many?"

She shook her head. "I daydream a lot."

"Why only daydream?"

"Because," she answered without pretense, "it's no fun to travel alone."

Something warm and reassuring flowed through Brendan just then. It was his life's blood, he knew, but it was infused with new vigor. He felt suddenly stronger, more buoyant. He felt as though the future was definitely looking bright.

The feeling lasted for six hours. During that time he and Caroline ambled slowly through Georgetown, pausing to browse in the shops or eat or find a comfortable spot to sit and talk. At the end, though, they reached her door. She invited him in, but he had to return to his loft to organize his papers and thoughts before his trip the next morning. When he invited her back to his place to read or relax while he worked, she smiled—a little sadly, he thought—and said that she'd better catch up on her own chores. So they kissed with a brief, sweet passion and parted.

In hindsight, Brendan realized that they'd been foolish in not choosing one of their lofts and staying together. He didn't get much done that evening. He tried, but his gaze regularly wandered through the open French windows and across the courtyard. Whenever he caught Caroline's eye, he went to the window and indulged in that special, silent communication they shared.

The game they were playing was a torturous one. The night was humid, and he was hot in every sense of the word. Kneeling on her window seat, with her hair caught at the top of her head, the skin of her face and neck visibly moist, her thin shift simultaneously covering everything and nothing, Caroline was even more the innocent seductress than she'd been before. Because now he knew her. Now there were open smiles and meaningful gestures. He knew what it felt like to plow his fingers into her hair, to catch trickles of sweat with his tongue, to explore the feminine curves beneath her shift. She had merely to rest her head against the window frame or scoop loose strands of hair from her neck or arch her back in a hot, lazy stretch and he was on fire. Everything about her was simply sultry.

But she was there and he was here and because of that he felt uneasy. He cursed the timing that was engineering a separation so early in their relationship. He had no doubts about his feelings for her. After weeks of daydreaming, he'd only had to meet her briefly to know that she was the woman for him. But he needed more time to convince *her*.

He knew that she felt something for him. What they'd experienced that weekend had gone far beyond the sexual marathon they'd joked about. If it had been only sex, they'd never have been able to talk as they'd done. And there was something else—he had to smile a little slyly when he thought of it—something that was promising. Caroline had insisted on taking his spare key so that she could drop his mail in his apartment each day. He'd made vague sounds of protest, but she'd said that she really wanted to do it, that it was something she'd do for any good friend and certainly she considered him that. He refrained from pointing out that "doing things" was what she'd wanted to avoid. He suspected that she truly did enjoy being generous with her time and effort—when she didn't feel taken for granted. And he took care to see that she didn't.

The fact of the matter was that he liked knowing she'd be checking into his loft each day. It was a small thing, a link, and it gave him solace at a time when he was needy.

His greatest fear—it came to him in cold flicks of emptiness—was that someone else would discover her and steal her away while he was gone. He knew he was being silly, because while he was gone she'd be going to work, seeing the same people she always saw, and if nothing had clicked with any of those people before, there was no logical reason why it would now. But it seemed incredible to him that she *hadn't* been discovered before. She was so perfect. Didn't the rest of the world see it?

Four days. That was all he'd be gone. But, damn, he wished he weren't going at all.

His greatest frustration, he decided, was that he couldn't share his greatest fear with her. If he'd had his way, he'd have already bared his heart and begged a commitment. But that wasn't part of the bargain he'd made with her—which was also why he'd been evasive when Mrs. Cooper had asked about his intentions toward her daughter.

Intentions seemed an old-fashioned word to him, and he'd never thought of himself as an old-fashioned man, yet what he felt for Caroline was old-fashioned through and through. He wanted the whole thing—flowers, double rings, the wedding march, the bridal suite—and he wanted it yesterday.

But he'd wait. He'd wait until Caroline acknowledged what he already had—that along the line of their unorthodox introduction, what they shared was totally and wonderfully unique. He'd wait if it killed him—not that he'd be twiddling his thumbs in the interim. He'd work on her subtly but steadily. She wouldn't know what had hit her until she was well and truly hooked.

Caroline knew very well what had hit her. She couldn't deny that when she went to work Monday morning her spirits were soaring. To some extent, she was feeling relief. She'd called Elliot the night before, and though he'd been miserly with words himself, she felt that she'd explained herself well and smoothed over at least one or two raw edges.

In greater part, though, her light spirits were due to Brendan. For the first time in her life, she had an ally. He was someone to talk with and play with. He'd proven himself capable of listening and offering compassion and advice. He'd even taken on her mother—something that they'd laughed about afterward but that had meant the world to her. A little help, a breather once in a while—that was all she asked. And Brendan seemed more than willing to provide it. He'd told her to use him. She didn't even have to feel guilty when she did it.

So, life seemed a little easier. The knowledge that she'd be talking to Brendan, then seeing him later in the week was the touchstone she needed when those little frustrations piled up. And they did that.

When he phoned on Monday night and asked about her day, she readily told him about her mother's call. "The phone rang at seven o'clock this morning, Brendan. That's six o'clock her time, and mother's never been a naturally early riser. She was probably counting the hours all weekend."

"What did she have to say?" Brendan asked. He had a good idea what the answer was, but he wasn't about to offer a guess when he knew that Caroline needed to let off steam by relating it all herself. Besides, he took pleasure in hearing her voice.

"She wanted to know where we went this weekend, what we did and what time we got back."

"Did you tell her?"

"I told her what time we got back."

"She wasn't satisfied with just that, was she?"

"No. I kind of fudged the rest."

"You could have told her the truth."

"Are you kidding? And open up a whole other can of worms?"

Brendan chuckled. "She doesn't actually think you're still a virgin, does she?"

"She pretends I am. I told her that particular truth quite bluntly years ago, but she chose not to hear, and it's occurred to me since that I'd be wise not to press the point. Do you have any idea what would have happened if I'd told her what we really did this weekend?"

"What?"

"AIDS. She would have gone on and on about AIDS."

"Oh, no."

"Oh, yes. She would have asked how well I really knew you and did I know whether you'd had many women before me and was I positively certain you weren't bisexual and giving me something that could well be fatal."

"Damn good thing I ruled it out at the start," he mumbled in a Lord-help-us tone. "Has she done that sort of thing before?"

"She's made general statements about every other sexually transmitted disease. She tells me about so-and-so who contracted such-and-such, and she babbles on for such a long time that I *know* there's a direct message in there for me."

"She must have known you were sleeping with Ben."

"She tried not to."

"Did she like him?"

"Like him?" Caroline echoed tongue-in-cheek. "How could she like him? She never got past the point of wondering whether he was a spy infiltrating the diplomatic corps on behalf of the KGB."

Brendan didn't want to think what the woman would say when she learned that he dealt with terrorism. "She really is an alarmist, isn't she?"

"Oh, yes. What bothers me most, I think, is that she should trust me to know what I'm doing and she doesn't." Caroline took a deep breath. She'd been annoyed all day by the call from her mother, but somehow, after telling Brendan about it, she felt better. Unburdened. A tiny smile played at the corners of her mouth. "By the way, she said that you had a nice voice."

"She did?" he asked, pleased with that.

"Uh-huh. She said that it was compelling in a gentle way—then she went on to warn me to be careful because men with low, charming voices weren't always to be trusted. She said that I should be on my guard, that you might try to con me into something."

He heard the smile in her voice. "Are you? On your guard, that is?"

"Sure am," she said, but the softness of her tone hinted that she wasn't terribly worried. She trusted him, which was one of the reasons why, when he called on Tuesday night and again asked about her day, she found herself telling him about Paul Valente.

She was disturbed by the meeting she'd had with Paul that day. Without mentioning names, she briefly filled Brendan in on the situation between Paul and his wife. "He canceled their appointment last week, and this week he came in alone to say that she'd left him. He was really down. I was a little surprised."

"That he was so upset?"

"No, no. I knew he'd be upset. I just didn't think he'd express it as openly as he did. Other than isolated minutes before or after a session, I've always counseled them together.

He comes across very differently when he's with his wife. Alone, he's a more sympathetic character."

"It sounds like he got to you today."

"Yes. I feel really bad. He doesn't want this separation. He wants to work things out."

"Is there any chance of that?"

"Not unless he can somehow convince his wife to sit down and talk, but since communication has never been their strong suit as a couple, the chances of that are slim."

Brendan knew what she wasn't saying. He could hear it in her discouraged tone. "I think you're blaming yourself for not being able to do more."

"Yes," she said quietly.

"I'm sure you did what you could."

"It wasn't enough. You know," she went on plaintively, "it wouldn't be so bad if he'd have come to me and said that they were separating but that it was the best thing, that he felt relieved because they were really making each other miserable. In a situation like that, I've failed but I haven't. I can tell myself that therapy served a purpose in clarifying their relationship for them. I can look back on it as a last-ditch effort to save something that in the end neither partner cared enough to save. That might have been true for the wife in this case, but not for her husband. He does love her."

"So you feel that you've personally failed him," Brendan concluded with compassion. "But the burden of responsibility wasn't totally yours, Caroline. The fellow's *wife* failed him, because she reneged on certain vows she'd once made. She was the one who gave up on the marriage, not you."

His words soothed her. The plaintive quality had left her voice. "But maybe I could have prevented it," Caroline argued more calmly, then tacked on a bewildered "somehow."

"You tried your best, didn't you?"

"I thought I did at the time."

"Isn't that the bottom line?" he asked softly, then raised his voice a notch. "Hey, I know exactly what you're feeling. When I was a prosecutor in the D.A.'s office, there was many a case I lost despite weeks and weeks of preparation. I could be totally convinced, I mean convinced beyond a shadow of a doubt, that a person was guilty of the crime for which he was being tried, but if that jury found him not guilty, there wasn't a damn thing I could do about it."

"Did you ever question your own competence?"

"All the time. After I lost a case like that, I'd sit down and review everything. There was learning value in it. Sometimes something would come to me in hindsight—something I'd done or hadn't done that could have been pivotal. When I first started, I made some mistakes. But as time went on, the problem was more often in the evidence itself. In other words, the case as I'd been handed it was not quite strong enough to win that conviction." He paused for the briefest of breaths. "Maybe the analogy fits here. Maybe the case you were given by this couple just wasn't strong enough. Certainly, if you tried your best, no one can find fault. The fact that the husband came in to see you today shows that he doesn't hold you responsible for the separation."

Caroline was feeling better because he did have a point. "If you were in his situation, Brendan, what would you feel? Would you be angry at me?"

Brendan tried to answer as honestly as possible. He respected Caroline too much to do any differently, and he wanted her respect, as well. Telling her only what he thought she wanted to hear would be counterproductive in that sense.

"Yes, I'd be angry, but only at first. I'd need to blame someone, and you'd be there. But when I stopped to think rationally, the anger would fade. I'd realize that I couldn't blame you for something you didn't create. Hell, you don't enter the picture of a relationship until it's in a shambles. Through the course of therapy, you can point out what's wrong, which I presume you did in this case. You can make suggestions for improving things, which I presume you did, also. You can even try to put those suggestions into effect during your sessions, but when you have only one hour a week to do it—" he exhaled a loud breath "—the odds have to be against you in those tough cases."

"It doesn't seem fair," Caroline concluded quietly.

"Life isn't, that way."

Those words were to echo in her mind the next day. When she spoke with Brendan on Wednesday night, she was particularly discouraged. "Karen called this morning in a panic. Her doctor has ordered her to bed until the baby is born."

"To bed? What happened?"

"She started bleeding. It doesn't have to do with the baby directly, but if she stays on her feet she's apt to bring on premature labor."

"When is she due?"

"That's one of the problems. The doctor says that she has another eight weeks to go, but she's convinced she conceived a month earlier. I'd almost agree with her. She's huge. She's been so uncomfortable for so long that we've been expecting the baby momentarily."

"Don't they have tests to determine that kind of thing?" he asked. He wished he knew more about the subject. Unfortunately, he was a virgin when it came to pregnancy and babies—not that he wasn't eager to learn, but eagerness alone couldn't provide the facts with which to offer Caroline comfort.

Caroline was every bit as naive. "Your asking me is like the blind leading the blind. I asked Karen the same question. She said something about an ultrasound test—that produces a picture of the baby. From the size of the skull they can tell the stage of gestation but only working up to a certain point in the pregnancy, after which it determines nothing more than the size of that particular baby. Anyway," she said with a sigh, "Karen didn't think to have the test done in time."

"Oh. Poor kid."

"The baby?"

"Karen. It won't help if she panics now."

"That's what I told her, too. But she really is distraught. She was planning to work right up to the end. Now she'll have to miss that many more weeks. She's convinced that she's blown a partnership."

"Nah. I can't believe that."

"Me, neither, but she does."

That he could believe. "Firms foster that kind of paranoia. They hold partnerships as the be-all and end-all, the carrot dangling in front of the associates' noses. You don't bring in enough cases, you don't get a partnership. You don't bill enough hours, you don't get a partnership. You alienate one of the partners, you don't get a partnership. They seem to think it increases productivity, when in the end it only fosters resentment and ill will."

"You sound happy to be away from it."

"Very. Large firms today are more like businesses than the professional institutions they used to be. Let me tell you, if Karen's firm denies or even withholds her partnership simply because of maternity matters, she could sue them for discrimination."

"What a pain."

"Mmm. If her firm does that, she'd be just as well free of it."

"The problem is that she doesn't want to be free of it. She's worked so hard to get where she is, and when it came to this pregnancy, she desperately wanted everything to work out. To have something like this happen . . . something she has no control over . . . she feels thwarted and very frustrated . . . I feel so bad for her, Brendan!"

"I know you do," he said gently, then added, "Hey, maybe you could visit her this weekend. That would probably calm her down . . . or perk her up . . . or whatever she needs by then."

Caroline had thought of that. It had been one of the first things to come to mind after Karen had told her the problem, and she'd barely kept herself from blurting out the offer. But she'd held her tongue. She didn't want to go to Karen's for the weekend. Not this weekend.

"I could do that," she said quietly.

Brendan heard her hesitance and, regardless of its cause, was pleased. He didn't want her spending the weekend with her sister. He wanted her spending the weekend with him.

Still, he knew that she'd be torn.

On the other hand, there was one way to satisfy them

both. "How about I drive you up there?" he asked, then went quickly on. The plan was formulating fast, and he liked it. "Philly isn't so far. We could leave early Saturday morning, which would give you plenty of time to visit with Karen and Dan. After that we could drive just a little farther to one of those special inns you have in your book and spend the night, then return to see Karen again on Sunday before we head back here."

It was a super idea, if he did say so himself, and he couldn't help but smile in a self-satisfied, smugly male sort of way. But the smile faded quickly as it occurred to him that there was possibly one small flaw to his plan.

Caroline might not be ready to introduce him to her sister.

"Actually," he rushed on in the hope of compensating for that flaw, "I have friends in Philly myself. If you preferred, I could drop you at your sister's Saturday and pick you up there on Sunday. My friends have been nagging me to visit for months, so if you'd rather be alone with Karen, I would certainly understand."

"Brendan—"

"It wouldn't be any kind of a problem for me. And that's the truth."

"I liked your first idea better," Caroline said.

He paused for a single heartbeat. "The one about the inn?"

"Yes."

"Really?"

"Uh-huh. If you're sure you wouldn't mind."

"Mind? Of course I wouldn't mind! After what I've been going through here and what I'm bound to find piled up on my desk when I return, I'll look forward to the break!"

Brendan's meetings on Thursday were scheduled through to four o'clock in the afternoon. He'd warned Caroline that they might run late, and if that were the case, he'd have to take a later flight home. She had fully reconciled herself to simply seeing him on Friday after work. After all, she reasoned, that was how two good friends who just happened to be lovers would handle a brief separation. There didn't have to be any late-night reunion. They were both far too level-headed for that.

Caroline began the evening at her own place. She'd come home earlier than usual, a fact that she didn't stop to ana-lyze, other than to tell herself she could as easily do paper-work at her kitchen table as at her office desk. That reasoning became moot, though, when the phone started to ring.

Her mother called, all in a stir about Karen's problems, but Caroline was able to fudge the facts enough to make her feel better. When, soon after that, Carl called in alarm be-cause Madeline had suggested to him that Karen might not make it through childbirth, Caroline was able to set his broth-erly heart—which she was pleased to see still functioned—to rest. She then called Karen herself and was relieved to hear her sounding a little calmer. Karen asked if she'd come to visit. Without a word about Brendan, Caroline said she'd try.

When the phone lay quiet at last, she returned to her work. She was determined to catch up on every last bit of paper-work so that if she did get to Pennsylvania for the weekend she could do so with a clear conscience.

Good intentions notwithstanding, she didn't do much catching up. She did a lot of looking at her watch and glancing across the courtyard and wondering whether Brendan had made the six-o'clock flight or had had to reschedule. When Timothy, who lived in the apartment beneath Connie, came up to borrow laundry detergent, she welcomed the momen-tary diversion. She did not welcome it, though, when Ben called a few minutes later to ask if she was ready to see him. She couldn't believe the man's gall.

After calmly telling Ben what he could do with his ego, she decided that she'd had enough of the telephone for one night. Turning on the answering machine, she went to sit at the window. She felt odd, filled with a sense of anticipation that was new to her. Anticipation . . . and restlessness. She got up, wandered around the loft, returned to kneel on the window seat . . . only to repeat the circle ten minutes later.

Then inspiration struck. Slipping into a pair of sandals,

she grabbed her key and Brendan's and crossed the court-yard to his building. She hadn't picked up his mail that day when she'd come home from work; it hadn't made sense, since he would be returning himself. But she did it now, brought it upstairs, then opened the windows and turned on the fan to move the air in the loft a bit.

Standing in the middle of the room, she looked around and sighed. She'd done what she'd set out to do. There was no reason why she shouldn't return to her own place.

Except that she'd be bored and restless there.

She felt better here.

It was the change of scenery, she told herself. For the past three nights she hadn't budged from her apartment. It was nice to be out. The fact that Brendan's apartment was hotter than her own didn't matter. She really did feel better here.

For several minutes she stood where she was, smiled, then sighed. She tacked loose wisps of hair into her barrette. She smiled again. She wiped the beads of sweat that dotted her nose. She sighed again. Then, nonchalantly, she scanned the apartment.

His cleaning service had been in while he'd been away, she decided, because the place was spotless. She smacked her lips together and let out a small, idle hum. So she couldn't waste a little time by cleaning.

Strolling casually toward the refrigerator, she pulled the door open and looked around. But no, she couldn't cook dinner. She had no idea what time Brendan would be arriving or whether he'd have already eaten, and anyway, *she'd* already eaten. Besides, it was hot. Not to mention that the contents of the refrigerator consisted of a carton of cottage cheese, a bottle of ketchup, a pitcher of orange juice, a half-empty box of glazed donuts that were probably stale and a sealed package of bologna. True, his freezer, like hers, was filled with frozen dinners, but she couldn't prepare him one of *those*.

She sank down on the sofa, kicked off her sandals and

waited. When, no more than five minutes later, a knock came at the door, she quickly sat forward. Her heart skipped a beat or two, then settled. Brendan wouldn't knock at his own apartment.

She peered through the tiny viewer on the door, then debated for the space of several additional heartbeats. Feeling only a glimmer of unsureness, she slowly opened the door. On the other side stood the same blond-haired woman she'd previously seen only from a distance.

At the sight of Caroline rather than Brendan, Jocelyn Wills's smile got lost in a look of confusion. Her eyes flicked to the number on the door, as though she wondered whether she'd come to the wrong apartment by mistake. "Is . . . Brendan here?" she finally asked.

In that instant, Caroline could see why Brendan had felt the need to protect Jocelyn in a new city. She was lovely in a down-home, innocent, almost fragile kind of way. For that reason—and others that she didn't stop to dissect—Caroline didn't feel at all threatened by the other woman's appearance.

"You must be Jocelyn," she said with a smile that was gentle and came easily. "I'm Caroline. Brendan's told me about you."

Jocelyn dipped her head a fraction and gave a nervous smile of greeting, then sent an uneasy glance past her and repeated, almost timidly, "Is he here?"

"No. He's been out of town all week, and he's due back tonight, but I guess he must have missed his original flight if he isn't here yet."

Pressing her lips together, Jocelyn nodded. "I just wanted to say hi," she murmured, and turned to leave. "I'll catch him another time . . ."

"Uh . . . wait!" Caroline called out on impulse, then had the horrible notion that she was making things worse. She could clearly see that Jocelyn was disconcerted to find a woman waiting for Brendan in his apartment. She could clearly see the impression Jocelyn had gotten; Caroline was barefoot, wore a T-shirt and shorts and looked perfectly at home. She could also see that Jocelyn was going to be mortified when she got over her initial confusion.

The woman seemed so utterly alone, standing there in the hall with a questioning look on her face, that Caroline wanted to drag her inside and explain exactly what was going on between Brendan and her, and how suddenly it had come to be, and apologize for upsetting her. But that would make it worse, she realized.

She pictured Elliot with that same expression of hurt he'd worn for a fleeting instant the Friday night before. Unfortunately, to mention Elliot to Jocelyn at this moment would possibly be the most insensitive thing Caroline had ever done.

So, instead, she said with an apologetic smile, "I'll tell Brendan you came by. I'm sure he'll give you a call." Whether it had been her tone of voice, her smile or her words, something she'd done had made Jocelyn feel a little better, because she nodded a bit more confidently and then went off down the hall.

Caroline felt like a heel, but there wasn't any remedy for it. Quietly closing the door, she returned to the sofa and wondered what Brendan would think about what she'd done.

She should never have answered the door, she decided at length, but she couldn't do anything about that, either. It was done.

With a sigh, she slid lower on the leather, crossed her ankles, propped her feet on the low coffee table and let her head rest against the charcoal-brown cushion. She thought more about Jocelyn and about herself. She thought about why she felt so at home in Brendan's apartment and knew that it had little to do with the structural similarities to her own. There was something about Brendan's loft that was . . . that was . . . Brendan. She felt as comfortable here as she did in his arms. There was the same aura of safe haven, the same kind of cultured strength. And there was the same mild and subtle scent of musk and man. Of Brendan.

* * *

There was nothing mild or subtle about Brendan as he took the stairs to his apartment two at a time. He'd just come from Caroline's loft, where repeated banging on the door had resulted in nothing. She couldn't be sleeping, not after his pounding, which meant that either she'd gone out or she was here. If she'd gone out, he'd be destroyed. If she was here he'd be ecstatic.

Dropping his bags so that he could fumble with his keys, he finally managed to unlock the door and shove it open. His eyes fell on the sprawled, sleeping form on his sofa and he said a quick prayer of thanks. He shifted his bags inside the apartment, quietly closed the door and, with barely a sound, crossed to where she lay.

It had been a hectic four days. He hadn't had the leisure to indulge in daydreams, but the nights, around his calls to her, had been filled with dreams. There had been times when he hadn't been able to believe that she existed. Hearing her voice had helped, but it was her skin that he wanted to feel and the warmth of her surrounding him.

He felt relief, and yes, he was ecstatic to find that she did exist and in his own apartment, no less. He also realized that he was nearly fully aroused. Looking at her did that to him. No, not just looking at her. Loving her.

He whispered those words as he bent and placed a warm kiss on her cheek. She was dead to the world, and if she did wake up and ask him what he'd said, he could play dumb and she'd think that she'd imagined the words. He whispered them again, this time with a kiss to her chin. Would she be receptive to subliminal persuasion? On the bare chance that she would, he whispered them a third time, against her neck now.

She stirred softly. Her eyes didn't open, but her arms rose to loop around his neck. She wasn't awake, exactly; she wasn't asleep, exactly. She was in that limbo between the two where pleasure could be prolonged simply by willing it so. And she did feel pleasure. Gentle kisses. Whispered words that were indistinct but infinitely reassuring. Touches and caresses that brought excitement and heat to secret spots.

She didn't have to look to know that it was Brendan who was touching her so sweetly. Her fingers told her as they wound through his hair, curved around his neck, pressed into his shoulder. Her tongue told her as it explored the inside of his mouth. Her nose told her as it inhaled the scent that had taunted her earlier but was now present in greater force, the scent that was uniquely his.

With his shirt thrust aside, she could identify him by the texture of his skin—just the right proportion of flesh to body hair to muscle and the most pleasing tone of each. She could smile at the familiarity of the small sound he made—a cross between a groan, a growl and a sigh—when she slid her hands through his open fly and touched him there in a very special way. And she could never mistake the gentleness with which he lifted her hips to free her of her shorts.

Only after he'd entered her did she open her eyes, and then it was to smile up at him for an instant before the rhythm he set caught her in its vibrant beat. With her arms coiled around his neck and her legs circling his hips, she met his fire with her own until they both succumbed to the driving heat.

That night, Caroline realized that what she had with Brendan went far beyond the simple relationship she'd envisioned at the start. It came to her in those brief, special seconds after she'd climaxed, when he was in the throes of his own powerful release and she felt the warmth he poured into her as a life force in every sense of the word. She'd never experienced as profound a sensation. She'd never known it existed—that sensation of joining with a man and, together, being part of a cosmic order.

On the one hand, it was exhilarating. On the other, it was disturbing, even frightening, because she liked what she had with Brendan. She didn't want anything to spoil it, least of all one of them taking the other too seriously. If she were, by chance, to fall in love with him, she knew that she'd be breaking the rules she herself had established.

Which might be good. Or bad. But, in any case, that possibility was going to take a lot of thought.

* * *

Unfortunately, Caroline didn't have much time for thought. She spent the night in Brendan's apartment, in his bed and his arms. When she returned to her own loft the next morning to shower and change for work, she found a message from her mother on the answering service.

This time the alarm was for real. While Caroline had been following passion's path to Brendan's arms, her mother had been pacing the emergency room of a hospital in Milwaukee waiting for word on her husband, who'd suffered a stroke.

9

In a response so natural she would have thought it instinctive had it not been so new, Caroline called Brendan. She'd left no more than ten minutes before, and no more than ten minutes later he was at her loft wearing a handsome navy business suit and an expression of concern.

"I managed to reach my mother," she told him in a voice that came higher and faster than usual. "She must have been driving the nurses crazy, because they sounded relieved that I'd called. She's being her own pessimistic self, so I can't get any kind of clear picture about what's going on except that the doctors are still with him. I'm going out there."

Brendan's voice was as understanding as his eyes, and both were as supportive as the hand that held hers. "When?"

"This morning. As soon as I can get a flight."

"Have you spoken with Karen or Carl?"

She shook her head.

"Do they know?"

Again she shook her head, this time sending him a look of helplessness. "This is the last thing Karen needs to hear, given everything else that's happened to her this week. And Carl—Lord only knows how Carl will react."

"They'll have to be told."

"I know," she said on an even higher, faintly panicky note.

"Want me to call them?"

"I couldn't ask you—"

"You're not asking," he interrupted, curving warm fingers around her neck. "I'm offering. If you take your shower and pack while I make the calls, things will be a little easier, won't they?"

"Oh, yes," Caroline said, and meant it.

"Would I be better to try to catch Karen's husband and have him break the news to her?"

She considered that, then nodded quickly.

"I can easily call Carl," he went on. "How about Diane?"

"She'll want to know, too."

"Should I call her first?" Brendan asked. Behind the caution in his tone was an unspoken, even shrewd suggestion.

Caroline picked up on it with a quick nod. "Call Diane and have *her* call Carl."

It amazed Caroline that she and Brendan could be scheming to get Carl and Diane back together at a time like this. More, though, it amazed her that she was scheming with Brendan, period. Without having met a single member of her family, he seemed to know all of them well. She wondered whether she'd really talked so much about them, or whether he'd been perceptive enough to fill in the blanks, or whether he was simply that kind of caring person.

Whatever the case, she was grateful. Again there was that sense of having an ally. Actually, now, it was more having someone to lean on, to ease a bit of the weight from her shoulders. She knew that Brendan couldn't take the whole load; this was her family, her responsibility. But knowing that he was here to help with the immediate arrangements made the broader worries about her father a bit easier to handle.

Sliding her arms around him, she gave him a tight squeeze in silent expression of her gratitude. He accepted it warmly, then held her back. "Phone numbers?"

She jotted them down on a pad of paper by the phone.

"Now, shower," he urged, kissing her lightly on the forehead.

She did so and was in the midst of drying her hair when he poked his head into the bathroom. "Dan says not to worry, that he'll hold off a little bit before telling Karen so that you'll have a chance to get out to Milwaukee and hopefully call back with some news. Diane says that she'll take care of telling Carl and, by the way, thank you for calling her."

Only after Caroline had stepped into the shower had it occurred to her that letting Brendan make the calls could pose an added problem. Neither Dan nor Diane knew who he was.

"Did either of them give you any trouble?"

Brendan knew just what she meant. "I told them I was a good friend and neighbor and that I was helping you out so you could be on your way. I also called the airport, by the way. You have a flight out in an hour. That'll give you another half hour here. Enough?"

She nodded. "Enough." Setting the hair dryer down, she gave little shoves to the shoulder-length tresses, first with her brush, then with her fingers.

"Lookin' good," he said. Unable to resist taking a minute to watch her, he stood just inside the door now. Still, he'd tucked his hands in the pockets of his slacks for safekeeping. She was wrapped in a thick terry towel that was knotted just above her left breast. He envied it.

She'd already reached for her makeup and was about to apply it when she suddenly set the bottle down on the sink and turned around. Putting a hand flat on either side of his face, she stood on tiptoe and gave him a warm, wet kiss on the mouth.

"Thank you," she said, moving her fingers ever so slightly on his cheeks. "You have no idea—" Her voice cracked and broke off. Strange, her throat had grown tight, almost as though she was going to cry. But that was impossible. She never cried.

Taking a deep breath, she steadied herself and released him, then returned to her makeup.

Brendan had sensed the emotion that, for a minute, had come very close to the surface. He knew what he wanted to attribute it to, but he didn't dare. As a matter of fact, there was an awful lot that he didn't dare do, and it was beginning to bother him. With each additional minute that he spent with Caroline he grew more sure of his feelings. He tried to remind himself that barely a week had passed since they'd first gotten together, but each time he was with her he wanted her more, harder, longer, deeper, and not only physically. Hiding his feelings was becoming increasingly difficult.

But it was necessary, he reminded himself, especially now. So he thrust aside his frustrations and the dire yearning to take her in his arms, tell her that he loved her and assure her that everything would be all right, and instead asked, "Will someone cover for you at work?"

"They'd better."

"Who should I call?"

This time she shook her head. "I'll have to. I can do it while I'm packing."

He watched her for several minutes, until she'd zipped the small makeup bag. Then he asked, "Would you like anything—coffee, O.J., eggs?"

Again she shook her head. "My stomach's feeling a little off."

"What can I do? Name it and it's as good as done."

She looked up at him, her eyes large and troubled, and whispered, "Just hold me for a minute." Wrapping her arms around his neck, she closed her eyes and held tight.

It was all he could do just then not to offer to go with her. But she hadn't asked him to do it, and he didn't want to put her on the spot. It was possible that she preferred to make the trip alone. She was going to have enough to handle between her mother's mania and her father's illness, he knew, without having to worry about explaining the presence of this new man in her life.

Ironically, it was for these same reasons that he ended up on a flight to Milwaukee early Saturday morning. Caroline had called the night before to say that while her father had suffered some paralysis, he was going to be fine. Madeline Cooper was the real basket case, and the doctors' vagueness didn't help. Karen was calling regularly, and Carl was planning to fly out. Between coping with them and her mother and trying to talk with the doctors and visit her father, Caroline sounded strung out after eight short hours in Milwaukee.

So Brendan was flying out to help her. He knew that he could. He could talk with Madeline, and even if he couldn't do any better than Caroline in calming her down, at least Caroline wouldn't be taking the brunt of it.

He could also talk with the doctors. His own experience with the medical profession, obtained when his mother had had major surgery several years before, was that occasionally a deeper, louder voice was heard more quickly. He had no doubt that Caroline would have her answers in time, but if he could shorten that time, so much the better.

He could help deal with Carl when Caroline had her hands full with her mother. He could pass news on to Karen when Caroline's head ached, as she'd said it had been doing last night.

Most important, he could let Caroline lean on him when she felt pushed to the limit. It occurred to him shortly before his plane landed in Milwaukee that, at the moment, all he really wanted in life was to be there for her.

Of course, whether that was what *she* wanted was up for grabs. He knew that she'd appreciated his coming over on Friday morning. She'd told him so several times with smiles and hugs, and he'd had no cause to doubt her sincerity. But whether she'd appreciate his flying halfway across the country on her behalf was something else. He purposely hadn't told her he was coming because he hadn't wanted to give her the chance to protest.

The prospect of such a protest unsettled him as the plane landed. During the taxi ride to the hospital, he ran through the many arguments he could make to explain his presence. By the time he'd located Allan Cooper's room, he was thoroughly prepared to plead his case.

He wasn't prepared, though, for what the sight of Caroline, looking tired and pale as she sat by her father's bedside, would do to him. His insides knotted up, and he felt as though something was squeezing his heart. It was lucky that she seemed equally stunned when she looked up and saw him at the door, because it gave him a few precious minutes to re-cover. By the time she'd risen and come to join him, he was composed enough to launch his campaign, albeit in a low murmur appropriate to the setting.

"I don't want you to say anything about my having flown all the way out. There was nothing I really wanted to do in D.C., and I was hoping that I could be a help to you here. I'll fetch coffee, buy magazines, call nurses. I'll hold your hand." He shot a glance past her, back into the room, where the woman he assumed to be Madeline Cooper had turned and was eyeing him warily. "I'll even hold your *mother*'s hand. But if I'm putting you on the spot by showing up—or if you'd really rather be alone—I'll disappear. Just say the word. Or if you want me to stay, you can explain me away as one of your partners or your secretary. You don't even have to tell your mom that I'm the same man who answered your phone when she called last weekend. We can make up a name for me. I don't care. I just wanted to be here—"

Her fingers silenced him, trembling slightly against his lips. "I have no right to want you here as much as I do," she whispered, but she didn't have time to say anything more, because at that moment Carl came flying down the hall. He held his daughter, Amy, comfortably on his hip. Diane was at his side.

Caroline hugged them all, then introduced Brendan to them as "a special someone," which seemed to satisfy them far more than the realization that they'd all been on the same plane without knowing it. Madeline, who joined them sec-onds later, was relieved enough to know that Carl was there with his wife and daughter to overlook the fact that Caro-line's "friend" had flown all the way from Washington to be with her. By the time she thought to ask about the nature of that friendship, Brendan was proving to be such a source of strength that she didn't bother to question and simply ac-cepted what seemed perfectly right and natural.

He was, in his unobtrusive way, like another member of the family. Madeline turned to him as nearly as often as she turned to Caroline, which didn't bother him in the least. He

was in a far better frame of mind to take Madeline's alarm-
ism than Caroline, who was busy trying to find out how
alarmed she should rightly be.

As it happened, Allan Cooper's stroke proved to be less
severe than it had seemed at the start. He had a slight paralysis on his left side that the doctors believed would respond
well to therapy, and he was awake, aware and easily able to
make himself understood by the time Caroline and Brendan
bade him goodbye on Sunday afternoon.

Caroline was surprised that she was able to leave so easily. She'd assumed that she'd have felt obliged to stay and
hold her mother's hand a bit longer. But everything was under control. She was convinced that her dad was receiving
the best of care and that Madeline would be a nervous Nellie
regardless. Besides, Carl had decided to stay on an extra few
days with Diane and Amy. Amy had proven to be the only
one capable of distracting Madeline for long, which was
working out conveniently. Carl and Diane had begun to talk
and smile with each other as they hadn't done in months and
months, and they could use whatever time they found to be
alone together.

But Caroline's thoughts weren't on her parents, Amy, Carl
or Diane as the plane took off and headed east. Her thoughts
were on Brendan. His presence had taken the weekend from
the ranks of an ordeal and transformed it into something a
little less daunting. She felt calm, and that was a definite improvement over the way her family usually made her feel.

Brendan was a diffuser. He'd taken the sharp tip off the
crisis and softened its edges. He was her friend and confi-
dant. He shared the burden of responsibility and helped her
put things into perspective. And he was a steady reminder
that she was more than just Caroline-the-last-hope-of-the-
needy. There had been times that weekend when they were
alone, when he would hold her hand or wrap an arm around
her shoulder or draw her head to his chest, and she would
feel valued and appreciated as a person in her own right,
totally aside from any service she had to offer. And when,
very late on Saturday night when the rest of the household

was asleep, he made hot, sweet, silent love to her, she felt positively cherished.

Brendan was wonderful, but that was precisely what began to bother her during that flight home on Sunday. He fit so easily into her life that thought of life without him was suddenly frightening. In little over a week, she had grown dependent on him. It wasn't a material dependence; she felt every bit as self-sufficient as she ever had in the sense of day-to-day, surface functioning. But emotionally . . . she'd quickly come to need him that way.

Theoretically, she reasoned, everything should be perfect. She'd met a man who interested and excited her, a man who was strong enough to stand on his own two feet and take some of her weight, as well. They could head off into the sunset and live happily ever after, knowing that between them they had a handle on the world.

But it wasn't as simple as that. For one thing, a mere nine days ago she'd announced—no, insisted—that their relationship should be fun and free. If, by her own decree, she'd ruled out thoughts of a future, could she simply reverse herself now and expect that Brendan would go along?

For another thing, life often got complicated when couples started thinking in terms of long-range commitments. General concerns became personal. Issues that had previously been overlooked suddenly came to the fore. Expectations changed and sides were taken. She knew that from her work. Time and again she'd counseled couples who couldn't understand why their relationship had been perfect until they'd gotten married.

She asked herself if her work had turned her off marriage and knew that the answer was no. She'd seen many long-lasting, happy marriages—her parents' included—but she knew, too, of the growing pains those relationships occasionally suffered. She didn't want *any* pains in her relationship with Brendan.

She asked herself if her experience with Ben was making her nervous, and again the answer was no. Ben was an egocentric man who had a way with words that had little to do with honest, gut-wrenching emotion. Ben was as different from Brendan as night from day, and just as there was no comparison between the men, there was no comparison between the relationship she had with each.

The trouble was that she couldn't define exactly what she wanted her relationship with Brendan to be. Was it to be laid-back and hassle free, or more intense? Could it be both? Could it *not* be both?

The plane landed in Washington without a hitch, but Caroline was still grappling with the dilemma that night as she lay in bed with Brendan. Tipping her head sideways on the pillow, she studied him in the dark. He had a strong profile—all the way from the dark spikes of hair falling over his brow to the blunt tips of his well-formed toes.

They'd just made love. His skin gleamed beneath a sheen of sweat that hadn't yet dried in the hot night air. His body hair was ruffled, left that way by the impassioned movements of her skin on his. His muscles were relaxed, his breathing steady. He'd fallen asleep.

She couldn't begrudge him that. He'd been a rock for her this weekend. He'd earned his rest. And besides, she didn't want to talk right now. She wasn't ready to share the particular thoughts in her mind.

So she wrestled with them silently for another hour, until sheer exhaustion wore her down. But before she fell asleep, she reached a decision. Brendan Carr was too good to be believed. He had to have a flaw. It was going to be up to her to find that flaw, before she was so head over heels in love with the man that she was beyond redemption.

During the next few weeks, Caroline and Brendan settled into a routine that wasn't so much a routine as a regular meeting of minds. They each went to work in the morning and brought work home to do at night, but there was variety in where they did that work—sometimes at his loft, sometimes at hers. There was variety, too, in when they did it—sometimes before they went to a late movie, sometimes after they returned from a restaurant, sometimes between snacks or phone calls or chores. They found the spontaneous little twists to be refreshing, and though they discovered small differences in their tastes, compromise was incredibly simple.

Caroline wasn't quite as gung-ho about looking for Brendan's flaws as she should have been. Too often she was so comfortable with him that she simply didn't think to look for flaws, and when she was tired after a day of work, she didn't want to look for them.

On occasion, though, when an odd, tiny inner unease nudged her, she would examine their lives together and search for a catch in the relationship. She'd wanted the freedom to come and go as she liked, and she had it. Brendan never made her feel guilty. He didn't say things he didn't mean or make promises he didn't keep. She was able to lean on him and find ready support, and not once had he treated her like his mother. When she looked for signs that she was being taken advantage of, she couldn't find a one.

Cooking dinner was a case in point. On those nights when they decided to eat in, she took charge, since it had quickly become clear that even she knew more about cooking than he did. But he helped. Even when she protested, he offered, insisting on chopping onions or tenderizing steaks or setting the table, and not once was she left to do the cleanup alone.

Doing laundry was another example. Without a second thought, Caroline offered to throw his laundry in with hers when she went to the basement washing machine. It was no sweat off her back, she'd reasoned; she was doing the wash anyway, and the addition of his T-shirts, shorts and socks was negligible. In turn, Brendan insisted on making the trip to the dry cleaner's that she would have also had to make. The following week, when she'd gotten her period and was feeling crampy and under the weather, he did both chores without pause.

No, she wasn't being taken advantage of. True, she automatically straightened things up when she was at his loft. But then, he automatically answered the phone when he was at hers. True, she took care of his newspapers and mail when he was out of town. But then, he called every night from

wherever he was, and when he came home he was more solicitous than ever, compensating for what she'd done while
he was gone.

It was while he was on one such trip, after they'd been together for nearly four weeks, that a knock came at Brendan's
door. Having left work immediately after her last appointment, Caroline had been waiting for just that knock. She said
a tiny prayer that was answered the instant she opened the
door and saw the pretty brunette who was no more than six-
teen and very, very nervous.

"You're Shelley," she announced softly but with an excited smile. Catching the girl's hand, she drew her into the
loft and quickly shut the door. "I'm Caroline. Thank goodness you've come. Your mother's been worried."

Shelley seemed a little perturbed by that. "She shouldn't
have worried. I left a note saying I was coming here."

"Still, Kansas City to Washington's a long way. How did
you do it?"

"Bus."

Caroline hated to think of the state of the nation's bus
stops, but at least the girl hadn't hitchhiked. "Your brother
will be relieved to see you."

Shelley glanced uneasily around the loft. "Is he here?"

"He's been out of town since yesterday morning, but
when he learned that you were on your way, he canceled his
meetings for tomorrow. He should be back here in an hour
or two."

Shelley nodded. Her gaze skittered off. She was using her
forefinger to pick at her thumb. She looked awkward. "Were
you the one who talked with my mom?"

"Uh-huh."

"Are you living here with Brendan?"

"No."

"But you must have something going with him if you
were here."

Caroline hadn't been sure how Shelley would react to
her. She was relieved to find that the girl was more curious

than hostile. "I had dropped some things off last night and happened to be here when your mother called."

"I'll bet Mom was surprised when you answered the phone instead of Brendan."

"A little, I think." Caroline's smile was crooked as she recalled how impressed she'd been with the older woman's aplomb. "She recovered."

"She always does. She's cool. I have to say that for her."

The awkwardness seemed to be easing. Caroline took advantage of that and suggested softly, "Think we ought to give her a call and tell her you arrived safely?"

"She'll probably be furious with me once she knows I'm safe."

"Because you left a note and took off, rather than discussing the trip with her beforehand? Maybe. But if you call right now and tell her that you just this minute arrived and wanted to call right away because you knew she'd be worried, I bet the anger will be minimal."

Apparently that made some sense to Shelley, because after a brief pause, she let her backpack slide to the floor and went to the phone.

In an effort to give her a little privacy, Caroline crossed to the French windows and stood with her back to the girl. She could easily begin to understand why Brendan held a soft spot in his heart for this half sister who was so much younger than he. She was adorable to look at—slim and petite, dressed in ankle socks and flats, a short denim skirt that was nearly hidden first by a large Banana Republic T-shirt, then by an even larger denim work shirt with sleeves rolled high and lapels flapped open. Caroline's trained eye saw a sweetness and a certain vulnerability in her, which fit well into what Brendan's mother had told her the night before.

Shelley wasn't rebellious. The girl's father—Brendan's mother's second husband—had died three years before, and Shelley and her mother were close. Shelley didn't drink or do drugs. She was a top student in school and, a late developer, had just become part of a social group during the past year. Her one fault, it seemed, was laziness, which was why she didn't have a job for the summer. She'd been spending her time between her girlfriends and her first steady boyfriend. Two nights ago, she and the boy had broken up, which was why she'd taken off in search of Brendan, whom she adored.

"Caroline?"

Caroline whipped around at the sound of her name to see Shelley holding out the phone. She quickly retrieved it. "Hello?"

"Well, she sounds all right," Elizabeth Plummer said without preamble.

"And she looks fine."

"She says that she'd like to stay with Brendan for a few days. I know that his place is small, so it may be a problem, but he'll have to be the one to decide. Would you have him call me when he gets home?"

"Sure thing."

"And you won't let Shelley budge from there until he does?"

"She's not going anywhere," Caroline said with a mischievous grin for Shelley. "I'm lonely. I need company." She shifted the phone away from her mouth to ask Shelley if she'd had dinner. When the girl shook her head, Caroline said into the phone, "We're both starved. Brendan has a London broil in the fridge that I think I'll do on the hibachi. If he times it right, he may walk in just in time for the feast."

"Thank you, Caroline," his mother said with sincerity. "Perhaps one day I'll be able to thank you in person."

"I'd like that," Caroline said with a gentle smile, then added a goodbye and hung up the phone.

Brendan did, indeed, time things right. He walked into the loft with just enough time to spare to give bear hugs to both Caroline and Shelley before sitting down to a feast of London broil, garlic bread and salad—all of which Caroline had picked up on her way home from work.

Shelley camped out on Brendan's sofa for five days, during which time Caroline stayed at her own loft. Though Caroline missed Brendan's loving and the feel of his long body beside her at night, the arrangements were for the best. Caroline's close relationship with Brendan was obvious enough to Shelley, who craved a little of her brother's attention. Granting Shelley that time alone with him minimized the possibility of jealousy.

Caroline and Shelley became friends. Ironically, while Shelley had thought Brendan would be the one to whom she would pour out her broken heart, she found that Caroline, being that much closer to her age and a woman, was even better for the role. Caroline had two other advantages: she was one step removed from family, and she knew what she was doing.

By the time Shelley left to return home—by plane this time—she had decided that her heart wasn't quite as badly broken as she'd originally thought. She had also decided that Caroline would make a perfect wife for Brendan, and she proceeded to tell it to her mother, who called and told it to Brendan himself, who said that he agreed with her and that he was working on it.

He was working on it. He was working on it. He'd told himself that so many times that he was sick of the words. Unfortunately, "working on it" most often meant sitting back and doing nothing but being himself in the hope that he could get far enough under Caroline's skin to force some kind of eruption of feeling. For a man who was used to action, the wait was tedious. But he had no choice.

Circumstance was on his side. The circumstance of Caroline's father's stroke had brought them to Milwaukee, where Brendan had been able to show Caroline not only that he could get along with her family but that life with them was easier for her when he was around. The circumstance of Shelley Plummer's broken heart had brought Caroline into contact with Brendan's family, with positive feelings all around.

But the circumstance of the birth of Karen's baby was the most emotionally enlightening for Caroline. The baby arrived, quite conveniently, on a Friday, three days after Shelley left. Caroline got the call from Dan at work and was beside herself with glee. She spent her lunch hour shopping for her new nephew, then insisted on dragging Brendan out that evening to pick up even more. Because he was so delighted that she was so delighted, he went without a peep.

The next morning, they drove to Philadelphia. Karen was ebullient. She'd found labor to be easier than pregnancy, and she and Dan were overjoyed with their son. They took well to Brendan, too, and the feelings were mutual. That helped Caroline, because with Brendan preoccupied with Karen and Dan, she had more time to spend on the phone reassuring her mother that the baby was healthy. When she wasn't doing that, she stood at the nursery window staring down at the small, snugly swathed bundle of life that was the product of the love between Karen and Dan.

Thin, purple eyelids shifting with each newborn dream. A tiny mouth that formed sweet shapes around nothing at all. Miniature fingers, like spider's legs, crawling idly across a pink cheek. A nose that was little more than a bump with two holes at the bottom.

He was precious, Caroline thought, and he touched her deeply. She recalled the time when her niece had been born four years before. She'd been excited then and a little frightened.

Now she was touched in a different way. It was no great mystery. She was a woman, with maternal instincts, and those instincts were making themselves known. She wanted to hold, to nurture and to love a baby that was every bit as small and helpless as this one. She wanted a baby of her own—one that was hers and Brendan's.

Caroline thought about that through what was left of the afternoon. She and Brendan took Dan out to dinner. Then, dropping him back at the hospital to be with his wife and son, they drove north into the country to the inn they'd picked from Caroline's book.

Brendan, too, was pensive. He was thinking many of the same things Caroline was, and he knew it. He'd seen her face—how could he have *helped* but see her face—when she'd been looking at that infant. He'd never seen such an exquisite expression, and while he marveled at the beauty behind it, he was annoyed that it wasn't *his* baby that she was looking at with such awe. She would make a magnificent mother; he'd known it even before he'd met her face-to-face, and his judgment hadn't changed. But, damn it, before they had kids they had to get married, and before they got married they had to declare that they were in love, and before they did that, Caroline had to realize that the relationship she'd *thought* she wanted wasn't enough!

Words and emotions swirled within him. Having no outlet, they coiled around themselves. By the time he and Caroline had reached their destination, a charming inn in Quakertown, he'd worked himself into a mood that was as lousy as it was uncharacteristic.

"I'm going for a run," he told her as soon as they'd been shown to their room. He busied himself digging a pair of running shorts out of his bag.

Caroline had been aware of his mood from that moment when it had crossed the line from disturbed to angry. It was almost as though she'd felt invisible fingers tapping on her shoulder, telling her that something was brewing. But to know something was brewing was one thing; to act on that knowledge was something else. She had a vague idea what was on his mind. She just wasn't sure she was ready to discuss it.

"It's dark out," she said.

"I often run at night."

"These roads aren't lit like the ones at home."

He'd pushed down his jeans and was sitting on the edge of the bed trying to work them over his sneakers. When the denim didn't budge, he gave an impatient growl. "There's a moon," he said as he tugged off the sneakers, then the jeans, then pulled on the running shorts and went at relacing the sneakers.

Caroline hadn't ever seen him quite this way. She'd seen him when he'd been frustrated by something at work and had come home scowling. She'd seen him when he'd gone out one morning to find that the tires of his car had been slashed. She'd even seen him when Shelley had told him where she'd spent the night between Kansas City and Washington.

But he'd never scowled at *her* before—not that he was doing so now. He wasn't looking at her at all. And that was almost worse!

At a loss, she watched him finish with the sneakers, whip his shirt over his head and toss it aside, then leave the room. Turning out the light, she went to the window in time to see his shadowed form leave the shelter of the inn and take off at a rhythmic run down the drive.

She stood there long after he'd disappeared from sight, finally settling into a plush wing chair to await his return. After a while, it occurred to her that she was envious. He wasn't the only one in need of a little fresh air. Changing into her own shorts and sneakers, she nodded her way past the few guests who were sitting in the lobby and left the inn.

Once outside, she was faced with the dilemma of what to do and where to go. She wasn't a runner, and even if she were, she couldn't have known what direction Brendan had taken when he'd hit the main road.

She didn't want to miss him. Forget the business about getting fresh air; what she'd really come out for was to be with Brendan.

10

Caroline sat against the tall white pillar that was rooted to the front steps of the inn. Her hands were clasped between her knees, while her eyes systematically swept the darkened landscape for signs of life. She wondered where Brendan had gone and when he'd be back, but more, she wondered what he'd been thinking about when he'd taken off that way.

Nervously, she jumped up from the step and wandered into the yard, but the restless pacing she did there accomplished nothing. Minutes dragged by, and he didn't return.

The night was hot. Her skin was damp and sticky. She swatted at a bug, idly at first, then with greater determination when the bug persisted in hovering by her ear.

In a spurt of impatience, she marched down the broad walk to the drive, where she stood for several minutes, searching the night. Brendan had been gone, by her guess, for nearly an hour. She couldn't imagine that he'd been running the whole time. The air was nearly as humid as it had been in Washington, not ideal for a prolonged jog. Taking a page from her mother's book, she envisioned him passing out by the roadside and lying there unattended or, worse, being hit by a car. She went on to consider the possibility that he'd been accosted; violence was known to rise in the heat of the summer, and indeed, the moon was full.

All of which speculation was absurd, she scoffed silently. The man earned his livelihood tracking down terrorists.

That was dangerous. There was no danger on a quiet country road on a peaceful night beneath the stars. Most likely he was in town drinking a nice, cool beer.

Retracing her steps to the front porch, she sat down again. Something was wrong. Somewhere, somehow, she and Brendan had stopped communicating. That had been one of the basic rules she'd set—that there be honesty and openness between them. But right now there wasn't. She had the distinct feeling that Brendan was angry, and she wasn't quite sure why.

Once again she left the front steps, this time to wander down the drive and, in sheer frustration, start along the street. She didn't have to go far. No more than a three-minute walk from the inn was a low stone wall. Straddling that wall was her man.

She felt relief, then trepidation, but there was no way she could have turned around and left him alone. So she approached slowly. Moonlight glistened on his sweaty skin, and his hair was tousled. His breathing was regular, though; she guessed that he'd been sitting there for a time.

"Did you run?" she asked lightly.

He shrugged. "A little."

"Too hot?"

"Yeah."

Three feet of thick night air separated them. While Caroline found the air to be oppressive, the separation was worse. This was Brendan . . . her dream lover . . . the man to whom she could say anything and everything . . . the friend with whom she could carry on the most exciting of silent talks.

But neither of them was talking now, and there was nothing comfortable about the silence. She wanted to cry. Instead, she asked, "Are you hungry?"

"No."

"I'll bet you could use a cool drink."

He didn't respond to that at all but looked down, breaking eye contact for the first time since she'd come along.

Caroline moved closer. "What's wrong, Brendan?"

It was a long time before he answered. He plucked at

stray blades of grass that grew in spikes between the rocks, tossing each aside after he'd mangled it. She was beginning to wonder whether he planned to answer at all when his arms fell limply to his sides and he raised his eyes to the branches overhead. His voice came slowly and sounded distant.

"That was incredible today . . . seeing that little baby. I haven't ever seen a human being that small."

Caroline was surprised. She hadn't expected that he'd still be thinking of the baby. She watched him closely as he frowned, then lowered his head and, still frowning, concentrated on the stone wall between his thighs.

"It struck me . . ." he said, then hesitated. "Well, lots of things struck me, but the first thing was that that little boy is totally helpless. Without his parents or a nurse or some kind of caretaker, he dies. That's it. He just dies. Totally helpless. Totally dependent on others for survival."

He stopped talking. He brushed his thumb back and forth over the rock. His lower lip came out to cover its mate, sliding free at length. "And then I started thinking of survival, and it hit me that we really take having kids for granted. We don't think of it as propagating the species, but that's what it is. There's something primal about it, something raw . . . basic."

He paused for a brief, pensive minute. "We're like animals in that way, and I don't mean it in a negative sense. People regard 'animal behavior' as synonymous with lust, but the fact is that animals do what they have to, to keep their species from becoming extinct. The knowledge is built-in. Instinct tells them what to do and when to do it." He gave a soft snort. "It's ironic. We have the superior ability to reason, and because of that our timing gets screwed up. Not that there's a risk of our becoming extinct. . . ."

His voice trailed off. He remained still for a bit, only his thumbs moving on the rock. Then, slowly and uncertainly, he lifted his gaze to Caroline's. "I was terrified when I saw that baby. I was terrified thinking of the responsibility involved—not only to feed it and clothe it but to love it and educate it and raise it to be a productive individual." He took a breath, stopped, then asked, "Do you ever think of things like that?"

She nodded.

"I'll bet they don't frighten you."

"Sure they do," she answered softly. "Raising a child is a challenge no matter how you look at it. There are some things that start me shaking."

"Like what?"

"Like what happens if the baby's sick and crying and I don't know what to do and I can't reach a doctor."

"That's an emergency situation. Any normal parent would be scared."

"Some of the everyday, nonemergency things scare me, too. Like holding the baby when it's small and fragile and squirming. And protecting the soft spot at the top of its head. And making sure that it doesn't fall out of the crib or off the dressing table or down a flight of stairs." She took a breath. "The responsibility is awesome."

Brendan was studying her intently. His voice came out deeper, a little husky. "But then, in spite of those fears, you look at a baby like we were looking at Karen's today, and you know that you want one. That you have to have one. And you start thinking that if you should be struck by lightning and killed tomorrow or next week or next year—"

"Shh!" She cut him off with a sharp sound and a hand on his shoulder. Her hand remained tight on his flesh, though her tone softened. "Don't say that."

"But there's always the possibility. Life isn't forever."

"You're only thirty-eight years old!"

"Which is damned close to middle age—if I'm lucky. Hell, I don't know what the future holds—"

"Brendan!" she protested, but he went quickly on.

"It suddenly occurred to me that if I don't have a child, I really don't have anything to leave behind. A son or daughter is a person's legacy to the world. It's a little bit of him that lives on to be passed to another generation, and another. If I want to have that child and imprint it with *me*, I'd better get going."

Caroline had swung a leg over the stone wall and come down close behind him. "It's not like you to be so morbid."

"Not morbid. Realistic."

"Morbid," she insisted, sliding her arms around his waist. She proceeded to punctuate each word with a squeeze. "Nothing's going to happen to you. You'll have those children, and they'll do you proud."

He half turned his head toward his shoulder and vowed, "That's what I want, Caroline. I want to have kids, and maybe it's arrogant of me to say this, but they'll be great. They'll be bright and personable and enterprising." He dropped his gaze to the spot at his waist where her fingers were threaded and raised a hand to touch them. "When I was looking at that baby today, I could almost see my own. I could almost feel it, feel the way it would feel in my arms, the touch of its skin. That has never, never happened to me—" His voice broke and he fell silent.

"Oh, Brendan," Caroline whispered. Her eyes were closed and she was moving her cheek on his skin. She'd felt it, too—that elemental urge when she'd been looking at Karen's baby—and she felt the same elemental urge now. It was an ache deep in her womb, and there was nothing objective or detached about it. It was intricately connected to this man. She'd never been one to believe in predestination, but there was something so inevitable about her attraction for him that she couldn't have fought it if she'd wanted to. But she didn't want to fight it. She could still be honest in this. She'd always been honest in her physical need for him.

Her fingers spread over the warm, flat muscles of his stomach. She identified one rib, then another, and as her hands rose so did her excitement. Her name came as a quiet whisper on his lips, goading her on. She pressed closer to his back until her breasts were flattened. Her palms made slow, repeated crossings over his hardening nipples.

Brendan had never pretended to be immune to her touch, and he didn't now. But the pleasure was deeper, the need greater. Something of frightening force simmered just beneath the surface. In an attempt to keep it restrained, he inhaled sharply and pressed his palms flat to his thighs. But he couldn't keep his head from falling back in pleasure, or his back from arching, or his chest from swelling to her touch.

So many times in the past month they'd made love, yet for Caroline touching Brendan now took on new purpose. His responses were quick—the tightening of his muscles, the increasing speed of his pulse and shallowness of his breathing. They were prescribed responses, the wordless preamble to lovemaking. They were responses relevant to the biological drive not only to mate but to mate well.

Caroline understood the power of that drive. She'd already accepted the fact that if she were to have a baby, she'd want Brendan to father it. That knowledge, combined with the incredible inundation of sensation that came with the feel of his skin beneath her mouth, his taste, his scent, turned her on.

Her hands grew more active, venturing farther and more boldly. She wasn't thinking of teasing him or even of pleasuring him. She was simply arousing him to a state where he could fulfill his function as a man. And he was fast getting there. When she lowered her hands to his nylon running shorts, she felt the strained gloving of his sex. She caressed him there; he made a low, almost primitive sound. Needing to touch his flesh, she breached the band of his shorts and cupped him with both hands. He made another sound, one that she echoed. Touching him was setting her afire.

She wanted him desperately, but words would have shattered the precious silence of the night. So she showed him her need by making slow, undulating movements against him while her fingers drew him to his limits with silken strokes.

In a swing so gentle that it might have been made in slow motion, Brendan turned and brought her down to the grass on the hidden, meadow side of the wall. There was nothing slow about his fever, though. His mouth was open and hot on hers. His body was insistent. His large hands freed her of her shorts in the same deft movements with which he stripped himself. Claiming his place between her waiting thighs, he entered her with the sureness of divine plan.

Their lovemaking, then, became something fierce and

urgent. The pace was fast. Gentleness was something that neither of them could afford. Brendan's thrusts were deep and vibrant; Caroline met each with greater demand, then cried out when he gave her what she craved. She'd wrapped her legs high around his waist, inviting the deepest possible penetration, and he was there, touching the mouth of her womb, over and over again.

The night woods were a mute witness to the futile battle they waged. Their bodies grew wet with sweat and taut with need, and when the strain of passion erupted into a pulsing climax, they cried out.

But they'd failed. There would be no baby, because they were sane, responsible individuals who left nothing to chance when it came to conception.

Caroline was protected. A strange word, protected. In the aftermath of this night's passion, it was something to be resented. And a short while later, as Caroline and Brendan walked side by side back to the inn, they shared a sadness that compounded itself by their inability to discuss it.

They spent the night making fast, furious, demanding love. It seemed the only way they could express their feelings. There was a desperation to their coming together, an element of punishment in the fury of their coupling. And between bouts of passion, there was sadness.

By noon the next day they were back at the hospital in Philadelphia, and by five that afternoon, in Washington. They'd talked little during the trip. The silence was a knife twisting in Caroline, but she simply couldn't break it. There was so much to say that she couldn't say a thing, and what she had to say was of such import that she didn't know how to begin.

Brendan didn't have that problem. At her open door, he took her hand, whispered a soft kiss to its palm, then released it. "Go on in," he said softly.

"You're not coming?"

"No."

"Maybe later?"

"I don't think so."

The pain in his eyes became her own as understanding dawned. "It's not because you're tired or because you have work to do."

He shook his head.

"You want out," she said, trying to still the suddenly torturous pounding of her heart.

"No. But I can't go on this way. I need something more."

"I can't give you what you want?"

"You can, but I'm not sure you will. I want it all, Caroline. I want the commitment, the strings, the ties, the hassles. That bargain we made—it just doesn't work for me anymore."

The pounding in her chest had congealed into a painfully tight band that made breathing difficult. Her throat ached. Her eyes filled with tears. She pressed her lips together when they seemed prone to tremble and spoke only when she felt she had a modicum of control. "You want marriage."

"Yes. Marriage, kids, the works, and I want them with you. But you have to decide if that's what you want." His hand came up to trace the delicate line of her jaw, and he seemed a little awed for a minute. By the time he returned his gaze to hers, though, the pain was back. "I realize that I'm older than you are. I've been around longer, so I know what I want when I see it. You may not be as sure. That's why I think we should cool it."

She swallowed, trying to maintain a certain poise. "I don't understand. If you want to be with me for the rest of your life, why should we cool it?"

"Because when we're together, we don't think critically, and right now you have to think critically. You have to decide one way or another, Caroline. I can't wait." He thrust a hand through his hair. "I just can't wait. I told myself that I could. I told myself that if I was patient you'd reach the same conclusions I had. But you haven't, and there are times when I hurt so much inside from wanting you that I think I'll go mad." A little short on composure, he took in an uneven breath. "I want to say those words, Caroline. I know you don't want to hear them, because Ben misused them and one of the things you didn't want in our relationship was bartering with vows and promises. At some point, though, you have to trust me enough to know that when I say them I mean them." His voice grew pleading. "Can't you *feel* what I feel?"

She continued to look up at him through brimming tears. But she couldn't speak. She was afraid.

Brendan put the last of his cards on the table. "If I asked you to marry me right now, would you say yes?"

Marriage was the ultimate tie and could be the ultimate hassle if things didn't work out. She wished he hadn't done it this way. She needed a slower approach. She needed time to think. "We've only known each other . . . it's only been . . ."

"See? You're not sure. We could go on forever as we are now, and maybe you'd be happy, but not me. So what I'm suggesting may not make sense, but I don't know what else to do."

Caroline bit hard on her lower lip. She felt her nose running from the strain of holding in tears, and even then Brendan's face blurred. "Maybe you're right," she whispered as she lowered her eyes.

It wasn't what Brendan wanted to hear. He'd been half-hoping his suggestion alone would have been enough to force an admission of love from her. The fact that it hadn't done so left open the possibility that she didn't love him as much as he'd thought. She was obviously upset now, but he had no way of knowing if that was simply because she was losing a friend. His agony increased, but there was no turning back.

"Let me know when you've made up your mind," he said. Fearing for his poise, he leaned forward, kissed her lightly, even lingeringly, on the forehead, then turned and left.

Caroline suffered through Sunday night with an awful ache inside. She felt a deathly loss, and as many times as she prayed for numbness, it never came.

Going to work on Monday was a help. Her clients demanded the kind of concentration that offered a relief from her private thoughts, but no sooner had each client left than she felt the burden return like chain mail settling over her heart.

On Monday night she talked with her mother, who was in a snit about the bossiness of her father's physical therapist, and with Diane, who called to ask about Karen's baby. In the process of the latter, the discussion turned to Carl and issues of communication. Caroline was beginning to feel like a fraud by the time she hung up the phone.

On Tuesday, Elliot stopped in at her office to see her. He was meeting his brother for lunch, he said, and had just wanted to say hello. She sensed that he was testing the waters, but, if so, he was in for a disappointment. She was polite, but her mind was elsewhere. He'd have had to be blind not to see it and deaf not to hear it.

By Wednesday morning, Caroline felt as though she'd been rolled through a wringer. She hadn't slept well in four days. She wasn't in the mood to see individual clients, much less the group she had scheduled. So it was probably just as well that the sheriff chose that time to serve her. She took a good long look at the papers he presented, sank back in her chair in confusion, then rose in anger and, pausing only long enough to let Maren know she was leaving, took off.

She'd never seen Brendan at work, but everyone knew where the Justice Department was, and once there, she had no trouble finding his office. He was with another man. They both looked up when she appeared at the door. Brendan's eyes widened and his color faded a little. He turned to the man with him and asked in a voice of quiet command that belied the question, "Can we pick up on this later?"

The man closed his folder, nodded to Caroline and left. The instant the door shut, she advanced on the desk and slapped down the papers she'd been all but crushing in her hand.

Brendan had been too busy taking in her appearance to notice the papers. Her outfit, a soft, flowing skirt and a short-sleeved, lightweight cotton sweater, was appropriate for her work. But the strand of pearls around her neck was crooked, her hair was disheveled and high color stained her cheeks. She looked spectacular, vibrant and alive. She also looked furious.

He dropped his gaze to the papers. "What're these?"

She was standing straight, fists clenched at her sides. Her voice had that higher-than-normal pitch that it always got when she was upset. "I was hoping you could tell me. They were delivered to my office a little while ago."

Brendan read the papers, then looked up at Caroline in confusion. "Who is Paul Valente?"

"He's that client I told you about, the one whose wife walked out on our sessions. He's been seeing me alone since then—remember, I told you?—and now *she's* naming me in an alienation-of-affection suit! Have you ever heard anything so stupid?"

Brendan had heard plenty of things even more stupid when it came to the law and would have told her so, but before he'd had a chance, she was racing on.

"Nothing like this has ever happened to me before! It's insulting—to think that I'd actively pit a husband and wife against each other. I'm a *professional*. A professional doesn't do things like that!"

Brendan held out a hand to calm her, but she thought he was arguing, so she said, "I know what you're going to say—that the papers are full of stories of psychiatrists taking sexual advantage of their patients—but that isn't applicable here. I've only seen the man four times, and each time it was in the middle of the afternoon, with my partners in adjoining offices. Other than those four times, I saw Paul and Sheila together. I thought I had a reasonable working relationship with them both. How could she turn on me this way?"

Brendan was thinking of the adage about a woman scorned, which would explain some of Sheila Valente's fury, but he remembered Caroline saying that Sheila walked out on Paul, rather than vice versa, so the adage didn't apply. "She's probably—"

"There's no 'probably' about it," Caroline cried. "She's *crazy*, and the thing that bothers me most is that through all those months of therapy I didn't see it. I regarded her as an egotistical but basically rational woman. Now look what she's done!" She pointed a shaking finger at the accusatory papers. "Correct me if I'm wrong, but when someone is charged with 'alienation of affection,' they're being charged with more than talk. That witch is accusing me of chasing after her husband. The implication is that I *slept* with him, which is the dumbest thing I've heard yet!"

"Caroline—" Brendan began. He sensed that she was on the edge of hysteria, which wasn't like her at all. She might be a sight for his starving eyes, but that didn't mean that he couldn't see how tense she was.

"Do you know what this could do? This could ruin my career!"

"It won't—"

"If word gets out that I'm seducing my clients, I could be finished. I don't think I could bear that, Brendan," she said. Tears were quickly gathering in her eyes. "Because I'm not guilty of a thing. I tried my best with Paul and Sheila, and when Sheila gave up, I tried my best with Paul alone. Isn't that what you said—that what really mattered was whether you've tried your best?"

He was up and rounding the desk. She'd begun to tremble, and he needed to touch her. He'd gotten as far as clasping her arms when her composure started to crumble.

"I mean, the charge is absurd," she said brokenly. She was looking up at him, pleading, and the first of her tears had begun to trickle slowly down her cheeks. "The idea that I c-could have been with someone else . . . that I could have tried to seduce Paul or even wanted to do it . . . when a-all along I couldn't possibly think about any other man because I've been in love with you . . ."

With that, she lost it completely. She closed her eyes and tucked her head low. Her hands came up to cover her face and muffle the sobs she couldn't control. In the next minute, those sobs were muffled against Brendan's shirtfront as he wrapped her tightly in his arms.

"Shh," he whispered into her hair. "It's okay, baby, it's okay."

Incredibly, she began to cry even harder. Her arms slid around his neck, and she clung to him as though someone would be taking him away any minute. "Bren . . . dan . . ."

He held her tighter and murmured soft, soothing sounds. Her tears hurt him, but he knew that she needed the outlet. He'd seen how closely she'd guarded her tears on Sunday night, and he guessed that she hadn't let herself cry even after he'd left. He wondered when she'd last cried, really cried as she was doing now.

"Brendan . . . oh . . ."

"I love you, sweetheart."

"I've been . . . so . . . stupid. . . ."

"No, you haven't."

She burst into a new round of sobs, and he could do nothing but hold her tightly until she'd calmed a bit. At that point, he backed up to sit on the edge of the desk. Digging into the small purse that hung from her shoulder, he fished out a Kleenex. Then he shifted her sideways against his chest, handed her the Kleenex and watched while she blotted her eyes. He used the tips of his fingers to smooth her hair back from her face.

"Don't worry about the lawsuit," he said softly.

She sniffled.

"I guarantee you the charges will be dropped long before anything comes of it."

"Mmm."

"It's not uncommon for a husband or wife to go a little bit off the deep end in the course of a divorce. We'll explain the facts to Sheila Valente's lawyer, and if she persists in going forward, we'll threaten to countersue. She'll change her mind."

"I know."

"You do?"

Caroline nodded. Her head was still bowed, and the Kleenex was a tight wad in the fist that was pressed to his chest. "I just needed to see you." She took a breath that was so uneven he thought she was going to start crying again. She didn't. Nor did she look up. "It's been an awful week without you. Getting those papers was just one more lousy thing, but if it hadn't been that, it would have been something else. I've felt stifled not being able to talk with you. I've looked across the courtyard—"

"Only after you turned out the lights," he interrupted. "Before that, you never looked once. I was watching."

"After I turned out the lights," she admitted softly.

"Why not before?"

She thought about that for a minute. "Because—" she took a breath "—because I was afraid you'd see me looking, and I wasn't ready to say what you wanted to hear."

His hand fell away from her neck. "I don't want you to say only what I want to hear."

"That came out wrong," she said quickly. She began to fiddle nervously with the button of his shirt. "What I meant was that I wasn't ready to say what I felt, even though I knew it was what you wanted to hear."

"Why not?"

"I think," she said, "because things have happened so fast, and because what we have seems so . . . perfect . . . that I assumed there had to be a hitch."

"I thought you were an optimist."

"So did I. I guess I was nervous because nothing has ever meant so much to me before."

"Nothing?"

She shook her head. "Our relationship was like a dream. There were times when I knew that I wanted it to be forever, but I was afraid to think that way for fear of jinxing it."

"Superstitious, to boot?" he teased.

"No. Just dumb."

"What wised you up?"

"Missing you." She twisted the button back and forth. "And thinking about the struggles other couples go through." The backs of her fingers grazed his shirt, absorbing the warmth and strength of his body. "And realizing that I couldn't conceive of being with any other man but you."

"Caroline?" he asked in his softest voice.

"Mmm?"

"Why won't you look at me?"

She flattened her fingers over the button she'd been worrying. "I'm embarrassed."

"Because you've been crying?"

"No, because I've been a ninny. I'm supposed to know what I'm doing in situations like these. But I blew it."

"*Nearly* blew it," he corrected. The beginnings of a smile were in his voice and on his lips. "You've come to your senses in time."

Her head came up a little way, just enough so that she could focus on the pulse at his neck. "Then you forgive me for being dense?"

"On one condition."

Her eyes reached his mouth. "What's that?"

"That you stop taking the full responsibility for things that go wrong. You weren't the only one at fault here. We didn't talk. Neither of us. If I'd been open earlier about what I'd been thinking and feeling, I wouldn't have reached the point of frustration that I did."

"You're right," she said as her eyes touched his.

"I was a bastard to give you an ultimatum like that."

She considered that, then nodded. "You're right."

"Forgive me?"

"On one condition."

"Hmm?"

"The ultimatum sticks," she said with determination and promise. "It's either all or nothing. I've decided I want all. Can you give it?"

"Can I give it? Can I *give* it?" His eyes took on a breathtaking glow. "Oh-ho, baby, can I ever."

That night, Brendan wasn't wondering how much he could give but how much he could take. It was dark out. He stood before his window, staring across the courtyard into Caroline's loft. She was looking her seductive best, and it was driving him wild.

They had a date. They'd decided to dress up and go out for an elegant dinner to formally celebrate their love, but at the rate they were going, they'd never make it. Brendan was newly shaved and showered and had drawn on his dark suit pants, but those pants weren't feeling terribly comfortable at the moment. Fresh from her own shower, Caroline was leaning against the window jamb wearing nothing but a silk teddy. One of her arms was bent and braced against the wood by her head; the other rested loosely in the half lap she'd made by propping one knee on the window seat.

Well? he asked with a grin.

She returned the grin. *Well, what?*

Are we going out?

Sure.

His eyes made a sweep of her body, lingering at the swell of her breasts and the spot where her nipples pushed at the teddy. *You're not dressed.*

Her own appreciative eye wandered over his chest, leisurely following the tapering trail of hair to the spot where his pants waited to be fastened. *Neither are you.*

I can't get dressed when you stand around that way. It distracts me.

You don't look distracted. You look attentive. And warm.

So do you, he thought as she slowly brought her hand from her lap and curved it around her neck.

Brendan?

Hmm?

When we buy our house, can we get one with air conditioning?

You bet.

I want four kids. Is that okay?

Of course it's okay. Caroline, please get dressed.

Do you play baseball?

Baseball? What does baseball have to do with anything?

I have this image of you coaching a Little League team.

Sweetheart, I will do anything, anything you want, if only you'll put something on. This is torture.

Drawing her hand down her neck, she dipped two fingers into the hollow between her breasts. *I love you, Brendan.*

I love you, too, but if you don't get dressed soon, I won't be held responsible for my actions.

Do you really want to go out to dinner?

Caroline . . .

She took a long, slow breath that expanded her rib cage and lifted her breasts. *We could call and put the reservations back an hour. . . .*

He blotted beads of sweat from his forehead with his arm.

She smiled. *I could fix you something to tide you over.*

Tide me over? Ah, hell. Backing away from the window, he thrust his feet into his loafers, grabbed his shirt and made for the door.

Across the courtyard, Caroline, too, backed away from the window. With a smug smile, she turned and started slowly across the room. Before she reached the door, she'd turned off every light in the loft except the small one by her bed. Then she opened the door and waited for Brendan.

a special something

1

Hello?

How's America's answer to Michelangelo?

Feeling more like a frustrated David.

After last night?

After this morning. I was hoping to wake up with you in my arms. What time did you leave?

Just after dawn. You were sleeping so soundly I didn't have the heart to disturb you.

Some lover. Leaves me all alone to fight the Monday-morning blues wearing nothing but a bed-sheet and the very last of my Homme Premier cologne.

Mmm. Sounds enticing.

That's the point. When will you be back?

Tomorrow night. What would you like from New Orleans?

Just you. Dressed in soft pink. With a silky white negligee in your bag. And . . . darling?

Yes?

Bring a bottle of Homme Premier, will you? No David should be without it.

Rogue!

Fascinated, Leslie Parish stared at the advertisement for a long time. He was magnificent, this one whose lover had deserted him at dawn. A sculptor, his tools lay scattered atop the distant workbench at the base of a half-finished piece of art. A man, his studio apartment was a blend of muted browns and charcoals and sunlit whites. A lover, his bed was large and strewn with a sensual array of sheets barely covering one leg, and that part David hadn't tried to hide. Again and again Leslie's gaze returned to the taunting strip of flesh at his hip. Sucking in a wistful breath, she let her eye creep back up, over the broad and sinewed expanse of his lightly haired chest to his face.

Dark wavy hair, mussed by sleep, fell across his brow. His jaw bore the faintest shadow of a beard. His nose was straight; his lips firm, slightly parted. But what intrigued her most was the expression that the camera's soft lens had captured as he'd stared into his dreams with the phone cradled against his ear. A moment of vulnerability, an exquisite blend of lonely and loving that reached out to every woman on earth who had ever glimpsed a masterpiece and craved to touch it. . . .

"That's a crock!" The angry voice of Anthony Parish suddenly filled the room, startling her from her reverie, bringing her head sharply up. Her brother's hand gripped the phone, and his good-looking features were harsh in contrast to those of the face beneath her fingertips. "I don't care *how* long it takes to substantiate those facts! I'm paying top dollar and I want results!" He cast a glance at Leslie, then shook his head. "No, no. Not that way. Listen, you work on it. I'll be in touch later."

Replacing the receiver, he pushed himself from his chair and rounded the desk to take the seat beside her. Despite the flecks of gray that whispered through his hair, he was tall and lean, carrying his forty years well. "Sorry about that, Les," he murmured, "but someone's got to keep on top of them."

"I thought you had assistants to handle things like that."

Steepling his fingers, he leaned forward with a sigh. "The buck stops here. If I want this publishing house to make it in a struggling economy, it's *my* responsibility. Quality is the name of the game. At least for me it is. I want every story we print to be right." He shot a glance at the magazine that lay open on Leslie's lap. *"Man's Mode* has done well precisely because it's a notch above." He sighed again. "But that's not your worry—" he sent her a teasing smile "—unless you'd like to change your mind and join us."

Leslie held up a slender hand. "No, thanks. I rather like being the black sheep of the family. I mean, you've got the publishing end and Diane's got sporting goods and Brenda's tied up in computers, while dad sits up there as chairman of the board. No," she smiled, "I'll stick to my kids."

Teasing yielded to a moment's admiration. "You love your work, don't you?"

"Um hmm."

"I'm glad, Les. Hey!" The rotating file in Tony's mind must have given a sudden flip. "You've got a birthday coming up."

"Um hmm."

"A big one."

She'd been trying to forget. "Um hmmmmm."

"What do you want?"

She crinkled up her nose. "Nothing. Really."

"Come on. It's not every day that a woman turns thirty."

"Thank God."

"Leslie," her brother chided, "you're not feeling your age, are you? Hell, self-made woman and all, you're doing better than ever."

On the surface she was. Inside, though, there was a growing sense of restlessness. "I suppose," she said thoughtfully.

"So what's your pleasure?" He sat back in his chair and eyed her speculatively. "A watch? Better still—" his brown eyes lit up "—how about a fur jacket? Something soft and chic?"

"Really, Tony. I don't want anything. . . ."

He arched a brow. "I won't take no for an answer. You may be a successful professional, but you're still my little sister. In my book, that gives me the right to dote. So," he breathed, as though the matter was settled, "what'll it be? For your thirtieth—a special something. . . ."

Leslie thought for a minute. Her gaze dropped to the advertisement that still lay open on her lap. Her forefinger traced the swath of skin whose lightly bronzed color ran unbroken from head to foot. She chewed on her bottom lip, then smiled. "What I'd *really* like," she announced boldly, "is the use of the house on St. Barts for a week . . . and *him*."

Three weeks later she arrived on St. Barthélémy. Having woken up at four-thirty that morning to pack and catch the first plane out of JFK, she was tired. Wearing the wools that a frigid predawn February morning in New York had demanded, she was sweaty. Greeting the beauty of the Caribbean through hot, heavy eyes, she was miserable. To top it all, the taxi she'd taken from the airport had had a flat tire several hundred yards from the villa, and desperate to lay her head on a fresh, cool pillow, she'd taken her things and left the driver to deal with his jack and spare.

Toting a duffel bag over one arm and a bag of books and her purse over the other, she struggled along the narrow road, which wound uphill. Though she clung to its shoulder, where the succession of palm parasols might protect her from the strong midday Caribbean sun, she felt beads of sweat gather along her hairline, moisten her neck, trickle in a tiny stream down the valley between her breasts. For the moment the beauty of the island was lost on her. She simply wanted to lie down.

She sneezed once and sniffled as the road curved, then moaned aloud when the familiar structure with its red-tiled roof and white stucco walls emerged from its tropical camouflage. That was all the incentive she needed to quicken her step. Her legs felt like rubber, but she didn't care. Another two minutes and she'd be there, sprawled in her favorite room—in *everybody's* favorite room—with the overhead fan gently cooling the air, the palm fronds dancing on the skylight overhead, the sea strutting its lush azure stuff beyond the open sliding doors, from the sparkling white sands of the beachfront to the far horizon.

Fairly running the last few steps, she shifted from one

elbow to the other the heavy wool sweater she'd already stripped off and dug into her purse for the key. When it eluded her, she tugged the purse around and peered bleary-eyed into the scrambled abyss of its interior. She rummaged again, whispered a soft oath and peered a second time, finally shaking the bag to hear the telltale rattle that helped her zero in on the spot. Another minute's ferreting produced the key.

With a twist of her hand, the front door opened. As cool air enveloped her, she smiled her relief. "Thank you, Martine," she rasped softly, vowing to repeat it louder later in the week when she came face to face with the woman who must have been in earlier that morning in anticipation of her arrival. And a twist of fate it was that Martine was a morning person. Leslie's original plans had been to arrive that evening; only a last minute cancellation on the early-bird flight had brought her in at noontime.

Closing the door behind her, she stooped to let her bags fall from her damp and tired shoulders. Her purse and sweater slid to the floor nearby. Mopping her clammy forehead on her sleeve, she stepped out of her leather pumps and, with her fingers at the button of her plum-and-blue plaid skirt, started down the stairs.

After ten years of family vacations here, she'd come to take the villa for granted. Only a visitor would be entranced by its unique design. Nestled into the cliffs rising above the sands on the western end of the small island, it sprawled across three spacious levels. The top level, even with the road, held the front foyer, one wall of which was glassed and looked out toward the ocean, the other two walls of which opened to lateral bedrooms. The bottom level, to the right as the house followed the natural cropping of the cliff, held the airy kitchen and living room and opened on to a flagstoned terrace, itself graduated on two planes, the lowest of which was a hop, skip and jump from the beach.

It was the middle level of the house to which Leslie headed unswervingly. Connected to top and bottom by an open staircase, it was the one most coveted by whichever family member had the good fortune to arrive first, or, all too often and to Leslie's misfortune, needed the space. This level held an airy den and the exquisite master-bedroom suite, of which Leslie had every intention of taking sole possession for the week.

Bent on undressing and showering, she had her skirt unzipped and halfway down her hips by the time she reached the foot of the stairs. Quickly hopping free of the heavy wool, she tossed it over the back of a chair in the den, then reached down to pull her lavender turtleneck jersey from the elastic confines of her matching wool tights. Feeling more like a wilting violet than a stylish New Yorker, she padded toward the bedroom.

The door was open. Tugging the turtleneck over her head, she stumbled across the threshold, and was in the process of peeling the clinging fabric from her sweaty arms when she cried out in alarm and came to an abrupt halt. Clamping her teeth into her soft lower lip, she stared at the bed.

It was supposed to be empty. It was supposed to be freshly made and waiting just for her. It was supposed to be all hers for the week.

Instead, the covers were pulled back, and the rumpled sheets were draped—just barely—over a large body that was very definitely male and just as definitely sound asleep.

Sagging against the doorjamb with her turtleneck crushed against the pale mauve lace of her bra, she was seized by a wave of fury. Tony had promised! He'd said he would clear it with the others so that she might have the villa to herself for the week! Was this a friend of his? Or Diane's . . . or Brenda's? It just wasn't fair! The one time she'd wanted it . . . wanted it. . . .

Suddenly her anger faded as a memory seemed to mesh with the tableau before her. Decorated in white and rattan, with pillows and cushions of an imported Italian weave, the room glowed beneath the noontime sun, which stole through the palms above the skylight to lend a dreamlike quality to the air. The ceiling fan whirred softly overhead, augmenting the gentlest of breezes that danced off the ocean and whispered in through the open glass sliding doors. But it was to the bed that Leslie's eyes were riveted. To the bed . . . and the figure so carelessly spread atop it.

There was something familiar about him. Feeling a sneeze coming on, she pressed her hand to her nose in hopes of suppressing it as, entranced, she studied the limp torso and sprawled limbs. The length of lightly bronzed leg that extended from the sheet spoke of superior height. The firmness of his thigh and corresponding leanness of his stomach attested to commendable fitness. The solidly muscular structure of his shoulder hinted at bodily pride. He was, in a word, stunning.

He lay on his back with his head fallen to the side. One hand, fingers splayed, rested on his stomach. She couldn't help but note how comfortable it looked, cushioned by the soft ribbon of hair that narrowed from the more ambitious covering of his chest. His other hand was thrown out to the side in a gesture she might have seen as pure invitation had the man not been so very obviously asleep.

Hugging her jersey to her throat, Leslie dared creep closer. Eyes wide in disbelief, she stared. She'd seen that face before. Even in repose it held a certain expression of vulnerability that immediately conjured up images of another bed, another setting. There was the hair, dark and mussed by sleep . . . the nose, straight, almost aristocratic . . . the sensually enticing shadow of a beard. As her eye tripped down his body once more, her heart began to pound with understanding. Oh, yes, she'd seen that face before. *And* that body. This time there was no workbench in the background, no sculptor's tools, no half-finished piece of art. This time his sheet covered the strip of flesh at his hip that had so taunted her before. This time the bed was in no photographer's studio but in her family's own villa.

Without realizing what she was doing, she sniffed the air in search of the unique scent of Homme Premier. But her nose was so stuffed she only succeeded in sending herself in a paroxysm of coughing, from which she emerged in horror to watch the man on the bed begin to move.

First his chest expanded with a deep, indrawn breath. His lips thinned, his brow furrowed. He turned his dark head on the pillow, stretching the outflung arm up over his head. Leslie swallowed hard when the sheet slipped precariously low on his abdomen.

Her gaze returned to his face in time to see one eye open—and stare at her blankly. When it was joined by the other, she saw that they were a warm shade of brown. The man blinked, dusting thick mahogany fringes against the high line of his cheek, then frowned, then blinked again and stared at her. Finally, as though abruptly recalling something, he bolted upright.

"My God!" he exclaimed, thrusting his fingers through the thick swath of hair that waved gently over his brow. "I'm sorry! I was going to be up and showered and dressed long before you arrived!" Frowning again, he looked toward the skylight, then reached for his watch from the stand beside the bed and stared at it in confusion. "Twelve-forty? But you weren't supposed to be in until seven tonight."

"I got an early flight," Leslie droned in a near monotone, then shook her blond head in distress. "I . . . don't . . . believe it."

"What don't you believe?"

"You."

His expression was immediately endearing, as though his only purpose in life was to please her, and having failed that, he was crushed. "I've done something wrong already?"

"You're here. I don't . . . believe it."

All vestige of drowsiness gone, the man looked down at his body innocently, before breaking into a gentle smile. "I am here."

"An understatement," she muttered beneath her breath, then watched him hoist himself up against the headboard. He seemed to dominate not only the bed but the entire room. In turn, Leslie's eyes held dismay. "He really did it."

Her reference was clear. "Your brother? Of course he did it. It sounds like he adores you. Most likely he'd have given you *anything* you'd asked."

"But . . . a man? *You?*" Her dismay was fast turning to mortification. "I was supposed to be here alone," she said in a very small voice. Above and beyond all the special things she had planned for herself, she suddenly realized that this man was not only gorgeous, but he was a male model who was *paid* to be pleasing to women. In this case he'd been paid by her brother, *her own brother*, to spend the week with her! Her cheeks felt hotter than ever.

Beneath the sheet, he bent one knee out to the side. Leslie eyed its vivid outline with something akin to anguish, breathing only a marginal sigh when he safely adjusted the sheet over his hips.

"Alone is no fun," he countered softly. His eyes dropped from her face to her chest, taking in the straps of her bra, the disarray of the jersey, which she clutched more fiercely than ever to her breasts, the slender expanse of purple wool running from her waist to her toes. She assumed she must look like a lavender elf; in truth, she felt more like the court jester.

Following his gaze and for the first time realizing her state of dress, Leslie took a step backward. "Alone can be lots of fun," she argued, recalling the plans she had to read, to sunbathe in the buff, to amble around the island to her heart's content with no thought of any other living soul, for a change. It simply wasn't fair, she mused, then slanted him an accusing glance. "You're in *my* bed, you know." She felt on the defense both physically and emotionally.

But her brief spurt of belligerence was feeble and reflected her growing torment. Not only was she appalled that her brother had taken seriously what she'd said purely tongue-in-cheek, but she felt sicker by the minute.

"I thought this was the master suite," came the deep rejoinder.

"It is. And this time round, *I'm* the master." So she'd been telling herself for the past few weeks; it had been part of the lure of spending her vacation at the villa in solitude.

The man on the bed arched a brow and skimmed her defensive pose. "You don't look terribly masterful right now.

As a matter of fact—" his dark brows knit and he sat forward "—you don't look terribly well. Are you feeling all right?"

In no mood to be witty or subtle, Leslie simply shook her head. "I was up before dawn to get to JFK and had to wait forever sweltering on St. Martin to catch the island hopper here. I'm hot and sweaty and just want to get out of these things and into a cool shower. Besides that, I've got a splitting headache and one hell of a cold." She took a stuffy breath. "In short, I feel awful!"

When the man quickly pushed himself up from the bed, she shut her eyes. All too well she remembered the sliver of smooth flesh by his hip. She didn't think she could take that just now.

"You mean your normal voice isn't as nasal?" came the note of amusement not far from her ear. Simultaneously an arm circled her shoulder and propelled her forward.

Feeling perfectly stupid, she opened her eyes, careful to keep them straight ahead as the bathroom door neared. "No, it's not," she managed, struggling with the *n*'s.

"That's too bad," the man replied softly, teasingly. "It's sexy. Deep and . . . sultry. That's it. Sultry."

"Sultry, as in hot and humid. And sweaty." Sexy was the last thing she felt.

At the bathroom door he slipped a hand to her forehead. "And feverish. Wait here."

Sagging against the jamb, she closed her eyes. Then, hit by a wave of dizziness, she gave up even the idea of a cooling shower. Suddenly nothing mattered more than lying flat. Turning, she stumbled back to the bed. The thought that the man whose body had warmed its sheets moments before might have a god-awful social disease was totally irrelevant to the situation. Her legs simply wouldn't hold her any longer.

With a soft moan she curled on her side, then, forgetting her company, rolled onto her back, clutching her jersey to her stomach with one hand and throwing the other arm across her eyes. When, moments later, the same arm that had led her toward the bathroom lifted her to a half-seated position, she groaned.

"Let me rest," she whispered, but her protector had other ideas.

"First, aspirin," he said gently. "Are you taking anything else?" She shook her head and docilely swallowed the tablets, washing them down with the water he'd brought. "There." He took the glass from her and eased her back onto the bed. Then he reached for the waistband of her tights and began to shimmy them over her hips.

"What are you doing?" she cried in alarm and squirmed away. When she tried to sit up, though, a firm hand pressed her flat. For the effort she'd made, her only reward was the sight of the pale blue briefs that ringed his hips. With strong, knowing hands he proceeded to peel the tights to her toes and off.

"Better?"

By twenty degrees at least. "Oh, yes."

"Want a shower now?"

She shook her head and rolled to her side again, pulling one of the pillows against her for comfort. "Not yet. I think I'll just lie like this for a while."

"Then I'll shower. Where are your bags?"

Her eyes were closed, his voice distant. If the man wished to rob her, she couldn't stop him. Her total concentration was on finding relief from the aches and pains that seemed to have suddenly invaded her body. "Upstairs. . . ."

If she was aware of the pad of footsteps on the stairs going up, then down, she made no sign. Nor did she turn her head when the faint hum of an electric razor filled the air, or when the spray of the shower rang out, or when the rustle of clothes in a suitcase ended with the glide of smooth cotton over hair-roughened flesh. It was only when the aspirin began to take effect, when she felt just warm, rather than hot, when the pounding in her head had subsided to a dull throb, that she opened her eyes again.

Seated in a chair by the bed, wearing nothing but a pair

of pleated khaki shorts, was the man she'd been given for her birthday. A rush of mortification hit her anew. For, sitting there, his hair and skin damp and fresh, his chest broad and manly, his shoulders strong and inviting, he looked more magnificent than he had in his ad. By contrast she felt as though she'd been dredged up from hell.

"I don't believe it!" she moaned, then felt all the more gauche when the faintest of smiles curved his lips.

Propping his elbows on the arms of the chair, he threaded his fingers together. "I think you've said that already."

"I don't care! This is incredible!"

"What is?"

"This. . . ." She waved toward him, then herself, then extended her fingers to take in the situation as a whole. "I can't believe Tony would do this to me!"

"As I was told, you specifically requested it."

Her chest rose and fell as she labored to breathe. "It was a *joke*! I was being facetious! Tony must have known that." When the man opposite her slowly shook his head, she went quickly on. "And besides, the man I pointed to was a fictitious character."

"He had a face and a body. You had to know he was real."

"He was a paid model! I never, expected Tony to go out and track him down, then hire him to entertain me for the week!" The thought instantly revived her embarrassment. Pink-cheeked, she turned her face away and shut her eyes. "God," she moaned beneath her breath, "I feel so lousy. Maybe I'd be laughing if I felt all right. But I can barely breathe, let alone think straight."

The mattress yielded to another form. Though she tensed up, she didn't have the strength to move, even when a cool hand began to stroke damp strands of blond hair from her brow. Quite against her will, she found the gesture a comfort.

"How long have you felt this way?" the deep voice probed with such concern that she couldn't help but answer.

"Since last night."

"Sore throat?"

She shook her head, then opened her eyes and peered up

into his, which were studying her carefully. "You can't stay here, you know."

"Oh?" The twinkle in his eye spoke of his amusement.

"No."

"And why not?"

"Because *I'm* here."

The man made ceremony of looking around the bed. "We seem to be doing just fine here together." Anticipating her, he had a hand at her shoulder before she could begin to raise it from the bed. "Besides, I'm your gift. You can't just discard me along with the wrapping."

"What wrapping?" she quipped. "Seems to me you weren't wearing much of anything."

"I was wearing something."

"Not much."

"So you *did* notice. I was beginning to think I'd lost my touch."

Leslie sighed and closed her eyes. "You haven't lost your touch," she granted. It was moving in slow circles against her temples. "Great for headaches. . . ."

"And . . . ?"

Her eyes flew open. "That's all," she said quickly. "I meant what I said before. You can't . . ." Her voice trailed off as a sneeze approached. "Damn," she whispered, covering her mouth and sneezing. She sat up in time to sneeze a second time, then took the tissue he offered and blew her nose. "Do I ever feel lousy. . . ."

The same hand that had smoothed her hair from her brow now tucked random strands behind her ear. "Why don't you take that shower? In the meantime, I'll fix you a cold drink."

"You can't stay. . . ."

"Have you had any lunch?"

"Lunch? I haven't had any *breakfast*. Feed a cold, starve a fever . . . I've got both. What do I do?" She raised her eyes to those above her. They were reassuring and confident.

"Don't worry, sweetheart. I know what to do. Here, you stay put." He pushed himself from the bed and reached for her bag. "What do you want to put on?" Unzipping the stylish duffel, he began rummaging inside. "Is there a nightgown in here?"

Leslie recalled the ad that had started this farce. Her voice held more than a trace of sarcasm. "Nightgown as in silky white negligee?" She shook her head. "Sorry."

For a minute the man raised his head and eyed her strangely. Then, as understanding dawned, he cast her a punishing glance and turned his attention back to her bag.

Perhaps it was her reference to the ad that did it. Perhaps it was simply the aspirin clearing her head. But in the moment's pause it occurred to Leslie that she was lying on a rumpled bed in nothing but scant wisps of mauve lace, watching a total stranger fish through her clothes.

"Here, let me do that," she said crossly as she pushed herself up. Within seconds she'd managed to extract the oversize T-shirt she'd come to think of as her Caribbean negligee. A very pale aqua from too many washings, it was likewise soft and comfortable. Easily reaching her thighs, it would be suitably unappealing. "If it's sexy you're looking for," she muttered, "you've come to the wrong place."

Mustering her pride, she snatched her bag of toiletries from the duffel and headed for the bathroom, totally unaware of how truly sexy she looked. The man watching her, however, was not. He stood holding the picture of her in his mind's eye long after the bathroom door had closed.

On the other side of the door, Leslie pressed her palms to her hot cheeks, then slid her fingers up to push her hair away from her face. A mess. She was a mess. The entire situation was a mess. How had she ever managed it . . . careful, conservative Leslie?

Angrily plopping the bag of toiletries atop the vanity, she dug inside for makeup remover. Makeup? Hah! What a wasted effort that had been. She'd looked deathly regardless. But New York was New York, and one didn't show one's face in public unless it was suitably protected from the elements. Lips thinning with sarcasm, she squeezed a gob of cold cream onto her fingers and began to scrub at her cheeks. Protected from the elements? More likely camouflaged. Hidden. Shielded from the world by a manufactured sheen. How phony it all was!

With a vengeance she tissued off the cold cream, then bent low to rinse her face with water. There she lingered, savoring the sensation of coolness on her cheeks and eyes. At last she straightened and pressed a towel more gently to her skin.

She should have known . . . should have known never to even joke with Tony about the state of her love life. He'd been after her for years to marry, have an affair, get involved, live it up. Wasn't that what he'd been doing since his own divorce six years before? Not that she criticized him. He'd married young and had been faithful to the letter to Laura. In the end she had been the one to run off with someone else, leaving him to cope with three growing children. He was a hardworking, devoted father who needed time off once in a while; Leslie certainly couldn't fault him for his own choice of outlet.

On the other hand, she reasoned, as she turned on the shower and stepped beneath its tepid spray, he should have known not to foist something as . . . as preposterous as this pretty boy on her! Hadn't she spent the past ten years trying to show the world how different she was? She'd had her fill of high society back in high school. And in college, well, Joe Durand had soured her on men, period. But then, Tony knew nothing about Joe. She hadn't spoken of him to anyone. The self-reproach with which she lived was bad enough, but to air her folly for the sake of others' enjoyment . . . *that* she didn't need.

Adjusting the water to a warmer temperature, she shampooed her hair, then soaped herself. It was several minutes later when she stepped from beneath the soothing spray. After toweling herself as vigorously as her tired arms would allow, she drew on the T-shirt and a fresh pair of panties and blew her hair nearly dry. Then, standing opposite the misted mirror, she studied herself. Even the mist couldn't soften the image.

"Pale, Leslie. Too pale," she announced, then sneezed and reached for a piece of Kleenex. By the time she faced herself again, the mist had begun to clear, and what she saw gave her a jolt. Oh, the features were fine—soft amethyst eyes that were large and, if anything, set a bit too far apart; a nose that was certainly small enough to balance the delicacy of her mouth and chin; hair that was an enviable shade of blond, cut into long bangs across the brow, trimmed crisply an inch above the shoulder, cropped stylishly at the sideburns and falling into place as Diego had promised. No, the features were fine, taken one by one. Put together, however, they formed the image of a lost and lonely waif.

Reaching up, she brushed her bangs from her eyes. What was she going to do? Granted, it was unfortunate that the one week she'd chosen to spend in the sun should be hampered by a mean winter cold. That, though, she could live with. And the sun, the warm weather, would be potent medicine.

But this man, this, model . . . this very handsome model . . . was something else. Never in a million years would she have sought such a man on her own. Indeed, pausing to think of the man's occupation, of the many women he must have serviced over the years, she was appalled. And embarrassed. She wasn't that type at all! She wouldn't know what to *do* with such a man. . . .

Shaking her head half in regret, she left the sanctuary of the bathroom to find the bedroom immaculate. The man's suitcase that had lain on the low glass table was gone, as were odds and ends atop the nightstand. The bed had been freshly made, its covers turned back invitingly. Padding barefoot to the walk-in closet, she peered inside, then turned. There was no sign of him.

While urging herself to simply climb into bed and be grateful she'd been left alone, Leslie headed downstairs toward the kitchen. He'd said he'd make her a cool drink. Well, she was thirsty.

Indeed he was in the kitchen, though his attention was not on making a cool drink. Rather, he stood before the open window, his back to her, his arms crossed over his chest, one

bare foot propped on the low rung of a nearby stool. He wore
the same shorts he'd put on earlier, and all in all, he presented
a perfect image of reflective masculinity.

For a lingering moment she studied him. Though his hair
was thick and on the long side, it was well trimmed. From
the sturdy nape to the soles of his feet, he looked clean.
He also looked older than she'd imagined him to be, despite
the prime condition of his body. From where she stood she
caught shadings of silver following the gentle curve of each
ear. Rather than detracting from his appearance, these silver streaks lent him an air of dignity that puzzled her all the
more.

In short, there was nothing unsavory-looking about him.
She wasn't sure what she'd expected from a gigolo. Certainly not . . . this.

With practically no warning she sneezed, ending her moment of invisibility. The man by the window turned quickly,
his features instantly released from whatever thoughts had
held them taut.

"There you are," he said, taking the few steps necessary
to end their separation. "Feeling better?"

She had been, she'd thought. Now, though, looking up that
great distance into a face that seemed so gentle, so knowing,
she felt suddenly small and utterly insignificant.

"A little," she murmured, adding "self-conscious" to the
list. What had made her think that a T-shirt would protect
her from the eyes of a professional lover? When those eyes
began to wander across her chest and down, she slithered
from their touch and took refuge on the stool by the window.

"Why aren't you in bed?" he asked softly.

"I felt like seeing what you were up to," she answered
defensively, then turned her face to catch the ocean's gentle
breath. "Where's that cool drink you promised?" Even to
her own ears her tone held a touch of arrogance. It bothered
her. She didn't much care for hired help . . . certainly not of
this sort!

After a pause came a murmured, "Coming right up."
Only when Leslie heard the refrigerator door open did she

dare look back to find her attendant on his haunches sorting through the packed shelves. "It looks like someone was far more prepared for your arrival than I was," he said, pushing aside a bushy head of lettuce to get at a carton of eggs. "I wouldn't have believed they had all this fresh produce down here."

"Some of it is home grown, but most of it's imported. And it was Martine who did the marketing. She's a marvel. She comes in to clean once or twice while we're here and keeps an eye on things when we're not. All it takes is one call from the States and the house is open, cool and stocked to the hilt."

"You don't ever rent it out."

"No. Friends use it sometimes. But more often it's just us." She tried desperately to be tactful. "We were very lucky to get this land. It's on a prime part of the island. Most of the space is owned by small inns. In fact, there's a quaint one just around the bend. You could probably get a room there. . . ."

Ignoring her suggestion, he added a quart of milk and a package of neatly wrapped cheese to the growing assortment in his arms. "Nice cheese. Any lemon? Ah, there." When, arms laden, he stood at last, his knees cracked in protest. He flexed them gingerly as he deposited his armload on the counter.

Leslie focused in on the knees. "How old are you?"

"Thirty-nine."

"That old?" Even with creaking knees and the twin streaks of gray behind his ears, she would have given him no more than thirty-five. "Aren't you a little . . . beyond this type of thing?"

"Beyond cooking?"

"Beyond modeling. And. . . ." She waved her arm in a gesture to indicate his dubious role as her supposed birthday present. "I always thought you had to be younger. . . ."

"To bring pleasure?"

"To do it . . . like this. . . ." The heat on her cheeks soared when he turned teasing eyes her way.

"Are you trying to say something, Leslie?"

"Yes," she declared in frustration, growing clammy all over. "You can't stay here for the week! You've got to leave; it's as simple as that!"

Reaching for a skillet, he put it on the stove, added a dollop of butter and lit the gas. "While you're under the weather? No way. As it is, I've got to redeem myself for not being up and ready when you arrived."

She held up a hand. "No apologies. I'm sure someone in your . . . field . . . is used to sleeping late." It had been twelve-forty, for heaven's sake! She couldn't remember the last time she'd slept that late herself. On second thought, she could. It had been the summer before, when she'd been hooked on *Noble House*. Not that she'd loved it that much, but she made a practice of never leaving a book midway through, and there had been another book she'd been dying to start. "Late nights and all. . . ."

"And all."

"So—" she sent him an accusatory glance "—you've found your way around the island? Gustavia has its lively spots. When did you say you arrived?"

"Yesterday. And I haven't been anywhere but the airport and here. Actually, I was up late reading. I was in the middle of a book I didn't really care for and I wanted to start another, but I have this practice of never leaving a book midway through, and it wasn't until five this morning that I finally finished it."

Leslie swallowed hard, sneezed again and put her palm to her head. Things weren't going as she'd planned. Not by a long shot.

"What are you doing?" she cried when she felt her feet leave the floor.

"Getting you back to bed. Don't worry. These weary old bones won't drop you."

"That's not the point."

"Then what is?" He took the stairs two at a time, carrying her as though she weighed no more than a small child.

The point? What *was* it, anyway? Her head was suddenly muddled again so badly that Leslie neither knew nor cared.

When she felt the coolness of the sheets she breathed a sigh of relief and, curling onto her side, closed her eyes.

She must have dozed off. By the time she awoke, the face of the sun had shifted from the skylight overhead to the sliding doors, lower and farther west. Blinking away her grogginess, she followed its rays to the tall figure propped casually in the chair by her bed.

Deep in thought, he didn't see her at first. His legs were sprawled before him, his elbows bent on the cushioned arms of the chair, his hands fisted inside each other and pressed to his lips. She wondered what thoughts held him in his distant world, then shuddered when she realized how very far that world was from her own. The faint movement was enough to bring him back.

The slowest of smiles gentled his lips. "Hi, there."

"Hello."

Reaching to the stand beside him, he lifted two more pills and an ice-filled glass. Without a word, she swallowed the aspirin, washed it down with several gulps of what proved to be fresh lemonade, then drained the glass. When she leaned back, it was to rest against the pillows that he'd newly puffed.

"Not bad . . . the lemonade, that is." In truth, what she'd been thinking was how nice it was to have someone taking care of her for a change. A small luxury . . . a birthday gift. Her expression grew exquisitely soft. "When I was a child I loved Steiff pets—you know, those little stuffed animals—" she reached up and caught the upper part of her ear "—with the tiny tag right about here? They used to come with names attached to their ribbons." She moved her hand to the hollow of her throat, then, almost timidly, raised her eyes to his. "Do you have a name?"

For a heart-stopping moment, he held her gaze. She felt drawn to him, much as earlier she'd been drawn to the kitchen when she'd known she should have stayed in bed. He had power. It had touched her from the pages of *Man's Mode*. It had touched her when he'd stood at the kitchen window with his back to her. It had touched her moments before when his eyes had been distant. A kind of dreamlike quality. A depth. A puzzlement.

Slowly, with the corners of his eyes crinkling in a most effective way, he smiled. "Oliver Ames, at your service."

Oliver Ames. Her heart skipped a beat.

2

"Oliver Ames." She said it aloud, testing it on her tongue. It flowed without any effort at all. Just right for a model—or a playboy. "Is that your . . . professional name?"

His mouth twitched at one corner. "Yes."

"And your real name," she asked more softly. "What's that? Or . . . is it off limits?" There were rules governing this sort of thing; unfortunately, she wasn't well versed in them.

Oliver smiled openly, his lips mirroring the dance of humor in his eyes. Sitting forward now, he was fully attentive. . . . *As rightly he should be*, Leslie mused. Wasn't he paid to be attentive? He was also paid to be attractive: bare chested, bare legged, large and vibrantly male—she found him disconcertingly so.

"No," he allowed lightly, "it's not off limits. As long as you don't spread it around."

"And who would I spread it to?" she snapped in response to the unsettling twist of her thoughts. "In case you haven't noticed, I'm not too . . . comfortable with this situation. Not much of a chance of my running back to Manhattan shouting the name of the guy my brother *bought* for me." She grimaced. "No woman wants to think she can't find someone on her own."

For an instant, when his dark brows knit, she feared that she'd offended him. Yet when he spoke, his voice held only curiosity.

"Can't you?"

"I'm not looking."

"And if you were? Surely there are men in New York who'd give their right arms for a Parish."

Leslie's lips grew taut, her expression grim. "If a man needed a Parish badly enough to sacrifice his right arm, I'd say he's sold himself short. And yes, there are many men like that around. Funny how money can screw up priorities." Closing her eyes, she slid lower on the pillows.

The creak of the rattan chair gave warning that Oliver Ames had moved. It wasn't until the bed dipped by her side, though, that she felt alarm. Eyes flying open, she found him settled near her hip, his arms propped on either side of her, hemming her in.

"You sound bitter," he observed. His voice was deep and kind and not at all taunting, as it might as have been, given the fact that it was a Parish who had dreamed up the very scheme that had brought him to St. Barts. "You've been hurt?"

She shrugged, unwilling to elaborate. For she couldn't think of the past when the man before her dominated the present. What was it about him, she asked herself, as she stared into eyes the texture of warm chocolate, that made her want to forget that he was what he was? What was it that made her want to reach up and brush the hair from his brow, trace the firm line of his lips, scale the gentle swell of his shoulder? What was it that stirred senses on which she'd long since given up? What was it that affected her so, that even now, as she lay in bed with a stuffy head and clenched fists, entranced her to the point of distraction?

"Your name," she whispered, then moistened her lips with her tongue. "Your real name. What is it?" Her expectant gaze fell to his lips and she waited, admiring the strong shape of them, until at last they moved to form the words.

"Oliver Ames," he mouthed, then gave a boyish grin.

"You're making fun of me," she contended soberly. "It was an innocent question."

"And an innocent answer. My name *is* Oliver Ames. Personal. Professional. Oliver Ames." He tipped his head to the side. "Perhaps you're the one doing the mocking. Is there something wrong with Oliver Ames?"

"Oh, no!" she breathed. "It's fine. It's more than fine. I like it. It's just that . . . well . . . it flows so easily I thought you'd made it up." She was babbling and she knew it. He seemed so close, his voice so deep and smooth that she felt rattled.

"My parents made it up. You can thank them one day."

Embarrassed, Leslie wrinkled her nose. "Oh, I couldn't do that. . . ." Her voice trailed off. A lover for hire . . . and his parents? Great! Then she grew curious. "Do your parents . . . do they know what you do for a living?"

"Sure."

"And . . . they don't mind?"

"Why would they mind?"

She shrugged and fumbled. It didn't help that Oliver had moved his hands closer, that his thumbs had slyly found their way into her sleeves to ever so faintly caress the soft skin of her upper arms. "Oh, you know. . . . Modeling, and . . . this. . . ." She waved one arm half in hopes of dislodging his hand. The gesture only seemed to solidify his grasp. And Oliver Ames was more amused than ever.

"Actually," he offered wide-eyed, "they're quite proud of me."

"Oh."

"Uh huh." He grinned. "A parent's love is all-abiding, wouldn't you say?"

She couldn't say much. A breathy, "I guess so," was all his closeness would permit. Her gaze fell briefly to his chest, but the sight of the light furring of hair there was all the more unsettling, so she forced her attention back to his eyes. Her insides burned; much as she wanted to blame the sensation on the aspirin she'd taken, she couldn't.

"You'll catch my cold if you sit this close," she warned as she tried to sink more deeply into the bed.

"I don't mind," came the silky reply.

"But . . . then where would you be?" she persisted, unable to free herself from his sensual spell, struggling against its hold by voicing frantic wisps of thought. "I mean, who wants a red-nosed model with glassy eyes? Who wants a lover with a stuffed nose and the sneezes? As it is there are already too many communicable diseases rampant in your trade—"

"Ah, so that's what frightens you—catching something from *me*?"

"I'm not frightened."

"Then why are you trembling?"

"Because . . . I'm sick."

To her chagrin he moved one hand to her forehead. "You feel cooler. You're not even as pale. No, there must be something else that's given you the shakes."

"I don't have the shakes!" she declared loudly, then clamped her mouth shut when even her voice belied her claim. It was sheer chemistry. She knew it, and it mortified her. Granted, he was a pro. But to be so totally susceptible to him appalled her. "And if I do, it's your fault. You're the one who's making me nervous. Damn it, you should be some kind of arrogant, unsavory creep, with little bugs crawling around here and there."

"I'm not," he stated, his voice calm. "And there aren't any bugs."

"I know," she replied miserably. It was obvious that the man was both clean and healthy. She didn't have to ask; she just knew. Besides, she trusted Tony. Though his sense of humor was sadly misguided, he did love her. And he was protective. Hadn't she kept her experience with Joe Durand from him partly out of fear of what he might do to Joe? No, Tony would never have invited anyone objectionable to spend the week alone in a villa with his little sister. Tony would have checked everything out. Strange. A male model checking out? A paid escort? In *Tony*'s book?

"Well . . . ?" Oliver asked softly, his face no more than a hand's width from hers.

"Well what?" she managed to whisper.

"The verdict. I can see those little wheels going round and round in your head. Will you let me kiss you . . . or am I going to have to be forceful about it?"

"Forceful? Truly?" she asked softly.

His forearms came to rest flush on the sheet, bringing his abdomen into contact with hers. Leslie caught her breath, aware of his warmth and of the precious nothings she wore beneath her shirt. Meanwhile, hidden high up her sleeves, his fingers cupped her shoulders and gently massaged their tautness. Her response, an instinctive coil of heat that sizzled its way to her toes and back, made moot the point. He would never use force. He wouldn't have to. He was good, she mused in dismay. Too good.

"Don't . . ." she heard herself say, then looked as puzzled as he.

"Don't what? Don't touch you? Don't kiss you? Don't take care of you?"

She wanted . . . she didn't. "Just don't. . . ."

"But I have to," he whispered.

Her voice was no louder, though tinged with regret. "Because you were hired?" The word stuck in her throat like a large piece of overcooked liver. She swallowed hard to dislodge it, managing to produce only a tiny moan. He'd been hired to love her . . . and it hurt.

When he slid his fingers to the back of her neck and pressed feathery circles in her skin, she closed her eyes and turned her face away. "What is it?" he murmured. She simply shook her head and squeezed her eyes tighter. "Come on, Les," he coaxed. "Tell me." His thumb slid across her cheek to stroke the taut line of her jaw.

"This is . . . humiliating. . . ."

"Why?"

"Because Tony . . . arranged for you," she said, feeling ugly and sick and sexless.

"And if I said that that had no bearing on this moment . . . ?"

"I'd wonder whether it, too, wasn't part of the act." Very cautiously she opened her eyes to find Oliver studying her intently. Then, easing up, he clicked his tongue against the roof of his mouth.

"So distrustful . . . and at such a young age."

"I feel about twelve. And, yes, I'm distrustful. I . . . I guess I just want more out of life than the buying and selling of favors."

He thought for a minute. "What if you thought of this as a fix-up? Haven't you ever had a blind date?"

"Oh, yes." Her lips twisted. "Charming invention, the blind date."

"It has been known to work."

"Not in my book."

"And why not?"

"Because a blind date is never really blind. I mean, the person who agrees to a blind date usually does so at the convincing of a salesman in the guise of a matchmaker." When Oliver frowned she grew insistent. "Really." She stared at the ceiling and spoke in a mocking tone. "He's in his late thirties, is tall, dark and handsome, is a stockbroker, drives a Porsche and has a horse farm in upstate New York."

Oliver nodded. "Sounds interesting."

"Sounds vile! Who gives a damn if he's tall, dark and handsome, and has enough money to put DuPont to shame? I certainly don't! And I dislike the thought that I've in turn been marketed, based on similarly meaningless data."

"Ah . . . the Parish curse."

"Among other things," she mused, then took a breath and, emboldened by indignation, faced her tormentor. "So, Oliver Ames, if you want to kiss me, do so knowing that I earn my own living as a preschool teacher, that I drive a four-year-old VW Rabbit, that I hate parties, love picnics and abide by intrusions into my privacy only with great reluctance." Energy waning, she lowered her voice. "Also know that I'm very conservative. I don't sleep around."

He pressed his lips together, stifling a grin. "Then I don't have to fear catching something from you?"

"Yes. A cold."

"Which I'll risk. . . ."

Certain her diatribe would have discouraged him, Leslie was taken by surprise. She tried to tell herself who he was, *what* he was, but the fact of his presence muddled her brain. He was so near, so vibrant. When his head lowered, she closed her eyes. Her breath came faster; she heard its rasping. Surely that would put him off . . . but no. His lips touched her left eye first, whispering a kiss on its lid once, then a second time before inching away. The bridge of her nose received similar treatment, then her right eye and its adjoining temple.

What astonished her most was the reassurance she felt from his touch. It was light and gentle, imbuing her with an unexpected sense of contentment. From her temple it fell to her cheekbone, dotting that sculpted line with a string of feather kisses before moving on to savor the delicate curve of her ear. The warmth of his breath made her tingle. Unknowingly she tipped her head to the side to ease his access.

"Nice?" he whispered against the high point of her jaw.

"Mmmmmmm."

"Relaxing?"

"Very."

"I'm glad," he murmured against her skin as he nibbled his way along her jaw, giving special attention to the delicacy of her chin before raising his head.

In a daze of pleasure, Leslie opened her eyes to find Oliver's, warm and alive, trained on her lips. His touch was a tangible thing, in the name of seduction doing something destructive to relaxation.

"I shouldn't let you . . ." she whispered meekly.

"But you can't help yourself . . . any more than I can," he answered, moments before he lowered his head and touched his lips to hers.

She stiffened at first, struck by the utter intimacy of the act. Only a kiss . . . yet it probed her entire being. Though his lips were gentle, they slid over hers with expertise— lightly at first, sampling, tasting, then with greater conviction as he sought her essence.

"Relax, Les," he whispered. "It's all right." His hands

emerged from her sleeves to caress her shoulders from without.

"No . . . don't. . . ." It felt too good. She didn't trust herself.

Again he raised his head, and she met his gaze. His eyes were more smoky this time; she badly wanted to believe that she'd excited him.

"Kiss me," he said in a shaky breath, his eyes on her lips, then sliding upward. "Kiss me, and then decide." When she shook her head, he took a different tack, dropping his gaze to his hands, which glided up her shoulder to her neck, then inched downward from the hollow of her throat, downward over her chest, downward to separate over the straining fullness of her breasts.

Unable to push him away, unable to invite his advances, Leslie bit her lip to keep from crying out. Her eyes begged that he free her from the prison of his spell, yet her breasts swelled toward his touch in primal betrayal. His fingers circled her, working systematically inward, coming at last to the turgid peaks that spoke so eloquently of her arousal.

In self-defense she grasped his wrists and put a halt to the torture by pressing his hands hard against her. "Oliver, please don't."

"Will you kiss me?"

"I don't want to."

"You might like it."

"That's what worries me!"

Silence hung in the air, made heavy by the honesty of her argument. Frowning, Oliver studied her as though she was a creature like no other he'd ever known. In turn, she pleaded silently. She was sick . . . and aroused. It was a disturbing duo.

"You have the eyes of a fawn," he said at last. "Has anyone ever told you that?"

The spell was broken. With a shy smile of relief, she shook her head. "No."

"Well, you do." He sat straighter. "The eyes of a fawn. I

could never hurt a fawn. So free and alive, so soft and vulnerable."

"You must be a poet. Funny, I thought you were supposed to be a sculptor."

"All illusion," he breathed magnanimously as he pushed himself off the bed. Only then did Leslie see what she wanted to. Very subtly and from the corner of her eye she saw sign of his arousal. Illusion? Not that. It was a heady thought on which to roll over and go to sleep.

She slept through the late afternoon and early evening, awakening only to eat the light omelet Oliver had fixed, to take the aspirin he supplied, to drink the juice he'd chilled. She felt lazy and pampered and stuffy enough neither to object to the attention nor to raise the issue of his leaving the villa again. There would be time aplenty to discuss the latter when she felt better. For the time being, having a caretaker was rather nice.

Not used to sleeping at such length, she awakened periodically throughout the night. Each time, Oliver was in his chair by her bed, either sitting quietly, reading, or, at last, dozing. Though she might have enjoyed the luxury of watching him sleep, her slightest movement roused him every time.

"How do you feel?" he asked softly, leaning forward to touch the back of his hand to her brow.

"Okay."

"Any better?"

"I think so."

"Want a drink?"

"I just had one."

"That was two hours ago. Another would do you good," he argued, bounding from his chair to return to the kitchen for juice. In his absence, Leslie marveled not only at the image of his moonlit torso edged in silver, but at the easy intimacy of their soft-spoken conversation. To her astonishment there was something warm and reassuring about it.

Then he was back, standing guard while she drained the entire glass.

"I'll float away pretty soon."

"I'm your anchor. You won't get far. Now, be a good girl and go back to sleep."

"Hmmph. 'Be a good girl.' Lucky for you I'm the docile type. What would you have done if you'd had a wildcat on your hands?"

"I guess I'd have had to tie her hand and foot to the bed. Are you going to go to sleep?"

"In a minute. What time is it?"

"Two-twenty."

"Aren't *you* going to bed?"

"Is that an invitation?"

"Uh uh. Just a touch of concern. After all, if you let yourself get run down, you'll catch this cold but good!"

"Hey . . . which one of us is the doctor here?"

"Funny, I didn't think we had one."

"Oh, we have one, and it's me! Now go to sleep."

"I'm not tired."

"Not tired? You've got to be tired. You're sick."

"But I've been sleeping for hours." She started up from the bed. "What I really feel like doing is taking a walk on the beach."

Just as quickly, her shoulders were pressed flat. "No way, sweetheart. The bathroom is about your limit tonight."

"Come on. It's no fun walking around the bathroom. No sand, no shells, no waves—"

"Right! That gives you great incentive to get well."

"Really, Dr. Ames. I'm *not* tired."

He paused then. Even in the dark she felt the brand of his gaze. When, puzzled, she raised her head, she saw him push himself from his chair and approach the tape deck.

"Then we'll have some music. What'll it be?"

Sighing her resignation, she laid her head back. "You choose." Then, recalling his occupation and suddenly fearing that his choice might be something loud and swinging, she wavered. "On second thought—"

"Too late. My choice it is."

Moments later the soft and gentle strains of Debussy

wafted into the air. Leslie lasted for all of five minutes before she fell back to sleep.

When she awoke it was dawn. Pale purples and blues lit the sky, filling the room with their opalescent hues. She was alone. Alone and unguarded. Quickly shaking off the last traces of sleep, she put her feet on the floor and stood up. Cold or no cold, she'd had her fill of bed. This was her vacation. Oliver Ames could do something quite pithy with his orders, *she* was going to the beach.

Walking stealthily, half expecting her keeper to pop up from around the corner and usher her back to bed, she left the bedroom. Finding the den empty she headed for the stairs, tiptoeing down their bleached wood planks and pausing on the lowest rung. Still no sign of him. The kitchen was empty. The tile felt cool beneath her bare feet as she sped toward the glass sliding doors. When she flipped back the lock, its echo made her wince. Looking cautiously behind her, she waited. Still nothing. Dallying no longer, she quietly slid the door open and stepped out onto the terrace.

A long, deep breath told her that her cold was better. For the first time since she'd arrived, she smelled the special aroma of the island. Fresh in the morning's first light, it was a blend of sand and salt and lush tropical verdancy, a bouquet evoking lavish thoughts of laziness and leisure.

With a smile, she crossed beneath the palms of the terrace, trotted down the few stairs to the lower level, paused once again to savor the setting, then took the last set of steps at a clip. Ahh, to be finally on the beach!

Her smile spread into a full-scale beam. There was nothing like it! She wiggled her toes in the superfine sand, squished forward several steps, wiggled her toes some more, then sat down. It was beautiful as always, the beach, the sea. Her lungs drank it in, her eyes devoured it. Every one of her senses opened greedily.

Sitting cross-legged with the cushion of sand conforming to the lines of her bottom, her thighs, her calves, she thrust her fingers into the fine white stuff, heedless of the grains catching beneath her nails, simply eager to feel it all close up. Her eyes tripped forward over the softest of sand to that damp area where the surf had recently played. Here and there small shells winked, half buried in the tawny beach. And beyond was the restful ribbon of the tide, swishing this way and that with each incoming wave, rhythmic and gentle and positively addictive.

Stretching her legs forward, Leslie dropped back onto her elbows. Facing west as she was, the sunrise was behind her. Yet far ahead across the turquoise depths, discernible to none but the most watchful eye, were the faintest pink reflections of the morning sky.

She was glad she'd come. She needed this—this sense of the warm, the familiar, the relaxing. She'd always been able to think here, to walk off on her own or sit on the beach and put things into perspective. She needed that now. She'd been troubled of late. Where was she going? What did she want in life? Oh, yes, the preschool thrived, and indeed she loved her work. But something was lacking . . . something with which she had to come to terms.

On impulse she swiveled around on the sand until she faced the villa. Arms now straight behind, supporting her, she studied the sprawling house set into the rocks. Where was he? Surely he hadn't given up so easily and left in the pre-dawn hours to find a more hospitable welcome in town. No, chances were he had simply made use of one of the bedrooms on the upper floor.

Her gaze rose to that level, slipping from one to the other of the large glass panes that marked each of the bedrooms in turn. Was he sleeping? Sprawled out in bed as he'd been when she'd first arrived? Wearing nothing but the bed-sheet . . . and his Homme Premier cologne? Today she'd be able to smell it. Would it be musky? Tart? Woodsy? Spicy?

What was she going to do about him? Her plans hadn't included a live-in companion, particularly one as tall and good-looking as Oliver Ames. The mere mention of his name set small butterflies aflutter in her stomach. She'd wanted to spend her time here in total relaxation, letting it all hang out, so to speak. Yet, sexy as sin, Oliver Ames intimidated her. What was she going to do about him?

Whirling around again in frustration, she hugged her knees to her chest. Moments later she scrambled to her feet and began to walk slowly, pensively, along the water line. The soles of her feet slapped the wet sand; distractedly she eyed the pattern of granules dislodged from beneath her toes. Bending, she lifted a tiny mollusk shell, studied its spiral design, tossed it lightly back into the surf. Then she turned to face the ocean head-on, wishing she could find something, *anything* offensive about Oliver Ames. To her chagrin, there was only one thing—his occupation. A paid smile. A manufactured daydream. Prepackaged virility. And, oh yes, bedroom eyes. No doubt he was good at his job.

Perturbed, she returned to the powdery sand of the beach, stretched out with her hands layered beneath her head and closed her eyes. The sky was brightening steadily; the sun wasn't far behind. A tan. That was one of the things she wanted this week. A soft, even tan. All over.

Oliver Ames would have to leave! He'd just have to! How could she possibly lie nude in the sun with him around? Smiling, she recalled the first time she'd gone topless on a beach. It had been the year before they'd had the villa built, when she and her father and Tony and Laura and Brenda and John had flown down here to scout around. She'd been eighteen at the time, confident of her youth, if not her future. In no time she'd discovered that on the beaches of St. Barts one was more conspicuous with a bikini top than without. In no time she'd discovered the delightful intimacy of the sun's warm touch on her breasts. And the rest, oh, she'd discovered that several years later, on the only other occasion she'd chanced to be alone at the villa. She'd felt free and uninhibited and sensual then. It had been wonderful. . . .

Opening her eyes a smidgen, she squinted toward the rooftop of the house. Another hour and the sun would scale it. Would he be sleeping still? Closing her eyes again, she pictured *him* bathing nude in the sun. Long limbs connected by sinewed bonds, tautly drawn skin, swells here, indentations there, a mat of hair extending in varied patterns from chest to ankle. . . .

Sharply sucking in her breath, she sat upright. Eyes wide, she dug her teeth into her knee, welcoming the pain. Then, when the slightest movement caught her eye, she lifted her gaze to the villa.

He was there, standing at the window of her room, hands on his hips, his dark head moving slowly from side to side. She stared for a minute, then hugged her knees tighter and lowered her head again. She could almost hear it. *What are you doing out of bed? And on the beach before sunup? If it's pneumonia you're looking for, you're on the right track!*

Hearing the patter of his feet on the planking connecting the terrace levels, she stood quickly, propped her hands on her hips and adopted her most belligerent stance. "I don't care what you say, Oliver Ames," she called to the fast-approaching figure, "but I'm here! And I'm fine! And I have every intention of making the best of my vacation!" She paused only for a breath as Oliver's long legs carried him toward her. "Now—" she held up a hand "—I do appreciate what you did for me last night, but I'm fine. Really fine. So you don't need to feel any further responsibility—"

The breath was knocked out of her when Oliver took her firmly in his arms. His eyes glowed, his body pulsed. "Damn it, but you look sexy," he growled, then took her lips in a kiss so masterfully gentle it shattered all pretense of fight. "Good morning," he whispered against her mouth seconds later. "Sleep well?"

Leslie stared at him in shock. "Good morning?" she echoed blankly, then watched him eye the sky in amusement.

"It is morning, I believe. And a beautiful one at that." His arms remained around her waist, holding her lower body snug against his.

"But . . . what are *you* doing up at this hour? I was sure you'd be out 'til noon. I mean, you didn't get to bed until after two-thirty."

"Actually it was closer to three-thirty. But I like getting up early. Morning's the best time."

Was it the velvet softness of his voice or the glimmer in his eye that lent deeper meaning to his words? She didn't know. She didn't want to find out. Coward that she was, she put light pressure on his arms. When he released her instantly, she was only momentarily relieved. When without another word he took off at a trot toward the water, she felt disappointed. When he splashed in to thigh level, then dived forward in a graceful arc and began to swim away from shore, she felt abandoned.

Lips on the verge of a pout, she sank down on the sand and watched the dark head turn rhythmically with each stroke. He was a good swimmer. *But why not*, she asked herself. Men of his ilk were bound to have access to villas such as these, or estates with pools. Indeed, part of his appeal would be the slickness of his limbs as they propelled him smoothly through the waves. Even now he was probably wondering whether she was watching. Perversely, she twisted sideways on the sand and studied the nearby palm. Tall and sturdy, graceful in a majestic kind of way, powerful, dignified, protective. . . . With a soft moan, she turned back to the sea.

Moments later Oliver emerged from the waves, his body wet and gleaming in the early morning light. Pulse racing, Leslie watched him approach.

"That was nice," he said breathlessly, rubbing a hand across his chest. Then, ducking behind her, he dragged a pad cushion from one of the lounge chairs tucked beneath the rocks and, returning to her side, spread the cushion flat. Within moments he lay on his back, his eyes closed, his hands folded on his stomach.

Unable to help herself, Leslie stared. Fit, indeed. His body was beautiful. Not perfect, mind you—there was a mole on his left shoulder, a tiny scar beneath his ribs. The gift of a jealous husband, perhaps? Or a scorned mistress?

Another scar caught her eye, this one slashing ever so slightly above the band of the slim-fitting trunks he wore. A low blow from a dissatisfied client?

"Appendectomy," came the timely explanation.

When Leslie's gaze shot upward, it caught Oliver's knowing smile. "I was wondering," she said hotly, "whether it was a battle scar."

He tucked in his chin to study his body. "This one is," he said, touching a finger to the small mark beneath the ribs. Then he moved the finger lower, following into his trunks and out again the faint ridge of the more daring scar. "This one's still pretty pink. I would have thought it should have faded more by now."

"When was it done?"

"Last winter." He put his head back down, closed his eyes again and gave a soft chuckle. "I'm not the best of patients. It was as much of a trial for the hospital as it was for me."

Somehow she couldn't believe it. Turning her head to the side, she eyed him askance. "You mean to say that the nurses didn't appreciate your presence?"

"Not by a long shot. I suppose I wasn't very cooperative, but after two days of being pushed and pulled, rolled and prodded, undressed and bathed and powdered, I'd had it!" He inhaled a deep breath through his nose. "I guess I'm just not meant to be pampered."

A shame, she mused, since he seemed the perfect subject. Lucky nurses, to have free access to that body. . . .

She cleared her throat. "So you prefer to do the pampering, do you? I suppose . . . if the reward's great enough. . . ." She took a breath, then shut her mouth and slowly exhaled through her nose.

Oliver opened one eye. "What were you going to say?"

"Nothing."

"Do you gulp air often?" he teased gently.

"Only when it's preferable to putting my foot in my mouth."

"Come on. You can say anything to me." When she simply turned her head and studied the waves, he reached out to slide his fingers around her wrist. "Come on, Leslie . . . anything."

"Actually," she began timidly, "I was just wondering why you do it."

"Why I do what?"

"Model. Rent yourself out. I would think you'd want something a little more . . . more lasting."

"You don't approve of my . . . avocation?"

Avocation. On the nose. Part-time hobby or source of amusement. "Perhaps I don't understand it. I guess I'm more attuned to occupations. You know, full-time career types of things."

"As in preschool teaching?"

"Uh huh."

"But what about fun?" he asked, suddenly up on an elbow looking at her. "You must have outside interests. There must be things you do on a lark."

"Is that what this is to you . . . a lark?"

For the first time there was a hint of impatience in his voice. "It's far more than that, Leslie, and you know it."

Of course. Tony had hired him. "Listen," she began, looking evasively at her toes, "this whole situation is extremely awkward. I appreciate Tony's thought in sending you down here, but now that we've had our laughs you can go on back to New York."

"I can't do that."

"Why not?"

"Because we haven't had our laughs. You stumbled in here sick as a dog yesterday. All I've had a chance to do is force liquid down your throat. Tony wouldn't be pleased."

"Tony doesn't have to know. You can go quietly back to New York, and I can tell Tony what a wonderful time we had. He'll never be any the wiser."

"And what about me? I've been looking forward to ten full days in the sun."

"Then I'll make a call and get you a room down the road."

"I don't want a room down the road."

"Don't you see," she exclaimed, growing more frustrated by the minute, "you can't stay here!"

For a minute he was quiet. His eyes roved her face, returning time and again to her eyes. "What are you afraid of, Leslie?" he asked at last. "There's got to be something hanging you up."

"There's nothing," she said quietly, all the while thinking how soft and coaxing his voice was.

"Look at me and tell me that."

She kept her eyes glued to the horizon. "There's nothing."

"Look at me," he whispered, his fingers tightening almost imperceptibly around her wrist. When still she didn't comply, he gave a gentle tug. Catching her off balance, he pulled her down onto the sand. Before she could begin to recover, he'd pinned her down. "Now," he murmured, his eyes an ardent brown, "look at me and tell me what's on your mind."

"You!" she cried. "You! You shouldn't be here, Oliver Ames! You're all wrong for me! I need . . . I need. . . ." Her voice trailed off, caught in her throat as the damp warmth of his body seeped through to her. "I need . . ." she whispered, mesmerized by the low glimmer of his gaze.

"I know what you need," Oliver whispered in turn, lowering his lips to her neck. "You need a man's loving." He pressed his mouth to her throat as she gave a convulsive swallow, then ran his tongue along an imaginary line to her chin. When he lifted his head to meet her gaze once more, he moved his body over hers. "You need me. . . ."

3

He was right in a way, she was later to muse. She *did* need a man's loving. But not just in the physical sense Oliver offered. She needed something deeper. A relationship—that was what was missing from her life. That was what she'd read in the ad. That was what she'd wanted when she had fingered Oliver's picture in response to Tony's magnanimous offer. She wanted love. A man, family, a home. And Oliver Ames, whose body was his prime negotiable commodity, was not the one to give it! Oh, yes, she found him attractive. Her body responded to him in precisely the way he intended. But there was far more to love than desire alone. Blinded by passion, she had made a fool of herself once. Never again.

"You need me," Oliver repeated in a husky whisper.

Leslie shook her head, her eyes awash with apprehension. "No. That's not true," she gasped, fighting his pull with every bit of determination she could muster.

Threading his fingers through hers, Oliver anchored her hands to the sand on either side of her head. "It is," he insisted. "Don't you see it? Don't you *feel* it?"

What she felt was the boldness of his body, hard and warm and aggressive, imprinting its maleness onto her. What she felt was the answering tremor of her limbs, the gathering of a heat deep within, the stoking of unbidden fires.

"I feel it," she cried softly, "but I can't, Oliver, I can't give in to it. Don't you see?" Her fingers clutched tightly at his, her eyes held a hint of desperation. "I can't view it the way you do. You may be able to jump from relationship to relationship, but I can't. I suppose I'm an anachronism in this day and age. But that's the way I am." Her voice lowered to a mere quaver. "I'm sorry."

With a harsh chuckle, Oliver rolled off her and sat up to stare at the sea. "Don't be sorry. It's really very . . . lovely."

Leslie watched the muscles of his back flex with a tenseness echoed by his jaw. Without a doubt, she'd made her point. What must he think of her now? Drawing in an unsteady breath, she sat up, then rolled to her knees. On a whim, wishing only to soften her dictate, she reached out to touch him, then thought twice and let her hand waver in the air before dropping it to her side. She'd wanted him to leave; now she'd simply given him further incentive.

Pushing herself from the sand, she headed for the stairs.

"Leslie?"

She paused, head down, her bare foot on the lowest rung. *Move, Leslie, move. Show him your grit. Show him you really don't care.* But she couldn't. Because she did care. Dubious life-style or no, she couldn't help but feel something for Oliver Ames.

"Leslie?" His voice was directly behind her now. She turned and looked up, then felt her insides flip-flop. His expression—so vulnerable, so very like that he'd worn in the ad. . . . But it couldn't be an act; there was something far too deep and needy. . . . "Listen, Les, I've got a proposition."

"Proposition?" *Oh, God, what now? He's imposing and appealing and powerful. A woman can only withstand so much. . . .*

At her look of fear, his gaze gentled all the more. "Nothing compromising," he soothed, his lips curving into the ghost of a smile. "Just practical." When she stood her ground, he went on. "This is your vacation. The week was to be something special for you." He lifted a hand to her shoulder, wavered, dropped it. She couldn't help but recall her own similarly thwarted gesture moments before. "What say we call a truce? You go your way, I'll go mine. You take the master suite, I'll take the bedroom I used last night. I'd like to explore the island, so I'll stay out of your hair. You can do anything you'd intended to do all by yourself . . . unless you change your mind. If that happens—" his gaze dropped to her lips "—I'll be here."

Leslie studied him, trying to equate what he was with what he proposed. "You're apt to be very bored," she warned.

He laughed gently. "I doubt that." He cast a glance behind him. "With all this—and a good book, and a kitchen at my disposal—how could I be bored?"

She wondered what the kitchen had to do with anything. There wasn't a spare ounce of fat on the man, so he couldn't be that much of a glutton. "I can't promise you anything. . . ."

"I'm not asking for promises."

"But . . . why? Why would you rather spend a quiet and uneventful week here than go to one of the resorts? I mean, I'm sure there'd be lots of women. . . ."

At Oliver's punishing glance, she shut her mouth. "I don't want lots of women. Or action. You may not believe it, but quiet and uneventful *do* sound perfect to me." He thrust long fingers through his hair, only to have the damp swath fall right back over his forehead. Leslie was grateful that something else dared defy him, and grew bolder.

"You're right. I don't believe it," she quipped lightly. "I'm sure your life is an endless whirlwind of pleasure back in New York."

He grew more serious. "Pleasure? Not always. Sometimes the whirlwind seems more like a tempest. Which is one of the reasons I jumped at the opportunity to come down here. I need the break, Leslie. I'm tired." Indeed, she heard it in his voice at that moment. "Maybe you're right. Maybe I am getting too old for this kind of—" a glint of humor returned to his eye "—rootless existence. Maybe a week of . . . abstinence will do me good. Build my character, so to speak. Reform me. Set me on the straight and narrow."

"Fat chance," she muttered, but her resistance was token. True, she'd hoped to have the villa all to herself. True, his presence would keep her on her guard. But there was something quite . . . appealing about him. If she had to share the villa, she could have done far worse.

"What do you say?" he prodded in earnest.

"What *can* I say? After your talk of character building, I'd feel like a heel to refuse." Her eyes narrowed. "You were counting on that, weren't you?" He simply shrugged and broke away to start up the steps. "Where are you going?" she called.

On the terrace and fast receding, he yelled back, "I'm disappearing. As promised." Sure enough, within seconds he'd been swallowed up by the house.

Smiling, Leslie followed as far as the lower terrace, where she sank into one of the deck chairs to track the progress of a fishing boat as it returned to Gustavia with its early-morning catch.

An hour later her nose twitched, rousing her from her peaceful contemplation of the beauty of the sea. At first she thought she was about to sneeze, then realized that the awareness was of something quite different. Lifting her head, she sniffed the air, then she stood up and moved hesitantly toward the steps. Curious, she climbed them. Stomach growling, she crossed the upper tier of the terrace. Only when she pushed back the screen and stepped onto the inner tile did she have her first glimmer of understanding of Oliver's attraction to the kitchen.

"What have you *made*?" she asked, mouth watering, eyes wide and hungrily homing in on the kitchen counter.

Oliver sat at the table, deeply immersed in a book. Before him was a plate containing the swirling remnants of some maple syrup. "Belgian waffles," he said without looking up. "There are two left. Help yourself."

Sure enough, on a plate covered by foil were two plump, warm waffles. In nearby dishes were strawberries, confectionery sugar, maple syrup and whipped cream. She felt as though she'd been treated to a breakfast buffet brought in from one of the local resorts. Had it not been for the waffle iron, well scrubbed and dripping dry beside the sink, she might have suspected he'd done just that.

His empty plate settled into the sink. "When you're done," he murmured near her ear, "just leave everything. I'll be in later to clean up." She looked up in time to see him turn. The next thing she knew, she was alone.

She hesitated for only a minute before reaching for a clean plate and helping herself to the feast he'd prepared. It was delicious. But then, she'd been starved. What had she had yesterday—one light omelet and twenty glasses of juice? Surely she was on the mend, what with this newfound appetite.

Without a second thought, she cleaned everything when she'd finished, then climbed the stairs to ferret a bathing suit from her bag. Though there was no sign of Oliver, she wasn't taking any chances. Her suit was one piece—albeit cut out in back with a bevy of crisscrossing straps—and appropriately demure. Satisfied that her appearance would preclude invitation, she armed herself with a bottle of suntan lotion and a towel and headed for the beach.

The day was utterly restful. She sunned for a while, returned to the kitchen for a cold drink and her book, then spent several hours back on the beach in a lounge chair, reading beneath the shade of the waving palm, even dozing to the gentle swish of the waves. In response to the sun, the warmth and the rest, her cold continued to improve. She felt stronger by the hour and more encouraged. For true to his word, Oliver had gone his own way. Or so she assumed, since she saw neither hide nor hair of him. She felt relaxed and free, almost as though she had the villa to herself.

She didn't see him again that day. When she finally left the beach at afternoon's end, she found a large brown bag and a note on the kitchen table.

"Dinner," it read, "if you're in the mood. I've taken the bike and gone exploring. Hear the sunset is spectacular from Castelets. If I'm not back by dawn, I bequeath you my bag of books. Particularly enjoyed. . . ."

Tuning out, she lifted her eyes in dismay. The motorbike. Of course, she wouldn't be able to hear it from the beach. But . . . to Castelets? Steep and jagged, the approaching drive had turned back many a cabbie in its day! So, she scowled and crushed the note in her fist, in the case of his demise, she'd inherit his books? How thoughtful. No doubt his choice of reading matter would fascinate her.

Then she caught herself. Hadn't she had similar thoughts regarding his choice of music? She'd been pleasantly surprised on that one. What if. . . . Bidden by curiosity, she straightened the crumpled note in her hand and finished reading. "Particularly enjoyed the new Ludlum. Why not try it?"

Indeed she'd had every intention of doing just that when she'd bought the book and put it in her own bag to bring to St. Barts. He liked adventure, did he? But then he probably lived it, while she was content to read it on occasion. With a wry headshake, she opened the bag on the table and removed, one by one, the small cartons. Langouste Creole, potato puffs, fresh pastry—from La Rotisserie, no doubt. Impressed by his apparent familiarity with the offerings of the island, she wondered for an instant whether he'd been on St. Barts before. Perhaps on another job? With another woman?

Fortunately at the moment hunger was a far greater force than jealousy. Setting aside all thought of Oliver and his lively if dubious past, she ate. Then read. Then slept, awakening only once, well before midnight, to hear movement on the upper level before smiling softly and closing her eyes again.

With the sun rising brightly, Sunday promised to be as pleasant a day as Saturday had been. Once more Leslie spent the morning on the beach. This day, however, even before she'd been able to drag herself from the sand to get a drink and a bite for lunch, she was brought to attention by the sound of footsteps on the planks leading down from the terrace. Looking up from where she lay on her stomach, she saw Oliver approaching, a large open basket in one hand, a blanket in the other.

"Hi," he said, placing the basket on the sand and spreading out the blanket. "How're you doing?"

"Not bad," she answered cautiously. She half wondered if she should excuse herself and give him his turn on the beach, then was too intrigued watching him unpack the basket to budge. "What have you got?"

"A picnic." He cast her a fleeting eye. "Hungry?"

"A little."

"Good." Within a matter of minutes, the blanket was spread with plates bearing a thick wedge of cheese, an assortment of fresh fruit, a loaf of French bread and a carafe of white wine. When he extracted two glasses, filled them and handed one to her, she accepted it graciously.

"Thanks."

"*De nada*."

"*Rien*," she corrected softly.

"Excuse me?"

"*Rien*. The island's French." Reaching out, she touched the bread with one finger. "Still warm? Don't tell me you baked it yourself."

"I won't," he said jauntily, producing a knife and moving to attack the loaf. "Actually—" he made a neat cut and handed her a slice, then made a similar incision in the cheese "—it was baked in a charming little bakery."

Sitting up, she grinned. "I know." Many times had she visited that very one. "But how did you? Have you been here before?"

"To St. Barts?" He popped a grape into his mouth, started to toss her one, then, seeing that her hands were full, leaned forward to press it between her lips. "Nope. But I read . . . and ask. Even guidebooks can be quite informative." Stretching his legs out and crossing them at the ankles, he leaned back on his elbow and took a sip of his wine.

He was wearing bathing trunks, black ones this time with a white stripe down each hip. If anything, his bare skin had an even richer tone than it had had the day before—richer and warmer and all the more tempting to touch. Stuffing a hunk of bread into her mouth, Leslie chewed forcefully. Only when she'd swallowed did she give a despairing, "Hmmph! Guidebooks. You're right. They give away every secret worth keeping. As a matter of fact, when we first started coming here, St. Barts itself was a secret. For Americans, at least.

Now, Gustavia's that much more crowded. Things have changed."

"It's still quite beautiful." His gaze slipped down the nearby stretch of beach. "And very private here."

Tearing her eyes from the dashing silver wings behind his ears, she followed his gaze. "Mmmmm. We're lucky."

He offered her a slice of cheese before helping himself to one. "You don't like crowds?" he asked, taking a bite as he waited for her reply.

"I don't mind them. I mean, I guess they're unavoidable at home. If one wants the pluses of a big city, one has to be willing to put up with the minuses."

"You live right in the city?"

She shook her head. "On the island."

"Is that where you teach?"

"Um hmm."

He paused to put a piece of cheese on his bread, ate it, then washed it down with his wine. Then he sat back and turned his avid gaze on her. "How did you get started?"

"Teaching?"

"Mmmm."

"I started in the city, as a matter of fact. It seemed like a good enough place to begin. I knew I wanted to work at the preschool level and, with the growing number of women working, there were preschool centers cropping up all over the place. After a year, though, I realized that . . . well . . . I wanted to be a little farther out."

"Away from your family?"

He was right on the button. "Uh huh."

"You don't like your family?"

"I love my family," she countered quickly. "It's just that . . . I needed some distance. And there were other challenges. . . ."

"Such as . . . ?"

She faced him squarely, filled with conviction. "Such as meeting the as-yet-untapped need in the suburbs. There had already been a slew of day-care centers established there, also to meet the need of the working woman. But those centers did just that: they met the women's needs rather than those of the kids themselves. What was required was something a step above day care, a very controlled environment in which children could learn rather than simply pass the time." She paused to sip her wine. Oliver quickly lifted the carafe and added more to her glass.

"So you found something there?"

"I made something there. Another woman and I set up a small center in a room we rented in a church, put together what we thought to be a stimulating curriculum, found a super gal to teach with us, and it worked. We incorporated a year later, opened second and third branches in neighboring towns the following year. Last fall we opened our fourth. Two more are in the planning stages."

He cocked a brow. "Not bad . . . for a teacher."

"Hmmph. Sometimes I wonder about that. There are times when the managerial end supersedes everything." Then she smiled. "But I do love it. Both teaching and managing."

"You love kids?"

"Mmmm." She tore off the corner of a piece of bread and ate it. "They're such honest little creatures. Something's on their minds and they say it. Something bothers them and they cry. No pretense at all. It's delightful."

"Doesn't say much for us big creatures, does it?"

"Nope." She reached for another grape, tipped her face up to the sun and closed her eyes as she savored the grape's sweet juice. "This is great. Thanks. I do love a picnic."

"So you said."

She blushed, recalling her stormy outburst. "So I did."

"That's pretty."

She opened her eyes to find Oliver's gaze warming her. "What is?"

"Your color."

"It's the wine. Or the sun." Far be it from her to admit that his presence might have an effect.

"You look good. You sound good. Your cold really is better."

"Yes, doctor," she mocked, then held her breath, mockery fast forgotten beneath the power of his lambent gaze. His heat reached into her, stirring her blood, quickening her pulse. She wondered whether any woman could be immune to this silent command of his, a command as vocal in his eyes as in the long, sinuous strain of his body. She bit her lip and looked away, but he was one step ahead, bounding to his feet and heading for the surf.

"I need a dip," he muttered on the run, leaving Leslie to admire his athletic grace as he hit the water and dived.

"You'll get a cramp," she murmured to the breeze alone, for he was well out of earshot, intent on stroking swiftly from shore. She glanced back at the food spread on the blanket, then up at the house. Old habits died hard, but he was trying. And he was sweet. Dinner last night, a picnic today. He really *had* left her alone most of the time. Once more it occurred to her to simply disappear and leave him in peace; he'd obviously had something quite different in mind for his vacation than the innocent cohabitation she'd agreed to. But he'd suggested it, and he could leave at any time, she reasoned, though she found the thought vaguely disturbing.

With a sigh of confusion, she settled back on her towel, closed her eyes and gave herself up to the soft caress of the sun. It was far less complicated than any man, she mused. Less complicated . . . less satisfying. Even now, with her body alive in heretofore forgotten crannies, she pondered the risks of each. While the sun could cause skin cancer, a man could break her heart. Yet here she lay, complacent as a basking lizard, taking her chances on the goodness of the sun. Could she take her chances with Oliver?

What she needed, she mused, was Oliver-block—something to optimize the pleasure and minimize the risk of overexposure to such a potently virile man. Did such a thing exist? She laughed aloud. It was the wine. Straight to her head. The wine. . . .

Moments later Oliver emerged from the sea. Eyes still closed, Leslie listened as he panted toward the blanket, caught up the towel he'd brought inside the basket, rubbed it across his chest and face, then settled down on the sand by her side. For a brief instant she felt her skin tingle and knew he was looking at her.

"All right?" he asked softly.

"All right," she answered, then relaxed when he closed his eyes.

They lay together in a companionable silence, rising every so often to munch on the goodies he'd brought, to dip in the water and cool off, to turn in the sun or move into the shade and read. It was Leslie who excused herself, first, gathering her things and returning to the house, phoning to have a rental car delivered, then showering. Donning a strappy yellow sundress and sandals, she drove into town to eat at a small portside café.

The sunset was beautiful, tripping over the harbor with its pert gathering of assorted small boats. Time and again, though, her eye was drawn to the couples surrounding her at other tables on the open-air terrace. Healthy and tanned, they sat close together, hands entwined, heads bent toward one another with an air of intimacy she envied. She wondered where they'd come from, whether they were married, whether the happiness they appeared to have captured was simply a product of the romantic setting or whether the setting had enhanced something that had been good from the start.

Leaving without dessert, she returned to the villa, only to find it empty. For a time she wandered from room to room making a pretense of admiring the fresh tropical decor before she settled at last in the den with the book she'd abandoned earlier. This was what she'd wanted, she reminded herself pointedly. Peace and solitude.

Three times she read the same page before finally absorbing its words.

By Monday morning her cold was nothing more than a memory. She rose in time to spot the dark-haired figure swimming in the early-morning sun, and, not daring to join him, retreated to the kitchen to fix a breakfast of bacon and eggs and muffins. There was more than enough for two. Quickly eating her share, she left the rest on the stove and returned to her room. Then, on a whim, she packed up a towel, a wide-brimmed straw hat, her lotion and a book and went into town to buy a newspaper, which she read over a cup of coffee before heading for the public beach.

Spreading her towel on the sand, she shimmied out of her terry cover-up, then, with a glance around to assure herself that the mode hadn't changed, gracefully removed her bikini top and lay down in the sun.

It felt wonderful, as she'd known it would. Strange that she could do this so easily on a public beach, while she'd persisted in wearing her one-piece suit in the privacy of the villa. But the villa wasn't totally private this time round, was it?

Squinting in the sun, she wrestled her lotion from the bag and squirted a generous dollop onto her stomach. It spread easily beneath her hands. She worked it up past her ribs, around and over her breasts to her shoulders, finally smoothing the remainder down her arms before lying back. Better. Warm. Relaxing.

Why *couldn't* she do this at the villa? Was there truly safety in numbers? Peeking through the shadow of her lashes, she scanned the growing crowd. The bodies were beautiful, few of them covered by more than slim bands of material at their hips. Men and women. Lean and fit. Well, she was lean and fit, too. What objection could she have to Oliver's seeing her like this?

Oliver was lean and fit. She recalled how he'd looked this morning with the sun glancing off his limbs as he swam. She recalled how he'd looked yesterday, lying beside her on the sand. His shoulders were sturdy and tanned, his hips narrow, his legs well formed. She liked the soft matting of hair that roughened those legs, the broader patch on his chest, the tapering line down his stomach. His body was every bit as beautiful as that of any man on the beach today. And his hands--those hands that had so deftly poured wine, sliced cheese, popped a single grape into her mouth—had those fingers touched her lips? She remembered how easily they'd circled her wrist to tug her back down to the sand. What might they have been like spreading lotion on her body . . . ?

To her dismay, she felt her breasts grow taut. Peering down in embarrassment, she flipped angrily over onto her stomach and silently tore into herself for the foolishness of her thoughts. Was she that starved for the touch of a man? True, it had been a long time since she'd been reckless enough to trust one to the point of making love. But she'd never known the kind of frustration that would make her body respond out of sheer imagination. Opening one eye, she skimmed the bodies nearby, pausing at that of one attractive man, then another. Nothing. *Damn him!*

Defiantly she rolled over once more and concentrated on her life back home. The preschool centers were thriving. Six by next fall . . . quite an accomplishment. What now? Should she continue to teach? Go back to school for a business degree? Focus on the managerial skills she'd inadvertently picked up? There were many options, not the least of which was to take Tony up on his offer of signing on with the corporation. Even in spite of the distance she purposely placed between it and herself, she was neither deaf nor blind. Had she not caught talk at family gatherings of the corporation's spreading interests, she had certainly read of them in the newspapers. There were new divisions forming all the time, any one of which she could take over if she showed the slightest inclination.

But she didn't. And she wouldn't. There was something about high power and the almighty buck that stuck in her craw. Misplaced values. Misguided loyalties. Marriages of convenience rather than love.

Look at Tony. He'd married Laura because she'd promised to be the kind of wife every chief executive needed. Only problem was that every *other* chief executive needed her, or wanted her . . . or simply took her, so it seemed.

Sensing the dry, parched feel to her legs, Leslie sat up and smoothed lotion on them liberally, then lay down again.

And Brenda—she was working on number two. Number one had been her high-school sweetheart and had unfortunately developed a penchant for gambling away every cent she earned. Poor Brenda. John had been a disappointment. Perhaps Larry would be better for her.

And then there was Diane. Slim, petite Diane, who'd wanted nothing more than to be a gymnastics star until she'd discovered that all the money in the world couldn't buy her the gold. Unable to settle for silver or bronze, she'd quit gymnastics and, by way of consolation, had been awarded the sporting-goods division of the corporation.

From the start she'd been in over her head. Even Tony had seen that. When she'd quite opportunely fallen in love with Brad Weitz, himself a senior vice-president of his family's development firm, things looked good. What with Brad's business acumen and that of the circle of lesser executives he helped Diane gather, she was able to focus her own attentions on the content of the Parish line, rather than its high-level management.

Unfortunately, while the business flourished, her marriage floundered. Brad wandered, always returning to soothe Diane's injured pride, yet inevitably straying again before long. More than once Diane had eyed Leslie in envy at the latter's unencumbered state.

If only she knew, Leslie reflected wryly as she turned onto her stomach and tuned in to the sounds of the gentle Caribbean air. They were soft sounds—the murmur of easy conversation from parties nearby, the light laughter of those near the water's edge, the occasional cry of a bird flying overhead. How delightful it was to be here, she mused, to leave that other world where it was. Soon enough she'd be back to face it again. Soon enough she'd have to decide where she wanted to go with her life. But for now she wanted to relax and enjoy. That was all . . . that was all . . . that was all. . . .

Lulled by the sun, she lay in a semisomnolent state, breathing slowly and evenly, savoring anonymity and the total absence of responsibility. When she felt hot, she stood and unselfconsciously walked into the water, swam about in the pale aqua surf, then returned to her towel. Stretching out on her back, she closed her eyes. It was divine. Thoroughly divine. She felt herself a part of the crowd, at ease and more in the spirit of the island than she had since she'd arrived.

Bathers came and went as the sun crept to its apex. Lathering her body frequently, Leslie knew she was beginning to blend in with the bronzed bodies all around. With a sigh, she closed her eyes and returned to her worship. Once, maybe twice a year she could do this. Any more and not only would she get bored, but her body would wrinkle like a prune. Once . . . maybe twice a year . . . it was nice. . . .

With a self-indulgent smile on her face, she turned her head slightly to one side and peered at the world through the shade of thick, tawny lashes. Then her smile froze in place and her complacency vanished. A man lay close by, sprawled stomach down on a towel, with his head turned away. Dark brown hair with a distinct C of gray behind his ear. . . . *Him!* When had he come? How could he have found her? His back glistened with suntan lotion; his breathing was even. It appeared he'd been there for some time, while she'd lain half nude, oblivious to all but the sun. . . .

For the second time that day she twisted onto her stomach in embarrassment. The first time she'd simply imagined him and her body had reacted. Now he was here, beside her. What was she going to do? Head turned away, eyes open wide, heart pounding, she examined her alternatives. She could nonchalantly slip on her top and as nonchalantly lie back down. But he'd know, and she'd feel more the coward for it. She could simply dress and leave, but then she'd be deprived of her time on the beach. She could lie where she was until he tired of the beach and left. But he wouldn't do that without a word to her, would he? Not after having so conveniently selected her body from all those others on the beach beside which to stretch his sexy six-foot-plus frame! Besides, was she supposed to lie on her stomach for the rest of the day?

There was one other alternative and, damn it, she was

going to take it. She'd come to the beach on her own and had
been perfectly happy and comfortable. Oliver or no Oliver,
she was going to stay. In the sun. And on her back, if she so
pleased.

On a rebellious impulse, she flipped back as she'd been
when first she'd spotted Oliver beside her. When her head
fell his way, she gasped in genuine surprise. He was looking
straight at her.

"Oliver!" she whispered, her breath in scarce supply. "You
startled me!" It was the truth. Somehow she'd been counting
on time to adjust to the fact of his presence.

As though relieved that she'd only been startled, he
smiled gently. "I'm sorry. I didn't mean to do that." His eyes
held hers without straying.

"How long have you been here?"

"Not long. Maybe fifteen, twenty minutes."

"Oh."

"Nice beach."

"Mmmm."

"Tired of yours?"

She turned down the corners of her mouth and shook her
head, felt her breasts shimmy and lost her courage. As gracefully as she could—and as casually—she rolled to her stomach again. Though the move brought her all the closer to
Oliver, she felt somehow let off the hook. "It's nice here once
in a while," she murmured, then managed to feign a relaxed
sigh. Facing him, she closed her eyes. His next words brought
them open in a hurry.

"I didn't think you'd do this, Les."

She knew precisely what he meant. "Why not?"

"You seem more . . . inhibited."

"I usually am," she confessed in the same half whisper in
which the rest of the conversation was being carried on. There
was something intimate about their talk; Leslie found she
liked the feeling.

Arching his back, he folded his arms beneath his chin.
"What makes things different here?"

Had there been the faintest hint of mockery in his tone,

she might have been put on the defensive instantly. But his voice remained gentle and curious, his eyes simply warm and pleased.

"I don't know. Maybe the other people. They're strangers."

"And safe?"

"I guess."

"Impersonal."

"Um hmm."

"Like . . . a gynecologist?"

"Come on, Oliver. What is this?"

"Just trying to understand why you'd bare yourself for them . . . but not for me."

"Oliver!" He had almost sounded hurt. When she opened her eyes in alarm, she indeed read that same gut-wrenching vulnerability written across his chiseled face. In response, she took her lip between her teeth. As quickly, he reached out a hand.

"Don't do that," he murmured, rubbing the tip of his forefinger against her lip until she'd released it herself. His finger lingered a moment longer in caress of her softly parted mouth. Then he put his hand on her back. The subtle incursion brought him inches closer. "God, your skin is hot. You'll be burned to a crisp."

"I'm okay." She felt strangely restful and raised no objection when he began to move his hand in a gentle kneading caress. For several seconds they just lay and stared at each other. "Oliver?"

"Mmm?"

"What's it like to model?"

His hand paused for only an instant before resuming its soothing motion. "It's . . . fun."

"You said that once before. But . . . I've always heard talk, of the trying pace—you know, hours doing the same thing over and over again. Is it like that?"

"I don't know," he said simply. "I've never had to do the same thing over and over again."

"You're that good?" She smiled in accompaniment to her

teasing tone and was rewarded by his total absence of arrogance.

"No. It just . . . works."

Her thoughts joined his on the set of the Homme Premier ad. "Is it ever . . . awkward?"

"What do you mean?"

"When you . . . I mean . . . you are nude, aren't you?"

He dared a tiny grin. "Yes."

"Does it bother you?"

"I like nudity."

"So, if this were a nude beach, you would . . . ?" Her brief glance toward his trunks said it all.

"No," he murmured without hesitation.

"Why not?"

"Because it would be embarrassing."

"Embarrassing? But you've got a beautiful body!"

Again that tiny grin. "How do you know? You haven't seen it all."

Again her downward glance. "There's not much left covered."

He arched a brow. "Some men might take offense at that."

"Come on," she chided. "You knew what I meant. Would you really be embarrassed to *un*cover it?"

"On this beach . . . beside you . . . yes."

"Because of *me*?" So she wasn't the only neurotic one?

"Yes." He inched closer. His lips were a breath from hers. "I don't think I could lie quite as impassively as—" he cocked his head "—most of these other men seem to be doing. It was bad enough when I first got here and saw your car in the lot. I've been to this beach before; I knew what the style was." His hand slowed its motion, coming to a rest just beneath her armpit. Leslie felt her breasts tingle at the nearness, but she couldn't move. His eyes held hers with binding warmth. "There are lots of pretty women here, Les, but I was totally unaffected . . . until I saw you."

"Sounds like the lyric to a song," she teased by way of self-defense, lifting her eyes and singing, "'Til I saw you. . . .'"

Then, recalling how boldly she'd been lying on her back with her breasts bare, exposed to the sun, she blushed.

"I'm serious," he said, brushing the back of his fingers against the swell of her breast. Suddenly she was, too.

"I know," she whispered. Had his earnestness been faked, something would have given it away—the glimmer of an eye, the twitch of a mouth, the rush to offer other lofty words. Oliver's expression, however, was solemn, every feature in harmony with the intensity of his gaze. He said nothing more, simply looked at Leslie as though imprisoned by the very charm that gave credence to his claim. Only his hand moved, sliding very gently along the side of her breast, up and back, doing ragged things to her pulse, damaging things to her composure. She felt his touch through every inch of her being. Her gaze dropped to his lips.

"You're very soft," he mouthed. He slid his thumb forward until it skimmed her aureole.

Leslie caught her breath, then, swept up in the sensual magic of the moment, released it and whispered his name. It was as though her entire life had been in a state of limbo . . . and only now took direction once more.

4

Her lips were parted. Stealing forward, he accepted their invitation, grazing her in soft, slow mouthfuls until she closed her eyes and yielded to his quiet fire. Her insides burned, and still he teased, growing evasive between lingering kisses, forcing her mouth to be more aggressive in its search for satisfaction.

"Oliver!" she whispered, angling her body just high enough to slip his hand beneath and press it to her breast. "I can't stand this!" she gasped, watching the slow opening of his eyes.

"*You* can't stand it?" he growled hoarsely. "They're apt to arrest us in a minute." He wiggled a finger against her throbbing nipple and took pleasure in the moan she suppressed. Her fingers tightened over his, yet she didn't pull his hand away. She couldn't. His touch felt far too good, as though that of a long-lost lover who'd just come home. Feeling suddenly light-headed, she gave a mischievous grin.

"Do you think they would?" She cast a surreptitious glance around. "I mean, there have to be other people fooling around here." Then she frowned. "Why don't I ever see it?"

"Because you're not a voyeur," he returned simply. "If you were looking, you'd find it."

"You did?" she asked, eyes alight, curious. "Come on, Oliver," she whispered conspiratorially. She tugged his hand upward and cushioned it against her cheek so that his arm fully crossed her nakedness. Their bodies were snug, side by side. She felt wonderfully alive. "Tell me."

"I will not. It might give you ideas."

"Ideas? What ideas?"

When he grinned, the groove at the corner of his mouth deepened. She hadn't noticed it before; it had a lazy sensuality to it. "Now if I told you that, you'd know what I've seen. I think I'd better go back to sleep." Turning his head away, he raised his hips and resettled them in a bid to ease his discomfort. Leslie appreciated the gesture, appreciated even more his attempt at self-control, appreciated most of all that strong, hairy arm that tickled her where it counted.

"Sleep?" she challenged. "Is that what you were doing?"

He turned back until their heads were intimately close. "No. I suppose not. I was lying here thinking. . . ." His tone was up; he seemed ready to go on. Then, expelling a soft breath, he simply repeated the word with a proper period at its end. "Thinking."

"Are you pleased with St. Barts?" she asked, nestling more comfortably against the arm he seemed in no hurry to remove.

"Yes." An affirmation it was, yet it dangled in the air.

"You don't sound convinced."

"Oh, it's fine."

"But?"

"Just about everyone's coupled up. It makes me feel lonely."

She sent him a look of doubt. "Does it mean that much to you to be with a date?"

"For the sake of a date? No way. For the sake of pleasant talk and easy companionship, yes. That's what I see here—on the beach, in shops and cafés. Warmth. I envy it."

"I know the feeling," she murmured half to herself as she recalled similar feelings she'd harbored the night before. She lifted her head for an instant to look forward. "Who do you think they are, Oliver? Friends? Lovers? Husbands and wives?"

His gaze followed hers, lighting on a couple lying on the

sand several yards away. "Some of each, I suppose." He tossed his chin at the pair. "They're married."

"Oh?"

"Sure. See his wedding band?"

"Where's hers?"

"Oh. Hmm, that shoots that theory."

"Oliver?"

He settled his head down again, returning his mouth to within a whisper of hers. "Um hmm?"

"Were you ever married?"

"No."

"Why not?"

"Never wanted to."

"Not even for the sake of that warmth?"

"The woman, not the marriage, brings the warmth."

"True. But what about kids?" Strange. By stereotype, she'd assume he'd have no interest in children. Somehow, though, she could easily picture him with a brood. "Wouldn't you marry for the sake of having them?"

"A bad marriage for the sake of kids can be disastrous."

"You could have a good marriage."

"I could . . . I suppose. It's been hard finding good women —" he smirked "—what with my job and all."

She nodded. "Your job and all."

"How about you?"

"*My* job's no problem."

"Then why aren't you married? You seem like a warm, affectionate sort." He moved one finger ever so slightly against her cheek. "And you love kids. Wouldn't you like your own?"

"To quote you, 'A bad marriage for the sake of kids can be disastrous.'"

"To quote you back, 'You could have a good marriage.'"

She grew more serious. "If only. It seems that wherever I look I see divorces piling up. Divorces, or couples in the throes of counseling or those who are simply miserable. Maybe you don't see it, or maybe you take it for granted in your line of work, but I see it every day and it bothers me. Not only has my family struck out, but many of the kids at the centers are products of broken homes. And many of them are suffering terribly."

Oliver studied the look of anguish on her face. "But now you're getting onto the issue of kids again. What about the marriages to start with? Why is it that they're not working?"

She thought for a minute, then shrugged. "I don't know. Too much ambition. Too little honesty. Too much independence. Too little trust. Maybe it's the times, and what we're going through is an emotional evolution of sorts. Maybe love has to take on different meanings to make it feasible in this day and age. Take that couple over there. For all we know, his wife may be off with someone, too. But if she's in love and they're in love, and all four are happy, far be it from us to criticize them, particularly if we've got nothing better."

As Oliver pondered her words, his brow furrowed. "You condone infidelity?"

"No, not really." She was frowning, too. "Maybe what I'm saying is that love is the most important factor, that it makes allowance for other slips. Only problem is that where love is involved, those other slips can cause terrible, terrible pain. . . ."

"You sound very sure."

"I am."

"You've had personal experience with that kind of pain?"

Realizing she'd strayed far from the beaten path and in a direction she loathed, she shrugged. "It's not important." She sighed and forced a lighter smile. "Besides, it all may be an illusion anyway. These people may not be in love, they might simply be swept up in the atmosphere of this place. There's something about a tropical island in the middle of winter. . . ."

"Something daring, like lying on a beach half nude?"

In that instant, the more serious discussion was shelved. Leslie grinned. "Something like that."

"Why don't you turn over?" he teased.

She fought fire with fire, enjoying the banter. "Why don't *you*?"

"Because I keep thinking of *your* doing it and I get . . . hot and bothered."

"Hot and bothered. Interesting."

"Tell you what. I'll go down the beach a way and pretend you're not here. If you do the same, we'll be all right."

"I don't know." She wavered, reluctant to lose his company. "Maybe we could do it here. . . ."

His eyes gaped. "Do what?"

"Lie cool and comfortable. . . ." She felt so very close to him that it seemed absurd, this modesty of hers. Avoiding his gaze, she released his arm and turned over with slow and studied nonchalance. "There," she sighed, eyes closed, body aware of far more than the sun. "Your turn."

He offered a pithy oath beneath his breath, then coughed away the frog in his throat. "I think I'll take that walk."

"Don't go," she whispered, turning her head and opening her eyes. "I mean, it's really all right. There's no reason you can't stay here. It's all a matter . . . of the mind."

His eyes pierced hers, then seared a path to her breasts. "Is that all it is?" he asked, his voice thick. "A matter of the mind?"

Leslie felt his gaze as long, sinewed fingers caressing her fullness, belying her claim. Her breathing was already disturbed when he pushed himself up on his forearms and put his mouth to her ear.

"You've got beautiful breasts, Leslie."

"So do three-quarters of the women on this beach."

"I'm not looking at their breasts. I'm looking at yours."

She felt the truth of his words. Her breasts were ready to explode. "Well, you shouldn't be."

He ignored her. "Need some lotion? I'm great at spreading lotion up over—"

"Oliver!" she exclaimed in strangled protest. "You could try, at least—"

"I'm trying. I'm trying."

"Sure. To get me aroused." She gave him a withering stare. "Now try to get me *un*aroused."

"What fun would that be?"

"Oliver," she warned, growing frustrated in, oh, so many ways, "you promised you'd leave me alone. You promised you wouldn't push."

Before her beseeching expression, he grew serious. "I did, didn't I?" She nodded, her face inches below his. "Then," he began slowly, a look of regret in his mocha gaze, "I guess I'd better take that walk after all." He kissed the tip of her nose and was on his feet before Leslie could respond. But it was just as well. Bracing herself on her elbows, she watched him jog toward the water, submerge completely in the waves, swim off his own arousal, then emerge and walk thoughtfully down the beach.

She would have loved to have gone with him. It would have been nice, walking side by side with the lace of the surf curling at their feet. It would have been nice to have talked more. She enjoyed talking with him. He was easygoing, quick to smile and curious. She would have assumed the beautiful model-type to be self-centered, yet he wasn't. He seemed far more interested in hearing her thoughts than in impressing her with his own. Come to think of it, he'd spoken little of himself in the discussions they'd had.

With a sigh, she dropped back to the towel. In this, too, it was probably just as well. Given the source of his income, the less she knew about his life-style the better. Hmmph, she mused, he had all the lines. Beautiful breasts . . . attracted to no body but hers—baloney! He was a pro, and hanky-panky or no, he was still on the job. The only problem was that she wanted to believe him. She wanted to believe that he found her breasts beautiful, that he was more attracted to her than to any other woman on the beach. She wanted to believe . . . how she wanted to believe. . . .

Abruptly sitting up, she put on her bikini top, tugged on her terry cover-up and gathered her things together. She'd had enough of the beach for now. A long, slow drive around the island would clear her brain. That was what she needed—a long, slow drive.

It filled the bill. By the time she returned to the villa she

had her mind in working order once more. She was Leslie
Parish, loner, spending the week at her family's villa. Oliver
Ames just happened, by a quirk of fate attributable to her
brother Tony and worthy of no further mention, to be staying at the villa as well. That was all. Each went his own way,
did his own thing. Period. She had it all straightened out . . .
which made it doubly hard for her to understand her continuing restlessness.

After her return, she fell asleep on her bed. At some point
during that time, Oliver quietly returned to the villa. When
she awoke, she found his sprawled form spilling over one of
the terrace chairs. He was reading a book.

Wearing the one-piece terry sunsuit she'd put on after her
shower, she walked slowly out onto the terrace, gave Oliver's
shoulder a gentle squeeze of hello as she passed, then stood
with her back to him at the railing overlooking the beach.
When several minutes passed and still she didn't speak, Oliver
took the first step.

"You got back okay. I was worried."

She turned to lean against the wooden rail. "You shouldn't
have been." But it touched her nonetheless. "I took a drive."
He nodded, and she felt a tinge of remorse that she'd left the
beach without a word. His thoughts were back there, too.

He dared a faint smile. "I had trouble finding my towel . . .
without your breasts to mark the spot."

"Oliver . . ." she pleaded.

"Sorry." He nodded once, then schooled his expression to
the proper degree of sobriety. "Couldn't resist that."

"I'm sure."

"I did miss you, though," he said, suddenly and fully sincere. "It was fun lying like that . . . talking. . . ."

Hadn't she had similar thoughts? She looked down at her
bare feet and crossed her ankles. "Uh, that was what I
wanted to talk to you about."

Far more jumpy than she might have imagined, Oliver
grew instantly alert. He held up a hand and shook his head.
"Listen, Leslie, it was no big thing. I wasn't out chasing you
or anything. I mean, I'd been to that beach the day before,

and when I saw your car I thought I'd look for you. I didn't mean to pester. Hell, I was only teasing about your breasts. . . ." His voice trailed off when he caught her amused expression. "What's so funny?"

"You are. When you get defensive, you're adorable. But that's beside the point. I was just wondering if—well, there's this quiet restaurant in Gustavia . . . very classy . . . and I thought, well, I don't really feel like going alone what with everyone else coupled up, as you said." She paused for a breath, wondering why he didn't come to her aid rather than sitting there with a bewildered look on his face. "What I was wondering," she began again, "was whether you'd like to have dinner with me."

"Yes," he answered instantly.

"I mean, you can think about it. I . . . I can't offer anything afterward. Just dinner."

A broad smile illuminated his face. "That's fine. Dinner will be just fine."

She took a deep breath and smiled. "Good. I'll make reservations for eighty-thirty?"

"Great."

She nodded, feeling awkward again. Pushing off from the railing, she headed for the beach. "See ya then."

The evening turned out to be worth every bit of her hemming and hawing in issuance of the invitation. She'd wanted stimulating company; stimulating company was what she got. Looking particularly handsome in a navy blue side-buttoned shirt and white slacks, Oliver proved to be an absolutely charming dinner partner. Ever solicitous to her whim, he deftly steered the conversation from one topic to the next. Not only was he conversant in the fine points of Wall Street, he was easily able to match Leslie's knowledge of politics, as well. He got her to talk more about her work, showing genuine interest and a flair for understanding the tenuous link between parent, child and teacher. Only when once or twice on impulse Leslie shot a personal question at him did he pull back. She assumed it was standard practice—the refusal to allow a client past a certain point. And though she was curious as to what made him tick, she appreciated the reminder about the nature of their relationship. With such an attentive and attractive man sitting elbow to elbow with her in the intimate confines of the small French restaurant, it was far, far too easy to forget. . . .

Tuesday was a day for remembering, a quiet day, a restful day. Leslie saw Oliver only in passing, and then but once, at noontime. They exchanged quiet smiles and hellos. He explained that he wanted to pick up something for his sister back home and asked for her advice. Stifling the urge to ask all about his sister, she suggested a small boutique in Gustavia, from among whose selection of hand-blocked prints and clothing she was sure he'd find something. Then he was off, with nary a word about the evening before.

Just as well, she told herself again. Just as well. She'd come here to be alone. Alone was what she'd get.

Unfortunately, alone became lonely at some point around dinnertime. With no sign of Oliver, she grilled a piece of fresh fish, sliced and marinated vegetables, made herself an exotic-looking drink, which was little more than rum and coke dressed up in a coconut shell with an orange slice across the top, and ate by herself on the beach. It was there that, long after the sun had set, Oliver found her.

"Leslie?" he called from the terrace. "Leslie?"

"Here, Oliver!" she answered, her heart suddenly beating more lightly. "On the beach!"

A random cloud had wandered in front of the moon. It took him a minute to find his way down. Only when he stood before her on the sand did the silvery light reemerge. "You're eating here . . . in the dark?" he asked, spying the tray behind her.

She looked up from where she sat, knees bent, arms crossed around them. She wore a gauzy blouse and skirt, the latter ruffling around her calves. "It wasn't dark when I ate.

I've just been sitting here thinking." For a minute she feared he would simply nod and, finding her safe, return to the house. To her relief, he hunkered down beside her.

"Mind the company?" he asked, suddenly cautious.

"No," she breathed softly. "As a matter of fact, it's kind of lonely here. The company would be nice."

"You should have called. I'd have come."

"You weren't here."

"I've been back for at least an hour and a half."

"Where all did you go?" He wore shorts and a shirt and looked devastatingly handsome.

"Oh—" he gazed out at the sea "—I was in Gustavia, then rode around for a while."

"Find something for your sister?"

"Uh huh."

"Have you eaten?"

"I grabbed something in town."

She nodded, feeling superfluous, then took a fast breath. "Hey, if you've got something to do. I don't want to keep you. . . ."

"You're not. I was the one who offered, remember?" His voice lowered. "You look pretty. Very . . . feminine."

Her blush was hidden by the night. She shrugged. "It's nice to wear something like this every so often." Last night, her dress had been as soft, but more sleek—to lend her an air of confidence and sophistication. Tonight she looked and felt vulnerable.

Attuned to her mood, Oliver kept his voice on a gentle keel. "It must be appreciated. I'm envious of those men you date at home."

Her heart skipped a beat. "You don't need to be. There aren't an awful lot of them."

"But you do date. . . ."

"Only when necessary."

He frowned. "What do you mean?"

"Just that," she returned frankly. "There are certain . . . social obligations to be fulfilled. Birthday parties, openings, receptions—that type thing. It's sometimes easier being with someone than without."

For a moment, only the gentle lapping of the waves broke the silence of the night. When Oliver spoke again, his voice held a deadly calm. "Was that what you felt last night?"

"Oh, no!" she exclaimed without pretense. "Last night was something different! Last night . . . it was . . . I wanted it. . . ." She stared wide-eyed at Oliver until at last he reached over and took her hand in his. Only then did she relax.

"I'm glad, Les. I enjoyed myself last night. More than I have in a very long time."

"A very long time?" she teased. "Doesn't say much for all those other women."

His fingers tightened around hers instants before his taut voice rang out. "There haven't been all those other women, Leslie. I think it's about time we clear that up. I'm not a gigolo."

"I never said you were," she countered weakly.

"But you've thought it. And don't deny it, because my thumb's on your pulse, keeping track of your lies."

"That's fear you feel. You're frightening me." Instantly his grip eased, though her hand was as much a prisoner as ever.

"Have you ever thought I was a gigolo?"

"I, uh. . . ."

"Yes or no."

"Yes. Well, what was I to think? You were my birthday present. My brother *bought* you for the week. For *me*. Isn't it pretty much the same thing?"

To her relief, Oliver's voice had gentled again. "I suppose. If it were true. But it's not."

"What's not?" She felt a glimmer of hope. "Tony didn't hire you?"

"Tony called me, explained the situation and proposed I come. Aside from free use of this house, everything has come from my own pocket."

Leslie's mind had begun to whirl, her relief nearly as

overwhelming as her embarrassment. Not knowing what to say, she blithely lashed out at Tony. "That cheapskate! I mean, I know that you probably do very well modeling, but I'd have thought that if the plan was his the least he could do was foot the bill!" Taking Oliver off guard, she tore her hand from his and tucked it tightly into her lap. She was sitting cross-legged now, the folds of her skirt gathered loosely between her legs. "I'm not sure whether to be more angry for his having gypped you or undersold me!"

"You weren't sold, Leslie! That's what I'm trying to tell you! I needed a vacation. Tony simply suggested a spot. As for the practical joke, well, that was to be frosting on the cake."

"Frosting, indeed," she mumbled. "All along I've assumed this was nothing more than a business proposition for you. But you speak very comfortably of Tony—do you know my brother?"

Taking a deep breath, Oliver settled on the sand facing her. "I met him about a year ago. We play tennis every now and again."

"Was it Tony who set up the Homme Premier thing?"

"No. As a matter of fact, it was sheer coincidence that the ad ran in his magazine."

"I see." Lowering her chin, she scowled at her skirt. She did see—more now, at least, than she had before. Yet while one part of her was elated to learn that Oliver Ames wasn't the horrible playboy for hire she'd thought him to be, the other part was mortified.

"Les . . . ?" came the soft voice opposite her. "What is it?"

"I feel foolish," she whispered. "Really foolish."

"But why?"

She looked up then, her eyes round and luminous. "I thought you were a gigolo." She paused, offering a spitting aside, "God, that word's disgusting!" before resuming her self-castigation. "You must think I'm a perfect ass . . . what with some of the things I said."

"Actually," he grinned, "they were amusing."

"At my expense!"

"At mine. I was a good sport, don't you think?"

"I think you could have told me the truth. Good sport, hah!" Swiveling on the sand, she turned away from him.

"Hey," he crooned, reaching out to take her arm. "Come on. There was no harm done. Besides, you really didn't say very much that didn't apply to a model as well. I've never thought less of you . . . for any of it."

She wanted to believe him, but simply shook her head. "I felt so humiliated when I first arrived, thinking that Tony was really paying you to keep me company."

"Sweetheart, nobody pays for my time in chunks like that," he drawled, then cleared his throat when Leslie eyed him questioningly. "I'm a free agent. I don't like to spend more than one day at a stretch on any given job. This is no job. Believe me, if I hadn't wanted to come here, I wouldn't have. Likewise—" his hand caressed her arm "—I could have left at any time."

Trying to assimilate this altered image of Oliver, she felt confused and unsure. A model. Just a model. Was that so awful? It was still a world away, and in many ways the epitome of all she'd fought for years. Illusion. Grand pretense. Wasn't that what advertising was all about? But then there was this man—his face, his smile, the vulnerability about him that mirrored her own. . . .

Turning her head, she looked up at him. Then, without thinking, she rolled to her knees, put her arms around his neck and held him tightly. Only after several seconds did she feel his arms complete the circle.

"What's this for?" he whispered hoarsely.

She closed her eyes and hung on a minute longer, drinking in every bit of his closeness before finally loosening her grip and sinking back against his hands. "An apology . . . and thanks."

"Thanks?"

"For not accepting money to pleasure me."

His voice deepened. "Am I . . . pleasuring you?"

She could barely breathe, the pull of him was so strong. "Yes. I've enjoyed having you here."

"Now, that's a concession," he said softly, then shifted to lower her to the sand. With one hand he propped himself over her, with the other very gently tucked her hair behind her ear. "You are beautiful, Leslie," he murmured. "Even if there had been all of those other women you'd imagined, I'd still have thought you to be the best."

"Must be the full moon addling your mind."

"You don't think you're beautiful?"

"No. Oh, I make a nice appearance. But beautiful?" She shook her head against his hand, liking the feel of its tethered strength. "No."

"Well, you are. And if you didn't turn all those guys away so quick, they'd be the ones telling you, not me."

"They tell me, they tell me! It's so boring when you know it's all part of the game."

Oliver's body grew tense, his eyes darker. "This isn't, Les. I mean it. To me, you are beautiful. Do you believe me?"

Strangely, she did. "I must be as crazy as you."

"Not crazy. Simply. . . ." He never finished what he was going to say, but instead lowered his head and took her lips in a kiss that was crazy and heady and bright. "Ahh, Leslie," he gasped, pausing for air before returning to take what was so warmly, so freely, so avidly offered.

Reeling beneath the heat of his kiss, Leslie could do nothing but respond in kind. Her lips parted, giving the sweet moisture of her mouth, the wet stroking of her tongue into Oliver's thirsty possession. With the freedom she'd craved— forever, it seemed—she thrust her fingers into the thick hair behind his ears and savored its vibrant lushness as she held him all the closer.

"Mmmmmmm, Oliver," she whispered on a ragged breath when he left her lips and began to press slow kisses against the fragrant pulse of her neck.

"You smell so sweet—" he breathed deeply against her skin "—so sweet."

Then he raised his head and kissed her again, moving his lips with adoration, his hands with utter care, his body with the gentleness she'd come to expect of him. He was lean and strong, his long frame branding its readied state on her, telling her of his need, inflaming her own. If this was illusion, she mused, it was divine illusion indeed.

"I need you, Les," he moaned, leaving one of his hard thighs thrust between hers as he slid to his side to free a hand for exploration. "I need to touch you here—" his hands grew bolder, spreading over her waist and ribs "—and here." Claiming her breasts with tender strength, his fingers circled her fullness, sending corresponding spirals of fire through her. "Feel good?"

She closed her eyes and nodded. "Oh, yes—" When his palm passed over her nipple, taunting it into a tight nub, she moaned and strained upward. Then, eyes flying open, she pressed her hand on top of his to stop its motion. "My God, Oliver, there's no end. . . ."

"There *is* an end, sweet. I'll show you."

He held her gaze; she held her breath. Slowly he released first one, then another of the buttons of her blouse and slipped his large hand inside. "I wanted to do this yesterday on the beach," he whispered, fingering her flesh, sensitizing her to his touch.

"I know. . . ." She sucked in a loud breath.

"Nice?" His fingers worked a heated magic, making everything feel so very right.

"Mmmmmm . . . Oliver?"

He put his lips to the upper swell of her breast. "What, sweet?"

"My breasts . . ." she managed through a daze of passion, yielding to a nagging force. "You said you were only teasing . . . that they were more appealing than the others on the beach. Were you?"

He drew his head up to eye her in earnest. "No, I wasn't teasing. I meant what I said, Leslie. Your body affects me in a way no other can." Leaning forward, he nudged her blouse farther aside, then took her nipple into his mouth and kissed it reverently.

She shuddered, sighed, arched ever so slightly closer. "I'm

glad. I don't like to be teased . . . not about a thing like that."
Her voice grew stronger. "Not about a thing like . . . us."

A nearly imperceptible quiver worked its disquieting way
through Oliver's long, taut limbs. He stilled for an instant,
then slowly, reluctantly disengaged his mouth from her
breast and gave a final kiss to the hollow of her throat before
setting his fingers to the task of restoring order to her blouse.
"We have to talk," he murmured against the warm skin of
her cheek. "We have to talk."

Very slowly, Leslie realized that the source of her pleasure was gone. With uncertainty coming fast on the heels of
passion, her limbs felt like rubber. When Oliver lifted her to
a sitting position, she docilely sat. Her eyes were wide, her
voice breathy. "What is it?" she asked, fearing she'd done
something dreadfully wrong.

"We have to talk."

"You've said that . . . three times."

"I also said I'd leave you alone. I haven't done that."

Hearing the self-reproach in his voice, Leslie was fast to
shoulder the blame. "What happened just now was more my
fault than yours. I was the one who threw herself into your
arms."

"That's beside the point," he grumbled, then shoved a hand
through his hair and took several steadying breaths. "Listen,
maybe you're right. Maybe it is the full moon." Standing, he
reached to pull her up. "Come on. Let's go inside. I could
use a drink." One-handedly scooping up the tray that held
the remnants of her dinner, he motioned for Leslie to pre-
cede him.

She did. It took everything she was worth, but she did, and
with each step she came closer to the understanding of what
had nearly happened. Even now her breath came in shallow bursts, her legs shook, the knot deep within clamored
for more. But her mind, ahh, her mind delivered a batch of
far different messages.

Passing through the kitchen, she made straight for the
living room, seeking shelter in a deeply cushioned rattan

armchair to weather the storm. For there was bound to be a storm of some kind, she knew. It had been building from the moment she'd arrived last Friday, had been denied outlet moments before, now ached for release.

Through troubled eyes she watched Oliver approach the bar. As attractive as he looked in his jersey and slacks, their fine fit fairly broadcast his tension. His shoulders were rigid, his back ramrod straight, his legs taut. He poured himself a brandy, shot a glance over his shoulder, poured a second drink, then crossed the room and handed her one. While he tipped his snifter and took a drink, she merely watched the swirl of the amber liquid in her own glass, her lips tight in self-disdain.

Legs planted firmly, Oliver stood before her. "Leslie, I want to tell you—"

She gave a violent shake of her head. "Please, no excuses."

"But there's something you should know."

Refusing to look at him, she continued to shake her head. "It must have been the moon. I don't usually forget that easily."

Embroiled in his own quandary, he swallowed more brandy, then stalked to the window. "This whole thing was crazy from the start. I can't escape it! Damn it, I can't escape it!"

"What happened just now was nothing more than sheer physical need," Leslie ranted on, no more hearing Oliver's words than he did hers. She lowered her head and put two fingers to her brow. "I can't believe I let that happen. I thought I'd learned. It was dumb. Really dumb!"

"All game playing—here, back there," Oliver growled. "I thought I could get away from it but I'm only in deeper." Whirling around, he stepped quickly forward. "Leslie. . . ."

She sat with one hand over her face, helpless to stop the tears that flowed. Legs tucked beneath her, body curled into itself, she was unhappiness personified.

"Oh, Leslie," he groaned from somewhere deep in his throat. Within seconds he knelt before her, gently releasing the snifter from her fingers and setting the glass down on the floor. Immediately she added her other hand to her defense. "Don't cry, sweetheart." He tried to pull her hands from her face but she fought that further exposure.

"I don't cry. What's wrong with me?" she whimpered between shuddering gasps.

Oliver slid his arm across her back and drew her forward. "I don't know that, sweetheart. You'll have to tell me." He curved his fingers around her neck, twining his long fingers through her hair. "Talk to me, Les. Tell me what you feel."

"I feel . . . I feel . . . very confused. . . ."

"About us?" he whispered.

"About . . . everything. . . ." When she dissolved into another bout of quiet sobbing, he pulled her down beside him on the floor, holding her close. With his back braced against the chair, he rocked her gently, stroking her arm and the silk of her hair as he let her cry herself out.

At long last she sniffled and grew quiet. "I'm sorry," she hazarded a shaky whisper. "Now I've made your . . . shirt wet."

"It'll dry. Do you feel any better?"

She nodded, sniffling again. "I don't usually do things like this."

"We all need the outlet every once in a while," he crooned, only then looking down to wipe the tears from her cheek. "Feel like talking?"

She thought about it for a long time, hiccoughing every now and then, blotting her lower lids with the fingers of one hand. Finally she looked up at him. "I don't think I can," she whispered.

"You can tell me anything. . . ."

But she shook her head against the warmth of his chest. "I can't tell you something I don't know myself."

"You can tell me your thoughts."

"They're all jumbled up."

"Maybe I can help unjumble them."

Again she shook her head. Somehow, with the expenditure of tears, she'd purged herself of much of her tension.

Now she felt . . . tired. "It's something I've got to work out, I guess."

"You're sure?"

With a sad smile, she nodded, then caught her breath. "But—Oliver?"

He smiled down. "Yes?"

"Can we sit here . . . like this for a little while? Just . . . sit here?"

He lowered his cheek to her head and gave her a tight squeeze. "Sure thing, Les. I'd like that."

They said no more for a time. Leslie nestled against him, finding quiet solace in the support of his arms, reassurance in the beat of his heart near her ear. Though her thoughts were indeed a jumble, she made no effort to unscramble them. There was too much to be savored in the utter simplicity of the moment. Just Oliver and Leslie. No past or future. Just . . . now.

Slowly her limbs began to slacken, and her breathing grew soft and even. Relaxation was a blissful thing, she mused as she snuggled closer to Oliver's warmth. Closing her eyes, she took a long, deep breath. Then something struck her.

"Oliver?"

"Hmmmm?" His eyes, too, were closed, his limbs at rest. She tipped her head up. "Oliver?"

He opened his eyes. "What, sweet?"

"I still can't smell it."

"Smell what?"

"Your Homme Premier."

"I don't wear it."

"You don't wear it? Ever?"

"Ever."

"Isn't that against the laws of advertising or something?"

He hugged her more tightly and closed his eyes again. "I thought you were going to sleep."

"I think I was . . . then I thought of that."

"Don't like the way I smell?" he mumbled.

"I *love* the way you smell," she murmured, burrowing against his chest. "All warm and fresh and . . . manly. . . ."

As though to make her point, she took a deep, long breath and sighed. "Mmmmmm. So very . . . you. . . ."

"I hope so," Oliver whispered, hugging her a final time before settling his head atop hers.

Leslie's next conscious thoughts were of the sun, the living room carpet beneath her cheek, the stiffness of limbs that had spent the night on the floor . . . and Oliver's hand on her rump.

5

It was the last that brought her fully awake. Squirming to a sitting position, she watched as that hand slid from her hip to the floor. Oliver was dead to the world. His tall form was sprawled prone on the rug with head turned away, his breathing slow and deep.

Stretching first one way, then the other, Leslie winced, then struggled to her feet. Her skirt and blouse were badly wrinkled, but then she'd spent the night in them. Putting a hand to her head, she tried to recall what had happened. Inevitably, her gaze returned to Oliver, and it all came back.

With sad eyes she studied his passive form. She was half in love with him, she supposed. Half in love with a man who prized his freedom, who resented being tied down for more than a day, who was no doubt the heartthrob of millions of women in America. It was a sad state of affairs.

Distractedly she made her way to the kitchen and up the stairs, finally sinking down on her bed. What other ads had he made? For what products? Wearing . . . what?

She knew the course of those ads. Not only would they appear in *Man's Mode, G.Q.* and *Esquire*, they'd appear in *Vogue* and *Cosmopolitan* as well, plus a myriad of lesser publications. His face, his body would be seen and savored by so very many eyes. In turn, he'd have his choice of the most exquisite of those admirers. Why, then, of all the places on God's green earth, was he here? And why, oh, why was he leading her on?

Rolling to her back, she stared wide-eyed at the ceiling. After all, what could he see in her? There was nothing slick or glittery about her; she'd made sure of that. Nor, despite what he'd said about her breasts, did she have a body to attract a man of his stature. So he wasn't a gigolo, as she'd originally thought. Still, he was the image of glamour, the striking playboy, the model. She, on the other hand, had chosen a different track to follow, a more quiet, private one. And she couldn't switch from it . . . any more than he could from his.

Realizing that no amount of deliberation could alter the facts, she dragged herself from the bed, showered and pulled on a clean sundress, then set out to grocery shop in Gustavia. By the time she returned to the villa, Oliver was on the beach. For a long time she stood on the terrace, unobserved, watching him. He lay absolutely still, a unified mass of bronze flesh broken only by the thin navy swatch at his hips. He loved nudity, he'd told her once. She'd love to see him strip. . . .

Frustrated by the single-mindedness of her thoughts, she whirled away, made herself a tall glass of iced tea, picked up her book and settled in a lounge on the terrace. It wasn't that she wanted to see Oliver when he left the beach, she told herself, simply that she felt like sitting on the terrace. This was, after all, her house. . . .

By a quirk of fate she dozed off. When she came to, it was with a start. Disoriented at first, she stretched and looked around, then jumped again on encountering Oliver's worried brown eyes.

"Oliver! You frightened me!"

Perched near her legs on the edge of the lounge, he smiled sadly. "We seem to have a way of doing that to each other. Are you all right?"

"I'm fine." Her hand went automatically to her wrist and, finding it bare, she frowned. "What time is it?"

"I'm not sure." He squinted upward. "I think about one." Then his gaze returned intently to hers. "*Are* you all right?"

The deeper meaning to his question didn't escape her this time around. Slowly beginning to relax, she offered a soft and helpless smile. "I think so."

Reaching out to take her hand in his, he made study of her small, slender fingers. "About last night, Leslie—"

On elusive butterfly wings, those very fingers slipped from his and touched his lips. "Shh, Oliver. Please. Don't say anything." Her smile grew pleading. "It's not necessary. Really it's not. I think we both got . . . carried away by—" she rolled her eyes to the palms overhead "—the atmosphere of this place. There's no harm done."

"I know, but still, there's so much I want—"

"Please," she interrupted more urgently. "Please don't. Things are . . . nice just as they've been. Why upset the apple cart?"

His chuckle was harsh. "To get to the rotten apple?" he mumbled, thinned his lips in frustration and shook his head. Then he, too, raised his eyes to the palms. "The atmosphere of this place—such a simple explanation. . . ."

"If there are others," she stated soberly, "I don't want to hear them." The last thing she wanted was glib words of excuse, or worse, of affection. It was obvious that Oliver Ames had one way or another gotten himself into an uncomfortable situation. She was simply trying to offer him an easy out. "Nothing's happened here that I haven't wanted to happen. I have no regrets."

"None?" he asked, his voice a bit too low, his eyes too dark.

She had the good sense to look away. "Well . . . none that can't be remedied." When she faced him again, her smile was forced. "Anyway, it's already Wednesday. I've got no intention of living with regrets for the rest of the week. Before I know it I'll be back in New York." Her voice cracked. "Let's not spoil things by analyzing them to death. Okay?"

A strange look appeared on his face, and he grew even more intense. His dark eyes held hers relentlessly, delving deep, finding secret paths to her soul, leaving her raw and exposed. She felt as though she'd been taken apart piece by piece and thoroughly possessed. When her heart beat faster, his gaze fell to her breast.

"Oliver?" she whispered. "Okay?" Her sense of bravado was a bygone thing.

Slowly his eyes returned to hers. "It's okay, Les. I see your point." Patting her knee, he stood up. "I'd better get dressed if I'm going to bike downtown."

"Take the car if you'd like. I won't be using it."

"No, thanks. I think I prefer the bike. Don't dare ride one at home." He threw her a cynical smile. "Wouldn't want to risk damaging the goods. The camera doesn't take kindly to gross blemishes."

He'd left before she decided just whom he'd been mocking—the camera, himself or her. But it didn't matter. Nothing did. As she'd told him, there was no point in endless analysis. And before long she would be back in New York. Strangely, this thought disturbed her more than any other.

Alone on the beach that afternoon, with the knowledge that Oliver was in town, she yielded to impulse and stripped off her bikini top. Her tan was really coming along, she mused, as she studied its golden hue while spreading lotion liberally over her skin. Would anyone see it? Not on her breasts. No one but herself—and she'd remember. . . . And grow warm just thinking about lying on the beach—beside Oliver.

It was a lovely memory, even if it had nowhere to go. Where were they now? Back to square one, each going his own way, leaving the other in peace. Funny how "peace" could take on such different meanings. . . .

For Leslie, a special kind of peace came that evening when, out of the blue, Oliver appeared at the door of the den. "Hi, Les."

She looked up with barely suppressed pleasure at the sight of the tall, casually lounging figure. "Hi."

"Whatcha doin'?"

"Crossword puzzle." She slapped her pencil against it. "Lousy puzzle. I'm really stuck."

"Need some help?"

"Oh, no." She held up a hand and pressed the paper to her chest. "I can do it. It may take me several days, but I'll get it if it kills me."

"You like word games?"

Most likely they bored him to tears. "I do," she said pertly, tipping her chin up in challenge. Wearing cutoffs and a open short-sleeved shirt, Oliver looked disgustingly virile. She needed something to dilute the effect of him; a challenge was just the thing.

"Are you any good?" he asked, eyes shining.

Leslie gave a modest shrug. "I've never won any championships, but I think I can hold my own."

"Got Scrabble?"

"Uh huh."

He tipped his head almost shyly. "Are you game?"

"Are *you*?" she countered in surprise.

"Sure."

They played Scrabble until midnight, broke for several rounds of Boggle and some coffee, then returned to the Scrabble board. Whether it was the lateness of the hour or the pleasure of being with Oliver, Leslie didn't know. But when, sometime around two, giddiness set in and the choice of words took a decidedly suggestive turn, she played right along. After all, it was a game, only a game.

SOFT. SENSUAL, LIBIDO.

"Good one, Oliver!"

BED.

"Come on, Les. You can do better than that."

"I'm trying. But I haven't got any vowels."

"Here. Let me give you a couple."

VIRILE.

"Very smooth."

CARESS.

"Not bad. I thought you didn't have any vowels."

"I just picked them. Go on. Your turn."

WARMTH. FLOW. WAIF.

"Thirty points, Oliver. You're good at this."

SPA. SIR. KEYS.

"Pure, Leslie. Very pure."

SEX.

"Oliver! That's a nothing word!"

"I wouldn't say that. It's got an *x*. That's worth eight points."

"But you didn't even get it on a double or triple score. You blew it."

"I'll say," he muttered under his breath. "Your turn."

AROUSE. GROAN. RAPE. BREAST.

"I don't know, Ol. This is getting pretty bawdy. Hey, you can't use *breast*. You've got two blanks in there that aren't really blanks. The other two are already on the board. That's cheating."

"Come on, Les. Where's your sense of humor? *Breast* is a great word!"

"It's bawdy. Try again."

BAWDY.

"That's not fair. I gave it to you."

"Uh uh, Les. You didn't have the letters. I don't like that gleam in your eye."

"Hold onto your socks. *Bawdy* is nothing. Look at this."

QUIVER.

"Triple word score, plus double letter on the *v*. Twelve . . . twenty . . . twenty-two . . . that makes sixty-six points. So you can keep *bawdy*, even though the *y* does run off the board."

For the moment she'd taken the upper hand. Then, in the last move of the game, Oliver struck.

LOVE.

No double or triple word score. Not even a double or triple letter score for the *v*. Nothing but the emotional clout of a simple four-letter word.

Strangely and mutually subdued, they called it a night after that.

Despite its poignant ending, the camaraderie they shared that Wednesday night carried over to Thursday. By silent agreement they spent the day together, starting with Leslie's mushroom omelets for breakfast, moving down to the beach for several hours of sun and surf, finally doubling up on the motorbike for a shopping expedition into Gustavia.

"You're sure you're up for this?" Oliver asked, strapping a helmet on her head before donning his own.

"Of course. I've taken the bike out myself many times."

"The roads are narrow."

"I'll hang on tight. Hey, are you sure *you're* up for it?"

Taking in her knowing grin, he returned with a pointed stare. "I will be soon," he growled, tossing his leg over the bike, reaching an arm back to settle her snugly behind him, then setting off.

To Leslie, nothing could have been more exhilarating. Wearing shorts and a T-shirt, she felt the sun's rays in counterpoint to the breeze whipping her skin. And Oliver—so firm and hard and strong between her thighs, against her stomach and her breasts—She held on for dear life, her arms wrapped around his lean middle, her hands flattened on his ribs.

"Okay?" he called back once, rubbing her hand with one of his own in a warmly endearing gesture.

"You bet," she returned, closing her eyes as she pressed her cheek to his back. To have a viable excuse to do this was . . . was ecstasy.

To her delight, the ecstasy continued long after they left the bike at the quai and began to stroll along the streets. Oliver kept her hand tucked firmly in his, holding her close to his side as they ambled idly in and out of shops in search of nothing in particular. Indeed, they chanced upon a kind of euphoria; they were a couple among many couples, yet were oblivious to all but each other.

Twice, as they browsed, they stopped at small cafés to sit and talk and further savor the atmosphere of the town. The few purchases they made were Leslie's—a bottle of imported perfume, a small enameled box and, on a whim, a soft pink pareo made of an original hand-blocked fabric that had appealed to her instantly. She knew that the three items would have special meaning for her, given the circumstances under which they'd been bought. Her only regret was that the bag holding them came between Oliver and herself during the airy ride back to the villa.

"How about a swim?" Oliver asked as he parked the bike next to the car.

Leslie smiled and stretched. "I don't know. I feel really lazy. I think I could go to sleep. What with late nights and fresh air and walking. . . ."

"Come down to the beach with me, then. You can sleep while I swim."

To her amazement, that was precisely what she did. She remembered seeing Oliver dive into the waves, watching him swim for a minute . . . then nothing. Once she stirred, finding the warm body near her in her sleep and snuggling closer. When she awoke, Oliver was there, sleeping beside her, his arms cradling her ever so gently. Turning carefully, she raised her head and looked at him. His face was the image of peacefulness. In turn, her own glowed.

"Oliver?" she breathed in a whisper.

"Mmmmmm?" He didn't move.

"You awake?"

"Sure," he murmured in a sleep-slurred voice. "Just have my eyes closed."

"Is that all?" she teased.

"Sure. Late nights don't bother me. Do it all the time." He smacked his lips lightly together once, twice, then his head lolled to the side. His eyes still hadn't opened.

Capitalizing on a rare opportunity, Leslie made a free study of his chest. She loved the smoothness of his skin with its soft mat of hair. She loved the way his nipples hid amid dark whorls of chest hair, camouflaged in apt reminder of a dormant sexuality. She admired the fluid span of his collarbone and the way the muscles of his shoulder had bunched to accommodate her head. She was fascinated by the more vulnerable skin on the underside of his arm and the silkiness of hair there. She raised her fingers to touch, momentarily resisted the temptation, then yielded.

"Hey!" Oliver came alive at once, capturing her hand with unerring aim. "That tickles!" One eye opened, deep and brown. "You must be bored."

"Oh, no."

"Restless?"

"A little."

"Hungry?"

"Mmm."

The double-entendre sizzled between them for a breathtaking minute. Then Oliver snatched her to him and hugged her tight. "My God, Les!" he exclaimed softly as he crushed her to his bare skin. She felt the tremor of his arms and knew an elementary satisfaction that was in no way lessened when he set her back.

"Let's clean up and go into town for dinner," he suggested in a deep voice. "I'm in the mood for something . . . hot and spicy."

"Creole? That's funny. I would have thought you'd prefer soft and subtle and classic."

The sudden smokiness of his gaze sent corresponding spirals smoldering through her. "Later," he crooned. "Later."

It was a promise that was foremost on Leslie's mind. When she bathed, it was with special care to leave her skin soft and aromatic. When she styled her hair, it was with attention to even the smallest wisps. When she made herself up, it was with the lightest hand, no more than the most subtle emphasis on eyes and cheekbones.

Come time to dress, there was no question of her choice. Padding from the bathroom into the bedroom wrapped in a towel, she took the exquisite pink pareo from its bag, shook it out, studied its gentle floral print for a minute, then turned to the mirror. Loosening the terry knot at her breast, she let the towel fall to the floor. Her eye slid from her naked body to the print, then back. With careful concentration, she straightened the fabric, held it up to herself and began to wrap it around the pliant lines of her body, finally criss-crossing the ends at the hollow of her throat and tying a loose knot at the back of her neck.

Then she turned to study herself. It was perfect. Had she picked it out with this in mind? She ran her hands down along her hips, eminently aware of the smooth, unbroken line. Soft pink. Just as the Homme Premier sculptor had requested. Soft pink. Just for Oliver.

When he met her at the front door at eight, he was very obviously affected. For a minute he simply looked at her, devouring every soft inch, every gentle curve. "You look . . . beautiful, Leslie. Absolutely beautiful."

She felt it. She felt beautiful. She felt . . . special. In spite of all their many differences, in spite of the more glossy women he'd surely known in his time, in spite of all the power and grace and raw virility that the man exuded in his fine-tailored slacks and designer shirt, he had a way of making her feel as though there had never been, as though there never would be, another woman for him.

Leslie barely knew what she ate that night, only that she sat at an intimate table for two, elbow to elbow with Oliver, and that he didn't take his eyes from her the entire time. They may have talked of interesting things, but conversation, too, was secondary to mood. Had she tried to classify it she would have used words like loving, needing and expectant. For those feelings permeated her being, blinding her to everything but Oliver.

Somehow, sitting there at a small table in an unpretentious restaurant on the warm, cozy island of St. Barts, she was ready to play the game she'd decried for so long. She was ready to believe that Oliver was as taken with her as she was with him, that they were positively meant for each other, that what existed between them would be right and good and lasting. What he was in real life didn't matter any more than did her own past or future. They were together now and, in the illusion, very much in love. That was all that mattered.

"Dessert?" Oliver murmured, fingers entwined with hers, eyes adoring her lips as the waiter stood nearby.

Entranced by the faint but roguish shadow of his beard, she shook her head. "No," she whispered.

"You're sure?" he whispered back, as distracted as she was.

She nodded.

Within minutes they were in the car headed back to the villa. There, Oliver led her on the long path around the house, holding her hand tightly, turning at times to circle her waist and lift her over a tricky patch of rocks. When at last they reached the beach, he took her in his arms.

It was as if she'd been waiting for just this moment all night, all week, all month, all year. Shorn of inhibition by the aura of love surrounding them, she stood on tiptoe and wrapped her arms around his neck. When her feet left the ground completely and he gently rocked her back and forth, she hung on all the more tightly.

"Ahh, Leslie, this is what I've wanted." Setting her feet back on the ground, he curved his body over hers and buried his lips against her neck. His arms crushed her to him with a fierceness that in itself thrilled her as much as did the feel of his long, lean lines. "So beautiful. . . ."

"Like you," she whispered as she ran her fingers through his hair. Inclining her face, she buried it in that vibrant shock. His scent was clean and rich, pure and unadulterated by fragrant colognes or balms. Breathing deeply, she was further intoxicated. It was only his straightening that brought her away.

His eyes were hot and intense, echoing the silver light of the moon as it shimmied over the waves. He raised a hand to her cheek, tracing its sculpted line, the curve of her jaw, her ear. "I want to kiss you, Les," he rasped. "I want to kiss you everywhere."

If his words hadn't sent fire through her veins, his restless hands would have done the trick. Straining closer, Leslie tilted up her mouth in sweet invitation, then gave him everything when he accepted her offer. There was no teasing, no feint and parry, but rather an all-out meeting of minds, of hearts, of bodies.

Her lips parted before his thirsty advance, moving with

and against him just as anxiously. When his tongue plunged inward, she opened to receive him and suck him deeper. She needed to know of his hunger, absolutely loved the feel of his consuming her, indeed wanted him to know every dark niche within.

All the while, his hands charted the outer landscape of her femininity, sliding around and across her back, over the gentle swell of her hips, the firm contour of her bottom. He lifted her, pressed her more closely, set her down and began again.

Deep within, a gathering of fire had begun. Never before in her life had Leslie known such an intensity of need. But then, Oliver's body was perfect. Arching against him, she felt its every contour. Her hands scoured him, mapping the breadth of his shoulders, the tapering length of his torso, the slimness of his hips, the solidity of his thighs. Around the latter her fingers splayed, sliding up and down as the sinewed cords beneath his slacks grew more taut. She felt the tremor that buzzed through him and found satisfaction that she could have caused it. But her satisfaction was quickly burned to a crisp beneath the flame of a hunger that flashed through her own limbs. When Oliver's voice came, thick and low by her ear, she quivered all over.

"You're not wearing anything under this, are you?" He drew back only to see her face. In the moonlight it had a pale silver glow and looked all the more fragile.

"No," she whispered, eyes strangely innocent.

"For me?"

She shrugged shyly. "I wanted to feel . . . sexy. I did."

"Do you now?"

"Oh, yes," she breathed.

"And . . . if I took the pareo off, would you still?"

Her pulse had taken such a giant leap that she could only nod. It was what she wanted, what her entire body craved. Somehow hearing his intent was all the more erotic. She reached back to the knot at her neck, only to have his warm hands pull her arms away.

"Let me," he murmured, dipping his head to kiss her slowly, languorously, before turning his attention to the knot.

His eyes held hers while his fingers worked, gently pulling at the ends of the cloth, steadily loosening them.

When she felt the fabric slacken at her chest, Leslie felt a moment's hesitation. There was nothing at all glamorous about her body. And though he'd seen most of it already, there was something very . . . special about that part he'd now see for the first time. But it was too late to go back, she knew. If the determined look on Oliver's face hadn't told her so, the soft tendrils of excitement skittering in the pit of her stomach would have.

Slowly he drew his hands forward, unwinding the fabric and letting it fall to the sand. As though sensing her need for support, he instantly put his hands on her shoulders, rubbing them gently as his eyes fell to delight in her.

"Oh . . . Les . . ." he managed brokenly.

She caught in her breath. "Is it . . . am I . . . ?"

Only then did he look back to see the unsureness on her face. While one hand tightened on her shoulder, the other slid up to her neck. "You were worried?" he asked in surprise.

"I'm not gorgeous. . . ."

Helplessly drawn by the golden sheen of her skin, his gaze fell, to journey with his hand in a slow descent. The texture of his palm was the slightest bit rough in contrast to the butter-smooth skin of her breasts. His fingers seemed that much stronger than her waist, her hips, almost able to circle her thighs. But when they feather-touched the golden curls he'd never seen before, his hands were all male and dynamite.

In response to their tender force, Leslie reached out to clutch his shoulders in support. "Oliver!" she whispered hoarsely.

"You were worried?" he repeated dumbly as his hands flowed down and around and back up. Everywhere they touched she felt ready to explode. Again she moaned his name.

Framing her face with his hands, he tipped it up to his. "You're magnificent, sweetheart. Every inch of you. So warm—" he brushed his lips to her nose "—and soft—" he licked the line of her cheekbone "—and full where you should be full, and moist just there. . . ." His lips became pulsing things then, capturing hers with a frenzy that spoke more eloquently than anything else might have done. And Leslie surrendered to their argument, giving herself up to the fire of the moment, choosing to believe she was indeed as magnificent as he'd claimed.

For a minute, held and holding breathlessly onto him, she savored the feel of his clothing against her skin. It made her feel naked and naughty and sensual. Yet when she burrowed her head against the column of his neck and opened her lips to the heat of his skin where his shirt fell open, she wanted more. Naked and naughty and sensual were very lovely narcissistic things to be. But what she felt for Oliver went far beyond narcissistic.

As she kissed the bronzed hollow of his shoulder, her hands worked feverishly at the buttons of his shirt, releasing one after the other, finally tugging the material from his pants and brushing it away. Then, with a sigh of delight, she set her hands loose on the playground of his chest, feeling as though in being able to touch him at will she'd been given the greatest gift of all.

"That's right," Oliver moaned, pressing his hands to the small of her back to keep their lower bodies close despite the inches that separated them above. "I've wanted you to touch me for so long—to feel your hands on my body. . . ."

"Tell me what you like Oliver," she whispered as she spread her fingers wide and ran them up his sides. When her thumbs grazed his nipples, he jerked. Returning to them, she circled their tips, tormenting them with the pads of her thumbs until he moaned again.

"Like that," he gasped, his eyes closed, his chest laboring in the effort to breathe. She found that to please him, to bring his body alive, was a joy in itself. Growing bolder, she bent her head and replaced her fingers with lips. With the tip of her tongue she danced along his flesh, dabbing the hardened nipple with a sensual moistness, grazing it with her teeth. This time in response his groan was one of sweet agony. Crushing her bottom with his hands, he ground his hips to hers.

His voice was a low, unsteady rasp, his eyes wild with fire when he tore her head up. "I don't know how much more I can take, Leslie," he warned. "I've needed you so badly all week—and now. . . ."

Setting her back, he attacked the buckle of his belt. It was released, along with his zipper, in an instant. But as he would have thrust the fabric down, Leslie reached out.

"Wait!" she cried, then at his stricken look realized his misconception. "No," she whispered, stepping closer, "it's just that I want to do it." Arching against him, her hands at his waist, she stretched to reach his lips. Her breasts strained against his chest, creating a heady friction that gave even greater heat to her kiss. Then, offering him her tongue by way of exchange, she slid her hands beneath the band of his briefs, sought and found what she wanted, and stroked him tenderly. Fully aroused, he was thick and hard. She found herself breathing as heavily as he was, needing to touch him, yet needing so much more.

Oliver moaned again, and a shiver shook his limbs. Setting her aside almost roughly, he thrust slacks and briefs down over his legs and cast them aside, then caught her again.

At the contact, she cried aloud. It was new, rich and electric.

"Oh, Les. . . ."

"Yes, yes. . . ."

"Come here!" The last was a command ground out from his chest moments before he slid his hands down the backs of her thighs and lifted her, spreading her legs, fitting them snugly around his hips. Then, poised on the brink of her, he dropped smoothly to his knees and gently lowered her backward. Only when she was fully cushioned by the sand did he retrieve his hands. With one he propped himself up, with the other he reached down to unerringly find her warmth.

"Please, Oliver . . ." she pleaded, moving against his hand in frustration.

"Do you want me?"

"Oh, yes!"

His fingers caressed her longingly. "You're ready. . . ."

"I've been ready for so long—I don't think I can stand much more. . . ."

"I can't," he grated hoarsely. Planting his other hand near her shoulder, he moved his hips against hers.

They looked into each other's eyes then, aware of the moment as of no other before. To Leslie, it was right—right in every way, form and fashion. Not only did her body want Oliver, but her mind and her heart did as well. Regrets would be nonexistent, regardless of what the future held. For the moment to come promised to be the culmination of something very special to her as a woman. Pulse racing in wild anticipation, she grasped his hips and urged him in.

Ever wary of hurting her, he rocked slowly, surging forward by degrees, conquering her by inches. Her mouth opened in silent exclamation at the beauty of it, the slow filling, the exquisite heat. When at last he was fully buried within her, he dropped his head back and let his breath out in a soulful rush.

"You have no idea, Leslie. . . ."

"But I do," she cried, lifting her hips and hooking her ankles together at his waist. "I do," she breathed, tightening herself, closing her eyes with the sweet, sweet pleasure of knowing that Oliver was deep inside.

On arms that trembled, he lowered his head to envelop her mouth. Then he began to move his hips, slowly at first but with growing speed and power as the flight of passion caught him up.

Leslie was with him every step of the way. Her lips answered his hungry nips, her hands roamed in greedy caress through the damp sheen of sweat rising on his skin. She felt his strength and the rock-hard boldness moving within her and, coaxed by instinct, caught the rhythm of his fire.

In those instants what existed between them was raw and primal and devoid of identity other than that of an all-consuming and mutual need. Labels would have been useless; Oliver was no more the glamorous male model than she the private preschool teacher. The pleasure they brought each other was direct and intense, unsullied by anything either of them might have been or done or wanted before in their lives. There were just the two of them, making love at that moment; nothing else was of consequence.

"Oliver!" she cried from a daze of passion, her body alive with a fire frightening in its intensity.

"That's it, sweet," he urged, plunging ever deeper, "more . . . oh, yes . . . there. . . ."

She cried his name again, strained upward, then dissolved into spasms of ecstasy. In the next instant Oliver, too, stiffened, then let out an anguished moan of joy as his pleasure went endlessly on.

At last, totally spent, he collapsed over her. Then, when her gasping grew as loud as his, he quickly levered himself up on his elbows to relieve her of the worst of his weight. His gaze its most tender, he looked down at her.

"Does that smile mean that you're happy?"

Her throat felt suspiciously tight. She nodded.

"I'm glad," he said softly, brushing his lips against a corner of the smile in question. "You are beautiful. That was beautiful." He paused for a breath between each brief burst of words, then slowly slipped to her side, leaving one thigh firmly over hers. "Well, what do you think?" His tone verged on the giddy, yet she knew that deep down he needed to know that he'd pleased her. She also knew that it had very little to do with ego, and she was enchanted.

She brushed the dark wave from the dampness of his brow, then repeated the gesture when it fell right back down again. "I think," she began with mock deliberation, "that for a professional ladykiller you do just fine."

"I'm glad," he murmured, "because if my past has been worth anything, it's been to make me better for you."

"That's a sweet thing to say."

"It's what I feel, Leslie." He was suddenly serious. "You do know that it's never been like that before, don't you?"

Because she wanted to believe him, she nodded.

"You also know that I'm now very sandy."

"You ain't the only one." Before she could say another word, Oliver was on his feet, dragging her up with him. "What are you doing?" she cried, then pulled back on her hand. "Oh, no, Oliver Ames, it's chilly in there this time of night! You're not getting *me* in there."

"It's only the air that's chilly," he chided, dealing with her resistance by sweeping her into his arms.

"Oliver! You're supposed to be limp and sleepy. You can't do this!"

"I'm doin' it." His feet were making definite tracks, and not toward the house.

"But, Oliver!" She held tightly to his neck when she heard the splashing at his feet. "Oliver!" He bounced farther into the waves. "Come on, Oliver!" When the water touched her bottom, she strained upward, only to slide helplessly down when he released her legs.

Even the placid light of the moon couldn't hide the mischief in his eyes. His hands went to his neck. "Let go of me, Leslie," he murmured silkily.

She shook her head and locked her hands all the more tightly. "No."

He spread his hands beneath her arms. "Let go. . . ."

"No."

Then he tickled her. On a reflex of self-defense, she lowered her arms . . . and tumbled helplessly into the waves. Never once did he totally release her, though. His hands were there at her waist to lift her as soon as she'd been fully submerged.

"That was a dirty trick!" she sputtered. Tossing her wet hair back from her face, she scowled, but he pulled her against him once more and she melted nearly on contact.

"Now you can hold on again."

"Uh uh. You'll only tickle again."

"I promise I won't."

"Yeah, yeah."

"Really."

She wanted to believe. "Really?"

"Uh huh."

She hesitated for only a moment longer. Then, sensual slave that she happily was, she locked her arms around his neck once more. The fit of their bodies was perfect. "Only problem is that you've still got sand on you, and now it's back on me."

"Oh?" He frowned, as though stymied by the problem. Then, with an innocent shrug, he twirled and fell backward into the sea, dunking them both.

This time she came up laughing. When Oliver grasped her around the waist and hoisted her higher against him, she looked adoringly down at him. "That was nearly as dirty a trick as the other."

"But we're clean," he murmured between nips at her chin, "aren't we?"

Her legs floated around him naturally. "Uh huh."

"Are you too cool?"

"In your arms? Never."

He tipped her back and looked at her then. The moonlight set his features in relief, giving them a masterful air in counterpoint to the tenderness of his voice. "Why is it that you've always got the right answers?"

"They're not necessarily right," she replied lightly, "just honest."

"You like honesty?"

"I need honesty."

"Spoken with the same vehemence I've heard from you more than once before." He paused. "What happened, Leslie?"

Her legs slipped slowly downward. "What do you mean?"

"You've been hurt. Something happened. I want to know."

"You don't really," she said, trying to make light of it.

"I do." His expression echoed his words. "I want to understand why you feel so strongly about some things. Why you put that certain distance between you and your family. Why you seem leery of men."

"I don't know, Oliver. It's really irrelevant . . . and very embarrassing." He would think her a positive fool!

"Then—" he swept her up in his arms, turned and started for shore "—you'd better talk quickly so that the darkness can hide your blush. I intend to hear about it . . . tonight!"

"Or . . . ?" Her arms were around his neck once more.

"Or else."

"Or else what?"

"Or else . . . I'll hold you prisoner, stake you spread-eagled out in the sun tomorrow morning, and let you fry until you talk."

"Mmm, sounds very provocative."

Out of the water now, he stopped dead in his tracks. "Primitive is the word."

She gave a playful growl. "Primitive turns me on."

"Leslie, you're not being serious—but you won't get away with it." He let her feet fall to the sand, holding her waist until he was sure she had her balance. "Now pick up your things, and let's get up to the house. We've got some talking to do."

She picked up her sandals and let them dangle from one hand. "Oliver?"

He was searching the night sand for a second sock, his body lean and glistening in the moonlight. "Mmm?"

Inching closer, she wrapped an arm around his waist. His skin felt slick and smooth; her flesh slid easily over it. "Wouldn't you rather make love?" she asked softly, her expression more heartfelt than seductive.

He popped a kiss on the tip of her nose. "That, sweet angel, will be your reward. Now up!"

6

Actually, they didn't make it beyond the upper terrace. Stubbing her toe on the corner of a lounge chair she hadn't seen in the dark, Leslie needed consolation. Much later Oliver was to tell her that she'd simply wanted to make love on every level. But he hadn't complained at the time. Rather, there had been a kind of poignant drive to his lovemaking that had surprised her, given the satisfaction they'd so recently found on the beach. It was almost as though he feared what he'd learn when they talked.

He wasn't deterred, however. After they'd reached Shangri-la and beyond, had lain savoring the sensations, then recovered enough to languidly leave the lounge and pick up their clothes once more, he ushered her into the den. He left her only to go in search of robes, returned to gently clothe them both, then folded his long frame into the chair opposite hers and leaned forward.

She simply stared at him.

"Okay, Les," he began, undaunted. "Let's have it."

"Aren't you exhausted?"

"Nope. Who was he?"

Leslie tucked her legs beneath her and wrapped her arms around her middle. "It's not important."

"I think it is."

"It's *my* past. I don't ask you about yours."

He took on the same mocking expression she'd seen more

than once before. "That's because mine is so lurid and filled
with such an endless stream of women that I wouldn't know
where to begin."

"Well," she prevaricated, "maybe mine's the same. Maybe
I have a hidden past. Maybe I'm not as pure as I let on."

He chuckled and sat back, momentarily indulging her.
"Funny, I never thought of you simply as 'pure.' Maybe pure
honey or pure wit or pure sensuality. Never just . . . 'pure.'
Besides—" he came forward again, his dark eyes narrowed
"—you were the one who informed me—albeit in a very
sexy voice—that you didn't sleep around."

She recalled the moment exactly, the Friday before, when
she'd first arrived from New York and had been sick and very
threatened by his presence. How far she'd come, she mused,
then abruptly realized she hadn't. If she stopped to think,
she'd know that she was still very threatened indeed, though
by something quite different now.

"So, Les," Oliver went on, reaching forward to brush his
thumb against the furrows on her brow, "tell me about it." His
voice was quiet, patient. "Tell me about honesty. Too many
times I've heard bitterness, then just now vehemence, in your
voice when you've mentioned it. You need it, you say. Why?"

Quiet and patient, yes. But there was also an unmistakable trace of cynicism underlying his tone. Disturbed, Leslie
tore her gaze away. "It's not relevant to anything, Oliver."

Though his stance remained casual, long bare legs set
nonchalantly, hands now crossed over his stomach, his gaze
was sharp. "It's relevant to us . . . and to what's happened
twice now. And it matters to me. I need to understand you."

It was the last that hit home. She mulled the words over
again and again. *I need to understand you . . . need to understand you.* Perhaps it was nothing more than a continua-
tion of the illusion born earlier that day and brought to
fulfillment on the beach. But she wanted so badly to believe
that he cared that at long last she yielded and spoke, softly,
slowly, eyes downcast, arms clutched tightly about herself.

"It's really very simple," she began. "I grew up a Parish,
always a Parish. Living in an exclusive area, going to a pri-

vate school, my friends were pretty much . . . people like me, people who'd had most everything they'd wanted in life." She lifted her eyes to find Oliver sitting back, listening thoughtfully. "Oh, I had friends. A couple of good ones I've kept. But at some point I became disillusioned with most of them. They seemed shallow. Boring. Quick to manipulate when it suited their purposes. Maybe it was natural for me to rebel. I was the youngest Parish and felt I had gone through life in the shadow of the others. I was seventeen and feeling my oats. Having always had the material things I'd wanted and knowing that they'd always be there for me, it was easy to turn my back on them."

"You became a flower child?" Oliver asked, faint amusement lighting his features.

She blushed. "Not really. Just a free thinker. I did little things to proclaim my individuality—like going vegetarian and boycotting the senior prom and donating my graduation money to Oxfam and biking across the country with three friends."

Again his eyes lit. "Bicycling?"

She lowered hers. "Motorcycling."

"And the three other kids?" he asked more pointedly.

"My best friend from school . . . and her twin cousins."

He caught the drop in her voice and interpreted correctly. "Male?"

"Yes." She raised a defensive gaze and went quickly on. "Not that anything happened between us. I mean, we were all good friends, but that was it. We didn't cause trouble, either. Our idea of adventure was in living as cheaply as we could. We camped out a good part of the time, stayed in our share of sleazy places. Just knowing how appalled our parents would have been enhanced our joy." She sighed. "We did see the country, I have to admit." Then she qualified the statement. "I mean, we'd all seen the country before, but never like that."

"Sounds like fun," Oliver ventured wryly.

"It was! It really was. We enjoyed mocking everything we'd always had. Then the other three went right back to it when the summer was over."

"And you?"

"I went on to college. Berkeley." When he winced, she smiled. "It wasn't so bad. Actually, I'd already gotten much of the rebelliousness out of my system, so I was pretty receptive to learning. I felt confident and in control and loved the idea of being three thousand miles away from all of the other Parishes."

"They didn't keep close tabs on you?"

"Naw. They trusted me."

He arched a brow. "Should they have?"

She thought for a minute, then nodded. "My intentions were good. I was idealistic, bent on making a very serious, independent way in the world. I would never have done anything to disgrace them." She paused, then frowned. "Not knowingly, at least."

Silence sat between them for a time, broken only by the gentle murmur of the night surf on the beach as it accompanied the softest of breezes through the open glass doors. Leslie let herself be momentarily lulled, then, eager to get out the worst, she went on.

"I had a great freshman year. I loved school and did well." She cast him a sheepish look. "It was an awakening to find myself among so many people who were legitimately serious and independent. In many ways, it was humbling. I guess I withdrew a little, letting the place itself speak for my rebellion while I got reacquainted with the person I was inside. I liked myself. I thought I'd found a nice blend between 'way out' and 'way in'. . . ." Her voice trailed off as her eyes reflected a distant pain.

"Then what happened?"

As though she'd forgotten his presence, she came back with a start. With a shrug she looked down at the pleats her fingers were nervously folding into the terry fabric of her robe. "I met a fellow. A med student." She tossed her head to the side, keeping her eyes downcast, safe from Oliver's intent study. "He was tall and good-looking and bright and funny . . . and very high on life and himself." Her voice took on a gently mocking tone. "He was going to be a doctor. You know, heal the world?"

"I know the type," Oliver injected, but Leslie was too immersed in her story to hear the dryness in his tone.

"Anyway," she sighed, "we started to date and . . . things got pretty heavy. We couldn't see each other often. I was busy studying, and his schedule was ten times worse. I think it was the time we spent apart that aided his cause more than anything. I was young and starry-eyed and spent those times away from him imagining all the wonderful things he was going to do." She lowered her voice to a self-conscious murmur, "All the wonderful things we were going to do together. He was talking about the Peace Corps. That fit right into my scheme of things—noble, stoic, commendable. I spent those days alone dreaming about how, after graduation, we'd both go to South America or South Africa. He'd doctor; I'd teach. It was perfect." She paused to recall that particular illusion, then shook her head in dismay. "Things didn't quite work out as as I'd dreamed."

Oliver propped his elbows on his knees and prodded gently. "Why not?"

She looked up then, vulnerable and in pain. "He was married."

"Oh. And you didn't know."

"Of course not!" she cried, doubly hurt. "I'd never have knowingly had an affair with a married man! For all my ballyhooing about rebellion, I'd been pretty conservative about sex; it was enough for me to have had the affair in the first place! I honestly thought that he was busy studying all the time. I mean—" again the mocking tone "—between classes and rotations, a med student has to be the most put-upon person in the world. Hmmph," she mused aloud, "no wonder they go out into the world and keep patients in their offices waiting for hours. Revenge, I'm sure. Simple revenge."

Oliver let her anger gradually seep away before he spoke. "Not all doctors are that way, Les. There are ones who do serve time in the Peace Corps, or who keep ungodly hours as staff physicians well after their med-school days are over, or who go into private practice and make a point to see all their patients on time. How they are as doctors can sometimes be very different from the way they run their private lives."

"I'm not so sure about that," she retorted bitterly, "though I'll concede you the point. For all I know Joe's become an excellent doctor. And for that matter, I may have been as much at fault for what happened between us as he was." At Oliver's puzzled look, she explained. "Idealistic young thing that I was, I accepted everything on faith. He explained that when he was free he wanted to get away from it all. So he always came to my place, rather than the other way around. Sucker that I was, I believed him."

"Did you love him?" came the quiet follow-up.

"What I knew of him, yes. He was truly charming— great bedside manner, if you'll excuse the pun." Her lips thinned. "We'd been seeing each other for nearly six months when one day I thought I'd surprise him and bring a home-cooked dinner to his apartment. I knew his address in Palo Alto, though I'd never been there before." She swallowed hard, trying to accept all over again what she'd learned that day. "It was a lovely dorm not far from the medical school. Prettier than most—you know, small balconies with hanging plants and a baby swing here and there. When I went into the lobby to buzz him, I understood why. It was a married students' dorm. 'Dr. and Mrs.' all along the roster—the Joe Durands right up there with the rest. I turned around with my shattered dreams and went home."

By way of offering comfort, Oliver took her hand, but it lay limply under his gentle massage. "Did he ever follow you?"

"Oh, yes," she spat out with a harsh laugh. "He hadn't known I'd come and didn't know anything was wrong. He assumed his little game could go on indefinitely. When he showed up several days later, I'd had time to cool off and gather my thoughts. I was really quite . . . good."

"I'm sure," Oliver remarked tightly.

"I was," she insisted, raising her eyes in a burst of courage. "It was actually funny. I threw myself into his arms and told him how much I'd missed him, how much I loved him. After he tossed back those same hollow words, I told him about my brainstorm. It had occurred to me, I told him, that he'd be able to save all kinds of money if he moved in with me. I could cook for him and do his laundry and take care of him in between my own studies. After all, why not, since we loved each other so much?"

"That was mean," Oliver scolded, though he couldn't completely hide the glimmer of admiration in his gaze.

"It was intended to be," she rejoined without remorse. "I was brokenhearted at the time. I felt used and dirty. I had to score some points, and since I didn't have the heart to resort to blackmail, I simply wanted him to squirm."

"Did he?"

"Oh ho, yes," she answered, neither pride nor pleasure in her tone. "He hemmed and hawed about how he'd never get any studying done if we lived together, and he'd feel all the more guilty about having to put me off when he did need to work. I insisted that it wouldn't bother me and that it would be better watching him study than not seeing him at all."

The fire in her eyes spoke of an inner strength. Respecting it, Oliver grew more grave. "How did he handle that?"

"Very predictably, actually. On the pretense of being overcome by my offer, he took me in his arms and tried to put off the whole discussion by making love."

"You didn't—"

"No. I brought my knee up hard, and then told him to go home and *try* to make love to his wife."

Oliver jacked forward as though in physical pain himself. "You really did that?"

"You bet I did," she breathed, "and I haven't regretted it for a minute. I was hurt and angry. The look of surprise, then disbelief, then sheer terror on his face was the small satisfaction I got out of the affair. That . . . and the determination never to be made a fool of again." With the last of her venom trickling into thin air, she spoke more gently and with an awareness of Oliver once more. His face was racked by pain; she was touched by his sympathy. "It's okay, Oliver," she said, forcing a smile. "It's over, and I survived. In hindsight, I guess I was most disappointed in myself—disappointed that I'd been fool enough to be so completely taken in. I really did love a part of Joe. I thought I'd found someone different—someone down-to-earth, someone more concerned with doing and living than clawing up the social ladder." Her voice grew sad. "I was wrong. His greatest fear, when he discovered I knew the truth, was that I'd blow the whistle on him and somehow hurt his chances for a future in Boston. Not Kenya. Boston." She sighed, her tone a mere whisper. "Boy, was I wrong."

For the longest time, Oliver simply sat and stared at her, his chin propped on his fist, his face a mask of dismay. When she could no longer stand the silence, Leslie pushed herself from her chair and paced to the window.

"So now you know what a clever lady I am," she called over her shoulder. "Now you know why I'm wary."

With the sound of his bare feet muffled in the carpet, she didn't hear him approach. When his arms slipped around her to draw her back against him, she resisted. But he was insistent. And in the end she needed his support.

"I'm sorry," he murmured so sadly that Leslie turned in his arms to face him.

"You're sorry?" she asked, bemused by his almost anguished expression. "It wasn't your fault!"

"But still . . . in some ways I identify with . . . your Joe."

"He's not my Joe, and that's ridiculous. Aside from the fact that you both wear pants, you're nothing at all like Joe. He was a two-timing liar. You're not. You've never made promises or said things you couldn't see through. You've never made any attempt to deliberately sweeten the image of what you do, even when I've thought the worst." Her ardent claim did nothing to ease his pain.

"But you know so little about me," he began, his voice heavy and low.

"I know the essentials," she pointed out quietly. "And Tony knows you. If there was something grossly unsuitable about you, he would never have suggested you come. Be-

sides, I know that you were kind enough not to laugh at me
just now."

"Did anyone laugh?" he asked, brows lifting in a touching challenge. Was he truly a knight in shining armor, prepared to defend her virtue?

"No one laughed," she murmured, "because no one knew.
And if anyone finds out," she warned only half in jest, "I'll
personally knock you off that white steed of yours."

Attuned to the analogy, he grunted. "Better to fall from a
horse than to be kicked in the balls. Hell, you're a dangerous
woman."

"Only when I'm pushed. I don't really want to be dangerous."

Oliver's expression took a soulful twist as his arms tightened around her back. "Oh, Leslie," he murmured, his gaze
clinging to each of her features in turn, "I wish . . . I wish. . . ."

"Shh." She pressed a finger to his lips. His entire body felt
tense; she began to rub his shoulders and back in an attempt
to loosen him up. "Please don't say anything. Life here is
so . . . basic. So simple." Her voice dropped to a whisper.
"It's like lying bare on the beach. Unadorned and lovely."

"But there's still New York—"

"Next week," she vowed more strongly. "Not now."

"Then where's the honesty you claim you need?"

"What's honest in New York, New York can have. I just
want to enjoy what's here. Now." Her eyes grew beseeching.
"Can you understand that, Oliver?"

"Oh, sweetheart, only too well," he murmured with a sudden fierceness. Then his lips sought hers, transmitting that
fierceness through her body in the name of passion. His kiss
was long and possessive, enduring even as he swept her off
her feet and headed for the bedroom. Only when the large
bed took her weight did he raise his head. Trembling as he
leaned over her, he sighed her name several times and with
reverence. "Leslie, Leslie, let me love you the way you should
be loved. . . ."

Stunned by the aching depth of his plea, Leslie could find
no words to express what she felt. Oliver Ames had to be the

most gentle, most compassionate man in the world. Opening her arms, she reached up to him. For just a minute he held her, embracing her with the same fierceness with which he'd kissed her, then gently pressing her away. With unsteady fingers he untied her robe and, spreading it to either side, proceeded to worship every bare inch of her body with his hands, then his mouth, then his tongue. Helplessly she writhed at the havoc he caused, loving every minute of it, loving him all the more. For there was something supremely tender about his lovemaking this time, something that went far beyond the gentleness he'd shown before. It was as though in this abandoned adulation he sought to apologize for what another man had done, to make amends, to tell her what an exquisitely feminine wonder she was.

And she believed. She believed. How could she not, with the warmth of strong, manly fingers stroking her hips, with the wetness of a long, sensual tongue adoring her breast, with the length of lean, sinewed flesh branding her cherished? If she'd thought to protest that it wasn't Oliver's apology to give, her need for his loving was far too great to deny him his penance. His entire goal seemed to be giving her pleasure; yet she reveled in the sound of his own moans and sighs, in the quaking of his limbs when he finally drew back to remove his robe.

Then, wanting to absolve him of guilt for all time, she opened her thighs and welcomed him. The ensuing fire was purgative, cleansing, propelling them onward to a climactic point where it seemed their souls would fuse forever. When, after wave upon wave of glory washed over their straining bodies, they finally cooled, exhaustion took its inevitable toll. Deliriously happy and at peace, Leslie fell asleep in her lover's arms, awakening only when morning had fully established itself over the island.

"Happy Birthday, sweetheart."

She snuggled closer, eyes closed, a smile on her face. "Mmm. You remembered."

The arms around her tightened. The voice by her ear was

a deep, lazy hum. "Of course, I remembered. Thirty years old . . . oops, what's this?"

She felt the hair being lifted from her neck. "What's what?"

"This line."

"What line?"

One long finger sizzled around her throat. "This. Must be your age. They say the neck is the first to show it, love."

Leslie tipped her head back, arched a brow and opened the violet-hued eye beneath it. "Is that so?" she asked smartly.

Oliver nodded, trying his best to keep a straight face. "Uh huh. I should know. In my business, the face is everything. We worry about important things like lines around the mouth and receding hairlines and sagging chins."

"Do you now?" she teased. "And what'll you do when your day is done?"

"Oh, I've got no cause for concern," he stated outrageously. "Men don't get older; they just get more dignified-looking. It's women who have to worry. Say, Les, I wouldn't scowl like that. It'll only bring out lines on your forehead." He ducked in time to avoid the playful swat she aimed at his head, then grabbed her and kissed her soundly. She protested for only an instant before surrendering to his morning pleasure. When he came up for air, his eyes were dark and earnest. "Somehow," he said softly, stroking the delicate lines of her face, "I don't think you have to worry about wrinkles. You sure as hell don't look thirty. I may not have known you five or ten years ago, but I'd guess that you're one of those women who's getting better, not older."

"Oliver Ames," Leslie scolded gently, "this sounds like a living advertisement. Next thing I know the cameramen will pop out from behind the drapes."

"There aren't any drapes."

"Then . . . from under the bed."

"Heaven help anyone who was under this bed last night. Poor fool would have a concussion."

She shook her head and sighed through a grin. "You are incorrigible."

"Better incorrigible than late for breakfast. Come on," he announced, dropping her onto the sheet as he rolled out of bed, "I'm hungry." Then he looked down at her. "On second thought, you stay put. For the birthday girl, breakfast in bed."

The birthday girl, however, was suddenly and acutely aware that she'd never seen Oliver nude in the daylight. Beneath the bright sun streaking through the skylights, his body looked very strong and very male.

"Les?" He leaned over her. Startled, she raised her eyes. "You do want breakfast, don't you?" he whispered.

She swallowed once and realized how silly he'd think her if she said she just wanted to look at him, to touch him. "Sure."

As though reading her thoughts, he sat back down on the sheets. Taking her hand in his, he pressed it to his hip, moving it gently over the very strip of flesh that all the world had seen. "Maybe I'm feeling my age, after all," he teased. "You gave me quite a workout last night." Leaning forward, he kissed her forehead. "We'll have breakfast and then go . . . exploring. How does that sound?"

The deep velvet of his voice sent shivers of excitement through her, as did the smoothness of his flank. She grinned. "I'd like that." Slipping beneath the sheet, she watched him leave the room and closed her eyes, awaiting his return.

Return he did, bearing a tray filled with all sorts of breakfast goodies. They ate to their hearts' content, then explored as he'd promised. It was nearly noon before they finally climbed from bed, showered together, then headed for the beach wearing nothing but oversize towels, which they proceeded to spread on the sand and lie upon.

"This is indecent," she remarked, eyeing the solid length of Oliver's naked body stretched beside her, "but I love it."

He opened one eye. "You're very daring for a conservative lady. Topless on the public beach, nude here. Say, you never did finish the story of the flower child." He closed his eye and flipped onto his stomach, propping his chin on his hands in time to see her bob up.

"Wait," she said, "if you're going to switch on me, you

need more lotion." She had the bottle in her hand and was kneeling at his hips, grateful for the excuse to touch him. He shivered when she drizzled a line of cream down his spine. "Wouldn't want your butt to get burned."

"God forbid," he muttered, burying his face in his arms to endure the agony of the hands working so diligently over his skin. It was a full minute after she'd finished and lain down again before he thought to look up. Shifting in a vain attempt to make himself comfortable, he cleared his throat. "Your story."

She was on her back, arms and legs restful, eyes closed, face to the sun, As an afterthought, she rubbed the lotion lingering on her hands over her stomach and breasts, then fell still. "Not much more to tell."

"Did you transfer back east to finish school?"

"And jeopardize my independence? No way."

"It didn't bother you to be out there with memories of that fellow all around?"

"I was so angry at the time that I was thinking only of the discomfort he'd feel knowing I was there. When the anger faded, I realized that there wasn't an awful lot left. Yes, I was hurt and embarrassed and more than a little disillusioned. But I knew that it'd be worse to fly back home with my tail between my legs. Besides, I liked Berkeley and what with the course load I took on, I had plenty to keep me busy. I graduated a semester early and taught for six months before going back to grad school. By that time I'd accepted what had happened with Joe."

"So you came home."

She nodded. "I'd done a lot of growing up during those three and a half years. Not only was I the wiser for my experience with Joe, but I realized that I was a strong enough person to hold my own among the Parishes. And, as it happens, I love New York."

Eyes closed, he groped for her hand, finding it, enveloping it in his. "Look who sounds like an ad, now? And I thought you didn't like crowds."

"I don't . . . when it comes to going to work or the bank

or the dry cleaner or the supermarket. But I love museums and the theater, and there's nothing more delightful than bundling up and strolling down a packed Fifth Avenue at Christmastime. That's why I live outside the city but within easy reach. If I don't feel like reaching, I don't. I have the choice." Oliver's respectful chuckle brought her head around. "What about you? Doesn't it bother you—living right in the thick of things?" He'd previously told her that he lived in the city, though he hadn't elaborated either on where or on what kind of place he had.

He shrugged. "For the convenience of it, I'd put up with most anything. Besides, I have a small place in the Berkshires. Great for weekends."

She wondered what he did on those weekends, whether he had someone to play Scrabble with and . . . do other things with. But she didn't ask. She didn't feel she had the right. After all, there had been no lofty words of love or proclamations of undying devotion. She didn't want them. They could be so very shallow. *No*, she mused, *better to assume nothing than to pin false hopes on something that would probably never materialize.* It was far safer this way. Safer, if discouraging. . . .

"You're awfully quiet," Oliver whispered.

She tossed off his concern with a shrug. "Just . . . thinking."

"About what?"

"About . . . how beautiful it is down here and how much I wish I could stay another week." Though roundabout, it was the truth.

He was up on an elbow. "Can't you?"

Feeling his gaze, she shook her head and smiled, but didn't open her eyes. "The centers await." She gave an exaggerated sigh. "Ah me, the price of success. For us lady executives, the day is never done. They depend on us," she drawled. "They need us. Oh, to be a lowly errand girl—hey, what are you doing?" She opened her eyes with a start to find Oliver on his haunches by her hip.

"Lotioning you up." His hands were already at work spreading the cream he'd gushed on.

"But I'm already lotioned!" Feeling her body's instant reaction to his touch, she twisted to the side. Oliver simply straddled her hips to hold her still. "Oliver . . ." she warned, lying flat, looking up at him. His hands slid over her skin in a pattern of sensuous circles, teasing by sheer impartiality. "Oliver!" she whispered more urgently. "This is ridiculous! The oldest trick in the book—seduction by suntan lotion!"

"Guess I'm not terribly original then," he murmured, slithering his hands over the peak of her breasts again and again.

"My God!" she moaned. She bit her lip and arched helplessly into his touch.

"No, sweetheart, just me." Planting his hands on either side of her shoulders, he stretched his full length over her. His eyes held the lambency she'd come to know, the depth she'd come to love, the vulnerability that could touch her every time. "Just me . . . needing you again."

Leslie coiled her arms around his neck. "I don't know about these male model types. They're insatiable."

"Only with you," he murmured, seeking the honey of her mouth as he nudged a place for himself between her thighs.

And she believed . . . again. She believed because she had to, because the intense love that swelled within her came part and parcel with trust. If she was wrong, she'd be later damned. But for now she had no choice. No choice at all.

"This is positively decadent," Leslie remarked. "I don't think we've been properly dressed for two days."

It was Saturday morning, and they'd just emerged from an early-morning swim. She blotted her towel over her face, then glanced up to find Oliver just standing there, dripping wet, looking down at her. His towel hung, forgotten, in his hand, but she, too, forgot it in the face of his strangely uncertain expression. She'd seen that expression more than once in the past two days. It was not quite haunted, not quite pained, not quite worried, not quite fearful, yet it held a bit of all of those emotions and more, thrown together to produce something that cut to her heart, then twisted and turned.

"Are you all right?" she asked softly. She took a step forward, then was stopped by a sudden sense of foreboding. Shaking her head, she moved forward again. "Oliver?"

He blinked and inhaled. "Sorry, Les. I missed that."

Very gently, using her own towel, she began to dry his chest. "Didn't miss much. I was only being smart."

"Again?" His cockeyed smile was a relief, as was the mischievous eye that warmed her length. "You know, we really should get dressed," he suggested, tugging her against him. "It's been nearly two days. Think we'll remember how?"

At first she thought he was mocking her. After all, hadn't she just commented on their seemingly perpetual state of undress? But he looked so innocent and sounded so sincere. Where had his mind been then? She'd noticed his tension of late, a tension coming at odd moments such as the one just past. What was he thinking?

It was getting more difficult. Each day of bliss made it worse. *Think of today, only today*, Leslie told herself. But it didn't work. There was tomorrow, and the tomorrow after that . . . and so on until she was back in New York. Would she see Oliver then? Could she possibly reconcile her far slower life-style with his faster one? Did she want to? Did he want her to? All she knew was that she wanted Oliver. Very desperately.

"Hey, what's this?" he asked with exquisite tenderness as he dabbed a tear from the corner of her eye. Without awaiting her answer, he closed his arms about her and hugged her tightly.

"I don't think I like the idea of getting dressed," she said in a soft, sad voice.

"Neither do I, but we'll have to sooner or later. You know that, don't you, Les?" His deeper meaning was as glaring as the sun upon open waters.

"Oh, yes."

He drew his head back to look at her. His jaw was tight, his expression closed. "You also know that I'm not letting you go, don't you?"

His vehemence surprised her as much as it pleased her. "No, I didn't know that," she whispered.

"Do you mind?"

She shook her head. Mind? *Mind?* The first hint that he wanted to see her back in New York . . . how could she possibly mind? True, there'd be mammoth hurdles to clear. True, she might stumble and fall. But . . . what if she took it one day at a time, much as she'd tried to do here? Wouldn't it be better than nothing at all?

"Of course I don't mind," she answered, eyes misty, a smile on her lips.

"Good. Then what say we get dressed and go into town. There's something I want to pick up."

"Sounds fine."

"And brunch on the quai, a drive around the island, the afternoon on the beach?"

"Um hmm."

"And dinner . . . a last night out?"

She swallowed down the knot that was so very quick to form. "You bet."

He kissed her then, each eye in turn, then the tip of her nose, then her mouth. Sucking in a shaky breath, he hugged her tight, then, head down, moved back and took her hand. Leslie could have sworn he was as affected by the moment as she, but how much of what she saw was a product of what she wanted to see, she didn't know. Wishful thinking was a dangerous thing. Dangerous . . . though irresistible.

It was a busy day, this, their last full one on St. Barts. By unspoken design, they kept their minds occupied with the pleasure of what they saw, said and did. It was as though each feared the thoughts that, given idleness, might creep in and begin to fester.

Gustavia seemed more alive than ever. They walked, then brunched—then, to Leslie's horror, stopped at the jewelry shop Oliver had obviously visited earlier that week, to pick up a beautiful gold necklace he'd purchased. It was a serpentine chain whose central links had been removed to make way for a single amethyst. The stone matched her eyes perfectly. Only when he lifted the chain from its box and started to put it around her neck, though, did she realize he'd bought it for her.

"I can't accept this, Oliver," she breathed. "It's . . . it's too much!"

"Not too much. Just right. It was made for you, your birthday present. I'm sorry it's late." He deftly hooked the clasp, then straightened the chain and stood back to admire the way it nestled against her skin.

Leslie raised a trembling finger to touch the warm amethyst. "But you didn't have to—There was no need. . . ." Then, embarrassed, she scowled. "Tony didn't put you up to this, did he?"

For a minute she thought Oliver would hit her. His eyes grew dark, his features fierce. "No, Tony didn't put me up to it. I thought of it all by myself."

"I'm sorry," she said quickly, reaching out to grasp his arm, "that wasn't what I meant." In pain, she looked down. "It's just that it's so beautiful . . . and the thought that went into it. . . . I . . . I wanted, needed to know the thought was yours." Dropping her hand, she turned away. "I guess I'm not very good at accepting gifts. So often they've either been too easily come by, or given with an ulterior motive."

"Oh, sweetheart," he moaned and turned her to him. Placing his hands on her shoulders, he lowered his head to look at her. Her eyes lifted slowly as he spoke. "I want you to have this just . . . because."

"Just . . . because?" she echoed timidly.

"Just because you're you and I'm me, and together we've had a pretty wonderful week. I want you to have this so that when we get back to New York—" his features stiffened imperceptibly "—you'll be able to touch your throat and remember what we've shared."

"I could never forget," she murmured, entranced by the goodness he exuded. "Never, Oliver."

"I hope not," he rasped, then crushed her against him with a kind of desperation that was to remain with them through the rest of their stay. It poked its head through the palm fronds when they played on the beach that afternoon. It was propped between the salt and pepper shakers when they had dinner out that evening.

Later that night their lovemaking was slower and more intense than it had been. It was an expression of all the things they'd meant to each other during the week—of fresh lemonade, wine and cheese and Scrabble, of gentle and intimate talk about nothing in particular, of loving and living and counting one's blessings for the moment, of a gold chain with an amethyst at its heart. Particularly when they awoke again at dawn to desire and to each other was there a desperation in it, a kind of grasping and seeking and holding to something that might never come again. For that was precisely what Leslie feared. With the north would come the cold and the real world and all the differences she could only imagine to exist between herself and this man who'd made such a thorough conquest of her heart.

As a couple boarding the small island-hopper Sunday at noon, they were subdued. Transferring to the larger jet on St. Martin, they were distracted. Arriving in New York in the dark to subfreezing temperatures, they were visibly tense. Only when Oliver put Leslie in a cab headed for her home on the island, though, did she come close to breaking.

"Oliver?" She raised a frantic gaze to his, prepared to blurt out her love, prepared to plead, prepared to do most anything to prolong the inevitable parting.

"Shh. I'll call you. Okay?"

Don't call me. I'll call you. Her heart plummeted to her frigid toes. "Okay." She flashed him a plastic smile, swallowed hard, then turned and let the driver take her home.

7

Oliver stood at the curb for what seemed hours after Leslie's cab had pulled away. With his eyes he followed it as it dodged other vehicles and slowed, then entered the airport's exit road and sped forward, finally disappearing around the bend that would take it to the parkway and on to her home.

A part of him was in the cab. He wasn't sure how or when it had happened—whether he'd first fallen in love with her honest smile or her ready wit or her breasts in the sun or her mushroom omelets. Hell, it might have been the lavender leprechaun, stuffed-up and sneezing, for whom he'd first fallen. But he'd fallen. No doubt about that. He'd fallen hard. And, damn it, he didn't know what to do!

He'd made a mess of it with his whimsy of shaking the image and existing solely as a man. It had backfired! He'd simply been pigeonholed differently.

Leslie knew him as a model. Oh, yes, it had had its moments, and it was certainly flattering. Only trouble was that she loved him. He was sure of it. Leslie, who believed in, who needed honesty above all, was in love with a man who had deceived her from the start.

"Hey, fella, we're holdin' up the line. You wanna cab or not?"

Snapped from his brooding, Oliver looked down at the body sprawled from the driver's seat toward the passenger's window, at the face scowling up at him. With a curt nod he opened the back door, picked up his bags and tossed them in, then followed them. After giving his Manhattan address to the cabbie, he slouched against the door, his fist pressed to his mouth, and stared blindly into the arena of headlights and taillights they entered.

Was it deceit? Or simply evasion? He'd never lied, but had told only half the truth. He did model, though it was purely a hobby and something he did far less frequently than he'd let Leslie believe. If only he *could* model more often! But his practice was more demanding than it had ever been. Demanding, challenging . . . rewarding. Even now he wondered what bizarre messages he'd find awaiting him when he got home. Then his thoughts turned to Leslie, and he lost interest in bizarre messages.

She'd been as upset as he when they'd left St. Barts. A healthy tan notwithstanding, she'd looked as pale as her hand had felt cold. They'd said little to each other. He knew she'd hoped for something, but he'd been stymied.

He'd tried. He had tried. Even if she hated him when she learned the truth, she'd have to admit that he'd tried. And every time, she'd hushed him, saying she hadn't wanted to know, that it wasn't important. So why hadn't he pushed? He'd always been strong and convincing, never one to let a woman deter him when he'd had something to do or say. But . . . he'd never been in love before. And Leslie was a woman like no other he'd known.

The cab swerved. The cabbie swore. From his slouched position Oliver muttered an oath and thrust a hand through his hair. New York looked ugly, all dark and gray and spattered with mud from the snow that must have recently fallen. So different from the sunshine and heat of St. Barts. Damn, but he felt cold inside!

Seeking warmth, he wearily dropped his head back and conjured up memories from the week now past. It worked for a time. As the cab sped onward, snaking in and out of the parkway traffic, he thought of the villa, the beach, bubbling Gustavia . . . and Leslie through it all. The times he'd spent alone at the start of the week had mysteriously fallen from mind. The images that remained were of time they'd spent together—living, laughing, loving.

But Oliver Ames, more than most, knew that one couldn't exist wholly in a world of memories. In addition to past, one needed present and future. Present and future. The present was a dingy cab fighting its way across town now, through congested Manhattan streets. The future was a confrontation he feared as he'd never feared anything before. So much was at stake. So very much.

The cab lurched through the Sunday-evening traffic, forging steadily onward until at last it came to an abrupt halt at the door of his building. Oliver dug his wallet from his trousers' pocket, thinking how strange it felt in his hand after a week without it. He tugged out several bills and paid the cabbie, then hauled himself and his belongings from the cab.

The doorman was on the spot. "Good evening, Dr. Ames. Would you like a hand?"

Oliver dipped his head in response to the greeting, held up a hand in refusal of the offer, then headed through the door that the attendant had opened. Eighteen floors later, he was in his own apartment.

Leaving his bags by the door, he easily found his way in the darkness down the two steps into the sunken living room, where he collapsed in a sofa and dropped his head into his hands. Then, propping his chin on his palms, he studied the dark.

He missed her already. It was so quiet here. Not that she made much noise, but just knowing she might be in another room would have lightened the atmosphere of the place.

What was he going to do? For three days now, since Thursday, when they'd spent the day together and then made love and he'd realized just how deeply he was in over his head, he'd been trying to decide. He could call her right now and blurt out the truth, counting on her love to master her anger. Or he could make a date for tomorrow night or Tuesday night, and then tell her the truth. He could send her a letter of confession and follow it up with two dozen long-stemmed roses. Or he could storm over to her place and confess it all in person. As a last resort, he could always abduct her, break the news, then hold her prisoner until she forgave him.

Damn Joe Durand! It sounded as though Leslie had been leery enough of deception before Joe had come along, but his shoddy treatment of her had cemented her feelings. Now Oliver had inadvertently stepped in the muck Joe had left, and his feet were stuck. He felt like such a heel! A heel!

Eyes wide, he threw his head back, then gave a savage push and left the sofa. Flipping on the lights by the door, he grabbed his bags, strode angrily down the hall to his bedroom, tossed the cases onto the bed, then stood glaring at them.

"Damn!" Crossing to the bedstand phone, he picked up the receiver, held it midair for a minute, then scowled at it and slammed it down. He stormed back down the hall, paused overlooking the living room and stood, hands on his hips, frowning.

He lived in the lap of luxury in this coop with its prestigious East Side address. Maybe she wouldn't be surprised at it; after all, she'd assumed him to be a successful model, and they reportedly did well. Rubbing a tired hand against the taut muscles at the back of his neck, he slowly descended the steps and perched on the arm of a chair.

He liked this place. He'd certainly worked hard enough for it. Plush carpeting, cushiony upholstered sofas and chairs, lacquered coffee tables and wall units bearing unique mementos from one trip or another—a far cry from the cramped duplex his parents had rented all those years. He thought of the pleasant garden condominium he'd recently helped them buy, and smiled. They were comfortable; they deserved it.

In its idle wandering, his gaze tripped over loose pillows of the same rich browns and beiges and grays as the rest of the room before falling on the ancient brass spittoon he'd picked up in Wales. It was a planter now, bearing a small fig tree. Standing, he walked over to finger the oval leaves. It wasn't doing well—it needed sun and warmth. He snorted.

He needed sun and warmth, but his sun and warmth was Leslie. Did he look as despairing as the poor fig tree in front of him?

The jangle of the phone startled him. His head flew toward the kitchen. It was his private line ringing, not the business phone he kept in the den. In two strides he'd covered the distance and snatched up the phone.

"Hello?"

"Oliver, you're back! It's Tony. How did it go?"

"How're ya doin', Tony?" Oliver asked, trying to cover up his disappointment. For a split second he'd hoped it would be Leslie.

"Not bad . . . but tell me about *you*." His voice grew cautious. "She wasn't angry, was she?"

"As a matter of fact," Oliver began with a sigh, "she wasn't thrilled at first. But she came around."

Tony grinned. "I knew she would. You've got charm, friend. I knew you could handle her. It was a good week, then?"

"Great. You were right. The villa's gorgeous. So's the island. Bright sun every day. It never rained."

"Come on, Oliver. This is the guy you sweat with on the tennis court twice a month. I don't want a camp letter. I want some of that gut-spilling you guys love to provoke. Was it a good week?"

"It was a great week."

"And?"

"Any more is private."

"She's my sister, Ames. I wouldn't have sent you down there if I hadn't had hopes that you two might hit it off."

"Hit it off. . . ." Oliver smirked, rather amused by his friend's impatience. "You mean . . . *make* it?"

"I mean like each other." Tony grimaced. "The woman's impossible. I've tried again and again to introduce her to men I think she'll like, but she's just not interested. My happening to know the man in the Homme Premier ad was a bolt out of the blue."

Oliver shot a glance at the ceiling. "So it was a fix-up after all. Strange, I thought it was supposed to be a joke," he remarked grimly. Of course he'd known better than that. Tony Parish was transparent, at least when he, too, was sweating it out on the courts. But it didn't bother him to string Tony along. He needed someone to blame for the mess he was in.

"You didn't hurt her," Tony came back more quietly.

"No. I didn't hurt her. At least not yet."

Once more, deadly calm. "What are you talking about?"

Oliver rested one hand low on his hip and hung his head. "We had a wonderful week together. It was . . . unbelievable."

"So?"

"So—" he took a breath "—I think your sister's fallen in love with a man she believes to be a very glamorous male model."

"Male model? Didn't you tell her the truth?"

"That is the truth . . . albeit only a tiny part."

"And you didn't tell her the rest?" came the disbelieving voice.

"No."

Tony swore softly, then began to pace within the limits of the telephone cord. "You picked a great one to lie to—"

"I didn't lie."

"Then you picked a great one to be evasive with. Jeez, I don't believe it. I was sure you'd tell her everything within the first day or two. You're almost as straitlaced as she is!" He paced another round. "Do you have any idea what my sister thinks of deception? She's pretty opinionated on that score. Do you?"

"I didn't, then. I do now."

Tony had paused in his ranting long enough to hear the dejection in Oliver's voice. "Are you all right?" he asked, cautious again.

"No, I'm not!" Oliver exploded, his own frustration needing outlet. "I've got to figure out some way of telling Leslie what I do without having her positively despise me for not having told her in the first place. I'm *not* all right. It's become an emotional issue; she's apt to hate me."

The voice on the other end of the line was instantly contrite. "And that matters to you?"

"Damned right it matters! Not that I'd particularly want you for a brother-in-law knowing that you concocted this cock-and-bull scheme in the first place . . . !"

Satisfied, Tony sat down in his chair. "She was the one with the idea, Oliver," he said indulgently. "I simply set it into motion."

"Same difference. Damn, it's hard."

"Can I help?"

"Don't you dare. As a matter of fact, don't you dare repeat a word of this conversation to Leslie! I may have made a mess of things, but it's my mess, and I'll be the one to clean it up."

"She's got fire in her."

He gave a wry nod. "Tell me."

"Think you can handle her?"

"I'll handle her."

"Okay, pal." Tony was smiling broadly. "And Oliver?"

"Yeah?"

The smile grew more mischievous. "Good luck." If anyone could handle Leslie Parish, her brother mused, Oliver Ames could. Despite this minor and surely temporary misunderstanding, things had worked out well indeed.

Oliver wasn't in quite as optimistic a frame of mind when he hung up the phone. Love did strange things to otherwise rational people. It made them lose perspective and overreact. That was what he wanted to avoid.

Back in the living room, he opened the bar and poured himself a drink. Its warmth was the first he'd felt since . . . since he'd made love to Leslie so early that morning. Just that morning—it was hard to believe. He remembered every sweet moment; even now could feel the fragile shape of her in his hands. She'd been so honest and giving in her lovemaking. She'd lived true to her word. Not for a minute, though she hadn't said it aloud, had she hidden from him the fact of her love. And not for a minute did Oliver believe that he was vainly imagining it. He hadn't asked for love, hadn't gone looking for it. But feeling the all-consuming need he had to be with and share with and do for Leslie, seeing an identical desire written on her face time and again, he knew. Leslie loved him. He loved her. All that remained was for him to tell her what he'd done and why.

Bidden in part by determination, in part by the sheer need to hear her voice, he returned to the kitchen and lifted the phone. Information quickly gave him her number. As quickly he punched it out. The phone rang once, then a second time.

"Hello?" She sounded breathless, as though she'd come running.

"Leslie?"

A smile lit her voice. "Hi," she said softly.

"You got home all right," he ventured likewise.

"Uh huh. And you?"

"Fine." The sound of her voice was an instant balm. Perched atop his high kitchen stool, he felt himself begin to relax. "How are you?"

"Okay. I'm . . . cold."

"I know the feeling." It was only incidentally related to the abrupt change in temperature to which their bodies had been exposed in the past few hours. "Your house was okay? No problems?" She lived in a small Tudor home on a wooded lot, she'd said. He worried about her being so alone.

"Just quiet." Her voice fell to a whisper. "And lonely."

"I miss you," he murmured in lieu of taking her in his arms and kissing her loneliness away.

"Me too." She paused then and, sensing that she wanted to go on, he gave her time. "Oliver," she began again and timidly, "when will I see you?"

The utter smallness of her voice cut him to the quick. He could imagine how she'd fought asking. She'd want to be sophisticated and cool and unclinging. He hated himself for having forced her hand, though he found solace in this further evidence of her love.

"That's why I'm calling, sweetheart. I'd like us to spend next weekend together. Just the two of us at my place up north. I could pick you up Friday night and have you back Sunday. How about it?"

"I'd love to, Oliver." Her voice glowed. In turn he smiled.

"I wish it could be sooner. Friday sounds so far off. But this week will be crammed . . . after last."

Her laugh was a light, airy sound that made him float. "What is it this week . . . say, what *do* you do, other than cologne?"

His bubble threatened to burst. "Oh, clothing and stuff. Have you spoken to Tony?"

"Not yet. I'll have to give him a call to thank him for my . . . birthday present." Her voice lowered. "Thank you again."

"For what?"

"For . . . taking care of me when I was sick, for making the rest of the week so wonderful, for the necklace."

"Are you wearing it now?" Closing his eyes he pictured her as she'd stood before him last night, wearing nothing but the moonlight and that strip of gold with its amethyst eye.

"Yes. I'm wearing it," she murmured shyly.

"I'm glad." He smiled, then realized that he could sit forever saying small nothings to her. But he wanted to tell her he loved her—and he feared doing that. "Well, then, how does six on Friday sound? We can stop for dinner on the way."

"Sounds perfect."

"I'll be looking forward to it." His voice was suddenly lower and faintly hoarse.

"Me too."

"Take care, Les."

"You too. And Oliver?"

"Yes?"

"I . . . I . . . thanks for calling."

"Sure thing, sweetheart. See you Friday."

For several minutes after hanging up the phone, he sat where he was, basking in the glow that lingered. She was a wonder . . . so thoroughly lovable. And she'd had more courage than he. She'd nearly said it. I love you. Why couldn't he say the words? He admitted them freely to himself, had even implied them to Tony. Was it that he'd feel hypocritical telling Leslie he loved her while he knew he'd been less than forthright on other matters? Was it that he feared she might not believe him in *this* when he finally did confess to his deception?

The glow was gone by the time he stood up, replaced by a shroud of concern. He'd tell her this weekend after they arrived at his place. They'd be isolated and, aside from his own car, more or less stranded. She'd be stuck with him. She'd have to hear him out. And he'd have the whole weekend to prove his love one way or the other.

That decided, he returned to the front hall and picked up the thick pile of waiting mail. An hour later he retreated to the den, pushed several buttons on his telephone console and sprawled out on the dark leather sofa with an arm over his eyes to listen to the phone messages for the week.

An hour after that he was ready to return to St. Barts.

Leslie, too, had gone through her mail and then taken to the phone, but in a more active capacity.

"Tony?"

"Les! How are you?"

"Great." Silence. She was grinning like a Cheshire cat. "Thanks, Tony. It was a super birthday present."

"Liked it?" he asked smugly.

"Uh huh."

"I thought you would. He's quite a guy."

"Uh huh."

"So." It was like pulling teeth, in addition to which, he felt decidedly duplicitous. "Will you be seeing him again?"

"Uh huh." Her pulse sped at the thought. "He's got a place in the Berkshires. We're going up this weekend."

"Great!" he exclaimed. So Oliver had decided to make his pitch in the Berkshires. Secluded. Romantic. *Good luck, pal.*

"How's everything here, Tony?"

"Fine. Busy. Dad's still in Phoenix."

"Still? I thought he was due back last week."

"He was. . . ."

She smiled. "But the golfing was too good."

Tony chuckled. "Something like that."

"And the kids are well?"

"Raising Cain in the other room. You mean you can't hear the noise?"

"Why aren't they in bed?"

"Because it's back to school tomorrow. And the law of adolescence says that one positively cannot be awake and aware on the morning following a school vacation. Heaven forbid they should be in condition to learn."

She laughed. "Perverse little things, aren't they? So why isn't their father laying down a law of his own?"

"Because he's talking with you."

"Oh. Good reason. Well, then I won't keep you long. I want to give Bren and Diane calls anyway. They're both doin' all right?"

"Brenda's fine. The kids had a ball skiing. She and Larry have about had it with lugging skis and poles and boots back and forth to the slopes, but otherwise Vail was to their liking." He paused, frowning. "Diane's the one who's got me worried."

"What's wrong?"

"I'm not sure. She's been behaving really strangely. She took off by herself last Monday and Tuesday, had Brad worried to death until he finally found a note buried at the bottom of the mail."

Leslie, too, was worried. Diane had always been a little high-strung, and it was obvious that she hadn't been happy of late, but she'd never disappeared before. "Where was she?"

"In a hotel."

"In the city?"

"Uh huh. Just sitting by herself. Thinking, she said. I couldn't get much more out of her. When she came home Tuesday night she was pretty subdued."

"How have things been going for her at the office?"

Tony sighed. "According to Gaffney, things have been tough. She's difficult to work with and getting worse all the time. Demanding and unpredictable. Very temperamental. Why don't you give her a call, Les? Maybe you can find out what's bothering her."

Leslie gave a facetious grunt. "I know what's bothering her. It's Brad."

"Come on. Brad's not that bad."

"Tony, he's fooling around, and you know it!"

"What else is new?"

"Diane knows it, too. Discretion has never been one of his stronger points."

"Yeah, but a lot of the time it's just talk—"

"Which can be nearly as hurtful."

"Come on, Les. I can't believe that Diane would be threatened by talk. Brad wouldn't go out of his way to humiliate her."

"You're sure of that?" she asked skeptically.

Tony hesitated, then gave vent to his own frustration. "Of course I'm not sure! The guy may be a great businessman, but we've never been terribly close. I can't know what he'd do. All I do know is that if Di doesn't shape up, he may have just cause to wander."

"That's an awful thing to say, Tony, particularly since he's the thing preventing her from shaping up! Okay, I'll grant that Diane's had other problems. But can you imagine how she must feel when she hears about each of Brad's little . . . diversions? *Your* wife was a wanderer. How did you feel?"

"A low blow, Les."

"And well aimed. How did you feel?"

He pondered her question, then spoke with uncharacteristic seriousness. Gone was all pretense of the invincible male. Left was a man whose home life had fallen apart. "Angry. Hurt. Confused. Embarrassed. Insecure."

Much the same way Leslie had felt when she'd discovered that Joe Durand was married. Much the way she couldn't help but feel at the thought of Oliver with . . . other women. . . .

"Thank you for being so honest," she said more gently. "Now try to think of Diane living with, or trying to live with, those same feelings."

There was a meaningful silence. "Isn't that something she's got to work out with Brad? We can't give her much more than emotional support."

"Exactly. Let me call her. Maybe she'll talk to me. Sometimes just being able to air things helps."

"You know, Les," Tony breathed over the phone, "you're a good person."

"I'm her sister."

"There was a time way back then when you wanted nothing to do with the Parishes," he reminded her softly. "We thought we'd lost you to the West Coast."

"I needed breathing room, Tony. I still do. I guess I'm just fortunate in that I've found plenty of it."

She heard a riot of sounds in the background, then Tony's voice aimed away from the phone. "Leave him alone, Jason! If you boys don't. . . . Mark, go upstairs!" The voice returned. "Listen, hon, I've got to run."

"So I hear. Go ahead, Tony. I'll call Di. And . . . thanks again for Oliver."

Her brother smiled warmly. "My pleasure. And many happy returns."

Mirroring his smile, Leslie hung up the phone. Memories of Oliver warmed her for the moment. Then, unable to shake her concern, Leslie did put in a call to Diane. A disgruntled Brad announced that she was in her room reading and had left orders not to be disturbed. Reluctant to force the issue and possibly increase the tension between husband and wife, Leslie simply left word that she'd call the next day.

It was easier said than done. Round and about her own hectic schedule, she tried to reach Diane at the office three times. Each time she was out. It was not until after dinner that evening that Leslie finally made contact. What ensued was the most unproductive conversation she'd ever held with another adult human being.

"Di?" When there was no sound of recognition, she identified herself. "It's me. Leslie." When there was still no sound, she prodded gently. "Are you there?"

"Yes."

"How are you?" When again there was silence, she babbled on. "I tried you last night after I got back from St. Barts, but you were reading."

"I'm okay."

"Are you sure? You sound awful."

"Thanks."

"I didn't mean that in offense. Just concern." Silence. "Is everything all right there?"

"Yes."

She dared. "Brad's okay?"

"Yes."

"Hey, I'm not interrupting dinner, am I?" There had to be some excuse for her sister's curtness. Perhaps she and Brad were in the middle of a fight, and Brad was standing right there.

"No."

"Listen, maybe we could meet for lunch one day this week."

"Maybe. I'll get back to you."

"How about Wednesday?" Leslie blurted. Tomorrow sounded too obvious.

"I don't know. I'll have to get back to you."

"Will you?" Even in the best of times, Diane was notoriously bad at returning calls. It was one of the things her business associates were always yelling about.

"Yes."

"Try to make it Wednesday."

"I'll call you."

"Please, Di. I'd really like to talk." Leslie tried to make it sound as though she were the one with the problem. The subtle suggestion went right over her sister's head.

"I said I'd call you," Diane snapped back impatiently.

"Okay, Di. Talk with you then."

Diane hung up the phone without another word, at which point Leslie promptly called Brenda. Between them they were no closer to knowing what to do about Diane.

"Maybe something happened at the office?" Leslie suggested in trying to explain Diane's sudden turn for the worse.

Brenda sighed. "Possible. Not probable."

As Leslie had talked with Tony, she now raised the issue of their sister's shaky emotional state with Brenda. "So what do we do?" she asked: Of the three other Parishes, Brenda was the only one she'd ever leaned on. Capable and serious in business matters, Brenda had a level head on her shoulders. Ironically, the errors she'd made in her personal life were attributable to this very compulsion for order.

"We keep the lines of communication open. You'll have lunch with her Wednesday—"

"Wait a minute. I was the one who proposed Wednesday. Diane refused to commit herself. I'd put money on the fact that she won't even call me."

"Then you'll call her again. Try tomorrow night. Bug her until she caves in."

"I'm telling you, Bren, she really did sound like stone."

"I know. But she'll be all right."

"Maybe she needs professional help," Leslie ventured cautiously, though she could have predicted Brenda's response. None of the Parishes were fans of psychiatry, though Brenda was worse than the others. A computer person at heart, she believed there to be a sane, systematic, physical explanation for just about everything that happened in life. When her first marriage fell apart, she considered it a victim of the occupational hazard of being a full-time working mother. There simply had not been hours enough in her life to accommodate a demanding husband. Larry, her second, was a warmer, more easygoing man who was very satisfied to take Brenda when she was free. In turn, Brenda seemed free more often, though she'd never admit to the deep emotional need she had for Larry. He, saint that he was, was confident enough not to demand such a confession.

"A shrink?" Brenda asked with obvious distaste. "I doubt it. No, there has to be something more immediate that's causing her to clam up and act strangely. You're right. She's always been shaky. Which is all the more reason why something's got to have triggered her now."

"Well," Leslie sighed, discouraged, "I'll try to get her out with me. I'll let you know what happens."

As though her mind's computer had filed one document and called up another, Brenda's voice lightened. "Hey, you haven't told me about your trip."

Her trip. Mention of it brought an instant spot of warmth to her heart, an instant glow to her cheeks. "It was great." How much did Brenda know? Had Tony told her about his little "joke"?

"Lots of sun?"

Brenda's what-else-is-new tone said it all. She knew nothing. And Leslie wasn't about to enlighten her until she herself felt more sure of Oliver. On St. Barts he'd been unswervingly attentive. Back here, though, even in spite of a weekend date, it remained to be seen whether his seeming affection would hold up. Once he got back out in that faster, glittery world of his. . . .

"Yup," she answered with feigned lightness. "Lots of sun. I got a great tan."

"And rest?"

"That, too."

"Good. Okay, then, you'll keep me posted on Di?"

"Uh huh. Bye-bye, Bren."

Leslie hung up the phone thinking of Oliver. She'd been thrilled to hear from him earlier, after having spent the first agonizing hour at home convinced that he'd never call. Life on St. Barts had been so simple. Life in New York—ah, that was another matter. Theoretically, if she loved Oliver and he loved her, nothing could be simpler. But she could only guess at Oliver's feelings. He was a model and hence, to a certain extent, an actor. On St. Barts she would have sworn he loved her, but that had been part of the illusion she'd chosen to live. Back here, she just didn't know.

The weekend would only be telling to a point. He'd have had five full days to compare her with his other life. If he called on Thursday offering a lame excuse to cancel the weekend, she'd know. But even if the weekend went on as proposed and he was as wonderful as he'd been on St. Barts, would she be able to know for sure that he wasn't simply reliving his vacation fun, simply lusting his way through the weekend, using his home in the Berkshires as a substitute for the villa on St. Barts? Would she ever really know his feelings? More important, could she trust him fully enough to believe them? When she was with him, trust was automatic. But at moments away—at times such as these, of which there would be more and more—she doubted.

For Leslie, the week was a trying one, filled with highs and lows and very little in between. While it was wonderful getting back to work, wonderful being at work where her mind could be occupied, her free time was quite the opposite. She thought of the restlessness she'd felt so strongly before she'd ever left for vacation, and she realized—as she had on St. Barts—what ailed her. The house was quiet. Meals alone were not really meals at all. Despite a backlog of paperwork, evenings dragged. And an empty bed—an empty bed was cold and forbidding. Yet her thoughts of Oliver fluctuated violently. At times she was so very hopeful, so very buoyant and in love. At other times she was as down in the dumps as Diane appeared to be.

Ironically Diane's depression was the only thing that, in Leslie's free hours, gave her respite from her own love woes. As predicted, she didn't hear from Diane. Giving her the benefit of the doubt Leslie waited until Wednesday morning to call, striking out at the office, finally reaching her at home. No, she wasn't sick. No, she couldn't make it for lunch. No, she couldn't talk just then. Leslie hung up the phone more convinced than ever that something very definitely was wrong. On Wednesday night, with nothing better to do but brood about Oliver, she got in her car and drove to Diane's.

Brad answered the door. He was a man of average height, average looks, above-average business acumen and superaverage ego. Beyond that, he was thoroughly charming in a thoroughly contrived way.

He smiled broadly. "Leslie! What a surprise. We weren't expecting you. How are you?" He stood aside to let her in out of the cold but left the door conspicuously open.

"I'm fine. How are you, Brad?"

"Very well. Hey, nice tan you've got there. You must have been somewhere warm."

Diane hadn't told him. Well, Leslie reasoned, there was nothing so awful about that. Diane would have no cause to keep Brad informed of the details of her family's comings and goings. "I spent last week at the villa. It was beautiful. Is Diane in?"

He shot her his most regretful smile. "She's in but she's sleeping."

"Sleeping? It's so early. Is she all right?"

"Fine. She's fine. Just been working hard, and I think it's tiring her. She's been concentrating on some new designs for the fall line."

"I see." It wouldn't pay to say that Diane had been out of the office every time Leslie had called. "You're sure she's not angry with me? I've been trying to talk with her since I got back, and she's been practically incommunicado."

Brad gave a loud laugh. "That's Diane," he said, then feigned a conspiratorial whisper. "It's the prima donna in her. I'm sure she's not angry. She'll get back to you as soon as things clear up a little."

On the surface the words were innocent. Delivered by Brad, however, who stood with his hand on the open door, they bore deeper meaning. Leslie felt distinctly unwelcome.

She shifted her stance and fingered her keys. "Well, then, I won't disturb you. You will call me if there's any problem, won't you?"

"What problem could there possibly be?" Brad asked, throwing his arm around her shoulder in a spurious show of affection that successfully turned her toward the door. *Not as subtle as usual*, Leslie mused, then reminded herself that she'd never been a great fan of Brad's. Even before he'd launched his playboy routine, she'd found him far too pretentious for her taste.

"Well, if there's anything. . . ."

"She'll be fine. Take my word for it."

He sent her on her way with a brotherly kiss on the cheek. Once in her car, Leslie quickly wiped it off and pulled out of the drive, reluctantly concluding that she'd done her best. Yes, she was still worried about Diane. But if Diane didn't want her help and Brad didn't want her help, she could only butt in so far. Besides, she was suddenly in the mood for thinking about Oliver.

As she drove home, she thought of how much more handsome he was than Brad. While she lingered on her living-room sofa over a cup of tea, she thought of how much more sincerely he came across. When she climbed into bed with a book, she thought of how he, and he alone, electrified her senses. Finally, despairing of concentration, she turned out the light and, setting doubts aside, gave herself up to dreams of how beautiful the coming weekend would be.

Unfortunately her dreams were to remain unfulfilled. Leslie had barely stepped foot in the house after work on Thursday when the phone rang. She nearly panicked. Her relief at finding that it wasn't Oliver calling to cancel on her was short-lived.

It was Brad, in a state of panic himself. "You've got to get over here, Leslie! I don't know what to do!" Gone was all pretense of composure. He sounded frantic.

Leslie's stomach lurched. "What is it, Brad? What's happened?"

"She spent the day in her room. When I got home a little while ago I found that she'd been on a silent rampage."

"What are you talking about?"

"Her scissors. She's taken her scissors to the sheets, the pillows, the drapes, the clothes . . . it's a mess!"

Images of destruction had begun to form in Leslie's mind's eye. "Calm down, Brad," she said, trying desperately to stay that way herself. "What's she doing now?"

"That's the problem. Now she's in the dining room breaking dishes. She just stands there throwing them on the floor. When I try to stop her she aims at me! You've got to come over, Leslie! I can't seem to get through to her. Nothing I say registers. I don't know what to do!"

Nerves in a bundle, Leslie hung her head and pressed her fingers to her temple. "Okay, Brad." She thought aloud. "You stay there. I'll be right over. Did you call Tony?"

"What can Tony do? He's about as understanding as a bulldozer!"

Though on the surface brother and brother-in-law had always gotten along, Leslie could understand that Brad was, in his way, intimidated by Tony. "Okay. I'll take care of it. You watch Diane and make sure she doesn't hurt herself. I'm on my way."

Pressing the cut-off button, she punched out Tony's number. Since he'd taken over as president of the company, he'd also taken over as head of the family. It was the handing of power down a generation, with the senior Parish happy to hold no more than a purely titular position.

Leslie impatiently tapped her foot as the phone rang repeatedly. The receiver was finally lifted just as an angry voice finished its statement, ". . . always the one who has to!" The voice lowered. "Hello?"

"Mark?"

"It's Jason."

"Jason. This is Aunt Leslie. Is your dad home yet?"

"Yeah. Just a minute."

"Thanks."

She raised her eyes to the ceiling, praying he'd hurry. When she heard a rustle at the other end of the line, she readied herself.

"Leslie?"

"Tony! Thank heavens you're there."

"You sound hassled, Les. What's up?"

"It's Di. Brad just called. She's gotten worse."

"How . . . worse?"

"Violent."

"Violent? *Diane?*"

As calmly as she could, Leslie related what Brad had told her. "I'm going over there now. Brad doesn't have the foggiest as to what to do. Not that I do, but she needs *something*." When Tony remained silent, she prodded. "What do you think? Should we call someone? I mean, I'm not thrilled with the idea, but I'm nervous. It's fine and dandy to overlook strange behavior in the hopes it will go away, but when strange turns violent, it's scary."

Tony hesitated for only a minute. "I agree. Listen, I'll get on the phone. You go on over and see what you can do. I'll meet you there as soon as I can."

"Thanks, Tony," Leslie said, then quickly hung up and reached for the coat she'd discarded just moments, before. Tony was good at this type of thing—identifying resources, sifting through to find the cream of the crop. She felt assured that he'd come up with a qualified professional to treat Diane.

The scene at Brad and Diane's was gut-wrenching.

"Where is she?" Leslie asked the subdued Brad who answered the door. His face was pale, his hair disheveled. He bore a look of shock; she couldn't help but wonder how he'd managed to be so ignorant of Diane's mental state that he hadn't seen this coming. Then she chided herself for her insensitivity. The man's wife was falling apart. Cad he might be, yet he had a right to be upset.

"She's in the den," he said grimly.

Leslie glanced toward the dining room. Even from where she stood she could see shards of fine white china littering the oak floor and overflowing onto the rug. She frowned and looked around, listening. "She's quiet?"

"She ran out of plates. And steam, I guess. She's just sitting there crying."

Thrusting her coat toward Brad, she headed that way without a word. On the threshold, she faltered. Diane sat, a petite form in a long white robe, curled in an oversize arm-chair in the corner. Head bent, one hand to her face and another tucked against her waist, she was a pathetic figure.

"Di," Leslie whispered in agony, leaving the door and quickly crossing the room. She knelt before her sister's chair and placed her hands on its arms for support. "Di, what is it? Di?"

Diane's sobbing was quiet and internal, far different from the violent behavior she'd exhibited earlier. When she continued to cry, Leslie coaxed her gently.

"Diane, it's me. Leslie. I want to talk. Come on. Say something."

Very slowly Diane raised tear-drenched eyes. Time seemed to fly back to the day she'd been eighteen and had lost the most important gymnastic competition of her life. She looked crushed.

"Leslie?" she murmured in a small, high voice.

As though Diane were one of her preschoolers rather than actually two years older than her, Leslie reached up to tuck a long brown wave of hair from her cheek. "What is it, Di?" she asked gently. "What's bothering you?"

"Oh, Les," Diane began with a new rush of tears, "I've . . . made a mess of . . . things. I've really . . . blown it."

Leslie took her hand and held it firmly. "No, you haven't. Everything can be put to rights."

Diane was shaking her head even as Leslie spoke. "No. No. You don't understand. It's . . . everything. I'm lousy at the office. They override every decision I make. I'm lousy here. He finds his pleasure everywhere else—"

"No, Di—"

"It's true!" Diane cried, eyes suddenly flashing. "I hate him! I hate all of them!"

"Shhhh. You don't mean that—"

"I do!"

For a minute Leslie just rubbed the back of her sister's hand. If Diane were indeed four years old, she'd know what to say. Even now her temptation was to acknowledge that she had simply thrown one hell of a temper tantrum and now just needed a good talking to. But it wasn't that simple. Diane wasn't four; she was thirty-two. And her temper tantrum had involved acts that could easily have been harmful to herself. Then there had been the days of depression beforehand. . . . Where was Tony? Where was help?

"You may feel that way now, Di, but you're angry."

"I'm . . . not . . . angry. . . ." She dissolved into tears again.

Rising from her kneeling position, Leslie perched on the arm of the chair and tried to put her arm around her sister. When Diane resisted, burrowing more deeply into the cushions, Leslie had to settle for her hand again.

"Can I get you anything? A glass of wine? Warm milk?"

Crying softly, Diane simply shook her head.

"How about lying down?"

"I . . . can't. The room's destroyed."

"You could lie down on the sofa here." She started to get up. "I'll get a blanket—"

"No! I . . . don't want . . . to lie down!"

Feeling totally inadequate in the role of therapist, Leslie patted her hand. "Okay, hon. We'll just sit here."

"You don't have . . . to stay. . . ."

"I know."

"I'm . . . such a burden. Now to you, too."

"You're not a burden," Leslie argued ever so softly and urgently. Her face bore a pained expression. She didn't think she'd ever seen such dire unhappiness, such raw despair as she now saw on her sister's face.

Then she glanced up and, in a wave of relief, saw Tony stride through the door. Her gaze fell again to Diane, and she wondered what her reaction would be to seeing him.

"Diane?" Tony said, hunkering down before her much as Leslie had done at first. "Are you all right?"

Diane looked up in alarm. "Tony! You . . . shouldn't be . . . here!" she cried between sobs, wrenching her hand from Leslie's to cover her face with it. "I don't want . . . you to see. . . ."

"Diane, I've brought someone with me. He'd like to talk to you."

Only then did Leslie look up, her expression hopeful in a desperate kind of way. Then she froze. Her eyes grew larger. Hopefulness yielded to confusion, creating such a whir of sounds in her head that she barely heard Tony's words.

"This is Dr. Ames, Diane. He's going to help you."

8

Shocked, Leslie watched as Tony straightened and moved aside to let Oliver take his place. Dr. Ames. *Dr.* Ames? The man in question shot her a somber glance before turning his attention to Diane.

"Hi, Diane," he said in a low, gentle voice. "Not feelin' great?"

Diane looked up, first at Tony, then Leslie, her tear-streaked face accusing them of betrayal. "What is this?" she whispered.

Leslie couldn't possibly have answered. She felt numb, as stunned as Diane. Tony chose not to answer. It was Oliver who came to the rescue.

"I'd like to help you."

"But . . . you're a . . . psych. . . ."

"A psychiatrist. That's right." His voice was miraculously calm in light of the anguished expression he sent toward Leslie, who was far too busy comprehending his words to begin to see the pain accompanying them.

A psychiatrist? It had to be some kind of joke. This was Oliver of Homme Premier fame. Free heart. Golden boy. The man she'd once actually thought to be a gigolo. *Her* Oliver. His skin bore its familiar tan, his features their familiar shape. And the silver C behind his ear—it was there as well.

Yet something was different. Was it the tailored slacks he

wore, or the blazer or shirt or tie? Was it the air of authority about him? But he'd had that even on St. Barts. Now, though, it was . . . professional.

Stupefied, Leslie raised glassy eyes to Tony, who was looking directly at her. Obviously feeling Diane to be in the best of hands, his concern had shifted. In an instant Leslie realized that he'd known all along. Of course. They played tennis together, didn't they? They were friends. Tony had known just whom to call tonight.

Feeling superfluous at the moment and badly in need of fresh air, Leslie stood abruptly and started for the door. But Oliver caught her arm. His voice was calm, his expression well schooled. Only his fingers, fiercely circling her wrist, betrayed the intensity of emotion within him.

"Why don't you wait in the other room," he ordered softly. "I'll be out to talk with you in a minute."

Releasing her hand he turned back to Diane, to all appearances having done nothing more than offer support to the distraught relative of his patient. Tony knew better. He followed Leslie out, leaving Oliver to deal with Diane.

Feeling on the verge of suffocation, Leslie ran to the front door and opened it. She stood gasping the cold air when Tony reached her.

"Leslie?"

She shot him a look of bewilderment, then looked back out at the driveway, a bleak winter scene.

"It's all right, Les. There's really nothing so terrible about a psychiatrist."

"A psychiatrist?" she echoed dumbly. "I can't believe it. He's a model. A handsome model."

"No, Les. He's a handsome psychiatrist who happens to model on the side."

"But I . . . he can't . . . I never. . . ." She shook her head in confusion and slumped sideways against the door.

"Come on in, Les. You'll catch cold."

"I've already had my cold. He took care of me. A doctor . . . damn!"

"It's really no big thing—"

"No big thing?" she exclaimed, turning the force of her upheaval on Tony. "That's easy for you to say! You weren't the one who spent the week with the guy! You weren't the one who believed his lies!" And he certainly wasn't the one who'd fallen in love. In deep pain, she turned her head. "He didn't tell me," she murmured. "All that, and he didn't tell me. . . ."

Watching the agony his sister endured, Tony felt hamstrung. It would be so simple to tell her of Oliver's pain, but he'd promised his friend that he'd keep out of it. It was bad enough that the revelation had been forced upon them tonight; for that, too, Tony felt responsible. Too late he wondered if he might have been able to keep Leslie away from this house; unfortunately, at the time, he'd been more concerned with seeing that Diane was all right. Brad seemed useless. Even now he stood at the door of the den, his eyes downcast, his charm nonexistent.

"Come in from the cold, Les," Tony said again.

She looked up, uncomprehending at first, frowning in puzzlement. Then, as though suddenly given direction, she pushed off from the doorjamb and moved into the house, but only to put on the coat that Brad had dropped on a nearby chair.

Tony eyed her cautiously. "Where are you going?"

With her coat hanging open, she dug her keys from the pocket and turned to the door again. "Home." She felt numb and simply wanted time and space to consider what she'd learned.

"Wait, Les!. You can't leave!"

"Why not?"

"Diane. Diane needs you."

"Diane's got capable help. He is capable, I assume," she snapped sarcastically.

"The best. But she'll need our support, too."

"You stay here. And Brad's here, for what that's worth. I only know that I wouldn't be much good to her tonight." She was already outside and halfway down the steps.

"But Oliver said to wait—"

"Tell Oliver," she yelled on the run toward her car, "that I don't take orders from anyone! Least of all *him*!"

"Leslie . . . !"

But she had slammed the door and started the engine before he could say any more. He stood helplessly and watched as she whirled her car around and gunned from the drive, praying that she'd have the sense to slow down before she got herself killed. Glancing at his watch, he calculated the amount of time it would take for her to drive home. Then, vowing to call to make sure she was all right, he quietly closed the door and turned back toward the den.

Oliver had drawn a chair up close to Diane and continued to talk to her in a slow, soft reassuring manner. At Tony's return, he stood, squeezed her shoulder and walked to the door, where he gestured with his chin toward the hall. When Tony joined him there, he spoke in hushed tones.

"I think she's gotten the worst of it out of her system. She's tired and confused. I'll give her something to help her sleep." He glanced up briefly when Brad joined the conference, then swung his attention back to Tony. "Is there someone who can stay with her?" He frowned and looked around. "Where's Leslie?"

"She's gone home," Tony ventured hesitantly, at once aware of the way his friend's jaw tensed at the news.

Oliver thrust his fingers through his hair. "Swell," he muttered under his breath, then turned to Brad. "Your wife is upset. She'll need to rest and then talk with someone. I'll stay with her until she falls asleep. Can you get her to my office tomorrow morning?"

Unbelievably, Brad grew nervous. "You don't think she should be, uh, hospitalized?"

"No, I don't," Oliver decreed, his voice low and taut. "Hospitalization at this point would only upset her more."

"But what about what she's done?" Brad countered. "What if she wakes up and turns violent again?"

"She won't. She's let off the worst of the steam . . . and she's got our full attention. Now she needs our understanding and support."

"She doesn't want *me* to do anything for her," Brad went on in a sulking tone. "I tried before. She wouldn't let me near."

"That's because you're very much a part of her problem," Oliver stated with a decided lack of sympathy for the man who'd been so blind to his wife's worsening mental state. Tony had filled him in on the history of the Weitzes' married life, and though it wasn't Oliver's job to pass judgment, he couldn't deny his anger. Anymore than he could deny his need to get out of this house and go after Leslie. "Tony tells me you've got a housekeeper."

"Some help she is," Brad grumbled. "She's been hiding in the kitchen through all of this."

"Can I see her?"

"I guess so." With a parting glance of irritation toward the dining-room door, Brad stalked off toward the kitchen.

"Nice guy," Oliver couldn't help but observe.

"Yeah. But Diane loves him. At least she did."

"She still does or she wouldn't have gone off the deep end like this."

Tony grew more alert. "Has she, Oliver? What's the prognosis for this kind of thing?"

Oliver shrugged. "I've only talked with her for a few minutes. But between that and what you've told me, I think she's got very workable problems."

"You can help her?"

"In time." He frowned, his eyes clouding. "I just hope I'm the one to do it."

"Why not? You're the best."

He snorted. "Be that as it may, I happen to be emotionally involved with your *other* sister, and that fact could complicate my treating Diane." Hands in the pockets of his slacks, he crossed the hall to stand by the front bay window.

Tony was quickly by his side again. "Come on, Oliver. Don't make me go to someone else in a matter as sensitive as this."

Something in his voice, a note of urgency, pricked Oliver's curiosity. "Your family isn't big on psychiatry, is it?"

"Why do you say that?" Tony returned defensively.

"Because, among many families in your social stratum, psychiatrists have become standard fixtures. I'm surprised that none of you thought to call in someone earlier."

"We didn't want to interfere. We thought it was a matter between Diane and Brad. It wasn't until today that we realized how bad things were. Leslie's been trying to see Diane all week, but she'd put her off each time. . . ." When Oliver simply continued to stare expectantly at him, he scowled. "All right. We're not big on psychiatry. My mother was pretty unhappy during the last years of her life. We don't talk about it much, but I think we all agree that the guy she was seeing didn't do her much good."

"She was seeing a psychiatrist?" Leslie had never mentioned this. "Why?"

"Depression. Anger. Loneliness."

"With a husband and four kids?"

"It was the husband she wanted, and he was never around. What with business trips and all. . . ." He'd said enough, without elaborating on the "and all." "The kids could only fulfill certain needs. She had a slew of others that were never addressed."

"How did she die?"

"She didn't commit suicide, if that's what you're thinking. She had cancer. I think she just . . . gave up. Not much difference, I suppose."

Oliver was given no time to comment, for Brad returned with a shy-looking woman in tow. Introductions were made, at which point Oliver spoke kindly to the woman, asking her to check in on her mistress at intervals during the night. Diane was not to awaken alone. She was to be made comfortable and given food or drink or anything of the like that she wanted. And he was to be called if there was any further problem.

Returning to Diane, Oliver gave her a sedative and helped her upstairs to a bedroom at the opposite end of the house from the one she'd torn apart. All the while he talked quietly with her, demanding little, letting her speak as she wished.

The housekeeper brought the glass of warm milk he'd requested; he supported Diane while she drank. Then, denying the gremlins that thudded impatiently inside him, he sat by her bedside until the sedative took effect, leaving only when he was sure she was asleep.

Leslie wished she were out of it. Her mind was in a turmoil from which neither the sobering drive home nor her arrival at her own warm, familiar house nor a glass of her best and most mellow wine could rescue her. She picked up the mail, looked through it, put it down. She turned on the television, ran the gamut of channels, switched it off. She went to the refrigerator, stared at its contents, shut the door without touching a thing.

Wiping a single tear from her eye, she climbed the stairs to her bedroom and lay down in the dark. She felt hurt and tired, stretched taut by the emotions that gathered into a tight knot deep inside.

When the phone rang, she simply glared at it. Then it rang a second, a third and a fourth time and she realized that it might well be Brenda calling in concern about Diane.

"Hello?" she began cautiously, prepared to hang up if it was Oliver.

It was Tony. "Thank goodness," he breathed. "You got home all right."

"Of course I did," she answered in quiet relief, then growing irritation. "What could have happened?"

"The way you were driving, I wasn't sure."

"I'm all right."

"Are you?"

"Relatively speaking."

"He wasn't pleased that you'd left."

"Tough. How's Diane?"

"He took her to bed."

"Oh, great."

"He *brought her upstairs*. He gave her a sedative and said he'd talk with her until she drifted off."

"Then what?"

"Then he'll probably go after *you*."

Leslie scowled in frustration. "Then what does he have planned for Diane? One sedative and a good-night talk is hardly going to solve her problem."

"He'll see her in his office tomorrow."

"That's good of him."

"It is, given the fact that he's booked solid, and that he's got serious reservations about treating her, what with his relationship with you. Come on, Leslie. Ease up."

"Relationship with me," she muttered to herself. "*What* relationship? A relationship based on lies is nothing!"

Tony started to argue, then caught himself, fearing he'd only make things worse. "Listen," he said in his most placating tone, "Oliver will explain everything. I've got to run. I'll catch you later."

"Sure," Leslie murmured, hanging up the phone and lying back in the dark again. She didn't know how much time passed, only knew that she couldn't motivate herself to do anything but lie there and wonder how she'd managed to get hurt again. It hurt. It did hurt. As the numbness slowly wore off, the sting had begun.

When the front doorbell rang, she wasn't surprised. She'd known he would come. The male mind was very predictable when it came to bruised egos, and she'd bruised his with her refusal to hang around at Diane's house. No, it hadn't taken psychiatric wizardry to anticipate his move.

She lay in the dark listening. The bell rang again and again. When he began to pound on the thick wood, she simply turned onto her side and huddled in a tighter ball. When the back bell rang, again followed by knocking, she flipped onto the other side. She heard the vague echo of her name and found perverse satisfaction in his annoyance. His ego certainly was bruised; small solace for the tatters to which he'd reduced hers!

To her amazement, he gave up after several minutes. She grew more alert, listening closely for any sounds of his prowling outside. But what could she possibly hear? Her bedroom was on the second floor. It was the middle of winter. Snow blanketed the ground, providing a natural cushion for foot-steps, while thick storm windows blocked out not only the cold but extraneous noise as well.

It was spooky, she had to admit, lying here, wondering if she was being stalked. She sat up to listen. Slipping quietly from the bed, she stood at the door. Everything was still. Had he left, the coward? Had he tossed in the towel so eas-ily? Then it had been illusion, what she'd imagined he'd felt on St. Barts. Illusion and deception—all she detested.

A sound caught her ear and brought her instantly alert. A door shutting. In the kitchen? Then she heard footsteps and nearly panicked. Someone was in her house. Someone had broken in. The alarm . . . what had happened to the alarm? Had she actually forgotten to reengage it after she'd come in? Everything had been locked; she was sure of it. Hand on her thudding heart, she stood rooted to the spot, thinking she should call the police but waiting, waiting. . . .

"Leslie! Where are you? I know you're here!"

Her heart continued to thud, despite the wave of relief that swept over her. The footsteps came and went as he passed from area rugs to hardwood floors and back. He searched the living room, the dining room, the library, the den. On stock-ing feet she walked quietly from her bedroom door to the top of the stairs. Though the lower floor was bathed in light, she stood in darkness, waiting.

When Oliver reached the stairs and looked up, he saw her instantly. Hand on the end curl of the wood bannister, one foot on the lowest rung of the steps, he stared up at her for a moment.

"Come on down, Leslie," he said evenly, his manner tautly reined. "We have to talk."

"How did you get in?" Her voice was as tight as his.

"Through the garage. The lock on the inner door was easy to pick."

"That's breaking and entering, Oliver. Another of your surprise talents?" She hadn't moved, finding small comfort in the advantage of her raised position.

"The fact is," he snarled, whipping off his overcoat and

throwing it over the bannister, "that it was a lousy lock. You should be better protected than that. I'm surprised no one's broken in before."

"Someone has. I have an alarm system."

"It did one hell of a job just now."

"It wasn't on."

"Swell! Your insurance company would be real pleased! So you're one of those who feels that the little sticker on the front window is enough to scare away a thug?"

"It didn't scare *you* away. What would you have done if the whole system had gone off, and you'd found yourself surrounded by cops? It's hooked in to the police station, you know."

"I would have told them the truth. And I certainly would have had your attention."

"Oh, you've got my attention, all right," she spat. "You've had that since the first time I found you in my bed. Thing is that I could get you for perjury."

Oliver simmered. "Come downstairs, Leslie. I can't talk standing here like this staring up into the dark. I'd like to see your face."

Her fingers tightened on the wood railing. "Why? So you can gauge my reactions and gear your words accordingly? So you can analyze my frame of mind and plot your counterattack? So you can—"

"Leslie! Get down here!" he thundered, then swore softly and lowered his voice. "Please. It's been a long day for both of us. I'm tired and no more wild about this turn of events than you are."

"I bet you're not," she bounded on, driven by the anguish festering within. "I bet you'd have liked to have kept the charade going a while longer. Fun."

Oliver shot her a withering stare, reached up to loosen his tie, then turned and headed for the den. In her mind's eye, Leslie saw him approach the bar, remove a glass, open the small refrigerator below, extract the same bottle she had earlier and uncork it. Only when she heard the refrigerator door close with a thud did she very slowly start down the stairs.

He met her at its bottom holding two glasses, his own and the one he'd refilled for her. Head high, she took it from him without a word and padded softly into the living room. It was a larger room, not quite as intimate as the den and, for that very reason, never a favorite of hers. On this occasion, she mused, it would serve just fine. She needed the space. She also needed four-inch spikes; she felt suddenly much smaller and more insignificant than she had before. It took all her courage to settle calmly into the armchair and tip her head at its most arrogant angle toward Oliver.

She waited in silence, determined to do nothing to put him at ease. For ease was the last thing she felt. Looking at Oliver, vitally aware of his very presence in her home, she felt as though she were being torn apart. Strange, when Joe had come to her apartment that last time, she'd felt angry and strong and vindictive. Now, though, angry and vindictive were simply for show, while strong was nonexistent. What *did* she feel? She ached—inside, outside, everywhere.

Oliver took several gulps of wine, then tugged his tie looser and unbuttoned the top collar of his shirt. Anchoring one hand in the pocket of his slacks, he looked down at her. "I was going to tell you this weekend," he said quietly.

"Were you." It wasn't a question, rather a statement whose blatant mockery was quickly punished by the piercing arrow of his gaze.

"I would have told you as soon as we arrived in the mountains, once I'd isolated you from the world so you wouldn't be able to run out of the house and barrel off in your car. That was a dumb thing to do, Leslie!"

"That's strange." She gritted her teeth against the hurt. "I thought it was pretty smart. I wasn't needed there. Diane was well taken care of."

"And what about us?"

"We were well taken care of, too."

"Well taken care of . . . as in finished?" he asked, his voice grating. "Not quite."

She sipped her wine without tasting a drop. Then she took another sip, a larger one in search of the inner warmth that totally eluded her. She drew her legs up under her and wrapped her arms about her waist. "I think so," she murmured. "You've ruined everything."

"Only if you decide that I have," he countered firmly. His jaw was clenched, his shoulders rigid. "I'm not Joe Durand, Leslie. I did nothing immoral. And I didn't set out to hurt you. That was the last thing I wanted to do."

"You lied."

"I never lied."

"You said you were a model. Not a psychiatrist. A model."

"I am a model. You've seen my work. I pose every so often just for the fun of it. And I never said I *wasn't* a psychiatrist. I just—" his voice lowered "—didn't say that I was."

"And that's not lying?"

"Technically, no."

"Then you're splitting hairs, Oliver. You let me go on believing that . . . that . . . oh, what the hell." Eyes moist, she looked away and took a fast drink of her wine.

"Go on."

And give him the satisfaction of seeing how badly she ached? "No."

"You disappoint me," he taunted. "You're a woman of strong opinions. You mean to say that you've suddenly gone private with them? Where's the woman who asked point-blank why I'd choose to spend a quiet week at her Caribbean villa rather than live it up at a nearby hotel?"

"Maybe she's wary of the answers. Maybe she knows not to trust them anymore." Finding small satisfaction in seeing Oliver wince, she once again sank into a dark, brooding silence. Bowing her head, she didn't see him set his wine down on the nearby coffee table. Only when his hands settled on the arms of her chair did she grow aware of the large body bent over her.

"That's bull," his voice rumbled near her ear. "Her pride's been hurt, and she's vulnerable and in love—"

Leslie snapped her head up. "She is not!"

"No?" he hummed, his lips near her cheek.

Momentarily unable to function, she closed her eyes. He was close and warm and beckoning. His smell, clean and natural even at the end of the day, titillated her senses. All week she'd waited to be with him. She wanted him so badly. . . .

"No," she whispered, reinforcing the lie. If he could do it, so could she.

"I love you, Leslie," he murmured, his own eyes closed, his own senses absorbing her closeness. All week he'd waited to be with her. He wanted her so badly. . . .

"No!" she screamed, taking him by surprise and bolting past him. Oblivious to the slosh of wine over her hand, she ran to the fireplace and turned to face him. "No!" she cried, suddenly shaking all over. "I don't want to hear it! You had plenty of time to say it before. You had plenty of time to say everything before. Now it's too late. I can't believe any of it!"

"Leslie—" He started toward her.

"Don't come near me!" she yelled, cringing against the marble. When he continued forward, she tried to escape to the side, only to have her shoulders caught in the vise of his hands. "Let me go! I don't want you touching me!"

"You'll hear me out," he growled, then grunted when her foot hit his shin. Rather than releasing her, he slid his hands to her upper arms for better leverage, then with one hand relieved her of her endangered wineglass. "Childish, Les. Really childish."

"You must be used to it," she gritted, trying to push against his arms and free herself. "You're the expert on temper tantrums." She twisted and turned, but to no avail. Even when she brought her knee up, she was thwarted. Anticipating her ploy, he easily blocked the move.

"You told me about that little trick once before. Remember? You shouldn't have tipped your hand."

"I didn't think I'd need to try it on you. Let . . . me . . . go!"

"No way," he growled, all but carrying her to the sofa. "You're going to hear me out if it kills us both."

"And then where will Diane be? Where will your other

precious patients be? Where will the adoring public in love with the Homme Premier man be?"

Having shoved her into an upholstered corner, he stood over her, his hands on the sofa arm and back, barring her escape. "I don't give a good goddamn about anyone but you. And you will listen to what I have to say! Now, do I have to restrain you, or do you think you can try to behave yourself?"

"I am behaving myself," she said quietly.

He stared at her suddenly still form for a minute, then straightened. Taking a long, ragged breath, he walked to the far end of the room, turned back toward her, and tucked both hands in his pockets.

"When Tony suggested I spend a week on St. Barts, it sounded like a super idea. I was tired. I needed a vacation. When he told me about you and his little joke, I wasn't deterred. It sounded like fun, entirely harmless. Tony said you were the independent sort and that you'd probably go about your business as though I wasn't even there. Other than sharing laughs that first day, I didn't expect a thing."

"Got slightly more than that, didn't you," she murmured morosely.

"Slightly. I didn't expect an adorable purple elf with a whopper of a head cold bounding into my bedroom to wake me up."

"Adorable?" She screwed up her face. "As in puppy? Something you trick into fetching slippers solely for the sake of a stale biscuit?"

His tone softened. "Adorable as in fresh and pretty."

"Come off it, Oliver! I was sweaty and hot." The last thing she needed was his sweet-talking, given her peculiar susceptibility to it.

"Sweaty and hot, then fresh and pretty . . . and needing my care." He came several steps closer. "You don't know what that does to a man in this day and age, to feel needed."

She eyed him skeptically. "You're needed all the time! Look at the way Diane needed you, not to mention the crew of unhappy people who must have brooded around Manhattan while you were away."

"Professionally, fine. I was talking personally. And on a personal level, it's nice to feel needed once in a while."

"Polishes that image of the macho protector?"

His lips thinned. "The image of the macho protector is nothing compared to the one you're trying to project of the hard-bitten independent woman. Sarcasm doesn't become you, Les."

She had no smart retort. He was right. She didn't care for her tone any more than he did, and the fact that she was merely lashing out in anger did nothing to sweeten the bitter taste in her mouth. She dropped her gaze to the fingers clenched in her lap and listened as Oliver went on in a softer tone.

"You saw me as the man from the ad. To tell you the truth, I kind of enjoyed it." When she raised her head and took a breath to protest, he held up a hand. "No, no, Leslie. I'm not making fun of you. It was from a selfish standpoint that I enjoyed it. It was a new image for me. Believe it or not," he said less surely, "I needed that."

"I don't believe it," she said, but without sarcasm. She was puzzled. It didn't make sense. "What could possibly be wrong with being a psychiatrist?"

"Do you like psychiatrists?"

"No . . . but my situation is different. And my bias is strictly emotional. From an intellectual point of view, I respect the fact that you've had to make it through med school to get into psychiatry."

"Thank you," he drawled with a touch of sarcasm of his own, then grew more firm. "But most people don't think of that when they meet me. They think of how eager I must be to hear their problems, how good I must be at reading their minds, how neurotic I must be myself. When a psychiatrist meets people, they usually fall into two categories. There are those who treat him like he's got the plague, who are aloof, who won't go near him for fear that he'll see something deep inside that they'd rather hide. And there are those who flock to him and tell him everything." His face contorted. "Do you have any idea how boring that can be?"

"Don't you like your work?"

"I love my work . . . *when I'm working*. Not twenty-fours hours a day. Not when I want to relax. Not when I go to parties or dinners or the theater." In vehemence, his brows drew together. "It's damned frustrating to be constantly labeled. In the first place, I don't identify with many of my more eccentric colleagues. In the second place, *I'm a man*." His voice had risen steadily. Suddenly, as though a bubble inside him had popped, he spoke more softly. "At any rate, that was why I didn't jump to correct your misconception when you assumed that I was a model. It was my vacation. What better way to escape reality than by taking on a new identity?"

His manner was so sincere that Leslie could almost believe him. Almost . . . but not quite. He'd seemed so sincere about everything before. She'd believed then—and felt humiliated now.

"But you let me say so many things," she argued with a surge of embarrassment, "things about women and action and—" she tried to remember them all "—and aging. I even implied that your parents might be ashamed of your work."

To her relief, Oliver didn't laugh. "And everything I answered was honest. My parents are proud of what I do. And I do model, Leslie. Even though it's a hobby, I get a significant amount of money for it. I don't stick around long enough to see the glamorous side. You imagined that; I simply did nothing to disillusion you." He took a deep breath and walked to the fireplace, where he stood with one elbow on the mantel, one foot raised on the hearth. His gaze raked the cold, ash-strewn grates. "Modeling is an escape for me. To spend an afternoon doing something as light as that is refreshing. I need it from time to time."

His voice seemed to hover in the air, then drop into a chasm of silence. Leslie tried to find fault with his reasoning, but couldn't. Oliver tried to find reasoning for his fault, but couldn't.

"I should have told you everything."

"You should have. Why didn't you?"

He looked at her then, his expression one of vulnerability.

Not wanting to be affected, she lowered her eyes. But his words came to her nonetheless, accompanied by a note of urgency. "Because at first I enjoyed the role I was playing. Then, as the week went on, it grew stale. And about the time I realized that you were something very special to me, I got wind of your obsession with honesty."

"So why didn't you say something?"

"I was scared!" he bellowed, feeling angry and frustrated and embarrassed, just as Leslie had felt.

She wanted to doubt him. "You? Scared?"

"Yes," he answered somberly. "Me, scared. I wanted you. I needed you. You seemed to be everything I'd waited thirty-nine years for. I felt as though we'd gotten off to such a good start. I didn't know what to do. On the one hand, I didn't want you to know I was a psychiatrist. It's so . . . complicated sometimes. A model—that's simpler. On the other hand, I knew you'd be upset if I didn't tell you." He took a breath, then threw up a hand in frustration. "It was the old story. With each day that passed, it got more difficult. The longer the deception went on, the more I feared confessing to it. And in the end, the joke was on me. By the time we were ready to return to New York, I knew I loved you . . . and though I hated myself for having deceived you, I didn't know how in hell to correct the error without the risk of losing you completely."

He swallowed hard. His hand gripped the mantel until his knuckles were white. Gazing at Leslie, he hated himself all the more for having put that look of misery on her face. Somehow, some way, he had to convince her of his love.

"I tried to tell you, Leslie. Several times as the week went on, I tried to tell you. But you wouldn't let me, and I was happy enough not to push. There were times when I wondered if you knew. Once when you kiddingly called me Dr. Ames, another time when you begged me not to analyze things to death." His voice grew deeper. "Do you remember that time? We were on the terrace. . . ." He started to move toward her but she quickly rose from the sofa and crossed the room to stand at the window with her back to him. In tailored wool slacks, a sweater and blouse, she looked every

bit the successful businesswoman, every bit the caring
teacher, every bit the woman he loved.

"I remember a comment you made," she began in a distant voice, her mind, too, back on St. Barts, "when I thought
Tony had paid you to give me a good time. You laughed and
said that nobody paid you for your time in chunks like that.
I suppose I should have wondered what you meant, but I assumed you were talking of modeling. Deep down under all
that wariness, I was so . . . so anxious to believe." She shook
her head in dismay. "What is it about me?" she asked herself. "After Joc, I swore I'd never be taken in. One week with
you . . . and bam, I'm blind all over again."

Oliver came up from behind and stood at her side without
touching her. "Love is blind," he said, casting a sad smile
her way. "Haven't you heard that saying?"

She gave a meager excuse for a laugh. "Yeah. Dumb,
isn't it?"

"Not dumb at all. I let love blind me to your need for the
truth. I let it convince me to leave well enough alone." His
voice took on a husky timbre. "I do love you, Leslie. And if
you weren't so hurt and angry I think you'd admit that you
love me, too."

"But I am hurt and angry," she argued, the proof of her
words in her large violet eyes, which were open and pleading. "I feel . . . betrayed."

"Aw, Les," he moaned, "I haven't betrayed you." He
reached out to touch her cheek, but she flinched and he let
his hand drop. "Everything about me is the same as it was.
Psychiatrist and model, they're one and the same. If you could
love the model, why not the psychiatrist?"

"I didn't love the model!" she cried, grasping at the one
illusion that might save her from the power Oliver had. For
she felt it now—the need to touch him, to hold him and be
held, to find oblivion in the fire of his passion. "I got . . . carried away by the romance of the island. That was what it
was. Nothing more."

His gaze narrowed knowingly. "Is that why you were so
quiet during the trip home? Is that why you so readily agreed

to spend the weekend with me? Is that why you gave yourself to me with such abandon, why you'd do it again if I took you upstairs now? You 'don't sleep around.' Remember?"

Leslie's heart began to knot up. Whether it was his skill as a psychiatrist or simply that of a very perceptive man, he asked pointed questions. "You're good in bed," she heard herself say in a voice far cooler than the caldron heating within. "And I needed the escape. Maybe you weren't the only one trying to flee an image," she said, the words coming fast as the ideas formed. "Maybe I needed to shake the image of the down-to-earth schoolteacher for the week. Maybe I did have a ball. Maybe I was truly sorry to see my vacation end. Maybe my acceptance of your invitation for the weekend was nothing more than a wish to escape for two final days. Maybe I was playing a role, too."

She'd hit home. Oliver stood suddenly straighter. "I don't believe you."

"That's a shame. Funny . . . it seems to be a hazard of trips such as ours. When two people play for a week, it's hard to know afterward what's for real." Given strength by self-deception, she turned and headed for the front door. "I think you ought to leave," she said without looking at him. "The game is over."

"Not by a long shot!" Oliver exclaimed, coming from behind to whirl her around. "I don't believe a word you say. I know you, Leslie. I can see inside."

She pulled her arm from his grip. "Then you've got a double problem. Because if you want me to believe that, I'll have to believe all those stereotypes about psychiatrists. And if I do, I won't want to be around you. I've got secrets, just like everyone else. And I don't like the idea of being transparent." She took the few remaining steps toward the door and stood with her hand on the knob for support. Her legs felt like rubber. "Now are you going to leave, or do I call the cops and report a breaking and entering?" She crinkled up her nose in echo of her heart. "Wouldn't be good for the image, Ol. Either of them."

For a minute he stood staring at her. Though he hadn't

believed a word she'd said, his claims to that effect had only
hardened her. There had to be another approach, one that
would be more successful. Unfortunately, he couldn't think
straight. His insides were being chewed up; every bit of his
energy was needed simply to keep his cool. Almost as an
afterthought he remembered his overcoat on the bannister.
Head down, back straight, he retrieved it, then returned to
the door as Leslie opened it.

"This isn't the end, Leslie."

"I think so," she whispered, suffering behind a mask that
barely hid her pain.

He simply shook his head. Daring to touch her because he
needed to so badly, he lifted a hand to her face. When she
tried to draw back, he anchored his fingers all the more firmly
in her hair. "No, Les. What we had on St. Barts was unique.
Most people go through a lifetime in a futile search for it. I'm
done searching. All I have left to do is to prove that you are,
too." He let his thumb drift ever so gently along her cheek to
her lips. She wanted to pull back, to shake it off, to do anything but admit to herself how much she craved him. But she
was rooted to the spot.

Again he shook his head, this time with a smile to match
the tenderness of his touch. "We found a special something
down there, and I'll be damned if I'm going to let it go."

For a split second, she thought he would take her in his
arms. Her eyes widened. She swallowed hard. But while she
was still trying to decide whether or not to fight, he dropped
his hand, stepped away to put on his overcoat and left.

She stood in the doorway until his car was out of sight,
then went upstairs and cried herself to sleep.

9

It was a long two weeks before Leslie heard from Oliver again, two weeks rehashing all that had been said and done between them, two weeks of soul-searching. At first she'd been constantly on her guard, wondering when or where he'd show up . . . for she was sure he would show up. She'd seen that look of determination in his eye when he'd spoken of the special something he'd found, and her feminine intuition told her to beware.

At the start there was anger, anger that Oliver had deceived her, anger that she'd fallen for his ruse. And there was the hurt of betrayal. Yes, they had had a special something, but it had been built on delusion and was now destroyed.

The pity of it was that she'd wanted it, too, that special something. She couldn't deny it any more than she could deny that the mere thought of Oliver set her heart to beating with a vigor it lacked at other times.

Oh, yes, she'd wanted it. Before she'd ever gone to St. Barts she'd been aware of a lack in her life. She'd been restless and searching. Hadn't she debated going back to school, or worse, joining the corporation? But either of those options would have been stopgap measures for an ailment that went far deeper. She loved her work as it was. What was missing was a man, a home, children of her own. She wanted a relationship, a closeness, a warmth. She wanted love. She was thirty now; hadn't she waited long enough?

A special something. She had, indeed, found it on St. Barts. Illusion though it might have been, it had been divine while it lasted. Somehow in comparison the rest of her life paled dramatically.

By the end of the first week much of the anger and hurt had filtered away, replaced by an overwhelming sadness. She wanted to believe everything Oliver had told her that last night at her house, but she couldn't. She was afraid . . . afraid of trusting, then of being hurt all over again. What they'd once had had been so good; she felt as though she were mourning the loss of a limb or an ideal or a dearly beloved friend.

And she was lonely. So very lonely. Even during the hours she spent at one or another of the centers, she ached. There was some solace in the fact that Diane appeared to be responding to Oliver's ministrations. Though Leslie was unable to shake the vision of destruction at the Weitzes' house, regular phone calls to Tony, then to Diane herself, assured her of progress on that front. It was Brenda, however, who systematically homed in on Leslie's own malady.

"You sound down, Leslie," she commented during one evening's call.

"I'm worried about Di. You know that."

"And that's all?"

"Isn't it enough?"

"What about Oliver?"

Leslie stiffened, startled. "What about him?"

"Tony told me——"

"He had no business doing that!"

"He's your brother. He's worried."

"I told him I'd be all right."

"You don't sound it."

"Please, Bren. I don't want to argue."

But Brenda was insistent. "Is he very special . . . this Oliver?"

Very special? Ironic choice of words. For an instant Leslie wondered whether Brenda wasn't in cahoots with the man himself, then she chalked it up to coincidence. "Yes," she sighed wearily. "He is."

"Then give, Leslie. Give a little."

She'd already given her heart. What was left? "Brenda . . ." she warned.

"Okay, but just try."

"I'm trying, I'm trying," Leslie grumbled, and indeed she was; she was trying to envision her future, but it remained a muddle. Thoughts of Oliver tore at her endlessly. *Classic withdrawal*, she told herself. Persevere, and she'd be fine. But the ache persisted, and by the end of the second week she'd begun to despair.

Then the kitten arrived. She'd just gotten home when the doorbell rang. For an instant she stood frozen, wondering whether this was the time Oliver had chosen to pop back into her life. But it was a delivery truck on the drive, leaving a small brown-wrapped box in her hand when it drove away.

An F.A.O. Schwarz package? She had no idea. Then she peeled back the wrapping and unearthed the sweetest hand-sized toy kitten she'd seen . . . since . . . since she was seven and her own just like it had gone to the laundry and never returned. Her vision blurred as she stared at the tiny silver button in its ear. Steiff. And its name. Jigs. She smiled and sniffed and shook her head. Then, hands trembling, she reached into the box and extracted the card buried therein.

"Not a puppy to chase and fetch, but a kitten to purr and stretch and thrive on attention. I'd even indulge it its occasional bristling. All my love, Oliver."

Collapsing on a nearby chair with the kitten pressed to her heart and her head buried against her arm, she burst into tears. How could he remember such a small thing as that? How could he do this to her?

But he had. He'd sent her a teaser, then nothing. Another week passed without a word. Staring at the kitten each night, picking it up in her hands and holding it, knowing that Oliver had to have done the same when he'd bought it, she felt all the sadder, all the more lonely.

Predictably, with time, she grew used to thinking of Oliver as a psychiatrist. Unpredictably, given her annoyance that he should be something other than what she'd been led to expect, she grew curious. From model to psychiatrist—it was quite a switch. When she'd been on St. Barts she'd imagined what his life as a model was like. She'd never asked for details, feeling foreign enough, intimidated enough, to be wary of asking. He'd volunteered little. As she reflected on it, she realized that those few times she'd asked him questions he'd deftly turned the conversation around. At the time she'd simply thought him to be all the more modest, all the more attentive to her. Now she realized that his attentiveness had probably been not only habitual probing, but a diversionary tactic as well.

To think of him now as a psychiatrist conjured up quite a different picture of the way he spent his days. Rather than being in a studio, perhaps wearing a terry robe that he'd shrug off when it was time to climb into bed for the shooting of something akin to the Homme Premier ad, he'd be in an office, dressed in conservative slacks and shirt, tie and blazer, much as he'd been dressed when he'd come to Diane's house that night. Tony said he was skilled; indeed Diane appeared to have gotten a temporary handle on the more erratic of her emotions. Tony said he was busy. Leslie pictured him behind his desk, leaning far back in a chair, his long fingers steepled against his lips as he listened intently to his patient's words, interjecting questions or suggestions, concentrating fully on that one individual until the end of the hour, when, like clockwork, the guard would change.

To each patient he would seem all-attentive, fully engrossed. That would be part of his skill, making the patient feel wanted. Just as Leslie had felt wanted, and needed, and loved.

No sooner had she chased that thought from her mind than her curiosity went to work again. She wondered what time he went to work in the morning, when he got home at night, what he did evenings and on weekends. He'd obviously been free enough to invite her away. But certainly he had a social life, and most certainly it would be of a different class from that of a full-time model. Ironically, she assumed it would be similar to the kind of social life her family knew. Oliver appeared to be successful. He lived in Manhattan, had a place in the Berkshires, had been able to easily swing a trip to St. Barts, not to mention the beautiful gold necklace she wore, yes, every day. No doubt he lived well. No doubt he was part of that same social world she'd sworn off so long ago. . . .

As the days passed, she was prone to abrupt mood swings, high one minute and low the next. She'd miss Oliver with all her heart, then be glad he was gone. She'd be relieved he wasn't a model, then sad it should be so. She'd be proud to think of him as a psychiatrist, then furious at the way he'd so skillfully manipulated her mind. She'd be angry then contrite, indignant then forgiving. But through it all she was confused. Her future seemed more in limbo than ever before. She simply didn't know where she wanted to go, and the unsureness of it all gnawed at her constantly.

By the end of the fourth week, the unbuttoned ear of the small stuffed kitten had begun to show the imprint of her thumb. Much as she wished it weren't so, Oliver was never far from her thoughts. With March nearing an end, spring wouldn't be long. And spring, well, spring was a time for birth and brightness and love.

Had he had that in mind the day he sent the vase filled with violets? Violets . . . not drooping as she'd been that first day she'd arrived on St. Barts, but fresh and moist and gay. Had he known how desperately she'd needed word from him?

Her hand shook as she read the card written in the now-familiar bold scrawl. "I couldn't resist. I'll never see a violet without thinking of you. Care for them . . . please?" It was signed, "Love, Oliver."

She was more rattled than ever. Though ecstatic to receive his gifts, she was terrified to read too much into them. Worse, she was appalled at how much she wanted to read into them. She was wary and elated, distrustful and optimistic, and very much afraid of being hurt again.

Determined to view the violets as nothing more than a token, she put them in the center of her bright kitchen table and tried to go about her business as usual. She went to work each day at one of the centers, invariably brought paperwork home to do at night, had a pleasant if uninspiring dinner-date with a college professor she'd dated from time to time, spoke to Tony and Brenda, met Diane for lunch.

And the violets remained on her table. She gave them fresh water. She misted them. She recut their stems. She withered a little as each delicate face fell, dried up and had to be removed from the bunch. With no more than four or five flowers left, the vase began to look as lonely as she felt.

Then, on a rainy Wednesday evening that just happened to be April Fool's Day, Leslie came home from work to find a puddle of water accumulating in her basement frighteningly close to the furnace. Tired and discouraged, she was trying to get the sump pump going when the doorbell rang. Struggling frantically, she poked and pinched in vain. Then the bell rang a second time. Swearing at the stubborn machine, she brushed off her hands as she ran up the stairs.

The house, a brick Tudor, had an inner door, a small foyer, then a thicker outer door with multiple locks. Dashing through the first door, she stood on tiptoe at the second to peer out its single window. She was saved! Flipping the locks, she opened the door.

Standing in the cover of the meager overhang was Oliver. His hair glistened; his raincoat was wet. Collar up, he was hunched over as though trying to protect himself from the rain.

Without a pause she stood aside to let him step quickly in out of the rain. His breathing came fast; he must have dashed from the car.

"Hi," he said, shaking out his sleeves. "Man, is it pouring! Listen, I'm sorry to barge in on you like this, but I was worried you wouldn't see me unless I took you by surprise—"

"Thank heavens you're here, Oliver! Do you know anything about sump pumps?" She reached up to help him out of his coat.

"Excuse me?"

"Sump pumps!" She hung the coat to drip on the tall brass coat stand, then led the way into the house and directly toward the basement door. "Do you know how they work . . . or what's wrong with them when they don't?" She was taking the stairs at a clip, calling back over her shoulder to the bemused figure following her lead. "I can't get the thing to work and my basement's beginning to flood and if the water keeps coming in the furnace is going to be knocked out and then I'll be without heat and—"

"Keep still for a minute while I take a look."

Oliver hunkered down and peered into the small hole of the compact piece of machinery that was barely above the water line. Shrugging out of his blazer and handing it to her, he rolled up his shirt sleeve, then reached in to locate a part here, to jiggle a part there, to fiddle with still a third, while Leslie looked on.

"I can't believe this is happening!" she exclaimed. "I have a service that comes in twice a year to check both the furnace and the pump. They assured me both were fine. What do you think?" she asked, anxiously clutching his blazer. "Should I call the plumber?"

"I think," he grunted, reaching lower to tug at a lever that momentarily resisted him, "that the guy simply had the thing turned off. It's stuck. Wait. . . . There." Sure enough, with a final forceful tug, Oliver had the pump started. Removing his hand from the water, he shook it, then stood.

"It wasn't turned on," Leslie stated as though any fool should have known it right off the bat. With an expression of exasperation, she shook her head. "Terrific April Fool's Day prank. . . . Here, let me get you a towel." She would have escaped up the stairs had Oliver not caught her hand.

"The towel can wait. I can't." He drew her toward him.

The basement was gray, lit by a sole bare bulb hanging over their heads like mistletoe. Leslie looked up at Oliver then, and in an instant was hit by the fact of his presence. *He was here.* He had come. Or was he nothing more than a tall, dark and handsome April Fool's Day mirage?

"Heeey, don't look so stricken," he whispered. "I'm only going to kiss you." And kiss her he did, with one large hand curved to her throat, the other arm around her back holding her closer.

Leslie was stunned. In a matter of seconds, every one of the emotions with which she'd been wrestling for five weeks declared war. She loved him, she didn't. She needed him, she didn't. She trusted him, she didn't. She wanted him, she didn't. But . . . she did.

His lips felt wonderful on hers, bringing back thoughts of warmer, more carefree days on a distant Caribbean isle. His arms were strong, his body large and hard and just right to lean upon. Any thought Leslie might have had of denying her physical attraction to him was negated by the helplessness of her response. She needed to feel the hungry movement of his mouth, needed to respond to him for just that minute, just that minute . . . until sanity slowly returned. Only then did she put her palms to his chest and exert the gentle force that would speak for her.

Oliver instantly released her lips and buried his in her hair. Both of his arms circled her now, hugging her tightly for a minute. "Oh, Leslie, I've wanted to do that night after night," he whispered, then loosened his hold as she'd requested.

Looking up, Leslie met the same warm brown eyes that had so enchanted her on St. Barts. In self-defense, she averted her gaze and hugged his blazer tighter while she dug her free hand into the pocket of her slacks. Clearing her throat, she started for the stairs. "I'll get you that towel," she murmured, running ahead.

Oliver indulged her, though his hand had begun to dry on its own. She was nervous. Hell, so was he. God bless the sump pump for giving him entrée into the house; he hadn't been in the mood for picking locks tonight. It was dark and rainy and he'd had a long and trying day, not the least of which related to his anticipation of this visit. He'd planned it this way . . . almost. He'd guessed that she'd be better left alone for a while to quiet down, to put things into perspective. The kitten, the violets . . . they were simply reminders that he'd been thinking of her. Now came the test.

"Here you go," Leslie said as she handed him the towel. Then, not knowing what else to do, she stood back against the kitchen counter and waited for him to speak.

Unsure as to how he'd be received, Oliver was in no rush. He wiped his hands, rolled down his shirt sleeves, picked up his blazer from the chair over which Leslie had laid it and put it on.

Leslie's pulse raced as, arms hugging her waist, she followed each step of the dressing process. Damn, but he was handsome. Had he been this good-looking on St. Barts? His hair seemed darker; but of course it was wet. And the silver streaks seemed to have acquired several companions at his sideburns; or was that simply the reflection of her kitchen light? He looked leaner, which puzzled her, since she'd have thought that clothes would have made him look heavier. Perhaps it was the flattering fit of his gray slacks, the length of his legs, the thinning effect of the navy blazer he was slipping on. Beautiful material. Well tailored. But then, with his broad shoulders and tapering physique he was the perfect mannequin.

"There," he said with a final tug to his shirt cuffs. "Thank you."

"Thank *you*, I might have had a flooded basement had it not been for you."

"You'd have called a plumber," he said dismissingly. "It was a simple enough problem to solve."

"Well," she sighed, rubbing her hands together, "thanks anyway." She looked up at him, then away, intimidated by the intensity of his gaze. She didn't know what to say. She didn't know what she wanted to say. Oh, yes, she was glad to see him again. Even now, mired in confusion, she felt more alive than she had in five weeks. Why was he here? What did he want? At one time she might have believed that he wanted to be with her. Now she was wary.

"How've you been, Leslie?"

"Okay." She looked up shyly. "Thanks for the kitten. It's adorable. And the flowers." Her gaze wandered to the table where now only the empty vase stood. "They were beautiful."

"So are you."

Frowning, she absently rubbed at a small chip on the edge of the Formica countertop. Seeing her discomfort, Oliver instantly changed tactics.

"Listen," he said, clearing his throat, "I thought maybe we could go out for a bite."

"It's pouring."

"I don't mind if you don't. It's been a long time since lunch. Didn't I pass a place about ten minutes back, down the road?"

She nodded, biting her tongue. She could fix dinner here. But she wouldn't. Oliver Ames in her cozy kitchen would be far too much for one Leslie Parish to endure.

"How about it?"

She shrugged. "I don't know."

"Have you eaten already?"

"No."

"Then come on." He cocked his head toward the front of the house. "Keep me company. We'll just get something to eat . . . and then talk. I'll drop you back here afterward." When she hesitated still, he tipped his head and eyed her teasingly. "You're not frightened of me, are you?"

"Frightened of you? Are you kidding?" She was scared to death, though quick to point out to herself that technically she hadn't lied. She could play that game, too.

"Then why not dinner?"

Because being with you may be as painful as being without you. On the other hand. . . . She sighed her resignation. "Why not."

Within fifteen minutes they were seated across from each other at the steak-and-sandwich place Oliver had selected. Leslie remained quiet, letting Oliver take the lead. If he wanted to talk, let him do the talking for a change. She'd done her share on St. Barts.

As though understanding her silent request, he began to speak soon after their orders were taken. And if he'd been hesitant to discuss himself during their time on the island, he was no longer. Indeed he seemed to want her to know everything. In turn, Leslie couldn't help but respond to his openness.

"I always wanted to be a doctor," he began quietly, almost shyly. "From the time I was a kid. It wasn't until I was nearly done with medical school that I decided on psychiatry."

"Why?"

"Why did I wait that long?" He gave a self-conscious laugh. "Because I think I wanted to see myself in a more—" he frowned as he searched for the word "—flamboyant field. I'd had my heart set on surgery. I was going to be a surgical pioneer, improving on existing transplant processes, experimenting with others."

"What happened?"

"My surgical rotation was a disaster. Not only was I clumsy with a knife, but I also discovered that I wasn't terribly sorry about the fact. Scalpels are cold, impersonal, sterile tools. The major tool the psychiatrist uses is his own intellect—I kind of liked that. I felt there was that much more of a challenge in psychiatry. Perhaps not the glory of a transplant surgeon. But a good feeling right here." He tapped his chest in the region of his heart.

"Has the good feeling persisted?"

"For the most part. Sure, there are some patients who are either beyond my help or, for one reason or another, resistant to it, but I've seen progress."

"Diane seems better," she began on impulse, then caught herself. "I'm sorry. I know you can't talk about her."

"That's all right. It wouldn't be violating doctor-patient confidentiality for me to say that things are beginning to move. She's opening up." His brow furrowed. "She calls me often, which is normal for someone just making that transfer of trust. I don't want her growing too dependent, though. I'd been seeing her three times a week; I've just cut it back by a session."

"She sounds okay when I speak with her."

"She is. She really is. And she'll be fine."

Leslie nodded, thinking how ironic it was that Diane might trust Oliver so completely while she had to remain on her guard all the time. Maybe she was the one with the problem, she mused, then reminded herself that it was the truth. To sit with Oliver like this, loving him so very much yet trying to remain detached, was pure hell.

"You enjoy private practice, then?" she asked, needing to keep the conversation going as a detour from her thoughts.

The waitress brought a carafe of wine, from which Oliver proceeded to fill their glasses before answering. "I do. . . ."

His slight unsureness caught her ear. "You don't sound sure."

"I am," he said more firmly, but he continued to study the swirl of rosé in his glass. "I'm not sure I see myself doing it forever." When Leslie remained silent, he went on. "I'm on the Bellevue—N.Y.U. staff; I spend two mornings a week there seeing patients. In some ways I prefer that kind of practice."

Leslie was puzzled. In the social circles in which she'd grown up, private practice would certainly have been far more prestigious, not to mention lucrative. "Why?"

"The patients. The problems. They're more diverse, often more extreme. I'm needed—and appreciated—that much more. Those patients could never afford the hourly rates I usually charge." His was a straightforward statement, devoid of either pride or arrogance. Perversely itching to find the latter, Leslie prodded.

"If you don't find private practice as rewarding, why do you do it at all? Bellevue is a teaching hospital; surely they'd take you on full-time."

"They would."

"Then why not?"

His eyes held hers levelly. "The money. I want the money private practice can offer."

So he was like the rest, she decided, though she felt no elation at having discovered his fault. "That's noble," she murmured.

"Not noble. Just practical." His eyes pierced her shell of cynicism. His voice held conviction. "I want a wife . . . and a family. I want to be able to support them well, to have a nice home, to travel, to take them to fine restaurants and the theater, to buy them gifts. I've been saving money for the last ten years, investing it, reinvesting dividends. The way I figure it, another seven or eight years should do it. Then I will be able to accept a full-time position at a hospital, either Bellevue or another, without denying my family . . . or myself."

For a minute Leslie had nothing to say. He'd been blunt. And honest. She couldn't believe that he would have risked evoking what he knew to be her distaste for the calculated amassing of money had what he said not been the truth. To her amazement, she respected him.

"Tell me about your family, Oliver," she said with a new note of interest in her voice.

And he did. He told her of his parents and sister, of their modest roots and the relative comfort they'd finally achieved. Over thick steaks and hearty salads, he told her of his college years, inspiring laughter and sympathy in turn.

That weekend, over dinner at a more elegant restaurant in the city, he told her more about his work, outlining a day in his life, amusing her with the zaniest of his cases.

The following Tuesday, as they sat, heads together, in a dim theater waiting for the movie to begin, he told her about his experience as an expert witness in criminal cases and about the book he hoped to write.

The Saturday after that, strolling arm in arm with her through a sprawling suburban shopping mall, he told her about his few good friends, his addiction to tennis, his dream to one day charter a boat and cruise the Mediterranean.

And the next Monday he insisted on taking her to the reception her sister Brenda was throwing to commemorate the debut of the Parish Corporation's home-computer system. Leslie hadn't wanted to go. Receptions such as these, to which only the shiniest of brass and the biggest and most promising of clients were invited, bored her to tears. Between Brenda and Oliver, however, she hadn't stood a chance. As it happened, with Oliver by her side through the entire ordeal, it wasn't all that bad. Indeed, the only awkward moment came when, as a couple amid several hundred, they ran into Diane and Brad. Diane seemed stunned, then embarrassed, then plainly nervous in their presence; Oliver handled the encounter with grace and tact. As for Leslie, she pushed the confrontation from her mind the instant they left the hall.

All in all, she was so in love with Oliver that she was ready to burst. He'd been so open, so gentle, so very obviously honest that she simply couldn't doubt him any longer.

She was also extremely frustrated. Through the warm, casual getting-to-know-Oliver days, he never once repeated his words of love. After each date he'd drop her back at her house with a tender smile, perhaps even an affectionate hug, an extension of the hand-holding and elbow-hooking they did all the time. But though he had to have known she'd be more than willing, he didn't kiss her. Though her body seemed to ache endlessly for him, he showed no inclination to make love. And his words, other than to say that he'd call, were noncommittal.

Oh, he did call. Every night he called just to talk, to hear how her day had been, to tell her about his own. There were times when he was tired, when she could hear the fatigue in his voice, when it was her pleasure to be able to hear out his tale of woe, to commiserate, to soothe.

But he didn't say he loved her. And, fearing the breach of that last bastion, she said nothing.

"Hi, sweetheart."

"Hi."

"Good day?"

"Mmm. Busy. Three kids got sick and had to be sent home. Two of them needed rides to relatives without cars, so guess who drove. I did interview that woman for next fall, though. She's lovely."

"Think she'll be good with the kids?"

"She seemed it. I let her cover for me while I played chauffeur, then when I got back I was able to watch her in action. She's very warm."

"What's her background?"

"She just got a degree in special ed."

"No work experience?"

"Yeah. Six children of her own. Hey, how're *you* doing?"

"Not bad."

"Come on. You can do better than that. I thought the head banger at the hospital quieted down?"

"He did. A new one's into tap dancing."

"Tap dancing? You've got to be kidding."

"I'm not. Listen, babe. About the weekend. Should we, uh, should we try for the Berkshires again?"

"Do you want to?"

"Yes! But only if you do."

"I do."

"Good. Six on Friday?"

"Make it six-fifteen—I'm superstitious."

"Six-fifteen. I'll see you then."

"Sure thing. Bye-bye."

They nearly made it. It was five-thirty when he called. His voice was as tense as she'd ever heard it. She instantly knew that something was very wrong.

"What is it, Oliver?"

"I've got a problem here. I may be late."

"You're at the office?" She could always pick him up there.

"No."

"At the hospital?"

"No."

He'd been so forthright in the past weeks. His evasion only fueled her concern. "What's wrong?"

In other circumstances, Oliver would have simply named a later time when he'd pick her up. But he knew all too well that his tenuous relationship with Leslie was based largely on openness. "It's Diane, Les," he offered quietly. "She's acting up again."

"Oh, no! What's she doing?"

"It's all right, sweetheart. She's just being . . . difficult."

"You're there now?"

"Yes. Listen, this may take a while. Why don't I call you when I have some idea what's happening."

"Oliver—"

"Please, Les," he begged, "no more questions now. I've been looking forward to tonight since . . . since St. Barts. And if you think I'm pleased with Diane's sense of timing, you're crazy." She heard his desperation. "Let me call you?"

"Okay."

"And Leslie?"

"Mmm?"

"I love you."

"I love you, too."

There was a pause, then Oliver's broken, "I'll call."

With tears in her eyes, Leslie hung up the phone. He'd sounded awful. What could possibly have happened? *I love you*, he had said. And she'd answered him with total openness for the first time herself.

Likewise, for the first time, she felt no confusion at all. Suddenly everything Oliver had said and done made sense. She believed him. She trusted him. And she knew precisely what she wanted to do.

Within half an hour she arrived at Diane's. To her dismay, the driveway was packed. She recognized the Weitzes' cars, Tony's car, Oliver's car . . . was that Brenda's car? She bit her lip as she pulled in behind one she didn't recognize. What was going on?

A frazzled Brenda opened the door. "Leslie! What are you—"

"What are *you* doing here?"

"I'm . . . I'm trying to help out."

Leslie strode past her into the hall and dropped her coat on a chair. Keeping her voice low, she looked around. "Where are they? What's she done? Why wasn't I called?" At the sound of raised voices in the living room, she headed that way.

"Leslie, please—" Brenda tried to stop her but it was too late. No sooner had Leslie appeared on the threshold than every eye turned her way.

What she saw, perplexingly enough, was what looked to be a very orderly family gathering. There was sign of neither destruction nor tears, though the level of tension in the room was up near the danger mark. Diane, wearing a look of placid arrogance, sat regally in a high-backed chair, while her husband stood behind her, a hand on either sculpted post, an indignant expression on his face. One end of the sofa was occupied by a man Leslie had never seen before. To her eye, his hair was too perfect, his three-piece suit too flashy, his entire bearing too glossy; she disliked him instantly. Tony stood by the fireplace in a state of obvious agitation. And Oliver stood by the window observing the group from a more detached position. His composure was, for show, well intact. Only Leslie recognized the grim set of his lips, the shadow of worry on his brow, the stiffness of his casual stance.

It was to Oliver that she spoke, her voice a whisper. "What's going on here?"

"You shouldn't have come—" he began somberly, only to be interrupted by an irate Diane.

"And why not? The rest of the family knows. And *she* should know. More than anyone, perhaps. After all, she's the one who's been mooning over you. I think she's got a right to the—"

"Diane!" Tony broke in. "That's enough!"

Diane fumed, her eyes blazing. "She'll know when it hits the papers anyway. She's your sister. Don't you want to make it easier for her?"

"Make what easier?" Leslie asked, her stomach tied up in knots. "What are you talking about?" Her wide-eyed gaze swung back to Oliver for a minute. His lips were tight.

Brad's were not. "It seems that your boyfriend has made good use of his high-priced time to seduce my wife."

Leslie stared, aghast. "*What*?" She was aware of Brenda coming up from behind to give her support, but shrugged off the hand at her shoulder.

It was Tony who took over, speaking more quietly. "Diane is threatening a malpractice suit against Oliver. She claims that he forced sexual relations on her for the sake of therapy."

"That's the stupidest thing I've ever heard," Leslie stated with amazing calm. "Oliver wouldn't do a thing like that."

"And I'd lie?" Diane cried, rejoining the fray. "See. He's got you as brainwashed as he had me. Only I'm not so crazy about him that I can't think straight."

Leslie swallowed hard and tucked her fists in her, pockets. "That's a whole other issue. What does Oliver say to all this?"

Oliver's voice came deep and firm. "He denies it."

"Well, he can deny it in court," Brad countered, then cast a nod toward the slick man on the sofa. "We've retained Henry to represent us."

Leslie shook her head in disbelief. "You're serious! I'm amazed. You should know better, Brad. My God, it's not as though Diane's been the most stable—"

"Leslie!" Oliver cut in sharply, then lowered his voice, "Please."

The eyes that held hers said far more. *She's sick. Go easy on her. Besides, she hasn't got a case. Trust me. I love you.*

With the ghost of a nod, she walked to a free chair and sat down. She'd be quiet, but she'd be damned if she'd leave.

"Okay," Tony said with a tired sigh. "Where were we?"

Brad spoke up, looking down at his wife with a warmth that made Leslie nauseated. "Diane was just going through things chronologically. You were saying, sweetheart—"

"But what's the point of all this?" Brenda burst out, her gaze sliding from Brad to Diane and back. "I don't understand what you want. You're going to sue for damages? Neither of you needs the money."

Brad's jaw was set at a stubborn angle. "It's the principle of the thing. He's hurt our marriage and seriously threatened Diane's peace of mind."

"Now wait a minute," Oliver came forward. "Your marriage was on the rocks before I ever came on the scene. And as for Diane's peace of mind, it was nonexistent even then. Why do you think she spent an entire day cutting your bedroom to shreds?"

"That's beside the point," Brad went on in the way of the injured innocent. "What I'm concerned about is what happened *after* she started seeing you."

"But a judge and jury will take in the entire picture," Oliver pointed out calmly. "They'll ask about your marriage. They'll hear testimony about Diane's emotional state. Are you sure you want to put your wife through that?"

"For the satisfaction of seeing you lose your license to practice? Yes."

"That won't happen, Brad. Your allegations are absurd. You haven't a shred of evidence—"

"Other than my wife's testimony. Henry tells me that judges today lean heavily in favor of a woman who's been raped."

"She wasn't raped," Oliver scoffed impatiently. "Scandal is all you'll be able to create. Headlines. Innuendo. But no case."

Diane spoke softly. "Headlines and innuendo will be enough." She turned her smile on Leslie and crinkled up her nose. "Won't want to be seen with a guy who's got an atrocious reputation and no job, will you?"

"You're crazy," Leslie murmured.

"Di," Brenda said, "don't you think you're carrying this a little too far? I mean, headlines and innuendo could be harmful to the corporation, too."

"Not if I'm the injured party."

"But you're not," Tony injected, growing as impatient as Oliver, "and Brenda's right. This is foolish—"

"It is not!" Diane screamed. "You weren't the one who was—who was violated!"

Tony's tone mellowed to one of sweet sarcasm. "And you were truly violated?"

"Yes!" She tipped up her chin. "He took advantage of me! Maybe he takes advantage of every pretty girl who comes along. I don't know. That's something for the authorities to investigate." She arched a brow. "All I know is what he did to me."

"What did he do to you?" Brenda asked bluntly. "Tell us, Di. Tell us everything."

"He seduced me in the name of psychiatric treatment."

"Sounds like you got that from last month's *Post*."

"He did. He seduced me."

"Seduced—what does that mean?"

"Brenda . . . !" Diane protested in a whine.

"Seduced. Explain."

For the first time, Diane seemed to waver. "He . . . he . . . made love to me."

"Where?" Brenda shot back.

"Now just a minute," Henry the lawyer spoke up, Leslie thought his voice was as phony as the rest of him. "I don't believe my client has to answer your questions."

Brenda came forward, her hands on her hips. "Your client happens to be my sister. And the man she's accusing is a man who means one hell of a lot to my other sister. I'll ask whatever questions I want." She turned back to Diane. "Well? Where did you two make love?"

Diane shifted in her seat, keeping her gaze far from Oliver. "He made love to me, and it was in his office."

"On the desk?" Brenda came back as sweetly and sarcastically as Tony had moments before.

Diane scowled. "No." Her voice wavered. "There's a sofa there."

"Do you lie on the sofa during your sessions?"

"No. I . . . I sit in a chair."

"So how did he get you to the sofa?"

Diane grew petulant, reminding Leslie of a child who'd been caught in a lie and was trying to lie her way out of it. "He told me I'd feel better if I were to lie down."

"So you did."

"He was the doctor. Yes."

"And he just told you to take off your clothes?"

"Wait a minute—" Brad cut in, only to have Tony cut him off in turn.

"Let her answer. This is getting interesting."

"It's getting personal," Brad argued.

Tony's nostrils flared. "Isn't the whole thing personal?" Sucking in a loud breath, he turned to Brenda. "Go on."

Without pause, she resumed her relentless prodding. "What did he do . . . after you stretched out on the couch?"

Diane looked at the carpet. "He . . . he told me. . . ." She waved a hand and winced. "You know."

"I don't. Tell me."

"He said. . . ." She scowled in frustration. "You can imagine what he said, Brenda! What does any man say when he sets out to seduce a woman?"

Brenda pursed her lips. "I've only known two men in my life, and neither of them has tried to seduce me on a psychiatrist's couch. So my imagination's no good, Di. Tell me what he said."

Diane seemed to hesitate. She frowned, then gripped the arm of the chair. "He said sweet things."

"*Like what*?"

If Brenda's patience was wearing thin, Diane's was exhausted. With a sudden fury, she glared at her sister. "He told me it would be good for me, that it was a vital part of my treatment! He told me that he wanted me anyway, and that he'd make it good!" Her anger took on a touch of sadness. "He said that Brad must have been crazy to pass me by and spend time with women who couldn't possibly hold a candle to me."

Tears in her eyes, she bolted up. She was oblivious to the contorted expression on her husband's face. "He told me that I was still young and beautiful. That he loved me," she blurted defiantly. "And I loved him. He was kind and considerate and caring." Standing rigidly, she sent Leslie a gloating stare. "He's a good lover, Leslie. Very skilled and gentle. Not selfish like Brad," she spat.

Then, as the others watched in varying stages of anger, dismay and pity, she sank into her chair and let her head loll back. Astonishingly, her voice gentled along with her expression. She seemed to enter a dreamlike state. "His skin was smooth here, rough there. And he was lean and hard. He wanted me. He did. And I wanted him." She closed her eyes and breathed deeply. "I think I'll always remember that smell. . . ."

Leslie sat forward. "What smell?" she whispered, entranced by her sister's performance.

Diane opened her eyes and sent Leslie a patronizing

smile. "His cologne. Homme Premier." She shook her head. "He's so handsome. It's not every girl who's lucky enough to have a model as a therapist."

"He doesn't wear cologne," Leslie stated quietly.

"Excuse me?" Henry asked, twisting to study her.

She looked him in the eye and spoke slowly, with confidence. "I said that he doesn't wear cologne. I know. I spent a week with him at the villa on St. Barts." Rising smoothly, she walked to where Oliver stood and slipped her arm around his waist. Together they faced the gathering. "I know him far better than Diane ever will. Oliver doesn't wear Homme Premier . . . or any other cologne, for that matter. He never has. And if I have any say in the matter—" she looked adoringly up at him "—he never will." A slow smile found its way to her lips as a foil for the tears in her eyes. "He smells far too good on his own." Then, at the urging of his arms, she turned fully into his embrace. "I love you," she mouthed.

The moisture that gathered at the corner of his eye only enchanted his silent echo of the words. Then he smiled, and Leslie knew that everything would be fine.

10

Fascinated, Leslie stood staring at Oliver's sleeping form. He was magnificent. Dark wavy hair, mussed by loving, fell across his brow. His jaw bore the faintest shadow of a beard. His nose was straight, his lips firm. Lying amid a sensual array of sheets that barely covered one leg, and that part she now knew so well, he was the epitome of health, good looks and raw masculinity.

Again and again her gaze returned to the taunting, strip of flesh at his hip. It would always excite her, even now that her fingers had repeatedly conquered its velvet smoothness. With a sultry half smile, she let her eye creep back up, over the broad and sinewed expanse of his lightly haired chest, to his face.

"Where've you been?" he murmured sleepily, holding out an arm in invitation for her to join him.

Flipping off the bathroom light, she was across the room and in his arms, stretched out against him, in seconds. "I was just looking at you," she said softly, "remembering the very first time I saw you."

"On St. Barts?"

"In *Man's Mode*. You were so beautiful. Tony must have thought I was crazy. I kept staring at that ad, at the expression on your face." She nestled her chin atop the soft hair on his chest. "You wore such a look of vulnerability; you seemed lonely and in love. I wanted to reach out to you then!"

"Took you long enough," he chided, giving her a squeeze.

Her voice was mellow. She kissed his warm skin, then laid her ear against it. "I know."

"What was it, Les? What finally brought you back to me?"

Surrounded by the night sounds of the Berkshires, she pondered his question. It had been long after dark when they'd arrived, so she'd been unable to see the beauty of the hills. But the sounds—the rustle of wind through the forest, the murmur of nocturnal life along its mossy floor, the occasional hoot of an owl—gave her a sense of well-being.

"I think I never really left you," she confessed, experimenting with the fit of her hand to his ribs. "I was so in love with you on St. Barts. I'd never known anything like that before!"

"You should have told me."

"Did you tell me?"

"No. But that was because I knew I'd been deceiving you, and I felt like a louse. The last thing I wanted was to tell you I loved you, then, when you learned the truth about what I did, have you throw the words back in my face. With regard to those three little words, I needed you to believe me."

"I believed you. Oh, I tried not to. But I believed you."

"You said you didn't."

"I lied. I was angry and hurt. I felt so . . . naive. I'd had a complex all along about having to compete with the glossy women I'd assumed you were used to. Then when I found out that you were a psychiatrist. . . ."

"Do you mind?"

"Mind what?"

"That I'm a psychiatrist."

"Of course not. What's to mind?"

In the darkness she could just make out the gleam in his eye. "Psychiatrists are loonies, didn't you know? They're as crazy as their patients. They're—" he curled his mouth around and drawled the word "—strange."

"Not this one."

"You're sure?"

"I'm sure. You must be nearly as rational as my sister

Brenda." When he eyed her as though she were the strange one, she explained. "Your plan. It was brilliant. Those weeks you left me alone were awful. I missed you so terribly and kept trying to convince myself that I was better without such a lying devil, but it didn't work. When you sent that little kitten, I was overjoyed." Her voice dropped. "I love the kitten, Oliver."

"I'm glad," he whispered against her brow. His fingers idly traced the line of her spine. Her skin was warm and smooth; he'd never get his fill of touching her. "I had it all worked out. I figured I'd give you time to cool off and even miss me, then I'd let you get to know the real me. Then I'd bring you up here and start the seduction all over again." He paused. "But it was going to be slow and considerate, not fast and furious. I think I miscalculated somewhere along the way."

"There'll be other times for slow and considerate. Tonight I needed fast and furious. How did you know?"

"I couldn't control myself! I mean, it's tough for a man to be so turned on by a woman and not be able to go through with it."

"But you never even kissed me!" she protested, eyeing him in surprise. "You never gave the slightest indication that you wanted anything more than a squeeze or a hug."

"That was all part of the plan," he scoffed. "Let me tell you, you were gonna get it one way or the other over the weekend. Maybe it was good that Diane pulled her little act. She certainly brought things to a head."

His words gave them both food for thought. Leslie rubbed her cheek against his chest. He pulled her more tightly against him. Their voices were soft and intimate.

"Oliver, will she be all right?"

"I think so. I gave Tony a name of a colleague of mine who's very good. He'll be better able to treat Diane than I ever could."

"Why did she do that?"

"Ironically, it was probably her seeing us together at Brenda's reception that did it. It's not an uncommon phenomenon for a woman patient of a male doctor—in any kind of therapy—to think she's in love with him. She sees him as the source of her health, her confidence, her general well-being. I'd already begun to feel that Diane was growing too dependent on me; I told you that."

"I remember."

"I had just cut her sessions back from three a week to two. That may have bothered her. Brad was obviously still bothering her. He's a bastard." The aside was muttered under his breath. "A good deal of the time she feels she is unwanted and unloved. When she saw us together and, from what Brenda says, looking very much in love, she was jealous. Furiously jealous. Jealous of you. Furious at me. And Brad—well, with her cock-and-bull story she thought she'd be giving him the message that someone did want her, even if he did not."

"I feel so badly for her."

He drew soothing circles on her back. "So do I. She's very unhappy. I told Tony that I thought she and Brad should separate. Even her original outburst didn't faze Brad; Diane says that he's still seeing some little sweetie, and I think I believe her."

"Poor Diane. And we've got so much."

He hugged her, his arms trembling. "We do."

They lay together in silence for several minutes, each simply enjoying the presence of the other.

"Oliver?"

"Mmm?"

"How did you get to Diane's tonight? I mean, I'm surprised that she'd have wanted to give you a chance to defend yourself."

"She didn't. But she needed some sense of power, so she called Tony to tell him what she'd planned. He called me, then Brenda. He knew their lawyer was going to be there and hoped to nip the whole scheme in the bud."

"Why wasn't I called?" Leslie asked in a small voice.

Oliver planted a gentle kiss on her nose. "We didn't want you to be hurt. Diane's claim was pretty ugly."

"But it was false!"

"I knew that, but the words would have been hurtful enough. Besides, if we were successful, you'd never have been any the wiser to her threat." He paused then, hesitant. "Leslie?"

"Mmm?"

"Did you ever believe her?"

She brought her head up in surprise. "Believe Diane? Of course not. Were you worried?"

"That you'd believe her, a little. After what I'd done to you on St. Barts, I wasn't sure how far your trust would go."

"Were you worried that she would bring the case to trial?"

"I wouldn't be honest if I didn't say yes. She was right in a way. Headlines and innuendo could have easily damaged my career. Not destroyed it, but damaged it badly. Even if a person is found not guilty by a jury, the stigma of having been accused in the first place remains. It's a sad fact, one that our system of justice can do little to change." He grew quiet, pensive, his breathing even, close to her ear. Hooking his foot around her shin, he drew her leg between his and pressed her hips more snugly to him. Then he held her still, appreciating the beauty of the moment. "Thank you, Leslie," he said at last, his voice intensely gentle.

"For what?"

"For trusting me."

She laughed shyly. "It's nothing. You're an easy one to trust," she pinched his ribs, "even when you are lying through your teeth."

"I don't lie!" he stated with such vehemence that she realized he would always be sensitive about what had happened on St. Barts. She couldn't deny her delight; somehow she had managed to find the most straightforward man in the world.

"I know," she apologized gently. "I was only teasing." Then she grew more thoughtful herself. "A little while ago you asked what had brought me back to you. It was several things, I think. Time, for one. I was able to sort things out, to put things into perspective. I realized that what you'd said made sense. And I missed you so much I was very willing to give you any benefit of the doubt.

"When we started to see each other and I got to know you, I saw that what you'd said was right. Model or psychiatrist, you were the same man underneath. You were so open then, making up for all you hadn't said on the island. And right about that time I was beginning to feel like a hypocrite."

"You? A hypocrite?"

"Mmm." She breathed in his natural scent and was buoyed up by it. "For all my talk, I really wasn't any more honest with you—or myself—than I'd accused you of being. I did love you. I loved you back on St. Barts. When we made love, well, I played games with myself. I told myself that the only thing that mattered was the moment, that I didn't care about the past or the future. But I did. I should have been more open about my feelings then. I should have let you speak when I knew you wanted to." She raised soulful eyes to his. "It was my fault that you didn't tell me about yourself. But I was afraid—afraid of what you might say, afraid that it might burst the bubble of illusion we'd created. It was such a lovely bubble. I didn't want anything to happen." She looked down. "So you see, I was pretty bad myself. I created an illusion and clung to it as it suited me. But I was fooling myself to think that I could return to New York and forget you. I realized that during the cab ride home from the airport."

Oliver skimmed her cheek with the side of his thumb and brought her chin up. "I love you, lady. Do you know that?"

Seeing it written on every plane of his face, she smiled and nodded. "You know," she whispered through a veil of happy tears, "I feel sorry for all your female patients. If you'd been my therapist, I'd have certainly fallen in love with you."

"If you'd been my patient," he growled, rolling slowly over to pin her to the bed, "I'd sure as hell have been guilty of some mighty unethical thoughts."

"Only thoughts? No acts?"

"Nope."

"I'm not pretty enough? Or rich enough? Or thin enough? Why not?"

"If you want to know the truth, that sofa happens to be the most uncomfortable thing I've ever been on!"

"Oh? So you have . . . tried it out?"

He nipped her shoulder in punishment. "I've sat on it. I've fallen asleep on it once or twice."

"Have you ever *made love* on it?"

"No. Maybe we'll try it sometime."

"Aw, I don't know, Oliver. That might feel . . . unethical."

"But you're not my patient."

"I know, but. . . ."

"Tell me you're tired of me already."

"Are you kidding? It's just . . . well . . . even though Diane won't be suing you, I think I'll always remember her threat. I'd feel guilty making love in your office. Your patients have problems so much more serious than ours. . . ."

Adoring her sensitivity, Oliver felt choked up. When he could finally speak, his voice was a husky murmur. "You're amazing, you know that?" Before she could answer, he sealed her lips with his own in a kiss so gentle and loving that she could have wept for all she did have. "It doesn't bother you then," he mused against her mouth, "that I'm a psychiatrist?" He was thinking of her mother and what Tony had told him.

She sent her tongue in search of the corner of his lip, then smiled. "I'm proud of you."

"You will have to meet my parents," he quipped, recalling an earlier discussion about pride.

She remembered too and blushed. "I did wonder for a while there what kind of parents would be proud to have a gigolo for a son. Now that I know better, I'd love to meet them."

"And you'll marry me?"

"I'd love that, too."

He sucked in his breath, then let it out slowly as he raked the length of slender flesh beneath him. "You are beautiful. Not too thin. Not too rich. Just right. When we get back to the city I'm going to buy you a silky white negligee. I'd love to be able to take it off. . . ."

"Oliver!" she exclaimed, delighted by the very definite effect the simple thought of it had on him. "You must have this thing for nudity. What would Freud say about that?"

He moved more fully on top of her. "I don't give a damn. Freud was nothing but a constipated old—"

"Shhhhh. . . ." She put a finger to his lips, then let it wander to his hairline, into the thick waves, around his ear to trace that silver arc. "I like nudity, too. Knowing that you were naked beneath that sheet in your ad nearly drove me crazy. Oliver?"

He managed a muffled, "Uh huh?"

"Will you stop . . . doing that for a minute so . . . I can speak?"

"Doing what?"

"Moving like that." He'd begun to shift against her on the pretense of kissing her eyes, then withdrawing, kissing her nose, then withdrawing, kissing one earlobe, then the other. In essence his entire body was rubbing her in all the right places, and she'd begun to sizzle.

He stopped instantly, propping himself above her. "There. Better?"

Was frustration better? "Not really . . . except for speaking."

"So . . . what were you going to say?"

"I wanted to, uh, to ask you a favor."

"Shoot."

She raised her hands to his shoulders and followed their progress as they slowly descended over his chest. When her palms felt the unmistakable tautness of his nipples, she stopped. "It's about your modeling. When we're married. . . ."

"What is it, sweetheart?"

She shot him a glance, then retreated. "I know it's silly of me to even think of this—"

"Out with it, woman, so we can get on with it!"

"I don't want you posing nude! I don't think I can stand it! I don't want other women seeing your body! I want you all to myself!" Running out of breath, she lowered her voice. "I told you it was silly."

"It's not one bit silly, Leslie," Oliver returned gently. "It's sweet and loving and possessive, and it pleases me tremendously."

"Really?" she asked timidly.

"Really."

"Because I love your body." She slid her hands from his chest and ran them down his sides to his thighs. "I do love your body." Lifting her head, she pressed her lips to the turgid spot that her palm had just deserted.

"It's yours!"

"Just like that?"

"Just like that. There's just one little catch."

"Uh oh. Here it comes." She shut her eyes tightly. "Okay. Tell me."

"I want *your* body. That's a fair exchange, isn't it?"

"I suppose."

"What do you mean, 'you suppose'? You're supposed to be ecstatic."

"But . . . what about my mind? Don't you want that, too?"

"Your mind? Oh. That. Uh, well, let's see. We could always put it in a little box on the nightstand—hey, that tickles!"

"The ad was right, you know. You *are* a rogue."

"Any objections?"

She smiled and spoke with confidence, serenity and love. "None at all, Oliver. None at all."

**Read on for an excerpt from
Barbara Delinsky's upcoming book**

sweet salt air

In hardcover in 2013 from St. Martin's Press

Darkness was dense this far from town. There were no cars here, no streetlights, no welcoming homes, and whatever glow had been cast from Nicole's place was gone. Trees rose on either side, sharing the narrow land flanking the road with strips of field, and beyond the trees was the rocky shore, lost now in the murk.

But there was hope. As she walked, she saw proof of a moon behind clouds, etching their edges in silver and spraying more to the side. Those silver beams would hit the ocean in pale swaths, though she could only imagine it from here. But she did hear the surf rolling in, breaking on the rocks, rushing out.

When the pavement at the edges of the road grew cracked, she moved to the center. This end had always been neglected, a reminder that Cecily didn't invite islanders for tea. The fact that no repair work had been done said the son was the same.

She passed a string of birches with a ghostly sheen to their bark, but between the sound of the breeze in their leaves and, always, the surf, she was soothed. The gulls were in for the night, hence no screeching, and if there were sounds of boats rocking at moorings, the harbor was too far away to hear.

There was only the rhythmic slap of her sneakers on the cracked asphalt—and then another tapping. Not a woodpecker, given the hour. Likely a night creature searching for food, more frightened of her than she was of it. There were deer on Quinnipeague. And raccoons. And woodchucks, possums, and moles.

The tapping came in bursts of three and four, with pauses between. At one point she stopped, thinking it might be a crick in her sneakers. When it quickly came again, though, she walked on. The closer she got to the Cole house, the louder it was.

The creaking of bones? Skeletons dancing? That was what island kids said, and back then, she and Nicole had believed it, but that didn't keep them away. Bob and Angie had forbidden their coming here, so it was definitely something to do. Granted, Charlotte was the instigator, but Nicole wouldn't be left behind.

Feeling chilled now, she pulled the cuffs of her sweater over her hands as the Cole curve approached. That curve was a marker of sorts, as good as a gate. Once past it, you saw the house, and once you saw the house, you feared Cecily. As special as her herbs were and as healing as her brews, she could be punitive.

But Cecily was dead, and Charlotte was curious. A look wouldn't hurt.

Slowing only a tad, she rounded the curve. The thud of her heart felt good. She was alive; she was having an adventure; she was breaking a rule, like the irreverent person she was. The salt air held a tang here, though whether from the nearby pines or adrenaline, she didn't know.

Then, like a vision, Cecily's house was at the distant end of the drive. It was the same two-story frame it had always been, square and plain, with a cupola on top that housed bats, or so the kids used to say. But there were no bats in sight now, no ghostly sounds, nothing even remotely scary. A floodlight was trained on the upper windows, unflattering light on an aging diva. And the sound she heard? A hammer wielded by a man on a ladder. He was repairing a shutter, which would have been a totally normal activity had it not been for the hour.

Wondering at that, she started down the long drive. The walking was easier here, the dirt more forgiving than broken

pavement. An invitation after all? She fancied it was. The
house looked sad. It needed a visitor, or so she reasoned as
the trees gave way to the gardens where Cecily had grown her
herbs. In the darkness, Charlotte couldn't see what grew here
now, whether the low plants were herbs or weeds. She could
smell something, though the blend was so complex that her
untrained nose couldn't parse it. Tendrils of hair blew against
her cheek; wanting a clear view, she pushed them back.

Her sneakers made little sound on the dirt as she timed
her pace to the pound of the hammer. When the man paused
to fiddle with what looked to be a hinge, she heard a rustle in
the garden beside her, clearly foraging creatures alerted by
her movement.

Alerted in turn by that rustle, the man stopped pounding
and looked back. He must have had night eyes; there was no
light where she was. Without moving a muscle, though, he
watched her approach.

Leo Cole. She was close enough to see that, astute enough
to remember dark eyes, prominent cheekbones, and a square
jaw. She remembered long, straggly hair, though a watch cap
hid whatever was there now. He wore a tee shirt and paint-
spattered jeans. Tall and gangly then? Tall and solid now.

But thin-mouthed in disdain. Then and now.

"You're trespassin'," he said in a voice that was low and
rough, its hint of Maine too small to soften it.

"What are you doing?" she asked, refusing to cower. She
had met far more intimidating people in far less hospitable
spots.

His eyes made a slow slide from her to the window and
back. "What does it look like?"

"Repairing your house in the dark." She tucked her cuffed
hands under her arms. "Is that so you won't see the broken
windowpane over there, or do you just like being reckless?"

He stared at her for another minute. Then, holstering the
hammer in his jeans, he climbed down the ladder, lifted a
shutter, and, somewhat awkwardly given its bulk, climbed
back up. The shutter was wide, clearly functional rather than
decorative. Though he carried it one-handed, he stopped

twice on the way up to shift his grip. At the top, he braced it against the ladder's shelf while he adjusted his hands, then lined up hinges and pins.

He had one hinge attached but was having trouble with the second. She knew what this was about. She had worked with storm shutters. They were tricky to do alone.

Resting the shutter on the shelf again, he pulled the hammer from his waistband and adjusted the hinge with a few well-aimed hits. Then he tried the shutter again.

Watching him struggle, Charlotte remembered more about Leo Cole from her early days here. Not too bright, they said. Troubled. Stubborn. She had never known him personally; she was only there summers, and he ran with a different crowd. Actually, she corrected silently, he didn't run with a crowd. A lone wolf, he did damage all on his own, and it was serious stuff. The stories included stealing cars, forging checks, and deflowering sweet young things.

Those last summers she was on Quinnipeague, he was in state prison, serving time for selling pot. Rumor had it that Cecily was the one who grew it, and Charlotte could believe it, what with medical marijuana use on the rise. The islanders always denied it, of course. They didn't want the Feds threatening their cures.

Leo had been nabbed for selling grass on the mainland. Did he still grow it? She couldn't smell it now, and she did know that smell.

Having returned the shutter to the shelf, he was readjusting the hinge.

"Want some help?" she called up.

He snorted.

"Four hands, and you'd have that right up," she advised.

"Two hands'll do."

Charlotte looked past him toward the cupola. She didn't see any bats yet, didn't feel any ghosts. If Cecily's spirit was floating around, it hadn't cast a spell to keep Charlotte here. She remained because she was stubborn herself.

"I've done this before," she said now.

"Uh-huh."

"I have. I've built houses."

"That so." He didn't believe her.

"Half a dozen in El Salvador after the big quake there, and at least as many when tornados decimated parts of Maryland. I know how storm shutters work."

He continued to stare.

"All you need," she said, freeing a hand to hold back the hair that fluttered loose again, "is someone to steady it while you fit the pins in the hinges."

"Really. I didn't know that."

"Okay," she granted. "So you did. But you could've had that hung and been down five minutes ago. Aren't you cold?" She was appreciating every thick inch of her sweater, while his arms were ropy and bare.

"I'm a man."

She waited for more. When nothing came, she said, "What does that have to do with it?"

"Men run hot."

"Really." Refusing to be baited, she returned her hand to her armpit, shifted to a more comfortable stance, and smiled. "Great. I'll watch while you get that shutter hung. Maybe I can learn how you do it alone."

Apparently realizing he'd been one-upped, he said, "Fine. Since you know it all, here's your chance." He backed down, put the shutter on the ground against his leg, and gestured her toward the ladder.

"I'm not lugging that thing up," she said.

"No, but if you get up there, I can hold the shutter while you do the fitting. Assuming you can see. Your hair's a mess."

"Thanks," she said brightly and gripped the rail. Two ladders would have been better. She wasn't sure she liked the idea of climbing this one with him at her butt. She would be at his mercy. But she did have a point to prove.

So she began to climb, looking back every few rungs to see where he was. When she reached the top, she felt his shoulder against the back of her thighs. If she hadn't known better, she would have said he was making sure she didn't fall.

But she did know better. Leo Cole had no use for women,

or so the story went. If he was standing that close, he was toying with her.

She didn't like being toyed with—and, yes, her hair was in her eyes, but she wouldn't give him the satisfaction of pushing it back. Fortunately, she knew enough about hanging shutters to do it, hair and all. While he bore the weight of the wood, she easily lined up both pairs of hinges and pins, and that quickly it was done.

Nearly as quickly, he backed down the ladder. By the time she reached the ground, he was stowing the hammer in a tool box. The instant she was off the last rung, he reached for the ladder.

"You're welcome," Charlotte said.

He shot her a flat look.

"I'm Charlotte Evans."

"I know."

Coming soon...

Don't miss the next special two-in-one edition from *New York Times* bestselling author
BARBARA DELINSKY

LOVE SONGS

Perfect harmony. It takes two...

Available in January 2013 from St. Martin's Paperbacks

Look for these classic romances—now available as e-books—from beloved bestselling author

BARBARA DELINSKY

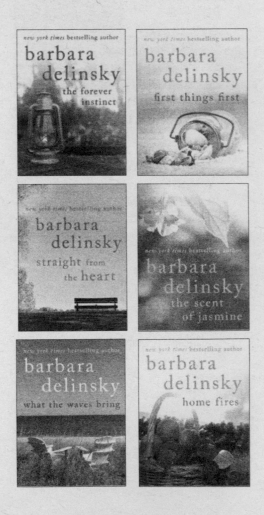

Coming soon...

SILKEN SANDS
HOLD MY HEART
Available in November 2012

CALL MY NAME
AMBER'S EMBRACE
Available in January 2013

From St. Martin's Press